Forever Yours

Melissa M. Marlow

For those Youthful Feelings!!

M M Marlow

authorHOUSE®

AuthorHouse™
1663 Liberty Drive
Bloomington, IN 47403
www.authorhouse.com
Phone: 1-800-839-8640

First published by AuthorHouse 11/24/2010

ISBN: 978-1-4520-8375-9 (hc)
ISBN: 978-1-4520-8376-6 (sc)
ISBN: 978-1-4520-8377-3 (e)

Library of Congress Control Number: 2010914959

Printed in the United States of America

This book is printed on acid-free paper.

Contents

Preface

My dad had moved up north to start his new business. It didn't matter to me, except this meant my mom and I would come up and spend our weekends there. We spent a couple of years going up to the cabin, which we tried to do on most weekends. I discovered I could be completely myself there. There wasn't the primping and pretense like there was in the city. I welcomed my new environment.

I was young, and still being a tomboy, I enjoyed everything my new life had to offer: boating, water-skiing, sledding, four-wheeling, and even the small mini bike my dad acquired. I had a fascination with speed and nothing was fast enough. This was my main source of entertainment, because I felt shy and awkward around people. However, part of me wanted to grow up and do the things I wasn't allowed to do because of my age.

My mom, Paula, was very down to earth and was very accepting of everything I wanted to do. My dad was a little more protective of me. They were both very outgoing and liked to socialize with the families who lived up there. We spent a lot of time at the small pubs, because it was good for dad's business. For him, getting to know the people and their needs helped him get more jobs.

I was able to meet a lot of new friends this way. I really enjoyed it. I played video games and pinball as much as I could. It was very homey and people looked out for each other. Everyone was like family, weird but true.

This is where I felt my true home was.

1. First Look

We ended up at Dice's Pub for dinner Friday Night. I had been there maybe once or twice before. Not many kids were there and it was off the regular path for kids to hang out. It was a great mom and pop place that had fantastic burgers. Dad intended to meet with one of the guys he had working for him to make plans for the week.

We were eating at the bar when he walked in. He reminded me of Tom Cruise, yes the actor, but a little more of a baby face. His face was very soft and young looking. I was only fifteen years old and yes, I had the hunger of having a boyfriend. Realistically, I was much too young for a real boyfriend. The desire was there, but only at the level of talking and holding hands.

I felt attracted to him immediately, but I really didn't know how to flirt. I was a complete dork. I was also very shy even though I didn't want to be. When he approached the bar on the other side of my dad and sat down, I went directly to finishing my burger and fries and hid my face, trying to stay out of the way.

Of course, dad introduced my mom and me. I was pleasant and smiled when dad said his name was Jason. I had always liked J names. He was interesting, but I hid behind my mother to block our view from each other.

I glanced around the pub, the bar was a horseshoe shape and we were off to one side with our back to the entrance door. Behind the other side of the bar there were a few more tables for people to sit and eat. There were neon and metallic signs of beer logos on the walls. At the end of the bar there was a pool table and another little room off to the side where they had a game room with pinball and some video games. This caught my attention since that was where I spent most of my time when we were at the pubs.

I tried to sit still but I was getting antsy. I peeked around my mother to get a look at Jason. To my surprise he caught my look right away and smiled back at me. He was sitting talking to my dad. Dad didn't seem to notice, but I hid behind my mother and tried to busy myself by paying more attention to what was in this pub.

I noticed the coasters stacked in piles around the bar. There was a cup full of matches in case someone had a need. A few boxes of pull-tabs were available for the asking. Once in a great while my mother would give those a try. A set of deer antlers hung behind the bar next to a door that led back to what I assumed was the kitchen.

When my gaze brought me back to him, I noticed he was looking at me. My stomach curled and now I was definitely very nervous. I turned to my mom and asked for some money, so I could go play video games. It was my way to escape, so I would not be caught taking my little peeks at him. She handed me some money and I got up and went to the game room.

To my relief he did not follow and I wondered how much more time my parents would have to spend here. Most nights it would be the whole night. But I didn't want to be here anymore. I was too uncomfortable. I played video games and pinball. Before I started another game of pinball I peeked out to see if they were still talking to Jason. I wanted him to be gone so I could go back to being my dorky, bored self.

They were still talking and it took a few moments before he caught me watching them. I quickly turned and focused on playing pinball. I was doing quite well due to spending a lot of time playing these games. It wasn't until I ran out of money that I finally went back to sit by my mom. I was really bored now.

Jason didn't pay attention to me when I came back. He and my dad were carrying on a great conversation. This amazed me. I thought maybe he was about eighteen or so, and how can someone that age get along with a dull old man. Maybe my dad was much more interesting than I gave him credit for.

The bar was very quiet and I asked if I could play the jukebox. My mom loved music so she gave me more money along with a few requests. The owner of the pub, Don, and his wife Mary, shouted out a few requests too. As I was searching for the items they were calling out, I realized Jason was by my side helping me look. When he stepped next to me looking down at the list, I felt a jolt of energy and the nerves set in. I think he sensed this and tried to make small talk.

He was friendly and asked, "Which one are we looking for now?"

I was in such a tizzy I blurted something out. My legs were a little weak so I leaned on the jukebox for support. I tried very hard to look like I wasn't nervous in a carefree way, but I think he knew I thought he was cute and interesting. I just didn't understand how someone his age could spend a few hours talking to an old man.

He turned more to me and asked, "Would you like to play pool?"

I smiled and looked shyly away, "I'm not very good at it, but I will give it a try anyway."

"Hmm...," he said with a little smile on his face. He moved to the pool table to set it up. I stayed at the jukebox and tried to find the songs everyone had picked out. When I finished selecting songs I followed to the pool table.

Jason was more mature than me so he was better at trying to make conversation. He tried to get me out of my shell. I was in for it now because the questions started. He raised his eyebrows and asked, "How often do you come up north to be with your dad?"

"We come up here nearly every weekend, so my mom can see my dad." I smiled with a little embarrassment because they liked to be together.

"Where do you live?"

"We live in Bloomington, just south of the Twin Cities."

He nodded and smiled at me. I wanted to melt when he asked me, "How old are you?"

I really didn't want to answer this one. I was just starting to feel a bit of an attraction between us, and I didn't want to blow it because I was too young. I responded anyway, "Fifteen."

"Oh," he said. His face did not have a cute, flirtatious smile anymore.

The questions dropped off a little after that and my hopeful heart sank a little. I could see this would be a crush on my side and that would be it. I relaxed and started to have a little more fun. My pool game was improving and I was feeling pretty good.

The questions came again but with a little more space between them and with no more pursuit on his side. I think he was being polite now, so his disinterest was not obvious. I knew I was too young, and not capable of having any kind of relationship anyway.

He continued with the small talk, "So what grade are you in?" He flashed a polite grin.

I cringed inside but replied, "Tenth grade."

Smiling again, "Do you like school?"

"Sure, most of the time, but I find having friends is hard because we spend most of our weekends up here."

He laughed a little at my response, "That is a good thing, spending time up here with your dad."

"Yes and no." I tried to not look at him with this reply, but I think he understood what I was thinking, which was that I was so hungry for someone to be friends with and to hang out with. I was really enjoying our time together, but I was still too timid to ask him a lot of questions. In my head all I could think about is – *Do you have a girlfriend?* But I didn't even know this guy, so why would it be any of my business. I was too young.

He was very polite and kept up the small talk, "So what do you do while you're up here?"

"Not much." I really didn't want him to know I like to do boy things. That might really show how young I really am.

"Do you play any sports?"

I thought to myself, *if you considered riding motorcycles, four-wheeling, boating, and water-skiing sports then, Yes,* ran through my mind, but I said, "No."

I was doing very well at pool. I was down to the eight ball and so was he, but I was up. I was a little nervous about this, because if I get it in I win. I knew boys like to win and that was hard for me, because I like to win too. I took my shot and missed, so I ran around the table and pushed it in to the pocket I had aimed for.

His eyebrows lifted as he smiled and said, "You can't do that!"

"Of course I can, I just did!" I gave him a great big smile.

He shook his head in disgust, but was smiling when he looked away at my dad. My parents were really enjoying each other's company. I think he could tell this was going to be an all night thing, so he looked at me again and said, "Another one?"

I almost fell over! *Why was he being so nice to me?* I would understand if he had to move on. He had a life that I was too young for yet. I don't know if he could see the excitement in my eyes, based on my cool, relaxed form, but I said, "Sure!"

I watched as he set up the next game. He placed the balls in the triangle and rearranged them then rolled them into position. He was bent over the table looking at me through the top of his eyes. He gave me a flirty smile and said, "I suppose you think you get to go first, thinking you won the last game?"

I smiled, "It doesn't matter, and I really didn't win. If you think a *boy* should go first than be my guest."

He gave me a disapproving smile and motioned for me to go first, but reminded me, "Try to get them broken up good. I don't want this to be a long game."

I was really disappointed with this comment. I guess he was just being polite after all. I felt the urge to tell him that he could go. I was used to this, but I really didn't want him to go. I took a deep breath and broke them up as best as I could.

"Not bad," he said lifting his eyebrows and giving me an approving smile.

I didn't get any balls in with the break so it would be *his* game now. I would leave it to him to lead again. As he leaned over the table he looked up at me again and smiled that flirty smile and asked, "So, do you have a boyfriend?"

Why was he asking me this? I really *did* look as young as I was, not totally developed yet. I was still a young girl, really no figure to speak of. I felt myself grin a little looking at him directly and said smiling, "I am not in one place long enough to have any kind of relationship, friendship or otherwise."

He laughed at me. I was hurt. I tried to not look up at all. I thought he was being polite and keeping it light, but this was too real and letting him into my world was not easy. But he wasn't going to be part of my world. At least that is what I kept telling myself to keep from getting hopeful.

Suddenly, he was bending down with his face close to mine, "Your turn."

This startled me because he was so close. Butterflies were fluttering now, and I kind of gasped and reluctantly got up and moved around him to take my shot. I was too involved in my own head to really keep the conversation going. *What was I thinking?* I was being stupid really. *Oh, can't the night just be over?* I want to go home and never think of Jason again. I was completely embarrassed.

When the game was over he walked over to my dad, and put on his jacket. *Did he know what I was thinking?* But I noticed that my mom and dad were getting ready to call it a night. I panicked and looked around for a clock. My heart sank, it was 1 a.m. The bar was closing.

He waited to walk out with us, but my parents were taking their time talking on their way out the door. Jason was behind me, but I noticed he walked a different direction toward a motorcycle. I couldn't help but watch as he prepared himself to get on the bike. My dad walked over and shook his hand.

Jason looked right at me and said, "Do you want to go fishing tomorrow?"

My heart leapt at this. I was yelling to myself *yes, yes, yes and on the motorcycle please.* I composed myself and looked at my mom. She gave me an approving nod. So I looked at him as reserved as I could and said, "Sure."

I wondered the entire way home how this would go the next day. I really was not in any shape to have a friend that was a guy. I was too shy, and too young.

2. Anticipation

The next day I woke up early. With no running water I was determined to wash my hair and look good before he showed up. I was looking at what I had to wear, and realized I was still just a little girl. I had nothing that would make me look like I had a figure. Oh well, he was probably just being nice to the little girl of his boss.

Time moved really slowly, like I could hear the tick tock of an old grandfather clock that we did not have. I sat on the couch and tried to watch TV. I would bounce to the kitchen and look out the window then I would retreat to the fridge for something to nibble on. I didn't find anything that I could eat. Besides, I had already brushed my teeth, and everything was such a chore without running water. I didn't want to be caught off guard. I went back to sitting on the couch. At about 9:30 a.m. my patience was wearing thin. I went out to the pole barn to check on my dad.

"Hey dad, can I use the mini bike and go through some trails?" We had a homemade mini bike my dad had acquired and it was really close to the ground and had very wide tires. You couldn't tip it over even if you tried.

Dad looked at me and gave me a half smile, "Are you sure you want to do that? You might get dirty and Jason is pretty good about being on time."

I looked at him with a question on my mind, because I didn't realize there was a time that we were expecting Jason.

Dad noticed my questioning expression and added, "Jason said he would be here by 11 o'clock."

Now my mind raced. *Did dad talk to Jason before we arrived and ask him to entertain me? Or did Jason talk to dad about what time his arrival would be before he asked me if I wanted to go?* I wanted answers, but didn't want to ask. I didn't want him to know I was really excited about this, and now there was some tarnish to my excitement.

Jason showed up right at 11 o'clock, but of course dad had to chitchat with him about the job plan again. Wondering when he was going to get things done with dad, I tried to listen out the kitchen window of our trailer. I listened for my father to embarrass me by implying my age, and how he should be very careful with his precious baby or he may have hunting season early. To my surprise nothing of the sort was inflicted upon this young man. I was so relieved.

I pulled myself together enough to make it out the front door. My nerves were on the brink of falling apart, but I held it together and bopped out the front door. He didn't pay me any attention when I approached them and my mom had already joined into their conversation. So I felt way out of place.

I tried to stand still and be patient, but I was fidgeting where I stood. Jason was very patient speaking to my mom and dad. He was not in a rush at all. He seemed more comfortable with them then I did. I kept telling myself he's not interested in me. I was just a little girl he was being nice to help entertain me for a while so mom and dad could have time together alone. He is just being nice, he's not interested.

Finally Jason looked at me. I thought I was going to turn to mush or run away to the safety of the trailer. He flashed his quirky smile and asked, "Well, are you ready?"

My heart leapt, but I tried to remain calm and said, "Sure."

Dad did ask him, "So, where are you taking her fishing?"

Jason smiled at me then looked at him and said, "Sampson's Creek if that's okay?"

Dad replied sternly but with a little laugh, "Well that's a good place, don't be gone too long. I don't want to have to come looking for you."

I wanted to die! I looked at Jason and he gave me a reassuring smile because we both knew what he meant. *She's our girl, so don't try anything funny.* I looked at Jason sitting on the motorcycle and gave him the, *I know and I am embarrassed look.* He handed me the helmet. I gave a look of disgust. I had never worn a helmet! That was part of the rush. I liked feeling the wind.

Jason gave me an encouraging look like he wanted to tell me to be a *good girl and put the helmet on.* Jason seemed to have a better feel for how my dad was thinking, and he wanted to show responsibility so dad would trust him to bring his little girl home in one piece.

I hopped onto the motorcycle as soon as I could climb on. I rested my hands on my thighs. I was very calm but excited. I loved to ride and I knew I could relax, because I wasn't being watched or judged with his back to me. I could just sit there and enjoy the ride.

Now the fishing was not something I was looking forward too, so I hoped for a long ride. Our trailer was off a dirt road so the first part of this trip was very slow, it was gravel and all. Not easy with a motorcycle, but he seemed to know what he was doing. I could have driven it faster, but I could feel Jason being extra careful thinking about my dad and all.

Just before getting to the tar road he stopped. My heart was pounding a little not knowing what this was about. I thought I was just going to be able to relax. Jason turned a little in his seat and looked at me.

I looked right at him and said sarcastically, "What?"

He chuckled and asked, "Do you really want to wear the helmet?"

I blinked a couple times and said awkwardly, "Not really."

With a half a grin he got off the motorcycle and helped me with getting the strap undone. He walked to the back of the bike and secured it there. When he came back in front of me, he looked me in the eyes with a very serious look and asked, "Is that better?"

"Of course it is!" I replied with a great big smile on my face. I was beaming now.

He had a serious look now and said, "No funny business though. Promise me?"

I nodded my head, "None, I promise." I really didn't know what he meant, but I smiled at him in relief to not have to wear the helmet.

"You still have to do me a favor though." The slight grin on his face as he looked at me made my stomach panic a little. My mind raced, I wondered *what he could possibly want from me?* He frowned and looked at me like this was going to be really bad, but how bad could this be? I thought he might be taking me home now. He didn't want to deal with a little girl who was rebellious.

He said, "Make sure you keep your face behind me and your mouth shut, it's not that great when you get a bug in your mouth."

I was completely relieved with this. I was so relaxed now and smiled, "I can do that!"

We were off again, still going slow even on the tar road because it was a residential area, but he swayed a little back and forth. I wondered if he thought maybe I was too comfortable on the motorcycle and wanted to put a little fear in me. I moved my hands to hold on to his shirt at each side of his waist. I hoped this would make him feel like he was accomplishing the *fear thing.*

I wasn't very fearful at all and I quite enjoyed the movement. When we turned onto the county road he was able to go at a better pace. I wanted to keep my head up and I closed my eyes, and felt the air move around me. I remembered what he said about the bugs, so I decided to tuck my face a bit and leaned against his back. The bug thing was not something I wanted to experience.

We moved around the curves of the road with ease. I knew how to shift my weight and lean into the curves so the ride was very smooth. Pretty soon we were turning onto the highway. I was excited. That meant more riding time. I watched everything as we turned. I had never been this way before, so I did not know where I was. Maybe I shouldn't close my eyes again, but I was enjoying the ride so much I eventually tucked my face behind his back again and closed my eyes.

Feeling his movement allowed me to move correctly to enhance the bike movement. I wished I could do this all day. This was wonderful. I didn't have to be stared at, asked any questions, and I felt completely free to enjoy the moment. I moved my hands to wrap more around his waist. I realized this could be construed to be something other than completely enjoying the ride. It just felt so good to cuddle into this moment of complete bliss.

When he slowed down, I opened my eyes to see if we were turning or what was going on. I raised my chin a little still trying to keep my face behind his back, but I moved my hands back to holding his shirt on his sides again. There was no objection to anything I did and I couldn't see his face, so I didn't know where I stood. Hopefully, nowhere, I thought. I was just comfortable on the motorcycle, and that was it. As we pulled off the road my heart sank. I really didn't want to stop riding. We had arrived at our destination. There were lots of rocks and a good size creek.

I really didn't enjoy fishing, and now I would probably have to answer more questions. *Maybe even have a conversation!* But I did like his smile. It was very comforting. We came to a stop. *Oh yeah, this was panic time.* I took a deep breath and he waited for me to get off the bike first. I just stood there while he grabbed the stuff for fishing.

So, he was serious about fishing. Well, this might be a relief. Most guys in my life don't like to talk when they're fishing. They think *the quieter—the better.* He walked over the rocks down to the creek, and I kind of just stood there.

He looked back at me and said, "Are you coming?"

I took a deep breath and followed him. I noticed there was a little current to the flow of the water, but the water was completely clean so you could see the bottom. I didn't see any fish, so I shook my head and found a rock I could sit on. He moved farther away from me and started setting up whatever he was doing. He would look back to see what I was doing, but I was just sitting there taking in the scenery.

He asked, "So, do you want to fish?"

I looked at him uncomfortably and said, "That's okay, you go ahead. I will watch."

He chuckled and continued to mess with his stuff and get situated. Finally he sat on the rock about thirty paces from me. I was pretty sure that was due to *little girls'* babbling, and he really liked the peacefulness of not talking. Better fishing that way, I am sure.

He stood up and moved along the creek until it brought him closer to where I was sitting. He really didn't seem to pay attention to me. He was trying to pay more attention to what he was doing. Walking on the rocks you really have to watch where you are stepping. That is why I sat on the rock. If I moved around too much I would probably trip and fall in. I brought my knees up to my chest and laid my head on my knees and enjoyed watching the stream.

When I looked up I realized that he had moved even closer to me. Now the questions would resume.

"So, do you know how old I am?" he asked with a smirk on his face.

I was still relaxed and turned my head on my knees to look at him smiling and guessed, "I don't know, eighteen?"

He gave me a great big smile and shook his head no. So was he older? I was really out of my league before, and now I was extremely out of my comfort zone.

"So, am I supposed to keep guessing or what?" I was kind of giving him that disapproving tone, "Well I'm just going to go up by a year so you could just tell me, couldn't you?" I was a little cocky now.

He smiled at me with the flirty smile he had. He couldn't be *that* old. He just didn't look it.

He looked away and cast a line out and said, "I'm twenty."

I guess five years apart wasn't *that* much except when you look at fifteen and twenty together that was just wrong and we both knew it. He looked over his shoulder out of the corner of his eye to see my expression. I was very comfortable on the rock and must not have shown what I was thinking about the age difference.

I think he felt like he needed to say something, but it wasn't the comment I was expecting at all.

"I could wait a few years." The puzzled look must have shown on my face because he continued, "I mean we could be friends for a few years, if that works for you."

I got it now. He *was* interested in me. I felt completely flushed, but smiled at him and put my head on my knees again. I was trying to look calm. Underneath it all I had become very excited that he wanted to spend time with me even though we couldn't explore the relationship we both wanted. I was now holding my knees to my chest to hide the tremors I was now feeling in my hands, arms, and legs. I couldn't even get up if I tried, but I felt the need to say something.

"So, is it time to go home then?"

His face went really serious now. He didn't look at me but said, "If that is what you want?"

I really wanted to stay where I was. I wanted to ponder how this turned so quickly into what I was hoping for. I took a deep breath and asked, "Can we stay just a little longer?"

He didn't look at me, but I could see the smile on half his face. "We can stay as long as you want. Did you want to fish a little?"

"No, I just want to sit here."

The funny little smirk on his face was now a grin. He wanted to keep up the conversation, "So, why did you come with me today?"

I wanted to play it cool, "You know my dad really well and I thought you were being nice to me so my mom and dad could have alone time."

"So, it really doesn't matter what my age is? You came with me to give your mom and dad a break."

I let my guard down a little, "Well I didn't think you were that old, you have a nice smile, and the motorcycle."

He chuckled at this, "So you were using me for my bike?"

"No!" I said abruptly.

He grinned and raised a questioning brow, "I was meaning to talk to you about that. Most people lean out of a curve and you leaned with. How did you know to do that?"

I felt a little off the hook now and smiled, "I didn't know there was a right way to ride."

Still looking at the creek he reeled in his line. Then started putting it away and grabbed the rest of his stuff then came over and sat by me. "Ahh, this is better," he paused. "You must be a natural at riding motorcycles."

The jig was up! I am a tomboy. He never put it into those words though. Looking straight ahead, with his legs pulled up to his chest and arms across the top, much more of a man's position, he turned his head toward me, "How do you see me?"

Okay, the nerves came back. *How was I going to reply to this, should I be cool, sarcastic, flirty, or what?* "I guess I was just happy to get some attention. I usually keep to myself and no one actually sees me when I am with my mom and dad. A little bit of me was hoping you were, at the most seventeen." Okay, I guess the truth works too.

A sly grin came to him and he looked directly at me and said very serious, "Trust me. People see you."

"What do you mean by that?" I was offended but curious.

He looked forward and smiled knowing this may or may not be good for me to hear, but he said it anyway, "You are a very pretty girl and the boys up here, especially really young ones, don't know how to talk proper about girls. The word gets around here fast and I had to come and see for myself."

Now I was embarrassed because I didn't feel that great about myself. I didn't have a figure, and I was kind of homely compared to the girls at my school. I was *nobody* back home. No one saw me as cute, at most a smarty.

I was reluctant to ask, but know I needed to know, "So you think I'm pretty?"

He chortled and turned his head, "For as young as you are, yes."

What the #!@ does that mean? Do I really look like a little girl to him? Well that was a great let down.

He stood up and was on his feet now looking at me waiting for me to get up too, "I think I need to get you back home now. If I don't your dad may never let me take you again, and I couldn't deal with that."

I half-heartily smiled and took his hand to help me up. I followed him to the bike and climbed onto the back. I was kind of sulking that this had to end, especially since I really wanted to know more about what these boys were saying about me. I was sure he wouldn't divulge this info though. Maybe because he thought I might look at *them* instead of him, and they were closer to my age.

Whatever the reason was I knew this was over, at least for today. He didn't get on the bike right away. Instead he looked out over the creek. After a few moments he turned his head to look at me, "I just want you to know if you were a little older, I wouldn't be able to bring you back." He kissed my forehead and turned to get on the motorcycle without a response from me.

My heart was pounding so hard it hurt. I was afraid to lean into him for protection from the bugs again, but I did it anyway. I sat closer to him spooning my body to his. I leaned my head on his back and wrapped my arms around him. I was in total bliss for the day.

3. First Kiss

That night all I could think of was Jason. I thought about how I was too young for this and he was right to bring me home. I would leave the next day not knowing if I was going to see him any time in the near future, but there was hope. He worked for my dad, so I would have to see him sometime, wouldn't I?

I think two weeks passed before we went back to see dad. It was early fall and I couldn't wait to get up there. We found dad at a different pub this time. This was on the main strip and everyone goes there. It was called Makley's. It was Friday night and really packed. There were kids my age hanging around by the video games. I stayed close to mom and dad hoping to see Jason. I really didn't want to hang with people my age. I was so unsure of myself around people my age. Jason was fun and I felt more comfortable around him. I spent the whole weekend worrying about whether or not I would see him.

Dad finally noticed that I wasn't doing much but watching for something or *someone.* He looked at me and said, "He's working with his dad this weekend. I kept him too busy this week and he had to help out around his folks' place." *Well that's great,* I thought. *It's nighttime why would he be working now?* Not much to say about that. I spent the rest of the

15

weekend sulking. I really didn't do a whole lot but sit around and wait. I went home feeling depressed that night and my mom took notice on our way home. I think she felt she had to say something to cheer me up, "We're going back up next weekend, if you're up to it?"

I smiled a little and didn't say anything. Knowing that we would come back the next weekend helped. I felt like a loner again and didn't pay much attention to anything around me.

During the coming week I immersed myself in my schoolwork. I really didn't like to hang out with friends at all. But the memory of my new friend I had crept into my thoughts and made me look forward to the weekend.

Friday came pretty quickly, and I was so excited to get back up north. It felt like I had a different life up there. We arrived late and had a burger at Timbers Lodge and Resort. Their food wasn't as good as the place where I had met Jason, but it was fancier. My dad wanted to treat mom to a nice dinner. The restaurant was on one side of the building, the bar was in the middle and the game room was on the opposite side of the building. I ordered my food and went to the game room. I wanted to pass the time as quickly as possible. I didn't want to be gloomy the whole weekend even if I would not get to see him, 'Jason.'

Mom came and got me when our food was served. My parents were so great and loving, everyone loved to be around them. They knew how to have a good time without getting too rowdy. We ate and moved to another little dive in the area. This was the best place. It was a small bar called Sherburn's Resort. They had a few cabins, a bar, a store, and kids about my age. Their older son, Brian, was a year older than me and drop dead gorgeous. He had a younger sister, Danelle, who was six months younger than me and a grade lower in school. I thought she was devastatingly beautiful. You could tell that Danelle was going to grow up to be quite compelling to look at, and I was already so jealous of her good looks. She was more grown up than I was. She could run the family store on her own.

They had living quarters behind and above the store. It must be a tough life because she seemed to spend all her time there working. I found myself wanting to hang out with her and help her anyway I could. I actually didn't mind not seeing Jason tonight. I was with kids my age and we hung out and played pool. Brian had a friend with him named Pat. I enjoyed the company I was with. It was a fun and playful evening. I didn't have to act older or more mature. I could be myself.

Saturday was a new day and there was hope of maybe seeing Jason. Dad offered to have a bonfire for us kids. Brian invited some of his friends and Danelle came too. She and I hit it off really well. She was so smart and direct. She didn't put up with all the bullshit that came with teenage boys. I liked the way she carried herself and she wasn't worried about what people thought of her at all. I admired that about her.

Most of the kids had to call it a night at about 10 p.m. We were all pretty young. By now the guys that worked for my dad hand begun to show up. He had quite the gathering. I was outnumbered by age again. Jason was not there and I really didn't know anybody. I decided to call it a night about 11 p.m. with no hopes of seeing him.

The bonfire was at the back of our property and I had to walk to the front where the trailer was. As I was walking I noticed a few more people were showing up in a pickup truck. Everyone was getting out and being loud. They were being rowdy and excited to get back to the bonfire. The driver took his time getting out, I hadn't noticed yet, but it was him.

I heard a voice from the darkness, "So, where are you going?"

I paused. I thought I remembered this voice, but I wasn't sure. I stopped dead and turned to look to see if it was my Jason. There he was leaning over the front of the truck looking at me with a flirty smile that would make any girl melt.

"I was on my way to bed. Everyone here is a lot older than me, and I feel out of place."

He frowned at me and asked, "Are you sure you want to do that?"

I looked at him with a bit of a smile, and a smirk on my face. No matter how bad I wanted to stay I knew it would look funny if I went back after he showed up, especially if he paid any attention to me. We would get so much crap. So I just shrugged my shoulders and said, "I really kind of have to now."

He gave me a pout, while he moved toward the back of the truck. He gestured for me to follow him. I looked toward the bonfire at the back of the property and no one seemed to notice that he had not made his way back there yet. I questioned him, "Do they know why you're here?"

"Of course they do. We are here to be polite and hang with the guy who gives us work." He had a very mischievous smile and motioned with his finger for me to come over.

I knew he could see the fear in my eyes. I looked again at the hill to the back of the property and the adrenalin kicked in. I walked over to the back of the truck not knowing what I was doing. I looked at him innocently and said, "You should go up there or they will be suspicious."

He smiled and looked at me and the tingling started in my stomach. *I couldn't believe he was here with me.* He assured me, "They won't notice anything. They probably think I'm going to the bathroom.

I looked at him doubtfully, "It doesn't take that long."

He pouted a little and moved closer to me, "Then why did you come over here? Why didn't you go inside?"

I tried to relax. I really didn't want to tell him that I wanted to yell at him for not showing up the last time I was here. These feelings stirring inside me were all new. I tried to be calm and not show him how nervous I was. *How can he play it so cool when I was a mess when he was around?*

It was quiet for a minute and finally he said, "You didn't answer my question."

I didn't know what to say, so I turned to go inside the trailer without saying a word. He grabbed my arm and pulled a little, "Wait!" The pull was enough to turn me toward him. "Why are you going inside? Don't you want to hang out with me?"

I looked right into his eyes, and then I was gone. I really didn't know how to find my voice. I lost my smile to a very straight face. I was nervous now and my lip was going to twitch if I tried to smile. I looked up the hill, and gave a guilty look, like he really needed to go up and be with his friends.

He smiled at me, "I'll see what I can do to get rid of them."

I shook my head in disbelief. It was already getting late. *What was he going to do? How could he get rid of them?*

He hadn't let go of my arm and was staring at me, "Can I try something?"

I was confused. He pulled me to the other side of the truck, which was farther away from the group. My back was to the truck, and I was looking up at him with uncertainty. He let go of my arm and put his hands on the truck on either side of me. My heart was pounding and I felt a lump in my throat. All I could think was *shit, shit, and shit! Okay I can handle this I think, oh maybe not.* I was too nervous for this and I looked down. Jason leaned into me with his mouth close to my ear. He whispered, "Please?"

I had a problem looking up into his eyes, but I found myself wanting to trust him. I didn't know how to do this and there were so many mixed emotions that I didn't know if I was standing. He put his lips to my face searching for my lips. I wanted to kiss him so much, but I couldn't quite let myself. I let him kiss me without refusing.

Glued to where I was standing I had forgotten everything around me. I lifted my head a little, but closed my eyes. I did not want him to see the fear stirring in me. His lips found mine and the kiss was gentle, more like a soft trace with our lips slightly parted. I found myself kissing his lips back. It was only for a moment and he pulled back away from me to look into my eyes.

I was nothing but putty now. He stood and stared at me. *Did I do something wrong? Did he realize how innocent I was? Did he realize that this could never be?* I was yelling in my head–*Please say something, anything. Don't leave me standing here feeling really stupid.*

He leaned in again, but to my ear and whispered, "Thank you. It was exactly what I thought it would be, perfect."

He let his arms drop and stood there. My mind was racing–*What do I do now? I want to try that again, that was the most wonderful feeling I have ever felt!* I looked at him with pleading eyes, begging for him to tell me what to do. My knees wanted to give way, so I couldn't move at all, and I just stared at him. He seemed to study my face looking for something to say to me to bring me back to life. I was surely gone.

He grabbed my hand and we sneaked around the back of the truck to the front door of the trailer. I was so unsure of what was going through his mind. When we got to the door he gave me a great big smile and said, "I will get rid of them somehow, just give me a little time."

My heart sank. I didn't want him to walk away. I wanted to feel the softness again. I wanted to beg for him to just stand there with me a little longer. I think he knew that I was yearning for him to stay. He took two steps up to me and kissed my lips quickly and looked into my eyes. He reassured me, "I will be back in just a little bit." Then he left at a sprint to meet the guys by the fire.

I went inside and collapsed on the couch. I was unable to move for a good twenty minutes, just thinking about what had just happened and reliving the moment. I did not want it to end. After I calmed myself I flipped on the TV. I tried to find something to preoccupy my time. I paced a little and looked out the front window when more people showed up. *How was he going to make it back to me?* He shouldn't come back. This was wrong on so many levels. I was not supposed to be having these feelings, not yet. This was for somebody older! I have to stay away. This wasn't right.

Okay, if he did come back, I was going to have to put an end to this. *I can't have these feelings!* This is too soon for me. My head was telling me *I didn't want these feelings,* but other parts of me were telling me *I did.* Okay, I would have just one more kiss and then say goodbye. I remembered how it felt so wonderful. I really had to have one more. Then more people showed up. This is never going to end. I should give up and go to bed. That way he would stay away longer and this would be easier to let go.

I changed into some shorts and a t-shirt to sleep in. I grabbed a blanket and wrapped it around me. I curled up on the couch in front of the TV until I dozed off. My dream was filled with delightful images of the soft and innocent touching of his face on mine. I swear I was smiling in my sleep.

I was barely awake when I felt someone leaning over me. I was afraid to open my eyes. I wanted to stay in my beautiful dream. When I opened my eyes, he was kneeling on the floor in front of me. I sat up quickly and looked at him with surprise. If he had seen my dream I would have been embarrassed. He looked at me with an apologetic smile.

I blinked a little and asked, "Is everyone gone?"

His eyes dropped from mine when he replied, "No."

"Oh, then what are you doing? You could get caught in here and I would never see you again."

"I couldn't stay away. You're so close. I just needed to make sure you were okay."

My eyes brightened and I smiled. I took both of my hands and placed them on his cheeks. I pulled his face close to mine, so that our lips were almost touching, "You need to go. I don't want this to end yet."

He moved in to kiss me. I responded and the kiss deepened. *This was so amazing!* I thought I was losing my soul to him. I used my tongue to lure him in more. I wrapped my arms around his neck. I wanted him to be closer to me. I wanted him to feel my heart beat for him. He pulled slightly away and caressed my chin with his cheek.

I could see his frustration. He leaned in and whispered to me, "You are going to make this difficult for me to wait for you."

"Wait for what?" I was already here and the kissing was amazing. I looked at him confused. *What was I doing wrong now?* He was looking at me and he could see the distress in my face.

He leaned in again and whispered in my ear, "You're too young yet. You need to wait."

I was disappointed even though I wasn't ready for anything more than this. But I liked this and I wanted more kissing! I began kissing under his ear and around his jaw wanting and searching for those soft wonderful lips. He was still leaning over me and he lifted me toward him off the couch. The kiss was even deeper both using our tongues to taste each other. He lowered me and let go.

He stared into my eyes, "You are making this so difficult, but I have to go. I will be back."

I didn't know if he would be gone for the night or just a while. I closed my eyes and drifted back to my dream. In my dreams things went further than I would have wanted. I could see what he was talking about and I knew I was going to have to stay away. He was right. I am not ready for that. I enjoyed my dream at the kissing level never letting things go beyond that. I needed to grow up a little more.

I woke to the rumble of car engines starting up. My mom and dad were making their way into the house laughing and giggling. It was obvious they had a good time, and maybe a few too many. But that was alright since we were safe at home.

I asked, "Is everyone going home?"

On their way to the back of the trailer to their bedroom dad made the comment, "You may want to go to bed yourself. Jason is going to crash on the couch."

But I was on the couch! I sat there in shock. They had no idea I had my first kiss tonight. Either my face wasn't giving anything away, or they weren't that observant. I tried to focus to find a clock. I blinked a few times clearing the sleepiness from my eyes. I was able to make out 3 a.m. Jason came through the front door. I really didn't like when people were drinking and that kind of motivated me to get up and move to one of the beds in the back room.

I knew if he had been drinking his self-control would not be there, and I wasn't ready for where this might take us. I needed a few more years. I didn't want to grow up that fast. I tried to get up and walk, but I was still sleepy and stumbled. There he was in front of me, trying to steady me. I gave him a dirty look.

"Hey! What is that for?"

I just looked at him.

"What?" He said again.

I stared at him and finally found my tongue, "How could you drink so much that you have to spend the night while I waited here all night for you to come back?"

A smile grew on his face. He leaned into me and whispered, "I was pretending. I dumped most of them out just so I could handle being around you."

I gave him a distrustful glare.

"Let me prove it to you?"

I was mad! I didn't want proof! I just wanted to go to bed and I turned my face away from him. I didn't want to get caught up in him so easily. I wanted to stay mad, and I couldn't look at him for fear my anger would melt. I really didn't want anything to do with him if he had drunk too much. I didn't know if he would be able to stop with alcohol in his system. He moved his arm around my waist bringing me in closer to him. He raised his other hand to my face, his thumb under my chin. He traced his lips so ever carefully along my jaw line back to my ear.

"I will prove to you that I am in control, but then it stops."

He started moving his lips downward to my collarbone, tipping my head back more with his thumb ever so lightly. He raised my chin even more and he moved slowly toward the hollow of my neck up my chin then to my lips. My heart was beating out of my chest. I was going to collapse. With my eyes closed I allowed him to be more convincing.

He parted my lips with his tongue so very softly and kissed me more deeply. I couldn't help but respond. I wrapped myself around him letting his arm around my waist bring me closer to him. I put my arms around his neck while his hand pulled my face tight to his. I was lost in his kiss again, but he broke away.

He held me close and looked deeply into my eyes, "Remember, we have to stop now. No more. This is the line and we're done. Come sit with me for a while. We need to calm ourselves."

I allowed the release. I wasn't ready for anything but kissing anyway. He made it so alluring for me. I pulled the blanket around me again, took a deep breath and flopped down on the couch next to him. I wanted it to stop too. I was thankful he took control and didn't press things further.

He closed his eyes and said, "Movie?"

We didn't get much for stations on the TV. I shrugged a little and said, "Sure." I must have sounded disappointed because he shook his head no, and turned to put something in for us to watch. He came and sat in the corner facing me. One foot was still on the ground the other was on the couch. He tapped his chest for me to come to him. My lip was quivering. I leaned into him, facing him.

He showed his disapproval, "You need to turn around. I will just hold you, if that's okay." I could tell he was better at this then I was. I turned my back to him with a sigh. "You're sleepy and you'll forget this in the morning, just close your eyes."

What would I forget? He for sure didn't mean the kissing! I really enjoyed that. Did he mean what was going to happen? I didn't want anything more except maybe more kissing. Okay, what was I getting into? He said that was the line and we had to stop. My mom and dad were in the other room. I just couldn't...

He wrapped his arms around me. I tipped my head to the backside of the couch. He used his right hand to stroke my cheek, my hairline, and my neck. I tried to turn to him to kiss his sweet soft lips again. He held me tighter and with a very firm voice he said, "No! You need to behave and sleep."

I complied and closed my eyes and enjoyed the moment. He continued to trace my features with his fingertips. He nuzzled his face against the back of my neck. I could feel his warm breath glide over my skin. The soft whispers in my ear reminding me, "*Go to sleep...*"

I tilted my head back and twisted in his arms so I could try to coax another kiss from him. I wanted to feel those lips again. I wanted to lose my every breath into him. He held me firm using his legs and left arm so I could not turn into him.

"You don't want to do that. I am just a guy. You need to close your eyes." I decided to close my eyes and let the evening take me. I was very relaxed with him tracing my face and breathing in my ear.

When I woke in the morning I was in a panic. I was still on the couch. I sort of jumped to see if he was still there. No Jason! I looked around the room searching for him. I jumped up to look out the window and his truck was gone.

My poor heart dropped. I was so confused. *So what was going to happen now? When was I going to see him again and where would we go from here?* My mind raced knowing we were going home today, and I had no answers. I calmed myself and went to the outhouse. To my surprise there was a note for me on the door.

Sarah,

I just wanted you to know I will be thinking of you every minute of every day we are apart. It will be a long while before I can see you again. I need to behave myself and that is so hard to do when you're around. So take care and I will be back.

Jason

I wanted to break down and start crying. *How long was he talking? How long did I have to go without seeing him?* I had no way of getting a hold of him. It was completely up to him to see me. I had to wait and there was nothing I could do about it.

We headed for home and I hadn't gotten to see him at all before we left town. This was going to drive me crazy wondering what this meant. I kept my composure, but was sullen during the ride home. When we got home I went straight to my room and cried.

I continued this for many days afterward. I would tell my mom I had a lot of homework and world go to my room to cry myself out. I knew we would not be going up north to see dad as much as winter approached.

4. Sherburn's Resort

The next time we drove up I was extremely excited. *What did my weekend hold for me?* It was Thanksgiving now and we were going to spend it with dad. I had four glorious days up north and I was so thrilled. *Would I get to see him? How could he refuse with this much time allowed?* He had to stop by at least to say hello.

Dad arranged for us to have dinner with the Turners. This was the family that owned and ran Sherburn's Resort. I loved being around them. They were a great family. The mom, Laura, was the most striking woman I had even seen. She seemed totally unaware of her beauty. She had a great personality that attracted both good and bad people, but she could hold her own. She was a great cook and could even make fish taste amazing. Her husband, Paul, was a very easygoing fellow. He was very sweet and went out of his way to make sure everyone had a good time.

The Turners had two kids. Danelle was my age. She was a thirty-year-old trapped in a fifteen-year-old body. The aura she gave off made me want to spend as much time with her as possible. She stood very firm and sure of herself. She didn't put up with all the crap that goes on in bars. She took after her mother a lot. And there was Brian, who I was developing a crush on just because of his good looks. When his friends were around he was kind of a jerk, because he knew he stood out from the rest. When he was alone with Danelle and me, he was actually quite nice. I knew there would never be anything between us because he was way out of my league, but the little crush was still there since he was a delight to look at.

We arrived at their place around 1 p.m. and Laura already had things cooking in the kitchen. It smelled so good. I got to hang out with Danelle and Brian in the pool table area listening to tunes and playing pool. Laura and Paul had pulled all the tables together to form one long table. There were a few other people joining us. That is why I loved this family so much. They actually cared more about other people than making money.

The food was magnificent. I was really hungry, but it was very hard for me to eat in front of people. I was afraid of looking like a pig. I watched Laura eat, and she must feel the same way. She was very skinny, and she only picked at her food. I wanted to stay this way the rest of my life, so I tried to just pick at my food too.

We stayed the whole night. More people kept showing up after all the family things were over. I think at about 7 p.m. the bar was getting packed. Brian had to help his dad restock, and I went to help Danelle do the dishes. This was her least favorite job. Brian would pick on her every time he passed her in the kitchen. I found this play fighting fun. I wanted to be part of it, but I really was not that comfortable yet.

Doing the dishes took us forever. There were more than just the Thanksgiving dishes that needed to be done. We finally finished them and went to where they had their living room to watch TV and hang out. I suppose the bar and pool tables got boring after a while. Now when Brian came through the house part there were three other guys with him. One was Pat, I met him once before. I also met Sam and Zach.

They were all a year older than me, and I found them childishly fun to be around. They pushed us out of the way to play video games. Danelle was pretty irate and threw things at Brian. Pat sat down next to Danelle putting his arms around her and said, "It will be okay honey. I'll take care of you."

I could tell that Pat was shy like me, but once he felt comfortable he came out of his shell a bit more. I focused more of my attention on him. He was mediocre like me and very sweet. I found myself watching him to see how he conducted himself. But Brian was so good looking it was addicting to watch him too. It was so cold outside and not enough snow to do anything, so I sat back and took in what was going on around me.

After several hours had passed, I figured it was time to go to the trailer. I walked into the bar with Danelle to discover the crowd at the bar had dwindled. I found my mom and looked around. I asked her very quietly, "Did Jason show up at all?" She looked at me with a smile and said, "No. I bet he is spending time with his family." I knew she was right, but I was just hoping.

We wrapped up the night and went to the trailer after bar closing. I went in to get a blanket to curl up on the couch to watch TV, and remembered the last time I was here. It didn't take long to fall asleep. I had the most wonderful dream remembering what had happened the last time I was on this couch. My heart was very sad, but at the same time racing as I slept.

The next day was Friday and I went out to try to find something to do. Dad had recently purchased a used four-wheeler. It would have been nice to get a new one, but we were not rich, so this was a happy medium. Of course dad couldn't refuse the glimmer in my eyes to get on it and go. I spent hours behind our trailer on the trails riding by myself. I had gotten out all the mischief I needed to and went back to the trailer to check in.

There was a different truck parked in our driveway. It was older than the one Jason had when he was here the last time. I was so excited that he didn't forget about me. I got off the four-wheeler and ran inside. I stopped dead inside the door. It wasn't Jason. It was some other guy talking to my dad. Dad noticed my surprise and introduced me to him. His name was James. He looked Native American and he was very stunning. Dad made reference that James was now working with him, and they were talking about what they were going to get done this weekend.

I couldn't tell if they could see the disappointment on my face, but I tried to smile and shake his hand politely. I said, "Excuse me dad, but can I go to Sherburn's Resort and see if Danelle can go riding with me?" I was getting bored all by myself.

He smiled without looking up and said, "I don't think Laura will let her, but you can try."

I smiled at the handsome boy sitting at the table with my father and turned to rush out of the trailer. I couldn't fall for another boy that was too old for me. My heart couldn't take it. I was on my way down the dirt road, trying to be as happy as a teenage girl could be.

When I got to Sherburn's, Danelle was watching the store. Her mom, Laura, was taking a nap. I think it was hard to have people over all the time and clean up after everyone left. There was no respect from people who drink, making a mess every day. Danelle asked, "Where are your parents?"

I said excited now, "They're at the trailer, but I have the four-wheeler and wanted to know if you could go riding with me!"

This saddened her because she knew better than to wake her mother when she needed her rest. Brian however jumped at the chance to go riding and said, "I'll go! Can I drive?"

I looked at Danelle for approval, but I don't think she was giving it to me. Brian grabbed my hand and led me out the front door. He held out his hand for the keys. I handed him the keys. He started it up and looked at me very excited and asked me, "What are you waiting for?"

So I hopped on and grabbed the sides of his shirt. I couldn't believe I was getting to ride with this gorgeous guy. I had a great big smile. He took off so fast with a wheelie I fell right off.

He stopped immediately, jumped off the four-wheeler and came to me. He picked me up laughing and said, "I am so sorry, maybe you should hold on tighter."

I was laughing at myself now and looking at the front door of the store. Danelle was standing there laughing too. I looked at her and shrugged my shoulders and she nodded. I got back on with Brian and this time he gave me a warning, "You really need to hold on tighter."

So this time I wrapped my arms completely around his waist.

He said, "That's better, are you ready?"

"Yep!"

He took me on the wildest ride, going down dirt roads, doing donuts, and other fancy moves. This was the most fun I had had in a long time. No talking, I could handle that. I was so shy I usually didn't know what to say anyway.

Then we were going down a dirt road and he started to drive slower. This four-wheeler was loud, and he half turned his body on the machine as if he wanted to ask or say something to me. My heart dropped. I couldn't handle anything more. I was trying to put guys out of my head, and I was really enjoying myself just riding. I knew he was not interested in me, because the little looks never indicated anything of the sort. So, I didn't understand what this was all about.

He yelled something, "Qwadg dkghao gaogidh!"

"What!" I yelled back.

He tried again, "Dgwad alcht kladsg!"

This time he looked back at me, but I couldn't make out what he was trying to say. I shook my head no, while I was pointing to my ear. Then he was stopping. *No, no, no!* I didn't want to stop! Why was this so important that we had to stop? Couldn't he just forget it and keep going? Okay, here we go. I just have to be polite and ask him to keep going, but I guess it wouldn't hurt to listen first. He smiled at me. He had no idea how gorgeous I thought he was. I melted, even though he wasn't looking at me this way.

Brian still half turned said, "Do you want to go see Pat?"

My face was confused by this question. *We were riding, why would I want to go see Pat?* He chuckled a little and said, "You know he kind of likes you."

I quickly replied, "No. He doesn't even know me. He's never really talked to me. How could he like me? That's just stupid."

Brian smiled and asked, "Are you sure?"

I rolled my eyes and said, "Can we just get back to riding? I would rather do that."

He shrugged his shoulders, turned around and took off again. I was still holding on for dear life. He was crazy and comfortable going very fast. This was probably slow compared to the newer models, but it filled our needs. We went on more trails than I knew existed behind all the cabins, and trailers in the area. We came up on one and he slowed into the driveway. He cut the engine and rolled forward.

I could hear him fine now even though he talked more quietly, "I'm sorry. I had to do this. He has a really bad crush on you."

I looked at him and was pleading 'No' with my eyes. His guilty smile gave me an apologetic look and he said, "I just have too, sorry."

Pat came out of his cabin with bright eyes, but looking at Brian a little angry. Brian jumped off the four-wheeler letting me sit there.

They said something to each other that I could not hear, and I was very uncomfortable. I tried to be observant of everything around me, ignoring what they were saying.

Brian turned to me and said, "Pat's going to come back to my place with us."

I really didn't care until Pat climbed on behind me. There wasn't much room for three of us, but we made it work. No one wanted to walk it was a little cold out.

When we got back to the resort Danelle came rushing out, she looked angry until she saw Pat. Then she smiled greatly. I couldn't tell if she liked him or if she knew that he liked me. Her smile was one of relief that her brother wasn't going to win this time. I got off the four-wheeler and sped to be with her. I was very uncomfortable being in the middle of them.

As we walked into the store she asked me where we went. I really couldn't tell her, because I had no idea. Then she looked at me with a smile, "But you ended up getting Pat."

"Yeah," I said. I didn't want to tell her what her brother said to me, because I didn't want to hurt her feelings if she liked him.

She leaned into me and asked, "Did Brian tell you? Pat has a crush on you."

I was immediately relieved. I said, "Yes."

She smiled and said, "So what do you think?"

I looked at her blankly and said, "How would I know, I really don't know him at all."

She looked disappointed. I tried to recover by saying, "He seems nice enough."

I didn't want to hurt her or his feelings, but in the back of my head I wanted to be riding with Jason or even kissing him. I shook this thought out of my head again. That was a lost cause, and I knew it would be a few years before we could actually be together. So maybe I needed to spend more time with Pat to see what he was about.

We spent the day hanging out, just the four of us. We played pool, watched TV and played video games. Brian flirted with me more than Pat did, but he wasn't doing it intentionally, that was just how he was. I didn't take it seriously, but I had a little crush that I knew I would never act on if I wanted Danelle to be my friend. Pat was very sweet, soft spoken, and respectful. He paid me more attention than I deserved.

It was an early evening and I went home with my mom and dad. Dad put the four-wheeler in the back of his truck. It was dark out and cold and he didn't want me on the road. It was already dark at 7 p.m. this time of year. Dad said James was stopping by in a little bit to talk over some more details about work. *Oh great! Another good-looking guy for me to ogle over.*

We got home and I plopped down on the couch to veg out. James showed up shortly after we got back to the trailer. My dad and James sat at the kitchen table and talked about work. I just ignored them.

I felt a weird sensation that James was watching me. I tried to ignore this feeling, but I wanted to look so see if my feelings were correct. His stare was straight ahead so my dad wouldn't notice, but he was looking right at me! He wasn't only looking, but *staring*. Like he was examining every movement I made. This made me very nervous. *What was it about older guys that excited me? Was it the maturity of the way they held themselves, or just the forbiddances of the age difference?*

Dad got up to get more coffee, this startled me a little and I jumped. Dad didn't notice, but James did. He chuckled a little. I tried to peek at him from the corner of my eye, but he caught me because he was now deeply staring at me. *How could my dad not notice? He was openly watching me!*

Dad sat back down, looked at James and laughed a little. He said, "Yeah, Jason was taken with her too, but she is too young. Put it out of your mind boy."

I tried to pretend I did not hear what my dad was saying, but I am glad he put his foot down. I was relieved that he saw the interest. James looked at my dad with a grin and said, "I know, it's just..." And his words dropped off. I could tell he was looking at me again. I must look better than I felt about myself. I was getting so much attention it wasn't funny. I wasn't used to this.

Dad chuckled, "I know she acts and looks way too old for her own good."

I was really embarrassed now. I didn't want to hear this at all, especially from my dad.

Then my dad stood up and said, "Oh yeah, James, I have something for you. I'll be right back."

He went out the front door, leaving us in the trailer alone. He was still staring at me. *Staring, staring, and staring.* I was getting angrier by the minute. I finally got up the nerve to be rude, "Do you really have to stare? You are making me uncomfortable!"

This relaxed him a little and he said with a smile, "Jason warned me, but I didn't believe him."

"You know Jason then?" I prodded.

The smile on his face was disapproving, "Yeah, I didn't believe him, but now I see what he meant."

This put me off. I said angrily and with attitude, "What did he say? And what the hell do you mean?"

He was a little shocked by this. The look on his face was of surprise. "Well, he said you were amazing, especially when you weren't trying. He warned me not to look at you, because I would be taken with you immediately, and if I touched you he would kill me."

This embarrassed me. I didn't think I was special at all and for him to give me this much credit was, *well this was just weird.* I took a moment and tried to compose myself.

"If I was that amazing then I guess he would be here wouldn't he?" I said this with a lot of attitude, and made it sound like Jason's loss.

James got up from where he was sitting and moved a little closer and leaned on the half wall that separated the kitchen from the living room. I studied him for a moment. He was much more mature looking than Jason. He had muscles that were amazing even under his t-shirt that was covered by layers of sweatshirts.

He looked directly at me and boldly stated, "I would be here all the time. You wouldn't be able to get rid of me. I'm not as soft as Jason, and whatever you wanted to do to me I would let you."

I gasped at this and it left me speechless. I can only imagine what Jason told him, and that was betrayal in my book. *How could he!* That was so special for me and for him to share that, I was really pissed! I looked a little angrier with him when I replied, "I don't know what you mean by all that, but it's none of your business, and I am not that way." He seemed to be watching my reaction with a funny grin.

Dad walked in, looked at James and said, "Settle down boy, not something you should be thinking about."

Did my dad hear this or was he just angry at the advancement he had made in a short time? I was steaming about this, but went back to watching TV, not really watching what was on at all. I was getting redder by the moment. *What was James implying? Why would Jason share that special moment with him?* James hung out the rest of the night with us, while I continued to fume. Dad and he both moved to the living room. Dad sat in his chair while James sat at the other end of the couch. Dad got up and went outside to get a couple more beers. Mom was already sleeping. She had a long day and was tired. So, there we were alone again.

I was looking at the TV, but felt the need to say something about the staring again, "Will you please quit looking at me?"

"I can't help myself."

"Please try, you're making yourself look foolish."

"Jason said that would happen."

"Can we not talk about Jason, and quit looking at me that way."

"Your just so…"

"What?" I was really getting irritated.

"He didn't say you had this much attitude, though."

I let up a little and asked, "So, what did he say that is making you look like an idiot?"

I think this helped him snap out of the trance of looking at me. His eyes softened, "He just said you were amazing."

"Nothing else?" My voice became softer.

"Not really, but I was wondering how somebody with your attitude could taste so sweet?"

I was back to being irate, "So, he did say more!"

"Did you kiss him or not?" He asked accusingly. I wasn't going to reply, because it wasn't any of his business. I huffed and turned my head away. I was going to ignore this question. He leaned forward to touch my foot, to get my attention again. I was holding back tears now, not wanting to discuss this any further.

He paused and inquired, "I was just wondering if I could maybe just…" and he looked down.

"No!" I was very insulted. I didn't want him to see that I was very hurt by this conversation. Dad came back in. We composed ourselves and I managed to successfully ignore him the rest of the night.

5. The Promise

It was Saturday and my long weekend was half over. The anticipation of whether or not I would see Jason has worn me out, so I was hoping for an uneventful day. If I could just get through today, I would be going home tomorrow. This time I was looking forward to leaving. For some reason I knew I wasn't going to get off that easily. I crawled out of bed about 9 a.m.

Mom was boiling water so we could wash up. We didn't have many of the conveniences like other people had. This trailer was an old hunting cabin my dad had shared with his buddies years ago. It still had most of the same furnishings from back when just the men used it. My mom had picked up a few more things to give it a homey feel. Nothing matched and it wasn't what you would call decorated, but it was comfortable and kind of charming.

She asked, "Would you like to wash your hair? I could help." It was pretty cold outside and I knew my hair would freeze when we did it, but it had already been two days since I last took a shower. I really needed it. So, I changed into a t-shirt and sweats, got the supplies stacked out on the picnic table, and grabbed a pail of steaming water.

I was throwing a tizzy while mom tried to help me, but it was too cold outside to be doing this. When we were done, I wrapped my hair in a towel, and flipped it up. Then I grabbed my stuff and turned to head inside. I stopped dead in my tracks to find myself being stared at. Here was my soft and tender, sweet baby faced Jason with that flirty smile on his face. Next to him was James. They were both leaning on the side of the back of the truck with their elbows resting on the edge.

They were staring at me when my dad said, "Guys! Pay attention here, we need to go over this for tomorrow."

Jason looked at me with that flirty smile of his. My heart leapt, but I decided to give him an angry glare. James chuckled at this. My glare moved to him. I smiled with attitude, stuck my tongue out at him, and went inside. I tried to peek out the window. Jason was paying attention to what dad was saying, but was trying to look up to the trailer for a glimpse. James was definitely more direct. He caught me and nudged Jason to give him an idea where I was.

I stormed to the bathroom determined to look better than I ever have. I would look older and prettier than I usually did. I would definitely give them something to ogle over. I left my long hair flow with ringlets of curls. I even put makeup on. I found my best tight fitting jeans and a really soft, sliming, low-cut v-neck (I brought with just in case). I put my short down jacket over top and took one more look in the mirror.

I needed my hiking boots. There! I was perfect, for how young I really was. If I didn't look older now, I would have to wait for time to do its job. Okay, I was ready to make an appearance and to blow them off for acting stupid. *Who was grownup now?* I had my pony binder around my wrist. I knew I would need this later. I bopped out the door and down the stairs. I didn't pay any attention to Jason or James standing by the truck and said, "Excuse me dad, can I take the four-wheeler down to Sherburn's? A bunch of kids are hanging out down there."

My plan worked! Jason stood there expressionless. I couldn't tell what he was thinking, but he kept his eyes on me the whole time. I looked directly at him with a great big smile on my face. He responded by giving me a disapproving look. James, however, gave me the response I was looking for. His mouth dropped open and he couldn't take his eyes off of me. *Now I gave him something to stare at!*

My dad looked up and took a double take. Then his fatherly instinct was to look at the two guys he had in front of him. He said sternly with a chuckle, "Easy does it boys."

I cracked a half smile. Dad looked at me again and said, "I think that's a great idea! Go hang out with people your age."

I smiled, got on the four-wheeler, and hit the throttle full force to do a 180 turn. Then I stopped and smiled, "Thanks dad!"

I sped off to the resort. I didn't even look back. As I drove away all I could think was – *I'm not playing games with those two anymore.* It was weird. The one thing I forgot was there would be more stupid boys where I was going, and I was really asking for the attention now. *Shit!* I didn't want that. I wanted to hang out and go unnoticed. Oh well this was still better than what I was facing at the trailer.

I got to Sherburn's and there was a large group of kids hanging together outside. I really didn't want to be with them. I didn't see Danelle, so I assumed she was inside manning the store again. Brian yelled at me to join them. Pat was looking at me pleadingly to join their group. As I headed into the doorway, I turned over my shoulder, gave a half smile and said, "I am going to hang out with Danelle for a while." Brian shrugged his shoulders as if to say *whatever.* Pat's face fell, I knew he was disappointed. I enjoyed hanging out with Danelle, because she acted more grownup then all the other kids put together.

When I got inside I asked, "Do you want someone to hang with you while you're manning the store?"

Her eyes brightened, but her words were different, "You *should* really be out there with them."

I looked at her and pleaded, "I would rather be in here if that's okay."

She smiled at me and said, "Sounds good to me!"

Since I was there I wanted to help, so she had me straighten the shelves a little and dust off products that were not a hot commodity. As we did this, the conversation was light, but her curiosity got the better of her.

"So, do you like Pat?"

"How would I know, I don't really know him. I just met him and he's so quiet."

She giggled a little and said, "So are you!"

I already knew I was quiet because of shyness. It was hard to believe anyone could be as shy as me.

Then she looked at me funny and asked, "Do you like my brother? It's okay if you do, *everyone* does."

I looked at her a little confused as I thought carefully about my answer. I tried the casual but forward approach, "Of course, who wouldn't? But he's way out of my league, so no worries here."

I looked at her hoping she would approve of this. Danelle didn't look at me, but I could see her small smile. I tried to recover more by saying, "I really liked riding with him the other day, and that would be the only way we could be together, not talking at all." She chuckled a little. I took it as approval.

Next, we went to help stock coolers in the bar. I was so much happier helping her than out with the group trying to fit in. Now, the group was moving into the bar. They all gathered in the back to play video games and pool. Danelle and I went back to the storage area for supplies. She looked at me and said, "You really don't have to stay with me. You can go hang out."

I rolled my eyes, "I would rather be here."

Her mom came out, "I've got the store. Can you two take the garbage out?"

"Uh mom, that's Brian's job."

Laura smiled and said, "But you have a helper today."

"No problem!" I replied, "We got this!" I nudged Danelle.

She was still not too excited about the task. I wondered – *How could it be that bad?* We dragged the first four bags out, and these weren't small bags either. There was a lot I'll have to admit. I happened to notice Jason going by slowly. I didn't have a free hand to wave, but I smiled as I watched him drive by. We went in to get the last three bags. Danelle grabbed two and I grabbed one.

She said, "It's the least I can do with you helping me."

I smiled to let her know I really didn't mind at all.

Jason was pulling in when we walked out. He pulled up to the dumpster. He rolled down the window and asked, "Can you go with me for a little bit?"

I looked at Danelle and asked her, "Do you mind? I promise I won't be long."

She gave me a suspicious smile and said, "No, that's okay."

"I promise. I will only be gone a little while!" I ran around to the passenger side and hopped in. I waived at her and smiled. I turned to Jason saying, "Only a little bit, okay? I promised."

He shook his head and started to drive saying, "It won't be long at all."

I felt saddened. I could tell this wasn't going to be pleasant. He wasn't looking at me, and had a very stern face, "What are you up to?"

"I was hanging out."

"No you weren't! I think they call that *working.*"

"I was *helping* Danelle."

"I know that. Why weren't you with the rest of the group?"

"I would rather help Danelle."

We hadn't driven far. I think he found the closest dirt road he could find. He pulled over and put the truck in park.

Why was he scolding me? "I wasn't doing anything wrong." I pleaded, "I'm not sitting around doing nothing am I?"

He got out of the truck and walked to the passenger side. He opened the door. I looked at him so confused. I really didn't know what I was doing that was so bad. I was just teasing earlier. I wanted a reaction, but his was a little different than what I was expecting. He pulled my knees around, so I was facing him. He pulled himself in between them. He placed his hands on each side of my face. *This* was what I was expecting. Now to those soft lips, but I was mistaken.

He said to me holding my face, "You need to hang out, and be with people your age."

I smiled and said, "Wasn't that what I was doing?"

"Well sort of, but not the *right* way."

"What do you mean?"

"Why are you hanging with Danelle? You should be with the group, guys your age."

I looked at him disapproving, but not saying a word.

"I know at least three of them that have an interest in you. I know. I have heard them talk about you and it wasn't innocent."

39

I tried not to show him that I was very uncomfortable. I didn't want to discuss how I felt. I just wanted the tingly feelings that he gave me when he kissed me. I found myself pulling away from his hands and his stare. I put my face down, and rested my forehead on his chin.

"Now what?" he said angrily.

I tried to push him away now. My eyes were filling with tears. Somehow I felt like this was rejection. I said quietly, "You can take me back now." I sat facing forward, but avoided his face. I was embarrassed. He closed my door carefully while not taking his eyes off me. He walked around the front of the truck, but stopped there in front of it and sat on the bumper.

Okay, I thought. We have already been gone long enough, and I promised it wouldn't be long. We wasted our time together arguing and now I had to get back, but he wasn't moving. My mind was racing, *what should I do? Should I get out and go to him? Should I sit here and give him some room. He was right I am too young to deal with this shit.* I decided to remind him that we were leaving. I opened the door of the truck and slowly got out. I didn't shut the door, because we would be leaving anyway. I walked slowly and carefully to the front of the truck. Still looking down I said, "I kind of promised Danelle I would only be gone for a short while."

He smiled and shook his head. He slowly stood up and looked at me really grinning now. I was nervous because his grin was not angry anymore. He turned toward me placing both his hands on the truck with me in the middle. He looked into my eyes and said, "You make me so crazy inside Sarah. There are so many things about you that fascinate me."

I gave him an angry look and kind of yelled at him, "That's why I have a hard time with people my age! They would never say anything like that."

He put one hand behind my neck, brought his body to mine and lifted me a little with his right arm, so I was pinned to the truck completely with the force of his body. He stared into my eyes looking for fear. I couldn't look at him, so I closed my eyes. His body had more pressure to it and then he kissed me. It was a lot harder this time and more intense. I found myself wrapping every part of me around him and replied by kissing him back. Our mouths moved together perfectly without even trying. His kiss slowed and I tried to nibble on his bottom lip to keep this going.

Oh, how I loved to kiss him, and now other parts of my body were tingly. I wanted more of this, but he stopped. I tried to lure him again by kissing his neck reaching to his ear and nibbling. He grabbed my face gently to pull it away from his. Resting our foreheads together he looked at me through his eyelashes and said very sternly, "You need to stay away from James."

I was in shock. What did *he* have to do with this? Why was he coming into the picture? Why did he have to talk about someone else? I was here with him, not James. Why would he bring him up? He waited only a few seconds and then repeated himself, "You need to stay away from James, and you need to promise me."

I tried to probe for more kissing. I didn't want to talk about James.

"I'm serious, please promise me?"

The intense kissing came with another rush. He pushed his body to mine more. He took my hands and pushed them back against the truck. He moved his mouth down my neck, putting his hands onto my waist, as he touching my skin. He wrapped his arms around me and his fingers traced my spine. His passion behind those lips was so intense I was completely lost in him. He moved his right hand back to my neck and down my chest bone, kissing every inch he had touched. He moved back up to my face. I couldn't open my eyes. Every possible inch of my body was excited. He traced his lips along my chin back to my ear and said again, "You need to promise me please?"

I was so engulfed with hormones that I said, "Yes, whatever you say", like a little zombie following orders. He was still kissing me, but a lot softer now. My eyes were still closed enjoying every bit of this.

His body loosened a little allowing me to be on my feet again. He stopped kissing me, and turned his body to lean sideways, pulling me to face him, "You need to open your eyes."

I slowly opened them, scared to see what he was thinking, but he smiled and traced his hand over my face.

He repeated himself again, "You promised me you were going to stay away from James, right?"

After a deep sigh I said, "Yes."

"You also said you would try to hang out more with people your age?"

I gasped, "I never agreed to that!"

He chuckled and said, "You are now."

I said, "Fine, okay. I will try."

"You know…James wouldn't have stopped."

Why did he keep bringing him up in our conversation? He kissed me long and hard, and broke away as he groan, "Uhhh…You are going to be the death of me. I have to get you back now, don't I?"

I said, "Yes."

As we drove back I wanted to touch him and tease him for more, but the little voice in my head said to me, *James wouldn't have stopped.* This kept me from pushing the issue with him. I didn't have enough gumption to ask him when I would see him again.

I assumed after today it would be soon.

6. More Competition

When I got back to Sherburn's I tried to not smile, even though I was in complete bliss over Jason. None of these little boys could have done that to me. *They wouldn't know how!* I found Danelle in with the group now. She was sitting on Pat's lap. I was almost next to them when they both noticed me.

Danelle tried to stand up, but I pushed her back down and sat down next to Pat saying, "I think that is sweet of you Pat."

He put his hand out for me to hold. It seemed harmless enough. I felt like I was betraying my feelings for Jason, but I did it anyway. This made Danelle giddy. The group was dwindling quickly, and there was only a handful left, including me. We sat around and joked.

I was heading to the bathroom and Danelle followed me. When I came out she was waiting there for me. She took my arm and pulled me to the back stairs, "Do you like him?"

I gave her a disapproving look and said, "I really don't know him, so how could I like him?"

She was a little angrier with me when she said, "Not Pat, that Jason guy?"

My heart sank, hoping it wasn't noticeable-*shit!* I smiled slightly more reassuringly and said, "Kind of, but he's too old for me. He encourages me to like someone my age and in this group."

She gave me the biggest smile now. I felt happier when she approved of me, but deep down I felt guilty for letting her think of him as nothing in my life.

I was all flustered the whole time I was there. I was exhausted from my time with Jason. I wanted to go to bed and dream about him. I was going to leave before it got dark so my dad wouldn't come looking for me. I agreed to give Pat a ride home. Only because I felt obligated to Jason to try.

We got to his cabin. He got off the four-wheeler, but stopped and looked at me with a question in his eyes, "Do you want to stay a while? We could play a game or something." At least he was less shy when everyone wasn't around. I smiled, trying to look more excited than I was, and simply said, "It's getting late and my dad…"

In his disappointment he replied, "Yeah, not a good idea." He stood there still a question in his face, "Who was that guy you left with?"

I was horrified that he noticed. I tried to play it off coolly, "That's just Jason, he works for my dad."

"Why did you go with him?"

"I was just keeping him company while he went to get a part for my dad."

"Do you like him or something?"

Oh yeah I did! But I didn't want him to know, so I said very calmly, "No, more like keeping an eye on me for dad."

"That's cool." He was smiling from ear to ear now.

I felt obligated to be polite and said, "So when do you plan on coming up next?"

He frowned a little and said, "I don't know, but I live in the cities. We could exchange phone numbers and we could call each other!"

"Great!" I forced my voice to sound eager. I wanted to be polite.

He ran into the cabin and came out with a notebook. He was scribbling something as he approached me. He tore the sheet out and handed it to me. I folded it as I gave him my phone number. He was beaming and said, "I'll call you this week!"

"Great!" I said with as much excitement as I could muster. I didn't want to hurt his feelings. After all, he was a nice guy.

I headed back to the trailer. It was already getting dark, so I knew I had to hurry. The daylight was ending earlier every day. I pulled up to the trailer. Everyone was inside including Jason. His truck was there, so I knew he was too. I was really nervous to see him especially after today's meeting with him.

I stopped at the outhouse. I thought I was going to be sick — *Oh how I hated having nerves!* My stomach was wrenching. I threw up then tried to compose myself. I took a deep breath, and headed to the trailer. I could tell they were up in the pole barn. I hurried to the trailer, so I could brush my teeth. *What was I doing to myself?*

Mom was preparing the potatoes for the oven, and said to me when I walked in, "Dad's going to grill, so the boys are out back getting it going."

"Boys?"

"Yeah, Jason and James are eating over. And Jason is spending the night. They're working early tomorrow, and he didn't want to drive home and have to drive all the way back so early. Oh, and by the way we're leaving early tomorrow."

I was done being cute for the day, so I went to put some sweats on. It was getting colder by the day now, and the trailer never really gets too warm. I grabbed what homework I had and curled up in a blanket on the couch to see what I could get done. I really didn't want to do any reading. I hated to read. I pulled out science. There was still reading, but also a workbook. I worked on it for about forty-five minutes.

I knew it would be time to eat very soon. Mom was sitting in her chair reading her book. Next I took out math. This was a no-brainer two pages with fifty-one problems. Thirty minutes later I was done. No boys yet. Grilling didn't usually take this long. I had one more choice before going back to reading. I pulled out history. It was almost as bad as reading. All I had to do was follow along the reading to find the answers.

Mom called from the kitchen, "Potatoes are ready, and the boys will be in, in a minute." I hadn't noticed she had gotten up. I was racing through the book as quickly as I could now, trying to finish. When the guys walked in, I gathered my things and put them back into my bag and put them away. James walked in next smiling, laughing, and being noisy.

He took one look at me and said, "All that and a brainiac too! What else don't we know?"

I gave him the nastiest look I could muster. I walked out to the kitchen and when I passed him I kind of gave him a shoulder shove as I passed by him.

"Oh and she has *attitude,* too!"

I moved around to the back of the table. Jason moved in across from me and said very quietly, warning me, "Don't encourage him."

The table was small and only meant for four people. I sat on one side and my mom sat next to me. Jason sat across from me and James was next to him. My dad sat on the end. I really hated to eat in front of people, so I cut my food up into the tiniest pieces. Dinner conversation consisted of my dad talking about work to the guys. This let me off the hook, or so I thought.

I was trying to avoid eye contact with either of them, but Jason tapped me on my foot. I looked up and he gave me a look and gestured next to him. I glanced over and James was completely staring at me again. *What an idiot, doesn't he know it was so obvious to my father? What the hell was he doing?* I looked at Jason a little confused and he gave me a disapproving look. I looked back at James and gave him an angry glare. He chuckled a little. I could see Jason shaking his head.

Suddenly my dad said, "We're good then!" I couldn't believe dad had not noticed the hostility at the table. Mom was always so happy and jolly that she didn't notice either. Even if she did, she didn't let on. I knew the business talk was over. Dad got up and moved to his chair to watch the 9 o'clock news. Mom followed to her chair and started reading her book again.

James got this very wicked smile on his face. I felt what was coming and it wasn't going to be pleasant, "So, I saw you hanging with all the little boys today."

I didn't even look up for this one, "Yep."

"Do you like any of them?"

I looked at Jason to search for the reply I was supposed to give, but nothing showed on his face, he wasn't even looking at me.

"Probably not," I replied. I felt a little guilty. I put my hand down and looked through my eyelashes at Jason to watch for a reaction. I reached in my pocket and pulled out a little folded piece of paper, and waved it in the air. Jason looked up for a moment. He chuckled a little and smiled approvingly. I snarled at James, since I wanted him to know I was irritated by all the questions.

James laughed a little and took a big mouth full of food and spoke again, "So do you have a boyfriend now?"

I squinted at him, to warn him, "I'm not answering anymore of your questions." I said abruptly. Jason moved to touch my foot again. James started laughing again. I just glared at him, blowing off Jason's warning.

I got up and started clearing the table off. I didn't have any plans of washing them, but I needed to do something. James was still eating. He was a bigger, more muscular boy and needed to fill those muscles with substance. Jason was just messing with something on the table. I stood on the opposite side of the table evaluating the situation. Neither of them had anything to say. I moved around the table to get stuff from in front of Jason. I could feel his touch, and only hoped James did not see it.

James continued to chuckle to himself and make wisecracks while he was eating. I started to take away food from in front of him, but he grabbed my arm softly and said, "Hey, I was still eating!"

I slapped his hand playfully and said, "I think we're done now."

He looked up at me, smiled and said, "The night is young and I have all night."

I took his fork away and scolded as a mother would, "Din din is done!"

He grabbed the fork back and huffed, "Not for me!" He lowered his voice and said in a whisper while looking at Jason, "Besides, I'm not leaving you two alone." A satisfying grin grew on his face, "…And things go bump in the night!"

I looked at Jason to search for help with this overbearing creep, but Jason just smiled, and was not looking at me. I took it upon myself to handle this, and I whacked him on the back of his head with my hand and stomped my foot at him gesturing to my parents. My dad must have recognized that things were escalating and yelled from the living room, "Knock it off kids!"

James was trying to hold his laughter in. I looked at Jason to do something, but he was holding himself from laughing too. Jason took the hint and asked, "Cards anyone?" I picked up two decks and dropped them on the table.

I could hear a little snoring from my dad's chair and mom got up and said, "Goodnight kids. Don't stay up too late." Then she walked back to the bedrooms. "By the way boys, you get the front bedroom. There is a bunk in there. Sarah, you can stay in the back room." My mind stopped when I realized they were both staying the night. *Great!* I sat down at the table to play cards, but I wasn't happy.

Jason asks, "So, what are we playing?"

James said, "Poker, strip poker that is."

I looked at him disapproving and said, "Can you stop this now, please?"

He was laughing again, and so was Jason. I realized I overreacted and kind of smiled too. I suggested 500 Rummy, since that was the only adult game I knew. They both agreed.

James started again, probing me more, "So you didn't answer me, do you have a boyfriend?"

Jason looked at me in a discouraging way.

I responded, "Not really."

"That's not a hard question. The proper answer would be yes, or no."

I glared at him, "No!"

"So whose number did you get?"

"Pat Hanson."

"How old is he?"

I really didn't know, but answered anyway, "I think a year older than me. Rummy!" I was out. They both went in the hole this hand. James was sitting on the end where my dad had been sitting earlier. Now it was a lot easier to look at Jason without it looking suspicious. As I was dealt the cards again, James continued his questions.

"Are you going to call him?"

I looked at Jason as I replied, "I suppose if he calls me first."

"So, you like a guy who makes the first move?"

I watched Jason intently, since I didn't know where this was going, "I am the girl. Guys are supposed to call the girls first."

"So, if you liked me, you wouldn't ask me out?"

"I wouldn't ask you, you're too old for me."

"I am only nineteen."

"Yeah, so?"

"Jason is twenty. Isn't *he* too old for you too?"

I was crushed. I looked at Jason sadly and said, "Yeah, I guess."

James was very pleased with himself.

"Rummy!" I won again and hoped this would put a stop to James' interrogation. They both went in the hole again. James was getting a kick out of this. As he dealt, the questions stopped, but it wasn't the end of them, "So, where did the two of you go earlier?"

I could feel my face flush. I couldn't help, but be embarrassed wondering if he already knew, "I don't know what you mean?" Not looking up at all.

"I saw you get in the truck and drive off together."

Jason very calmly said to me, "You don't have to answer him." He turned on James, "She doesn't have to answer that, and you can stop."

"I was just wondering. Rummy!"

Jason and I both got a few points this time even though James won the hand. He was chuckling to himself. He stood up, "While you are shuffling, I'm going to the bathroom, so you two can get the story straight. I wouldn't want to have to bring this up to *daddy dearest.*" He turned and walked out. Jason looked at me with very sorry eyes.

"Did he see us?!" I gasped.

"Maybe."

I leaned over the table, "Well, if this is going to end, I need to kiss you one last time!"

He came around the table so fast pulling me to the corner of the kitchen. He grabbed my upper thighs lifting me to the counter. I wrapped my legs around him. I could feel the heat of his body pressing into mine. His hands moved to my waist touching my skin, pulling me closer and harder. The kiss was extremely deep. It was like this had been building in him all night. It was so extreme it almost hurt, but in a good way. He stopped abruptly. I nibbled on his bottom lip, wanting more from him.

"He's back, you need to sit down."

Jason didn't move, so I dove under his arm and left him standing there looking angrily out the window.

James came happily in the door, evaluated the scene and said, "I guess I can't leave the two of you alone."

I looked at James with a glare, but noticed Jason. He was either really angry or still composing himself, I couldn't figure it out.

James laughed again, "Well, neither one of you can focus enough to deal could yah?"

I was relieved he was being more playful than accusing. I was sassy with James now, "Are you done with the questions now?"

He laughed, "Only if you two behave."

"Then I'm done playing." I walked out to the living room and tried to wake dad to move to the bedroom.

He got up and looked around, "Okay, okay, I'm up. Boys we have an early day tomorrow." As he walked to the back, I watched him tiredly move to the front bedroom. I felt my heart sink. *Great!* The guys noticed this too and they were both laughing. I grabbed the blanket off the back of the couch and wrapped it around me, not paying attention to what they were doing.

I knelt in front of the TV to put a movie in. I really didn't want a gushy movie, maybe something eerie. I grabbed one I thought would be appropriate in mixed company. I turned to sit and they were both on the couch, one on each end. Jason's expression was of apology. James expression was mischievous.

I moved to dad's chair with a smart ass remark, "You two look so cute together." I plopped down on the chair and grinned. James just stared at me not expecting I would choose the chair over sitting by Jason. I had already experienced too much for the day.

"Are you chicken?" James taunted at me.

"Of you? Of course, who wouldn't be?" I wrinkled my nose at him.

"What are you so afraid of?"

"Like I said. You!"

"I don't bite."

"Are you sure? I've seen your snarl."

Jason smiled at me and said, "I'll protect you."

James snarled at Jason, "You do bite. I need to protect her from you!"

"I don't need to be protected at all if I sit over here."

Jason glared at James, "We'll play nice, won't we?"

"Scouts honor." James put up his hand as if to motion the scout's pledge.

"*You're* not a scout."

"But I could be…" James patted the couch in-between them.

"Thanks guys, but I am fine right here. Remember boys, you have to get up early tomorrow." I flashed them a fake smile.

"So we're going to see who can out last each other?" James said with a smirk.

"You both can win. I have no problem going to sleep."

James was a little more arrogant, "Why don't you go to bed in the back then?"

"Okay."

As I started to get up they both said at the same time, "No!"

I chuckled to myself and sat back down falling between them on the couch. I found this playfulness enjoyable now, as long as they weren't arguing and James wasn't being nasty anymore. He was like a big brother and we could argue all day long. The only thing that bothered me was the staring. I slouched in the middle of them. They were both picking on me.

I was really tired, and it didn't take me long to fall asleep. I knew nothing could happen if they were both here.

7. New Feelings

I was awakened by Jason touching my face very softly. It startled me a bit, and I opened my eyes right away, "What's going on?"

Jason was looking at me very tenderly smiling, "James stepped out."

"Oh." I closed my eyes again to fall asleep again.

"We only have a little bit of time." He whispered.

I turned my head to face him, but I kept my eyes closed, almost falling asleep again. I was waiting for the kissing, but nothing happened. I tried to open my eyes again, kind of checking to see if I was awake or dreaming. Jason was there, but he wasn't doing anything but looking at me. I closed my eyes again.

I was so tired, but I wanted to keep him here so I asked, "Earlier in the kitchen, why were you so angry?"

"I was angry with myself."

"Why?" I yawned a little and tried to wake myself up more.

"I wanted to do things to you that are…" He hesitated.

"Are what?" I really didn't understand, but I was so sleepy I was dozing off a little.

"Things that are really bad because I wanted you so bad, but I couldn't, it wouldn't be right.

Still with my eyes closed I nuzzled into him, "Okay, but I like the kissing it makes me tingly." I felt him chuckle a little.

I reached with my face to his, so he could kiss me. He traced my lips with his fingers, slowly over the top then moving to the bottom lip. I bit his finger gently and said with gritted teeth, "Quit playing and kiss me. *Please?* I want to dream about this again, later."

The kiss came. It was softer than before, so much lighter on my mouth. Our lips moved with each other so smoothly, I didn't even have to think about it. I continued to turn onto my side and was leaning back more and more until I was lying down comfortably on the couch. His lips fit perfectly with mine as they moved together, slightly parted. The kiss stopped slowly. I was almost dozing off, so I opened my eyes a little to see him hovering over me but not touching me, but he wouldn't budge. "What are you doing?" I asked.

"I am trying *not* to seduce you."

"It's *not* working." I stretched a little now that I had more room on the couch. I opened my eyes in shock, "James!"

Jason's eyes saddened, "Do you want *him* here?"

"No! Isn't he still here?"

Jason smiled with a smirk, "He had to go see someone."

"Oh." I closed my eyes again. I was so relaxed and smiling now. He seemed to be closer to me, but I still didn't feel his body. His lips were quicker and more worked up. He would lower his body gently on mine and pull it away, to tease me. I grabbed at his shirt, and tried to pull him to me. I was so sleepy, and couldn't open my eyes, but I still wanted to feel his body next to me. He stopped kissing me and hovered. I had to work really hard to keep my eyes open, but I forced myself. I wanted to know what he was doing.

When I saw him still there I closed my eyes again, "What?"

He hesitated for a long time and then spoke, "Are you still awake?"

"No, not really, I think I am dreaming." I took a deep breath, stretched a little more and turned upward to face his body, almost dozing off again.

"I need to try something but you have to be awake for it to work."

"Can I keep my eyes closed?"

"Most people do," he assured me.

"Okay, I'm ready. What do you want me to do?"

He whispered to my lips, "Be very still and very quiet." He was kissing me slowly and softly. His hands were at my waist touching my skin, pushing my shirt upward until it was right below by breasts. He was careful not to take things too far. I nodded. I could feel his hands trace over my stomach. Then I could feel his mouth tracing over my stomach. My breathing was getting heavier. I opened my eyes a little and looked at him, with fear in them. "What are you doing to me?" I could hardly breathe without gasping. My breathing grew quicker with every touch he made.

"I am seducing you." I didn't feel any relief with his reply. He came back to my lips and said softly, "Do you want me to stop?"

"Yes... No... Maybe... not."

"Just relax. I won't do anything you don't want me too."

I took another deep breath and said, "Okay."

He moved slowly down my stomach again slowly kissing and tracing it with his mouth. My breathing was increasing again. He pulled my sweats down far enough to not reveal anything and traced my skin with his tongue and kissing. My stomach trembled and contracted. It was so hard to breathe and I had to open my mouth to breathe faster and harder. I closed my eyes. Something was happening to my body that I didn't know how to handle.

My body wanted him and I yearned for him to be inside me. I wanted him so bad, but my head was saying, *"No, I can't do this."* He came back to me to kiss me and hush my mouth. I couldn't even kiss him, my breath was too rapid. My heart was pounding so hard.

I gasped, "What are you doing to me?"

"Do you like it?"

"No. I can't control how I am feeling, and it's scaring me."

"Do you want me to stop?"

I looked into his eyes pleading, "I'm scared."

"It'll be okay," his voice sounded reassuring.

"What are you going to do?"

"Just relax. Nothing is going to happen tonight." He kissed me long and hard, "Close your eyes and try to enjoy this."

He moved back to tracing and kissing my stomach. Every touch was intoxicating. He kissed and teased my stomach at the edge of my pants, never advancing just taunting where he was. The contractions in my stomach quickened, my breathing became a moan from the pleasure. Then I felt something. I could not control it or stop it. I felt *a rush* run through my body! I sat up as I felt this. I couldn't stop it or myself from the trembling that filled my body.

Jason moved quickly to wrap his body around me and held me tight. I started to kiss him aggressively. This feeling overwhelmed me and I yearned for him. I wanted to feel him and every part of his body next to mine. I didn't care anymore if I was ready or not. I just wanted to feel him inside me. I was trying to pull his shirt off of him so I could feel his body next to mine. I wanted all of him and now. Jason held me and wouldn't let me attack him.

"You need to relax and enjoy this. Calm down and take a few breaths, and the urge will lessen. Just enjoy it please."

I didn't want to breathe. *I wanted to feel that again!* He held me as close and as hard as he could while I trembled. I tucked my face into his neck embarrassed by my reaction and emotions. I wanted to cry.

"What is wrong with me?"

He hugged me tighter and kissed my forehead, "This is supposed to happen."

"What was that?" I paused and looked at him pleading for an answer.

He smiled, "That is complete pleasure."

"So, that rush?"

"Normal."

"Does that happen when…?" I looked down. I couldn't believe I was asking questions.

"Not always, you need to be with the right person." I wanted him to make me feel this way again with him inside me. I was scared, but if it felt like that, I was definitely ready. I kissed him aggressively. I knew if we did this we could feel this pleasure together. I always heard it's like *becoming one,* and now I understood how this would be amazing to share with him. He squeezed me harder to hold me from doing anything.

"Why are you stopping me?"

"You are not ready."

"So? You *are* ready right now." I was so eager to have him. I advanced on him. I was kissing his neck, nibbling his ear, trying to push him back.

I pushed him onto the couch, sitting on him, I could feel him and this made me hotter. I pushed his shirt up and pressed my bare skin to his. I have not wanted anything more in my life.

He stopped me by tightening his arms around me, "You are not ready. Close your eyes and enjoy the experience you just had. This will not be the last time we are together."

"You're the one that did this to me."

He stated firmly, "Okay, then I get to undo it."

"Why do you get to call how everything goes?"

"I'm older and wiser."

"And you are a bad influence."

He was saddened by this and his lip came out like he was pouting.

I probed him some more, "If you think I am too young then why do you keep tempting me?"

"Yeah, I'm being bad."

"That wasn't the question I asked." I nuzzled my head into his neck and closed my eyes. I was calming down even more exhausted than I was before.

Jason held me more softly whispering in my ear, "Why don't you sleep?"

"I am still expecting an answer mister…"

"I already told you."

"You did?"

"Yes."

"Then how come I don't remember?"

"I want you to stay away from James."

"So, all this is about James?"

"No, it's about you."

"I don't get it, why me? I'm plain." I was grimacing.

"You're cute."

"I'm quiet." Putting my head down. Jason raised my chin.

"Your eyes are killer." I looked away.

"I'm a dork." He pulled my face back to look at him.

"You're quirky."

I looked at him suspiciously, "I'm a loner."

"You stand out."

I was shaking my head no, "You see me so different than I really am."

"You have no idea."

I was confused, "Of what?"

"How people see you."

"I think I'm…" I was kind of awake half sleepy and I couldn't speak anymore. I was completely relaxed in his arms. I closed my eyes while he traced my face with his fingertips.

…What kind of dream am I having? No pictures, but voices. I lay there very still and listened.

"So how was Karla?"

"Very good, if you know what I mean…"

"You are such a dog."

"I know. But they want me, so what can I do?"

"You can make a choice you know."

"Like you with her?"

"It's not like that."

"I can see it is."

"James, please don't! You would break her heart, she's too young."

"Then why do you?"

"I'm not sure, there's something…"

"I am seeing it."

"James please don't."

"So, how far did you go?"

"Not far-she's still too young."

James was chuckling a little, "She said no?"

"She didn't have to. She's way more innocent than you think."

"That's why I left."

"No, Karla was why you left. Not everyone is like you."

"I know and if she shows interest, I'm gonna…"

"No. Not this one, James."

I realized this wasn't a dream. "Guys…" I moved a little and opened my eyes. It wasn't long before they were in front of me kneeling. Jason was close to my face, while James was a little farther down.

James said, "Hey sleepy head."

Jason smiled at me, "What do you need?"

"Peace and quiet, can't you two sleep?" They both smiled at me.

I mumbled, "There are beds in the back, so help yourself because I'm not moving."

Jason lifted my head and upper body to move in and hold me. I nuzzled in to go to sleep. I could feel James lift my knees, and then he took my hand and messaged my fingers. I entwined them with his so we were holding hands.

"Sleep…" was all I could say.

Jason rested his head on mine and whispered, "I think I love you."

I was so sleepy I didn't know if what I heard was real. I didn't reply.

8. The Babysitter

When I woke the boys were gone. I got up and helped mom clean things from the night before. We finished the dishes and got everything put away. I got all my stuff together and loaded it into the car. Mom had said we were leaving early so I wanted to be ready. The weekend was very long and I was so ready to go back to my normal, boring life.

On our way out of town mom pulled into Lakeside (another tavern) I asked, "Why are we stopping here?"

"The boys are having an early lunch and I thought we would say goodbye."

"Are we eating too?"

"Not unless you're hungry?"

"Nope, but if you don't mind I'm going to stay here and start working on my reading."

"Are you sure?"

"Yep."

"I won't be long then."

"I'll be okay. I have a lot of reading to get done."

"It's cold out."

"I'll come in if I get too cold."

"All right then."

It wasn't even five minutes when someone was knocking on my window. To my surprise it was James. I unlocked and opened the car door. "Yes…?"

"What are you doing out here?"

"Homework."

"Did something happen last night, that I don't know about?" He was looking at me suspiciously.

"No. Not really. Why?"

James opened my door and was already pulling me by my hand out of the car, "Jason thinks he did something wrong."

"Okay, okay. I'm coming."

We were walking in hand in hand until Jason looked at me. James let go right away. They were all sitting at the bar.

I sat next to Jason. James made the comment, "She's too good to eat with us then she steals my seat."

I looked at him with a smirk, "Since when do we have assigned seating?"

When I turned to face forward I leaned my shoulder into Jason. He didn't budge.

James said, "Now look, you think you can push people around."

I nudged Jason again, but replied to James, "You just have to argue about everything, don't you?"

He replied smugly, "No, I'm just right."

I placed my hand on Jason's arm so he would look at me. When he turned to me, he looked miserable, completely depressed. I smiled at him. He looked away without acknowledging me at all. I was feeding on James' lead. He was being so good about trying to help me let Jason know I was not mad.

Jason looked at my dad, "I'll go get things ready." He walked out.

I looked at James with a question on my face like – *What should I do now?* James shrugged his shoulders, then a grin came over his face and he said out loud, "I chased *you* in here, now it's your turn. Go and drag his sorry butt back in here. Beg if you have too."

I looked at mom and dad to see if they approved of this. Dad said, "Yeah, someone should. I'm not done eating yet."

"Thanks James." I said with a bit of a sarcastic tone, but really meaning it. I got up and walked outside. Jason was sitting in his truck, but had his window down. I walked up to the truck, putting my forearms on the edge and resting my chin on my arms as I looked at him, "What's up?"

Jason didn't look at me. He was still looking miserable, "Are you okay?"

This surprised me, *what could be wrong?* "Yeah, I was doing great until I saw you like this. What is going on?"

"What I did was wrong, Sarah."

I was a little angry with this, because that was the best night of my life, "Why do you say that?

He shook his head and replied, "You're so young and I shouldn't have done that."

I grabbed his face between my hands so he had to look at me, "Don't do this to me. Don't push me away. That would break my heart." I said this remembering that is what he was lecturing James about. I moved to kiss his lips softly, and he was not responsive. I kept my eyes closed and whispered to his lips desperately, "Please?"

He started to kiss me back. I heard the truck door click, and I moved as he opened the door. I stayed connected to him as the door opened and I backed up until finally I couldn't reach anymore. I looked at him pleading, and then he grabbed my arm and pulled me around the truck door and into his arms.

Looking into my eyes he said, "Are you sure you're okay?"

I smiled, "You have no idea. It's just too hard to be close to you and not touch you, or kiss you when my mom and dad are around. It eats me up inside. I hate that I can't be with you when they are around and I feel like I can't control myself. One of these days I will jump you in front of them, with no self-control at all."

Jason wrapped me in his arms, "I was worried about how you felt. You need to tell me all your feelings even when they turn bad."

"I can't do that. I would be embarrassed all the time."

"Really?"

"Yeah."

The touch of his lips overwhelmed me again as he kissed me.

We could hear James coming closer, "You two aren't really kissing are you?" We broke apart immediately. James was chuckling and said, "You don't do as well as I do. We all better get inside or your mom and dad are going to think you two are doing what you were doing." We all laughed, and made our way back into the bar.

James said under his breath from behind me, "*I'm* not that hard to make happy."

"I bet… You make a lot of girls happy I'm sure."

Dad was finished eating and implied that it took us way too long. It was time to go. I looked at Jason. I wanted to hug and kiss him goodbye, but I knew that wasn't going to happen. We all walked out together. I gave dad a hug and kiss. Mom gave the boys a hug too. I walked to the car and both boys followed so mom and dad could say their goodbyes.

We got to the car and Jason opened the door for me. James said quickly, "I'll give you three seconds to block their view, so hurry up and kiss."

I smiled at him. He turned his back to us, as he was watching for my mom. I leaned into hug Jason and whispered in his ear, "I think I am in love with you too."

He looked at me shocked, wrapped his left arm around my waist to pull me close. He placed his right hand on my cheek, and then kissed me. It was one long kiss, not taunting. The tingling started again. I didn't know if it was the kiss or the memory of the previous night. I put my hands to his waist pulling him closer. He broke away. With his eyes closed in agony he said, "Don't! You'll get me going." I bit his bottom lip, but he just said, "Goodbye." I smiled.

James turned on us like it was a huddle, "Mom's on her way, sure hope you two are done."

I chuckled to myself and thought-*Why is he helping us?* I got in the car, closed my door, and waved. Mom and I were off.

Mom looked at me and asked, "What was the huddle for?"

I shrugged it off, "He's goofy."

The whole next week I found it very hard to concentrate. I wasn't paying attention in my classes. I kept daydreaming about the last weekend. I found homework unbearable, not remembering much of the class. Pat did call me on Wednesday. We mostly talked about up north and Danelle and Brian's family, and how they ended up having a cabin there. I was very polite, but didn't encourage any feelings, which was good.

Another week went by. This one wasn't quite as bad as the first. I could at least concentrate in class now. The only daydreaming I did now was when I was alone, which was every day after school. Pat called on Tuesday this week. We discussed plans about going back up north and set up tentative plans to go snowmobiling; nothing concrete since neither of us really knew when we would end up there at the same time.

It was now week three and I was getting impatient. *How long would Jason wait for me?* I wanted to have the tingles again. Pat called Tuesday and Thursday this week. We discussed homework, parents, friends, and he finally got to the *boyfriend* question, "So do you have a boyfriend?"

"No." I said with a bitter tone, "I'm really not ready for a steady boyfriend. Besides, we're never in the same place for very long, so it would be kind of pointless." I don't know why I didn't fess up, but really I didn't know what to call Jason and I was enjoying our conversations.

Week Four – It was Christmas time and we hadn't been to see dad for a whole month. Dad came home for Christmas. He was looking really rough. Through the conversations with my mom, I found out his business was slow, so the boys had to find other work. I wanted to panic. The only thought was – *When was I going to see Jason again?* I pouted through Christmas over this loss.

Finally a break, we were going up north for New Years! We went to Sherburn's Resort for the celebration. There were a lot of people around and tons of kids, thanks to Brian. We hung out in the back listening to music on the jukebox, playing video games and pool all night long.

Danelle and Brian were very good hosts, they had everyone in the group say their names and where they were from. There were kids from all over the state and some from Wisconsin too. Pat wasn't there. Danelle pulled me aside quietly and pointed out Pat's girlfriend Sue so I was aware. I put it into storage as an interesting fact.

Brian was a total flirt with me. I thought this was either because of the lack of options or he felt bad Danelle spilled the beans about Pat's girlfriend. I didn't really care. Actually, it was kind of fun this way. I still spent most of my time with Danelle. I did talk with Sue for a while. She had sandy brown hair with a very cute face. She was a little quiet, but very nice. I was glad Pat had a girlfriend. I could relax and just be friends with him. I never thought I should ask him if he had a girlfriend.

Danelle pulled me aside after I was done talking to Sue, "Did you tell her that Pat likes you?"

"Nope."

"Did you tell her that you two talk on the phone?"

"Nope."

"Don't you think you should?"

"Nope. I don't see what the point would be and besides that, she's so nice. Pat and I just talk on the phone about stupid stuff. It's not like we could ever be more than friends. This way everyone is happy."

"But he really, really likes *you*."

"Sounds like he doesn't know what he wants or *who* to like. Let's just leave it alone and have fun."

We walked back out, and Brian looked at me funny, "Girl gossip?"

"Yep."

He moved closer, enticing me away from Sue, "You're not going to say anything, are you?" He was trying to be flirty with me to keep my mouth shut. If I hadn't already decided not to say anything, this would have worked.

But I thought I could have fun with this, "Well I don't know...?" Danelle gave me a dirty look, which I deserved. I turned to Brian and reassured him, "I won't do that. She's too nice."

Out of the corner of my eye I saw James with mom and dad. I forgot everyone I was with and went running to him. I hugged him from behind his seat, "I didn't know you were here! How come you didn't come get me?"

"You were busy with the pups." He teased

"Don't start, grandpa. I feel like I could win today."

"I'm scared."

"I bet you are, and you should be." I could feel all the eyes from the group on me, but I ignored them, "So why are you here? Don't you have better things to do?"

"Nope."

"That's all you got for me?"

"Yep."

"You're not much fun today."

"Nope."

I leaned over and whispered in his ear, "Are you okay?"

He shrugged his shoulders. I grabbed his hand and lead him outside, "Okay, what is your problem? I expect you to argue with me!"

"Not in the mood today."

"So, I would win every time? Oh, do we have to argue now!" I didn't realize it, but I was still holding his hand. I was starting to shiver, too.

"I feel bad, and you look cold," he said with concern.

Okay this was a little more serious than I thought, "Why do you feel bad?"

He had his head down looking at me through his long eyelashes. He didn't reply.

"Please tell me," I pleaded.

"I'm here to baby-sit."

"Who would you be babysitting...oh, me, right?"

He looked up quickly to say, "But he didn't say it that way."

"I bet he didn't! If he was worried, why didn't he come himself?" My teeth were chattering together, and I was totally frozen now.

"He's still having Christmas."

"On New Year's Eve?!"

"I guess."

That's when I began to wonder. The tone in his voice told me that there was something else he wasn't saying. *Was Jason hiding something from me?*

James looked at me and realized I was convulsing from the cold. He put his arm around me and rubbed my arm for friction warmth, "You need to go back inside. You were having fun with the group and I could see that. Go have fun."

"Are you leaving?"

"Nope, I'm here all night."

"Okay, but you have to tell me when you are going to leave. Promise me."

"I promise."

We walked back in together. He went to sit with my mom and dad and I went back to the group. Brian was a little angry with me and a little concerned, "So, you're hanging out with the *older* crowd now? You know they aren't good people."

"He works for my dad, and he's like a big brother to me. I think my dad asked him to be here to watch over me. We argue a lot."

"So you don't like him, like him?"

"Nope." I smiled at Brian. It was almost like he was jealous.

Danelle whispered to me, "He really isn't the best person to hang out with, but I'm glad my brother got put in his place." She giggled a little.

"Honestly, there is nothing going on with him. He's like my babysitter, that's all." I had to defend him. It was like I was being protected from my protector.

It was near midnight and time for the countdown, "10... 9... 8... 7... 6... 5... 4... 3... 2... 1...*Happy New Year!*" All the grownups were kissing. Thank goodness none of the kids acted this way. There wasn't much time before we had to leave. I ran to James and asked, "Are you going home?"

"No, I'm going to your place."

"Okay!" I said excitedly. It was like having my very own playmate.

I rode with my parents back to the trailer. James was pulling up as we were walking in. I rushed to get something fun for us to do. I wasn't tired at all. I didn't know how I was going to react to the memory of what happened the last time I was here. I wanted to avoid thinking about Jason.

When James walked in I said, "Cards, movie, or board game?"

He chuckled a little and said, "Cards."

"Rummy?"

"Sure."

I was shuffling before he even sat down. He was a little leery.

Mom said, "Aren't you two tired? It's been a long night."

I was in heaven and wide awake, "Nope!" I didn't pay attention to how James felt. I wasn't going to give him a choice. I could do that with him.

James sat down, and looked at me suspiciously, "So what are you up too?"

"Nothing, I just wanted some company." I dealt the cards and we started right away.

Mom was on her way to bed and dad sat down in his chair to take off his boots, "How long do you two plan to stay awake?"

I said cheerfully, "As long as I can keep him up."

Dad moaned, "I'm going to bed, but…" He looked right at James, "I can trust you two to behave."

I looked at him mortified. "Dad! We will be good. James has lots of girlfriends. He's just being nice to me because of you, and I am taking advantage of that."

James chuckled and said to my dad, "Yeah, not a problem here."

We started the game by just playing, not saying a whole lot. I won three hands, and then James won a couple. We got to 500 in no time. I, of course, won. Guys didn't like to lose, so he was more determined to win the next round. As he was shuffling I could feel the questions building inside him, but he didn't pry. It was 2 a.m. He dealt the cards out and asked, "How long do you plan on keeping me up?"

"For as long as you will stay awake." I watched as he yawned, "Am I keeping you up now?

He smiled a little and said, "Maybe."

"Did you want to go to bed? I can be the winner of the night if you want?"

"No, I'm okay. Play on." I won two hands in a row. He was getting frustrated and yawned a few more times.

"Are you letting me win or are you that tired?"

"No, you're really winning, but it's because I am tired."

"Good, I'll have to remember to play cards with you every time you're tired."

As we started the next hand he looked at me funny, "Are you avoiding going to sleep?" He asked.

I was a little guilty of this, "A little."

"Why?"

"It's just this room and… Do we really have to talk about this?"

"Nope."

"Good."

"Do you want to tell me what happened here?"

"You said we didn't have to talk about it."

"We don't, but if you want to I am a really good listener."

"Guys talk, didn't Jason fill you in?"

"He said nothing happened, but when I saw you kissing at the bar, I knew *something* did."

"Oh."

"You really don't want to talk about this?"

"Not really." I gave him a pleading glance.

"Can we watch a movie instead? I am really tired and if you don't want to talk about things, I could use some sleep."

"Okay, what movie?"

He got up and moved to the couch, "Anything will do, I probably won't last very long."

I picked out a movie, then went to the back room and grabbed two blankets and two pillows. I tossed a blanket to James and wrapped the other around me. I sat down on the couch, pulled my knees to my chest and wrapped my arms around them. I put in an action movie, nothing scary at all, and definitely not mushy.

He sat at an angle with his back to the corner, his legs extended out in front of him. He crossed his arms on his chest. He looked very relaxed, but like he was flexing. The muscles in his arms and chest were so defined. I tried to ignore what I was noticing and turned to watch the movie. I think James was sleeping before the movie even started. I tried to get into the movie, but it was a total guy movie.

I found myself lying down curled up, but I used James' leg as a pillow. He didn't move.

9. The Turn Down

W hen I woke up it was really early in the morning. I think the sun had just come up. James hadn't moved at all. He was still in the exact position he fell asleep in. I got up with the blanket still wrapped around me and snuck outside. I sat on the stairs watching my breath in the cold. I heard the door open behind me. It was James and he sat down behind me with his legs on either side of me. He leaned forward so his mouth was by my ear.

"Did you sleep?"

"Yep."

"Not very much by the looks of it."

"I slept," arguing my case.

"Are you okay?" he questioned.

"Yep."

"Are you thinking about him?"

"A little, but I'm trying not to."

"That's good. You know he wishes you weren't so young."

"In a month I will be sixteen."

"Really, he's turning twenty-one in a couple months."

"Great." I said sarcastically, "When's *your* birthday?"

"In October."

"I missed it."

"Yeah. It was before I met you."

"So, how many girls are you dating right now?"

"None."

"I find that hard to believe. I thought you were a ladies' man?"

"They all found out about each other and dumped me."

"That won't last for long."

"Maybe, it depends on how hard I try."

"It can't help when you have to *baby-sit.*"

"Nope."

"Maybe you shouldn't agree to baby-sit me anymore."

"It's a nice break. I don't have to pretend I'm something that I'm not."

"I guess you have a point."

"So, are you going to tell me what happened?"

"Nope."

"So something did happen?" I really didn't want to answer him. He pushed further, "Did he hurt you?"

"Nope."

"Did you guys try to…?"

"Nope, and it's hard to not think of him when you keep wanting me to talk about it."

He grabbed my chin and tilted my head completely back, "Okay, okay, but if or when you need to talk, I'm here." And he kissed my forehead.

"So, are you on babysitting duty all day?"

"No, it depends on if your dad works me at all today."

"If you're not working and you have to baby-sit me anyway, do you want to go snowmobiling?"

"We'll see."

"Okay." I made it sound like I was hurt.

"Remember, you're supposed to hang out with people your age. I'm not supposed to interfere with that."

"So, I need to hang out with the group again?"

"Yep."

"But I don't really fit in. I'm kind of a dork."

"No, you're so cute they don't know how to talk to you."

"Great." Sounding disappointed.

"You said you would try."

"I am. It's just that you and Jason treat me differently."

"How is that?"

I turned half way on my butt to look at him. I didn't know exactly how to put it, "You two make me feel…*special.*"

"You are."

"How?"

"You tell things how they are, you don't play games, and you're fearless."

"Oh, I am scared all the time."

"It doesn't show. I meant that you're not devious and you don't have an ulterior motive."

"I don't get it."

"Sometimes you're more mature than the girls we date or hang out with."

"Do you mean just *you* or both of you?"

"Both."

"So, Jason dates?"

"I thought you didn't want to discuss Jason?"

"You're right. I don't want to know." I turned back to face forward, so he couldn't see me pout.

"You're upset now."

"No, I really don't have any right to be upset."

"But you are."

"Maybe a little, but it's not like he's a boyfriend or anything, right?"

"That's what I am talking about right there."

"What?" I gasped.

"You are so mature in the way you think, and reason out how you should feel, without playing mind games. It's innocent, like Jason said."

"I don't feel mature."

"That's what makes you irresistible."

"To who?"

"Jason…and maybe me."

I playfully shoved him with my back and said, "Right."

We sat there for a short while in silence, and then I was done feeling sorry for myself. I got up and look at him, "Hungry?"

"Starved."

"Cereal?"

"Sure."

We went back inside where nobody was stirring yet. I got a few different kinds of cereal out since I didn't know what he liked. He got the milk out. We poured ourselves a bowl and ate quietly.

I could hear my dad getting up. When he came out he looked at us disapprovingly, "Did you two sleep at all?"

"Yep," we said at the exact same time.

"You're eating already?"

"Yep," again we said at the same time. We both started laughing.

Dad shook his head, "James, are you going to work with me today?"

"I was hoping to."

"Good, I need some help."

James looked at me and said very quietly, "I guess I don't have to baby-sit today."

I hit him in the arm with my fist.

"Ouch!"

"Sarah, that wasn't nice," scolded my dad.

"He's picking on me!"

"It's not ladylike."

James was in on this, "Does that mean I get to punch her in the arm?"

"No, boys don't hit girls."

I stuck my tongue out at him and kicked him under the table.

"Can I kick her if she kicks me like she just did?"

Dad was getting irritated, "Stop it you two, or I'm going to separate you."

We both started laughing.

When I finished I started boiling water to wash up. Mom was up and eating now. Dad and James went out to get things ready for the day. When the water was ready I went to tell James and dad that it was ready for them to wash up. James came in and washed his face. We both grabbed a glass of water and went out to brush our teeth. When we were outside we both had the giggles. I nudged him, he laughed and hip checked me. I almost fell over. We were laughing again. I spit toward his feet.

"Oh, you *did not* just do that."

"What are you going to do? I'm so scared now."

He got an evil glare in his eye. He picked me up so quickly throwing me over his shoulder. He carried me to the deepest snow bank around and was trying to dump me in it. I clung to him with every muscle I had. I was not going to let go and be in a snow bank.

Dad yelled from the hill, "Put her down boy, we have got work to do!" I got down carefully to not end up in a snow bank and started to walk away.

"I win." I looked back at him with a smile. He shook his head and ran to help dad.

When they left, my thoughts turned to Jason and how he made me promise to stay away from James. James didn't make any moves on me last night. He was just like a brother. I had fun, plus Jason sent him to baby-sit, so it must be okay. Mom and I headed down to Sherburn's Resort about 2 o'clock in the afternoon. Mom and Laura were visiting in the bar. Danelle and I hung out with them. Laura was great and very funny. Danelle was so grown up that it was like we belonged there with the adults.

Brian and a couple friends, Zack and Tommy, were playing pool. At about 6 p.m. the guys decided to go snowmobiling. I didn't have anything with me so Laura offered to let me wear her stuff. I road with Brian, Danelle road with Zack, but only after Brian lectured him about being careful with his sister. I thought to myself—*Wow, James is like having a big brother,* and I smiled to myself. We rode all over the place; most of the time I didn't even know where we were.

We got back around 8 p.m. I looked really grubby now, but so did all of us, except for Brian, who was still as perfect as always. We stayed in the back and played video games. I really didn't want to be in the bar because I looked horrible. Brian and Danelle had to run out into the bar a few times to take food orders. Thank goodness none of them wanted to hang out in the bar.

Danelle had to go out for one last order just before midnight. When she came back she called me to the kitchen, "Your guy friend is here."

I got a little nervous and said in a very low tone, "Was it the one from the truck or the one last night?"

"The one from last night."

I took a deep breath in relief, "That's only James. He's like a big brother."

"I know who he is and he is a lot older and hangs out with some bad people."

"Really, I hadn't noticed. He usually doesn't have anyone with him when he's around my family and me. He works for my dad."

She was still looking at me disapproving.

"I'll go say hi and I will be right back." I ran out to him, putting my hands over his eyes.

He grabbed them and pulled them around him, "Did you really expect me to not know who it was?"

"Yes."

He was sitting next to my dad, but didn't reserve himself at all. He turned to me with my hands in his, "So what did you do today?"

"I hung out here and we all went snowmobiling. Now I am hanging in the back with Danelle."

"So, you got to do what you wanted today after all." He patted my head like a puppy and said, "You look a mess."

"Why thank you, because you look so much better."

Laura laughed and shrugged her shoulders, "She's right!"

He shook his head disapproving, "Okay, you go back and play with your little friends."

"Are you staying again?" I asked.

He looked at my dad.

Dad sighed and replied, "Well I guess so. I don't want you to drive so far when it's this late."

"Great!" I was excited about it.

James mustered a smile, "Great!"

As I walked away I said, "Board game tonight?"

Dad yelled after me, "Not all night again!"

James and I replied at the same time again, "It wasn't all night."

I continued to head back to the house part of the building. Danelle met me in the kitchen, looking at me funny, "He does kind of treat you like a little sister."

"I know. He doesn't seem bad, does he?"

"Maybe it's just when he's around *you.*"

"Well then that's a good thing."

"Do you like him?"

"No, he's just a lot of fun to hang out with especially when I'm stuck alone."

"As long as you don't *like* him."

"I do like him as a friend though."

She was persistent and scolded, "That's fine, but nothing more."

"Okay!" We went back in to play video games with the boys. It was getting to be bar closing so I went to the bathroom before going to the trailer. I hated using the outhouse, especially when it was cold out. When I came out Brian was standing there. I looked at him nervously, "Your turn?"

"No, I have a question for you."

"Okay, what is it?"

"You're not gonna want to answer me."

"Try me." My back was to the wall and Brian was facing me.

He leaned into me and asked very quietly in my ear, trying to be seductive, "What is the reason you like to hang out with the older guys?"

"What do you mean?" I grimaced at him.

"I saw you leave with Jason, and now hanging with James."

"Yeah, so they both worked with my dad, they're just around."

"Are you doing stuff with them?"

"No, and I really don't like what you're implying."

"I really don't like you hanging with them."

"That's not up to you."

"*I* would even be better for you."

"Yeah, well *you're* not interested, plus you have tons of girls that like you."

"Not really."

"Yeah, really! Besides the only reason you're giving me attention is because I am hanging out with older guys. You...think I'm easy."

77

"No, just more interesting."

"You know that's not true. Besides, Danelle is my friend, and this will never happen."

"Okay, maybe I wouldn't have noticed, but I am noticing now." He leaned into kiss me.

I stopped him and pushed him away saying, "This is not happening." I walked away. As I turned the corner to go back to the living area, Danelle was standing there hearing everything. I looked at her with apology. She waited for her brother. As he passed her she said, "Asshole."

We tried to get along long enough to get through the last fifteen minutes of the night, but it wasn't' easy. Brian was being a jerk, and Danelle just glared at him with anger..

I looked at Danelle and said, "It's almost bar close, and I think I will wait out there until mom and dad are ready to go."

Danelle came with me.

James looked at Danelle and said, "How come you don't look as bad as Sarah? She's a mess."

Danelle was embarrassed, and didn't say anything. I was happy he was trying to be nice. She was becoming my best friend.

10. Not a Date

W e got back to the trailer in no time at all. I ran inside and pulled out all the board games that we had. When I looked at them, they were all pretty childish. James walked in after dad. Dad was shaking his head, like he couldn't believe I was serious. Mom was getting ready for bed, but I think she was coming back out to read a little. Dad worked with the TV to try and get something in that would be watch-able.

I looked at James and said, "These all look really boring, would you rather play cards?"

"Whatever you want," he said wearily. I didn't know how long he would make it today. He was so tired.

I asked, "Rummy, again?"

He wrinkled his nose at me, "You always win. Can we try something simpler?"

"Sure! What are you thinking?"

"Maybe Kings in the Corner, I don't have to think for that one." He was yawning. I felt bad he was so tired.

My face turned down and I said, "You probably should get some sleep."

"No, I'll be fine for awhile. You can tell me about your day."

I was excited again. There would be so much to talk about. He would be proud of me. I think I did really well today. I was shuffling and realized that mom never came back out. I asked dad, "Did mom go to bed?"

"Yeah, she started really early today. I am right behind her. Sarah, don't keep the boy up too late. Try to let him sleep a little tonight."

"Okay, just a couple of hands."

James smiled at me as I dealt the cards. We started to play cards, but soon he was yawning every couple of minutes. I just couldn't force him to stay up with me. I was sad, but I knew I had to let him sleep. I took his hand, and he looked at me confused. I lead him to the couch and put the blanket over him, put his feet up, and tucked him in. Then I just looked at him.

He smiled and said, "What are you doing?"

"I am letting you off the hook because you need to sleep."

He sat up trying to refuse to give in to this, "But we haven't spent any time talking yet."

"It can wait. Nothing really exciting happened anyway." I pushed him back down firmly, "That's my final decision!"

"You are a very stubborn girl."

"Yep, I am."

"Okay, you win, but I just need a nap. Wake me in an hour so we can talk."

"If I make it that long."

He lifted the blanket for me to join him. I didn't know how to take that. I wasn't really comfortable with being hit on twice in the same night. He looked at me and could see my hesitation, "Do you really think I have the strength to try anything? Please."

"I guess not." I crawled in next to him with my back to him and my head resting on his bicep. James fell asleep before me. I could tell by his breathing. I closed my eyes.

The next thing I knew James was waking me up, "Sarah…Sarah?"

I didn't open my eyes at all but replied, "Yeah?"

"You should go back to one of the beds."

I opened my eyes, questioning him, "Why?"

"I don't think it would be good if your mom and dad got up to find us together on the couch."

"Yeah, you're right." I slowly sat up and tried to steady myself for a minute.

"Do you want help?"

"Nope, I just need a minute. I'm not really awake."

"Okay." He rubbed my back. I stood up and staggered a little. He was by my side, "Let me help you please."

"Okay." He walked me to the front bedroom which was empty. We stopped in front of the beds. I turned to him and hugged him so tightly, "Thank you."

"Yeah, no problem. Crawl into bed now." I did as I was told and he tucked me in.

"This isn't as comfortable."

"I know, but its better this way.

The next morning I woke up late. It was after 9 a.m. and we would have to go home soon. I couldn't wait to eat with James. I came out staggering, not quiet myself yet. Dad said, "Hi sleepy head. How late were you up?"

"Not late at all. James couldn't keep his eyes open." I looked around for my morning argument, but no James. My heart sank and I went to the kitchen. Mom and dad were making French toast and bacon. I was so hungry that I sat down to eat right away. I poured a large glass of milk and drank half before even eating. I sat waiting. I was not really awake yet. I grabbed my book for English class. I really hated reading. I put a slice of French toast on my plate and cut it into sixteen little bitsy pieces. I opened my book and James walked in.

"Oh my, you look scary in the morning."

I was giggling to myself, because that was the best sound, "I can see you got your beauty sleep."

"Yep, and don't I look pretty?"

I stuck my tongue out at him, "Great, I'm not going to get my work done now."

"The brainiac will get it done, just not now."

"Do you have something better to do?"

"Yep."

"So what are you planning?"

"Your dad said I could take you snowmobiling."

"Our sled?"

"Yep."

"Then *I* get to take *you.*" I was trying to get him to argue with me.

"Nope. He's loaning it to me so I can take *you.*"

"Fine, when do we go?"

"As soon as you're ready."

"Do I have to be presentable?"

"Probably."

"Give me fifteen minutes!"

"You can take longer than that. It might take some work."

"Don't need it." I grabbed a big glass of water and went to the bathroom. I brushed my teeth, pulled my hair back, and put on a headband. I decided I wanted to look my best, so I put long johns on so I didn't have to wear snow pants. I put on my white fur boots – I had a sweater vest with a fur collar to match. Then I put on my down Jacket over the top. I even put a little makeup on. I hurried back out to the front room, "I'm ready!"

"I'm not done eating yet."

"Okay, slow poke."

"I didn't think you would be ready so quickly. Most girls take at least an hour."

"I'm not most girls." I glanced over at my mom, "How long do we have?"

Mom smiled, "We won't leave until later. Maybe 5 or 6 p.m."

"Cool! Where are we going?"

James smiled almost scared to reply, "Where ever you want."

"I don't know where to go, so you'll have to surprise me."

"I kind of have an idea. We'll see how it goes."

"Are you ready yet?"

"No, let me finish eating."

"You're slow, hurry up, and let's go!"

"What are you in such a rush for?"

"I love to ride!" I took off my jacket and boots, grabbed my book and sat on the couch, "I guess I will just have to wait for you."

"Are you pouting?"

"No, are you being as slow as a *girl?*"

"I don't know if I want to take you anywhere, you're being…a pain."

I jumped up and ran to sit next to him at the kitchen table. He barely finished the piece he was eating and said, "Well, if we don't go now she's going to burst."

"That's not true, take your time."

They all laughed at me.

"Okay, I'm done." I grabbed his plate and put it in the sink. I set his glass of milk in front of him. He drank it in one gulp. I took it and put it in the sink. I asked mom, "Do you want me to help with dishes?"

"No, get out of here."

I grabbed James' hand and led him to where I left my boots. I put them on along with my jacket. I waited for him to get his stuff on. I could hardly wait to get out the door.

Once we were out the door I turned on James, "How did you get this worked out?"

"Your dad suggested it."

"Really? Oh, maybe they wanted to be alone for awhile. So now we have to stay away for a while."

"Yeah, I think so."

"You're really stuck with me now."

"That's not so bad, except when you're overly excited."

"Oh, like now?"

James started up the machine. It was a little old but it works well enough. I hopped on the back, wrapping my arms around his waist and we were off. I had no idea where we were going, but we were on our way. It seemed like a long ride, but we stopped at a small tavern I had never been to. The name was Sly's place. We went in and had a soda. James checked on me, "Are you cold?"

"A little."

"We'll go to the next one when you warm up."

"Okay."

"Why didn't you wear snow pants?"

"I hate them."

"So why were you in such a hurry to get out of there?"

"I'm not sure, but we didn't get much time together and I was just happy I get you for the day. I like being *babysat.*"

"So you're glad you get to spend more time with me?"

"Okay, I confess. Yes, you found me out!"

"Why do you think I asked?"

"I thought you said it was my dad's idea?"

"Yeah, but I planted the idea."

"You are such a bad boy." I smiled. "So what are you going to do with me?"

"I'm sure we can find plenty to do. Shall we go to the next?"

The next small tavern we stopped at took a little longer to get there. I was *very* cold. I decided to have some hot chocolate instead of soda. We played a game of pool and put some money in the jukebox.

James was a blast to be around. I think it had to do with knowing he was my *babysitter.* He was ordered to make sure I behaved. I found it kinda funny. I just needed to pout a little in order to get my way.

"You know you're really not that good at pool?"

"I know, but I can still win."

As he was trying to make a shot, I leaned over the table, rested my head on my hands, stared at him and blinking my eyes.

"That's not going to work."

"Shoot then."

"Come here I want to show you something first."

I moved around the table and stood next to him, "What?"

"See, there's a way around you," and he took the shot.

"I won't fall for that one twice," I warned. We both laughed. It was almost 1 pm so we headed to the next place.

I had been to this one before. When we went in we were discussing eating, and decided to share an order of French Fries. They took awhile to come so we sat and talked a little. James was very sweet, "Are you having fun at all?"

"Yeah. Aren't you?"

"I can think of a few things that would be more fun." I got a really eerie feeling. Was James going to overstep the boundaries we had set for ourselves.

I panicked, "Like what?" I had a little defense in my voice.

"Dancing, swimming, carnivals…"

"Oh," I chuckled in relief.

"What? Did you think I was going to say something else?"

"Kinda." I had a guilty smile.

"What did you think I was going to say?"

I was totally embarrassed now, probably turning three shades of red. I looked down to avoid his gaze, "I really don't want to say."

"Oh, I get it. Do you really think that is all I do when I am not with you?" he was very defensive.

"Yeah, with all the girls you have and your body is…*perfect.*" I still had my head down, but I was looking up at him with my eyes to see his reaction. I hadn't realized what I was going to say until it was already out of my mouth.

"So you think I have a nice body?"

I couldn't even look at him. I was so embarrassed. I didn't want him to get the wrong impression, but I would pay for that comment the rest of the day. He was going to torture me with it. James reached across the table with one hand and lifted my chin.

"Don't be embarrassed. That's what I like about you the most. You are brutally honest."

"Completely honest… Yes, I have noticed your muscles and they are *very* defined." Now with a little anger in my voice, "Are you happy now?"

He sat there stunned, not replying and took a minute, "Does that mean you like them or they're just there?"

"Do you really want to talk about your muscles, James?"

"I really don't. I was more curious to what you are thinking?"

"Shall we go?"

"You're not good at getting out of tough questions. Just answer me, honestly."

"Are you asking how I feel about your muscles, or *you?*" He smiled with my reply.

"See getting right to the point, no games. I guess this is too deep, shall we?" I was so thankful, I didn't want to tell him I really liked being around him, and I would miss him.

We had wasted a lot of time at the last tavern. As we drove things began to look familiar again. He slowed down and asked, "Do you want to stop at Sherburn's to say goodbye?" He was always thinking of what I wanted. I nodded my head. We pulled in. It was pretty quiet.

He asked me, "Do you want to go in alone or should I come with you?"

"You should come with me, of course." I said this with a question. I didn't understand why he wouldn't come in.

"You are supposed to have one of these kids as your boyfriend and I don't want to cramp your style."

I looked at him, "You're actually helping it. You have no idea."

"What do you mean?"

"Can I tell you later? Please."

"I won't let you go until you tell me."

"I will...just not now." I grabbed his hand and pulled him into the store area. Danelle walked out; she was working again.

"I had to come say goodbye. We're leaving as soon as I get back to the trailer."

"Oh." She looked at James and wasn't as friendly as she normally was.

"I don't know when I'll be back, but can I come help you again?"

She smiled at me, "Of course you can. Sorry about yesterday."

"You didn't do anything."

"I know, but Brian was a jerk."

"Awe that was nothing. I'm over it. Are you two talking yet?"

"Nope, but I told my mom how stupid he was."

"You didn't have to do that, I can handle it. You're my friend first."

"Thanks."

"No problem. Well, we better go. See ya!"

James and I walked out to the snowmobile. I got on and he just stood there and looked at me.

"Not now, can we talk about it later please?"

11. A New Development

He was pissed and he had no idea of what happened. I wasn't sure I should tell him what happened. We were on our way back to the trailer and I was getting cold again. James took some back trails instead of the road. I didn't understand why until he stopped. He turned the machine off and sat there for a minute.

"I'm cold."

"You're not getting out of telling me what happened."

"I told you I would tell you later."

"Yeah, but if I take you back home you won't tell me, because your parents will be there. So, you need to tell me what you meant and what happened."

"It's not as big of a deal as you're making it out to be, and you're getting angry and scaring me."

He started pacing to calm down. I sat there and waited, not saying a word. My teeth were starting to chatter. He looked at me with anger in his eyes, but it softened when his eyes met mine. He could tell I was cold. He came and sat behind me and put his arms around me to try and warm me a little, "Is this okay?"

"Are you done being mad now?"

"Not really, but I will behave."

"Then, yeah, it's okay."

"Can you please tell me what happened, and what you meant before we walked in to Sherburn's?"

"Yes, but I need to see your face so you stay calm."

"You think if I am looking at you I won't get as mad?"

"Yes."

"Fine." He got off the snowmobile and got back on in front of me, but facing me. He pulled my legs over his so we were sitting so close I felt the urge to kiss him, totally bad timing. He was rubbing my legs and arms to keep me warm, "Well?"

"Last night, right before the end of the night, I went to the bathroom and Brian was waiting for me when I got out." I paused and watched his eyes to see if the fury was coming back, but he was doing okay. I continued, "He sort of stopped me and asked me why I liked hanging out with older guys." I stopped again and waited for a reaction.

"Okay, what did you say?"

I was a little slow when I continued, "I feel really stupid and it's not that I don't want to tell you I just find it hard to talk about it, so please be patient. It's really not as bad as you think."

"Sarah, just be direct. That's what you're best at."

"He asked me if I was doing stuff with the two of you."

"You mean me and Jason?"

"Yes, but I told him I didn't like what he was implying." I was waiting for the anger to come and he just sat there.

"Is that it?"

"He told me that he didn't like me hanging with the two of you because you were bad for me and he would be better for me." I cringed when I said this. I thought for sure the fury would be coming; but nothing.

"So, did you say anything back?"

"Yeah, I told him that the only reason he was interested was because he thought I was easy, and the only reason he was paying me attention was because of you guys; otherwise he would have never paid any attention to me."

"Is that it?"

"No, he said he was mistaken and was noticing me now, and he tried to kiss me." I closed my eyes in fear.

James laughed, "So, what did you do?"

"I pushed him away and told him that this would not happen, and Danelle's friendship was more important than what he had to offer, basically."

He was laughing at me. He wasn't mad at all. I was totally embarrassed. I put my hands to my face and wanted to lose it. James hugged me tightly, "See, you are adorable and you just don't see it that way. It makes you even better."

I replied from my face in his coat, "But I'm not better. I'm just a stupid girl."

"Why do you say that?" he was trying to pull my face to look at him. I didn't budge.

"What are you so upset about?"

"Part of it was true."

"Which part?"

"Please don't make me talk about it; I really can't."

"Are you talking about Jason?"

I looked at him with pleading eyes, "Please, I can't talk about it?"

He paused for a long while and rubbed my arms more to try and keep me warm, "I'm sorry but you really need to tell me what happened."

"I can't. I am too embarrassed, and you're a guy."

"Did you two do it?"

I shook my head no in his jacket.

He lifted my face by cupping my cheeks in his hands. He was looking into my eyes so softly, so caringly. Tears were trying to run down my cheeks, but were freezing on their way down. He used his thumbs to wipe the tears away. Then he kissed my cheeks where the tears had run down to try and warm them with his lips. His face was so close to mine. I was tingly and I wasn't even kissing him. Why was I feeling this way, he was my *babysitter.*

"If you didn't do it, what are you so upset about?"

I couldn't reply. I was too upset.

"We can get through this together but you need to calm down."

I nodded my head.

"I'll count to three and we'll take a deep breath together. 1... 2... 3..." We both took a deep breath. It helped a little. "1... 2... 3..." We took another breath.

I closed my eyes with this last breath and whispered, "You'll think I'm easy too."

He pulled my face to his, "I won't ever think that. You need to talk about what happen or it will eat you up. I can see it's already bothering you."

"I know, but it's hard to talk about it."

"Why?"

I shook my head.

"I'm going to tell you something, but you have to promise to not get mad at me."

This helped me compose myself a little, "I'm ready."

"Do you promise?"

I nodded.

"No, you have to say it."

I looked at him suspiciously, "I promise."

"But you have to finish telling me what happened first."

"I'll try."

"Would it help if I asked questions?"

I nodded looking into his eyes trusting him to be careful.

"You can't laugh, because I might use some words that might make you laugh."

I shook my head eagerly to let him know I wouldn't laugh.

He paused and waited a moment then tenderly asked, "Did he touch your breast?"

I shook my head no and he smiled.

"Did he touch you down there?" I knew what he meant just by his gesture and I shook my head no, again. "And you think you're easy? I don't get it."

I looked at him pleading with my eyes.

"He did touch you?"

I nodded.

"We're going to try something else. I am going to say a sentence and you finish it. Can you try that?"

I nodded.

"He touched my...?"

I swallowed and replied, "Stomach."

His eyes got bigger. He was angry but trying to stay very calm.

"With his...?"

"Mouth."

His eyebrows furrowed like he didn't understand me anymore. "So, let me get this straight. You feel easy because he kissed your stomach?" My eyes widened. He just looked at me for a few minutes calculating it in his mind but he finally got it.

"One more sentence. Then I think I have it."

I waited for the worst sentence in my life.

"When he kissed your stomach you felt...?"

I cringed, "A rush."

He swept to my face so, fast I didn't have time to react and he kissed me one solid hard kiss. He got up, "I knew it!" He got off the snowmobile and was pacing around in front of me. I couldn't tell if he was happy or upset. "I knew it! You didn't! I just knew it." He looked at me and saw my confusion. This was the most humiliating thing I have ever had to confess and he was acting crazy.

He rushed back to me putting both hands on my face, "You are the most beautiful girl I know," and then he kissed me again. It was long and hard, but he stopped and looked at me, "I am so sorry; I shouldn't have done that."

I was still in shock.

"Do you realize you are the most pure and beautiful person in the world to me?"

"You don't honestly believe that?"

"I do!" He paused a minute looking at me, "Let me explain-you experienced the best feeling in the world. Most girls don't even do that when they're *having* sex, and you're still pure. Wow!" He stopped to ponder something in his head, and then said out loud without thinking, "He must be good if he can do that. It would have been almost impossible to do that and not go further." He looked at me very seriously, "Didn't that make you like want him really bad?"

I was so ashamed with myself that I looked down. I knew this would be a mistake to tell him but, "I tried to attack him and he wouldn't let me."

His excitement stopped he tried to lift my face to look at him, "I am a complete idiot. I am so sorry, but I told you I have to tell you something and you promised to not get mad at me."

I nodded.

"I have to do one thing to be brave enough to tell you, Okay?"

I nodded again.

His hands dropped from my face a little, so his palms were at my neck his thumbs were holding my chin up and he kissed me again. It was not luring but passionate and intense. I didn't know why I was doing this, but I replied by kissing him back. When he released our kiss he rested his forehead on mine.

"Okay, confession time – and you did promise me to not get mad."

I just smiled at him.

"You are so beautiful when you smile."

"Confession?" I reminded him. I wanted him to be as vulnerable as I was at this moment.

He put his arms around me tight, so if I did get mad I couldn't get away, "Jason didn't send me to baby-sit," he waited for a reaction. "I came on my own, but I have really good reasons: First, I couldn't get enough of you. Second, I was looking to see if you had any feelings for me at all. And third, I didn't want anyone else to have you. Not just sexually, I mean I didn't want you hanging around the little boys. I wanted you for myself." He waited for my reply.

I wanted this deep down, too. I had so much fun with James and all the time. I wrapped my arms around his neck and kissed him so hard. I was so relieved that this difficult part was over. He got up on his knees and pulled me with him. Our bodies were touching and he put his arm around my waist and pulled me as close as we could be outside in the cold. This kiss was taking my breath away; the passion was intense. When we stopped we both could hardly breathe.

"I do have one question for you?" I looked at him in wonder.

"What?"

"Why did you help me to be with him the last time? That must have been so hard?"

He was a little reserved when he replied, "Deep down I really like you and wanted you to be happy, no matter who it was with." He closed his eyes to be deep in thought, and then he opened them and looked deep in my eyes, "There is going to be something harder."

I was trembling, "What?"

"We'll have to be really careful and really slow, because I wouldn't be able to stop."

I kissed him so hard, but I used my whole mouth. I wanted him to feel this way about me and I was so happy. How was I ever going to leave?

"We have been gone a long time; we need to get back."

I moaned, "Yeah."

He started the machine and sat down. I wrapped myself around him as tight as I could. He gripped my arms at his front. I was completely trembling. I couldn't tell if it was cold or excitement.

We got back and dad looked a little angry. James addressed him very seriously, "We need to look at the machine, it stopped working and I couldn't get it started for over a half hour. It may have over heated." He didn't wait for dad's reply, "She's freezing we need to get her warmed up right away." It helped that I was trembling terribly.

He carried me to the trailer whispering, "Just play along, you're already trembling."

I smiled at him, "You are a bad, bad boy."

He grinned. He sat me on the couch and headed straight to the kitchen to boil some water. James noticed my dad was watching him and asked, "Cocoa, tea, something hot?"

Dad came out of it and moved, "Right, oh yeah right here."

Mom went to get more blankets, looking a little more worried then they needed to be. James came back to me and handed me a cup of cocoa as he pulled my boots off and rubbed my toes to warm them. He was really good at this acting thing. I was still trembling. I don't think it's from the cold anymore. When my trembling got better James settled down a little and sat next to me, "You are okay, right?"

I smiled at him, "Amazing."

Mom and dad both moved over to look at me, "Are you ready to go home now?"

"Sure."

James was still trying to look serious, "If it's okay with you two I'd keep her wrapped up and I will carry her to the car." They both backed off and let him carry me to the car.

"I don't want to leave."

He smiled at me, "Don't worry, I will be here when you come back. I'll be checking all the time."

"No phone calls?"

"How?"

"I know; I was just hoping."

"Beg and plead to make it soon. I'm not going to last a day without your face."

I was in heaven the whole way home. I kept daydreaming about his face.

12. Unwanted Surprise

Back to reality; my life was so much better up north. I am such a nobody in the cities. For a birthday present to myself I was going to work out and get fit. I needed to if I was going to take on James. I wanted to be able to defend myself against him.

First Week – Pat called on Monday and we talked about who was all up there and what we did. When I was going through the list of people, I had forgotten that Sue, his girlfriend, and said her name. He hesitated as he told me he had a confession to make. Nothing could faze me after this weekend.

"Okay," I said happily.

"Technically, Sue is my girlfriend. We email and I see her maybe four times a summer."

"I kinda found that out."

"Who told you?"

"It doesn't matter. She is a sweetheart and so are you. I hope we can still be friends and keep talking on the phone."

"You are so cool; why are you so nice to me?"

"I have nothing but time, and I really don't want a boyfriend I never see, so I am good with being friends." I filled him in on New Year's night and snowmobiling. The weekend wasn't that exciting."

School was so boring, but I noticed some of the people were being nicer to me. I really didn't have a lot of friends. Matt Erickson was my favorite person at school. He was a twin and lots of girls liked him. He was always nice to me and we always shared homework if there was something one of us didn't get. I wasn't stupid and sometimes I thought that was the only reason people paid any attention to me, to get help.

Second Week – Things had been very mellow. I was doing 100 sit-ups a day and 40 pushups. I wanted to look good. I spent most of my nights thinking about James and sometimes a little about Jason, but only about what I was going to say to him because I felt bad. I think he knew I would fall for James and that's why he made me promise. Oh shit, I broke my promise. I'll deal with that when the time comes. Pat called on Thursday. He was really behind in his classes, so he had a lot of work to make up. He said he would call next week.

Third Week – I was really missing my escape from reality. I was still working out every day. I hadn't noticed any change. I was miserable and I wanted to see James. I was going backwards instead of forwards. I closed my eyes every night and I could see him sleeping on the couch with his muscular arms folded over his chest, his strong face and his always tan body. I would love to have that color all of the time.

Fourth Week – My birthday is this week. Great, I was happy to be 16, but I hated being recognized for my birthday. I was still working out every day. *When does the transformation happen?* I'm still waiting. Pat called on Tuesday; he apologized for not calling the previous week. He was still restricted on phone privileges, so he couldn't talk, but he didn't want to leave me hanging.

I was dreaming every night replaying my time with James, playing pool, talking, riding snowmobile, playing cards, falling asleep in his arms, and his goofy outrage at my innocence. My dreams were moving to the daytime. I need to see him soon.

Dad called on my birthday, which was Thursday. He wished me happy birthday and said, "There are a couple of guys here who want to say hi."

Then Jason's voice was on the phone, "Happy Birthday!"

"Thanks."

"So, you're sixteen?"

"Yep, I heard you're turning twenty-one next week."

"How'd you hear that?"

"I'm amazing that way and a little persuasive."

"James told you?"

"I asked."

"So, you're coming up here this weekend?"

"Yep."

"I'll try to stop by."

"Okay."

"Bye."

"Bye."

James got on the phone, next. "Hi crabby girl!"

"Why am I crabby?"

"You told on me."

"I said I asked."

"Yeah, I'm getting dirty looks now."

"I'm sorry. I'll make it up to you."

"When?"

"I hope this weekend. Will I see you?"

"You know the answer to that one."

"So, Jason is in front of you right now?"

"Yep."

"So, if I tell you I wanted to kiss you so much right now, you couldn't say anything?"

"You're a pest."

"How about, I dream so much about you and it's moved into my days."

"That must be torture."

"You're going to hear about this from Jason aren't you?"

"Yep."

"I should let you go."

"Yep."

"I miss you."

"Happy birthday Sarah!"

"I can't wait to see you."

"Bye Sarah."

"Bye."

Dad got back on the phone, "Were you being hard on James?"

"Of course. I love ya dad!"

"See you this weekend! Can I talk to mom again?"

"Sure, bye."

Friday morning I was all happy. I went with my driving instructor in the morning to get my license, so I only had to tolerate a half day of school before we headed north. Driving was a breeze. I had been driving up north for nearly two years now. I was waiting for my mom to get home so we could get going. I was already packed and had everything in the car.

When my mom got home she advised me that I was going to drive. I had never driven that far before, but I was up for the challenge. It was cold and icy, but not snowing so I would be fine. I drove all the way to our trailer; it was still early when we got there. I figured we could put our stuff away before meeting dad.

I asked mom, "So, what are the boys up to?"

Knowing I really didn't like parties, she looked at me apologetic, "Sorry, I think a bunch of kids are coming here tonight."

"Mom, you know I *hate* parties!"

"I know, but dad set it up, so behave."

I walked up to the pole barn to see if dad wanted any help. I noticed all his machinery had been moved to the back part of the property. He had the bonfire stocked and ready to be lit. I walked into the pole barn and they were setting up speakers to stretch to all sides of it.

There was James; I ran to him and slugged him in the arm, "So you're in on this too?"

"Nope, this was, *all*, your dad."

"Dad, you didn't have to do this."

Dad smiled at me, "I had a lot of help, besides you only turn sixteen once."

"I heard you had help. Who's all coming?"

"I have no idea. I left that up to Brian and Danelle."

"So they're in on this, too?" There was no way out of this now, "Can I help?"

James grabbed my arms, turned me around, "No, it's a surprise so get lost before everyone finds out you know."

"So, what am I supposed to do?"

"I'll come up in a little while and then were going for a ride."

I looked at dad to make sure this was part of the plan. I think he thought I was worried about being alone with James, "It's only for a little bit, you'll be fine."

I went back to the trailer and went through everything I had brought with me, but I had nothing to wear that was warm and still cute. I wish I would have know earlier. I could have been better prepared.

Mom came in, "Would you like to open your gift early?"

I smiled, "Is it clothes?"

She smiled in return, but I knew it was.

"Yes please."

It was a brand new pair of jeans and they were great, just a little baggy, so I could be comfortable. Also, a sweater so soft that it was heaven to have it next to my skin. It was a v-neck with extra long sleeves; that might get a little cold, but I would deal with it. I hugged her, she was always the best.

When mom saw the pants on me she noticed they were a little big, "I bought your normal size, are you losing weight?"

"I have been doing sit-ups everyday it must be paying off. Does it look bad?"

"No, you look great."

I smiled at her. I went to the living room to wait. I didn't know when people were coming and I didn't know when we had to leave, so I sat down and turned on the TV.

James walked in, "Are you ready?"

"Yep, but I didn't see your car?"

"Nope. *You're* driving."

"What?"

"*You're* driving, but I'll drive us back."

"I just got my license today; aren't you scared?"

He gave me an evil grin, "I'll risk it."

"Are you sure, you might not make it back?"

"I can fend for myself."

"We'll just see about that, I've been working out."

"So you're ready to arm wrestle are you?"

"No, but I'm getting close."

"We need to go so we get back on time. Ready?"

"Yes, I'm ready."

I got in the driver's side and it felt really weird, "Are you sure you don't want to drive? I already drove enough today."

"Nope, you have to drive. You'll see why in a little bit."

"So, where are we going?"

"I'm supposed to make sure you eat."

"So, where do you want to eat?"

"Nowhere. I haven't seen you in four weeks."

"It wasn't up to me; if it was, I would have been here every weekend."

"I know, but before we eat can we stop somewhere?"

"Yeah where?"

"Any place will do."

"Help me out here." His hand was tracing my neck down to push my hair behind my back. I was getting tingles already without even kissing him. I pulled down the first dirt road I could find and stopped. As I shifted into park he started kissing me. He paused for a moment and looked at me adoringly.

"Meet me in front of the car because I have something for you."

I opened my door and rushed to the front of the car. He walked more slowly, making the anticipation so unbearable. He stood in front of me and looked into my eyes, "I have something very private and I can't tell you what it's for, but I will show you later. It has been passed from generation to generation. I am not a big believer in my Native American heritage, but you will appreciate it when I show you what it is meant for."

He put my face in his hands and kissed me very soft and gently. He moved his hands and arms around me to hold me. I wrapped my arms around his neck. This was the first real kiss we had. I was a little nervous. He was being so gentle, so respectful. This kiss was very slow and then he stopped with his lips on mine. It was as if he was breathing me in, "I just wanted to enjoy this moment with you."

I kissed him a little more luring than he did.

He stopped again, "Okay, are you ready for your gift?"

I nodded. He pulled my hands in front of me and turned them over. Then he reached up his sleeve. It was something wrapped in a silky material like a handkerchief. I unwrapped his gift. It was a single, large feather. It was very dark at the tip and got lighter toward the quill.

I looked at him a little confused, "Is it an eagle's feather?"

"Very good, how did you know that?"

"I don't know, but it's beautiful."

"It's even more beautiful when you know what it's for, but that's for later. Just bring it with you every time you're here."

"Can I bring it home with me?"

"Of course, but you need to bring it up here every time you come."

"I promise." I was very careful and wrapped it back up. I looked into his eyes to try and read what he was thinking. His face was a mixture of pleasure and embarrassment at the same time. I wrapped my arms around his neck again and put my lips to his cheek, "Thank you."

His kiss swept over me; I was lost in total bliss with every touch of his lips to mine. I was trembling a little everywhere.

"Are you cold?"

"I am a little, and nervous."

"Why are you nervous?"

"I can't believe this is real; I can't believe you are here with me."

"You really don't get how I feel about you?"

"No, and I don't understand why?"

"It started because of Jason. I really have to be thankful to him."

"Why, what did *he* do?"

"He talked about you all the time in agony. How you walked, not sexy at all but luring. How when you woke in the morning you were a mess, and you were still as precious as the dew on grass in the morning. How your insecurities came through on your face and your honesty to speak your mind. How you used your hands when you talked to explain the story behind your thoughts. The biting of the bottom lip when you're nervous, like you are now." He looked at me to see how I was taking this all in, "I had to see you, so I went to your dad and asked him if I could work for him. I didn't care what he paid me, it's never too much, but I had to see…" His lips moved to mine again. His kiss was so tender, I just about melted. "I was in love with every part of you, before I even saw you. I couldn't stay away no matter how much Jason threatened me." He smiled at me, "We'll, now you have it." He was studying my face, waiting for me to take this all in, "What are you thinking?"

"I'm not…I think you're expecting me to be better than I am, and that scares me." I looked to his eyes, pleading for him to not look at me that way.

"Why does that scare you?"

My eyes dropped from him; I didn't' want to say what I was thinking.

"Please tell me."

"You may be disappointed when you really see me."

"I do see you, and I couldn't stay away; that's why I'm here."

"But you had all those girls in your life, you could have anyone."

"I need for you to understand that you have ruined it for me. No girl compares to you."

"You're scaring me again."

"Don't be, I'm not going anywhere. My heart is set on you." He leaned into me, wrapped his arm around my waist pulling me to him, and pressed his lips to mine. This took my breath away as if I was dreaming. I found myself wanting him more than I would allow myself. I wrapped my arms around his neck, my hands running through his hair, parted his lips in mine, and the kiss grew more intense. He lifted me to his body, "Food?"

"I don't need food."

"But we need to stop, so food would be good."

I put my lips on his, "Okay, food."

"You look thinner. You are still eating, right?"

"Why would you say that?"

"You look different."

I put my hands on his well cut chest and traced them admiring every etched part of his chest. I looked at him guiltily, "I have been working out a little, sit-ups, and pushups, that kind of stuff. I thought I better get tough in case..." I looked at him a little longer than I needed to and then smiled at him mischievously, "In case I have to fight you off."

"You just might, you're kinda hot now."

"I wasn't before?"

"Actually no, you were almost frail looking. This is...," he pushed me away to look at me; "...this is hot."

"You're just feeding me a line. You really can't even see a difference."

"From my point of view, oh yes I can and if I keep looking you're going to have to fight me off right now."

"Food." I said firmly.

"Ah yes, food."

I leaned to him to kiss him and mouthed, "You."

"Oh, you can't do that. That will get you in trouble."

"Are you driving now?"

He looked at me suspiciously, "Nope, I don't trust you to behave yourself. You're driving."

13. The Rage of Kylie

We got back in the car and I asked, "Where too?"

"How about the first place we come to."

"Sounds good to me!" I pulled into Lakeside which wasn't far at all. We both ordered cheeseburgers, he got fries. We sat at a table off by ourselves, so we could talk in private, more like argue, we're good at that.

"I really don't enjoy parties."

"I figured that out."

"What do you mean by that?" I was defending myself.

"You have a hard time just hanging with kids your age. I didn't think you would like this."

"Not really. How come you didn't point that out, then?"

"Your dad said it was Brian's idea."

"Do you think he has an ulterior motive?"

"Yeah, I do."

I thought about it, "He wants all the guys in my life in one place at one time, kind of like how you got busted?" I grinned at him.

"Maybe. Or maybe it is something else."

I looked at him very seriously, "You do know no one else matters, right?"

He smiled at me.

"Can we…" I was hesitant, but I looked at him, adoring him so much, "Do you think we should come out tonight, together?"

"Not if you want your mom and dad to let us have alone time ever again."

"I think they already know I have a total crush on you. That's obvious. I am so much happier when you're around."

"I don't think they know."

I huffed a little and pouted, "So, do you know who is all coming to the party?"

"No."

"Great."

"You're funny when you're nervous."

"Thanks, you're quiet."

"I'm just enjoying the view." I made a smirk at him. His face went pale looking past me at the door, "Shit!"

"What?"

"Jason's here."

"So, I don't really care to see him. You know that."

"Yeah, but…" He looked sick; I turned to look at Jason, and he was walking in holding a girls hand.

I turned to James, "He had a girlfriend all along?"

He was studying my reaction and watching behind me at the same time, "Not exactly."

"You know I had no claim on him; it's okay, and I got the better." I was gleaming at him, but he wasn't looking at me. His eyes did not deviate from Jason. He was not angry, but he had intensity about him.

"Shit."

"What?"

"They are coming over here." His body stiffened, like he was going to get up and punch Jason.

"It's okay, I'm fine." I was trying to get his attention, but he never looked at me. I was really confused about how he was reacting.

Jason walked up to the table holding his girlfriends hand, "Kylie, you remember James."

"Yeah, hi James."

"Kylie this is Sarah, Sarah Kylie."

I looked up at her. She was very pretty, blond, blue eyes, and a very nice grownup figure, "Hi."

"This is Sarah?! The little bitch Sarah?!"

James was out of his seat so fast standing between her and me. He was backing her up and shielding me with his body; all while trying to move her towards the door, but she was still yelling profanities at me. James finally got her out the door, but he left me here with Jason, alone. I was completely stunned. I just sat there not knowing what to say or do.

Jason sat in James's spot immediately, "I have to explain."

"No you don't. It wasn't like we were boyfriend and girlfriend."

"I wasn't with her when…"

I interrupted, "Then why did she act that way? That really wasn't pleasant."

"I know. I'm sorry; we breakup and get back together a lot."

"That sounds pleasant, obviously you told her about me."

"It took a lot longer to get back together last time, because of you."

"You really don't have to explain."

"I really do."

"Jason it's fine; I'm fine."

"I wish you wouldn't do that."

"Do what?"

"Say my name, it melts me."

"Jason don't…"

"You did it again."

"I'm not going to play this game with you. You need to go to her because she's really upset."

"It's not a game. You're here with James?"

The waitress came with our food. I looked at her sorrowfully, "I think we've changed our minds. Can we get it to go?"

She smiled at me understanding. She took the food back with her. I looked at Jason and curtly replied, "Surprise party-James is occupying my time."

"That's all?"

"You have a girlfriend. Do you really think this is any of your business?"

"I was going to try and get rid of Kylie later so I could stop by."

"Why don't you bring Kylie?"

He gave me a disapproving look, "Yeah, right, probably not a good idea."

"Tell her I'm with James or something, just to make her not want to *kill* me."

"I don't know."

"Why did you bring her over here if you knew how she would react?"

"I needed to see you."

"Don't say stuff like that when you have Kylie."

The waitress brought a bag to me. I gave her cash, and I had to wait for change.

"I knew James would take care of her. He's gotten to be your protector, did you know that?"

"That's not fair to him, and no I didn't notice. But I'm glad. I needed it today."

"I am so sorry about that."

"You just shouldn't have."

"Why are you being so cold?"

"Jason, you have a girlfriend that almost attacked me and you want warm fuzzies from me?!"

"I just miss…"

"Don't do that."

The waitress brought me my change.

"Thanks." I didn't even look at it. I was so frustrated that I left all of it on the table. I looked at Jason. "I think I need to leave now."

"Are you okay?"

"I am fine, but can you please restrain your girlfriend so I can leave?"

"Yeah, sure."

Jason walked in front of me. He went straight to his truck where James was restraining Kylie. James was totally getting bitched out by her.

I got in the car, except this time I got in on the passenger side. I sat there in shock, and maybe a little numb. I wasn't really sure how I was feeling. James came running as soon as Kylie directed her rage at Jason. He got in the car with me and we just sat there for a moment and watched the two of them fight.

"I kinda lost my appetite so I got the food to go, hope that's okay?"

"Yeah, but are *you* okay?"

I was starting to shake a little, "I think I am in shock, but I'm still alive so I guess that's good, right?

He chuckled a little and shook his head, "You're still funny."

"I don't feel *funny* and I don't want to watch this. So, can we go?"

"Okay, we're gone."

James kept looking at me, but not saying anything. After the fourth time I was getting self-conscious, *"What?!"*

"Don't get mad at me. You're the one trembling."

"Am I?"

He pulled into an empty lot, and put it in park, "Are you cold?"

"No, I don't think so."

"Are you mad?"

"No, not really."

"Are you upset?"

"No. I don't really know why I'm trembling, maybe because of Kylie."

"Did Jason explain?"

"I didn't let him."

"He's gonna want to talk to you again."

"Great."

"Why didn't you let him explain?"

"It doesn't matter."

"But he went back to her to stay away from you. It was the age thing."

"Okay."

"What's going through your mind?"

I just sat there. I looked down and noticed the trembling. I held out my hand and it was worse.

"You are starting to scare me and nothing scares me."

I cracked a smile, "I really don't know what to feel and I don't know why I am trembling."

"Can I...?"

I turned to look at him, and noticed that he had moved closer to me and was staring at me. When our eyes met the tears began to stream down my face. He put his arms around me to hold me. I gazed into his eyes.

"What is it Sarah?"

"You left me." Now I lost it; I was sobbing.

"I had to, she would have killed you."

"But I *needed* you."

"He needed to explain things to you."

"But I *needed* you."

His eyes softened as he looked at me. He realized that nothing else that happened mattered. All that mattered was I needed him. A smile came to his face, "I thought you were working out so you could be tough?"

I smiled, "But you might let me win."

He chuckled a little, "I might."

"I am so sorry. Are you hungry?"

"No, not anymore." I could tell his concern was for me.

"Can we do that counting thing again?"

He held up one finger then two fingers, I nodded. "Ready? 1... 2...3..." We took a deep breath together, I kissed him. He gave me a disapproving glare. "1... 2... 3..."

We took another deep breath and I kissed him the most luring way I could. At first it was a touch then I traced my lips over his and then my kisses grew hungrier. He was replying. I found myself moving toward him making him lean back to the door. I moved to his neck keeping my hands on his well-defined chest. I was still moving closer and closer to him. He scooted down to the seat more. I was practically on him. I lowered myself to him. He interrupted, "We can't do this..."

I went back to his mouth kissing and nibbling in-between. He tried to speak, "You..." *kiss,* "need..." *kiss,* "to..." *kiss,* "stop..." *kiss,* "party..."

I laid my head on his chest and my body clung to his, "I know, but I am better now." I turned on my side a little and showed him my hand. The trembling was gone.

He smiled a little, "I still see a little, maybe..." *kiss,* "...a few more kisses." His kisses intensified. He moved his hand to touch my waist, "Will this make…" *kiss,* "…the trembling come back?"

We continued kissing, our lips gently moving together. He stopped and looked at my hand as I held it up for him to see.

I smiled coyly at him, "I think you're going to have to try harder."

"Later. We have to go or you'll be late for your own party."

I closed my eyes, "Promise you will be close to me all night?"

"I will be as close as you need me to be."

"Thank you," I looked into his eyes and he smiled at me. "Oh, there's one more thing. I told Jason to bring Kylie. I told him to tell her we were together so she wouldn't kill me."

"Why would you invite her?"

"He was planning on coming later without her. If she's there, he won't try to talk to me."

"You're good, but you need to finalize that relationship."

"I have enough to deal with tonight. Can we let it go for now?"

"We can do whatever you want, but at least I know to keep a close eye."

"I'll be keeping a close eye too, on you, that is."

He smiled, "Ready?"

"I think so."

"Let's go."

14. Birthday Party

When we got to the trailer it looked as if no one was there. He tied a blindfold over my eyes and led me to the pole barn. We tripped and stumbled the whole way, "You're not easy to lead."

"You're not easy to follow." I replied.

We walked into the pole barn and then he had me stop. Then he pulled off the blindfold and everyone cheered, *"Surprise!"* I found it really hard to act excited, but I tried. I think Brian made it his party since there were people there that I didn't even know. I hugged Danelle and she gave me a look that told me I was going to be sorry.

Brian came up and took my hand, "It's your party! I better introduce you to everyone."

I turned and looked back at James. He waved for me to go. I followed Brian as he dragged me holding my hand. The first group was all girls, "Mykala, Sherry, Jessica, Sammy, Theresa, Lori, Jill, and Michelle. I go to school with them."

"Thanks for coming. Does anyone like to dance?" Over half of them wanted to dance. I was pleased and told them, "Good I'll be looking for you guys in a little while."

As Brian pulled me to the next group, I looked around for James. I found his face; I love his face. He was with my dad and just watching. I looked at him pleading for him to come get me, but he smiled and shook his head no. Then he started to chuckle. Brian then led me outside. Most of his guy friends were out by the fire and the keg. He was still leading me by the hand. I wanted to acknowledge his efforts, "You know…this was very nice of you. I heard this was your idea."

"Yes, it was."

"Thank you." I really didn't mean it, but I was assuming he had good intentions.

Next he introduced me to the guys. "Guys, this is my good friend Sarah. Sarah this is Randy, Alex, Kurt, Seth, Frank, Jimmy, Jake, Steve, Pete, and John. You already know Pat."

I smiled at Pat and waved, "Hey guys, thanks for coming."

Brian pulled me to the keg, "Now, the beer bong."

"Oh, no, I am not doing that!"

"Oh, yes you are!"

I was pleading with Brian, "How about if I chug a glass, then will you leave me alone about this?"

"Yeah I guess." Brian handed me a glass of beer.

"Are you ready, *cuz this is it.*"

Brian was cheering, as I chugged the beer all the guys were cheering.

"Done, are you happy?"

"You drank the *whole* thing?"

"That's what the deal was, right?"

"I didn't think you could do it."

"We're good now, right?"

"Yeah, but you are going to do that again?"

"Maybe later."

"I'm going to hold you to that."

"Okay guys, have fun, and we'll see you later!" I went to find Danelle. As I headed back to the pole barn, James was in the doorway. I smiled so big. I wanted to kiss him right then and there. He was completely in the doorway so I couldn't pass.

"You're drinking?"

"Just one to get Brian off my back about the beer bong thing."

"You're really going to make me watch over you carefully."

"I was hoping so."

"You're going to drive me crazy."

I wasn't facing him and I was looking in the barn for Danelle. He was actually looking outside, so we didn't look like we were talking to each other, "That's the plan."

"You're purposely trying to make me crazy."

I glanced at him seriously just for a moment, "I only want to be here with *you*. Right now. Alone." I looked away to search the area to find Danelle. I had already seen her, but I was trying to buy myself more time with James.

"What am I going to do with you?"

"If you kiss me right here, right now, I wouldn't object." I looked into his eyes, "Please?"

He turned to me. It looked as if he was angry with me. He leaned in. My heart began to race. *Was I going to get what I was asking for?* He took the glass from my hand, "No more of this, you're getting too brave already. Now go play with your little friends. Later you'll have to deal with me."

I smiled, "Can't wait."

I walked in and went over to Danelle. The girls were all hanging around her asking her to talk about her brother. Most of them had a crush on him.

"Danelle, can you talk for a minute?"

"Sure!" She jumped up to talk to me by the stereo, "What's up?"

"I just drank a beer with your brother and the guys."

"I know. My brother's going to try and get you drunk."

"Great! Why?"

"He made a bet with the guys that you two would be making out by the end of the night."

"That's not going to happen."

"Good."

"So, which one of these girls would have the best chance with your brother?"

"Why?"

"Because I'm thinking she might get her way with him."

"That would be Mykala."

"She's pretty."

"But she knows he's a player."

"So, this maybe harder than I thought?"

"Not really. I think she likes him anyway."

"That's who I am going to work on then. How long do you get to stay?"

"Only 'til 9 o'clock. My mom and dad know there is drinking going on."

"I'm sorry."

"That's okay. People do stupid stuff when they're drunk and I don't like to watch."

"I bet you see a lot of stupid stuff at the bar."

"Every day."

We both laughed. I looked over at James. He was watching me while he was standing with a bunch of people I didn't know, but they were all with my dad.

Danelle caught my glance at James, "You know he hangs out with a bad crowd."

"Like, what do you mean, bad?"

"They do drugs and stuff. So does Jason."

"I didn't know that." My heart sank a little. I never saw that one coming. I looked at my watch. It was already 8:45 p.m.

Danelle noticed I was looking at the time, "I know. It's almost time for me to go."

"So, how are you getting home?"

"Brian is supposed to bring me home."

"He's already been drinking."

"I don't know then."

"If you don't mind, I could ask James to give you a ride home and I would come with you."

"But it's your party, and I don't know about...James."

"I really don't know that many people. No one will even notice I'm gone. Plus, my car is the closest vehicle here, and I've already had a beer, so I can't drive you myself. As far as James goes, he works for my dad, and I think he has to look out for me tonight, under my dad's order. I think he has to do anything I ask."

"Okay, if you're sure."

I walked over to James, "Excuse me."

I looked at James, "Have you been drinking at all?"

"No. Why?"

"Brian was supposed to bring Danelle home at 9 o'clock, but he has already been drinking. Could we run her home really quick?"

"Whatever you want to do is fine with me."

Mom was standing there also and she said that would be fine.

"Let's go."

I went to tell Danelle we could give her a ride. As we were walking over to where James was waiting she asked me, "Do you like James?"

"I do have a crush. He is just so...you know, but he's here to watch over me that's all."

"So you *do* like him?"

"Danelle," I felt embarrassed, "I told you before he's like a big brother to me. The nicest part about it is he won't let anyone win any bets tonight. It's like having a personal bodyguard. It's really kind of fun."

We walked up to James who was standing in the doorway then we all walked down to the car together. James tried to be casual by making conversation knowing I had already had a drink. "Why aren't you driving Danelle home yourself?"

I played along, "Oh, I forgot. I have my license."

"How do you forget you can drive legally now?"

Danelle chuckled a little, "But she's had a beer."

"You are in so much trouble little lady. Wait until I tell your mom and dad."

"They're the ones who bought it."

"But not for *you*."

"Everyone else is drinking."

"As your chaperone, I was told not to let you have any."

"You're kidding."

"No. I'm not."

"That sucks."

"Only for you!" James remarked.

Danelle laughed at this. I was so thankful he took this role with me while she was in the car.

117

"So why aren't *you* drinking if it's for the adults?"

"I'm not here for fun. I'm here to watch over you."

I looked at Danelle and we both started to laugh.

"What are you two laughing about?" James was confused by this.

"My brother doesn't have a chance."

"I told you."

James looked at me quizzically, "Sar-ah, you're not testing me are you?"

"Nope. I promise I'll be good."

We arrived at Sherburn's and I got out so I could walk Danelle in. James gave me a funny smile like he knew what was going on. I looked back at him, adoring him so much, but ran inside with Danelle. Laura and Paul weren't too happy with Brian, but were thankful we brought her home.

I gave her a hug, "Thanks for coming. See ya tomorrow!" I ran back out and got in the car.

"So, what was that all about?" James questioned.

"You played along so good I thought you knew."

"Knew what?"

"Brian planned on getting me drunk and taking advantage of me tonight." I could see this made James immediately angry. "I told her you were there to watch over me, so it wouldn't happen." That made him smile.

"Yeah, I knew what I was doing."

"You did not!" I accused.

"She doesn't like me much."

"She says you hang out with the druggie crowd."

He didn't say anything.

"So she's right?"

We were almost to the gravel road that leads to the trailer, but he turned off onto a dirt road. You could tell it wasn't used a lot. He stopped the car, put it in park, and looked at me. The pain in his eyes made me sad.

"Up here it's different, Sarah. It's everywhere and if you are with someone who does it, you pick up that reputation. I have tried it, but it's not for me. I haven't touched it for three years."

"Really?"

"I swear to it."

"That's good enough for me."

His serious and sad face eased a little, "So we're good?"

"We are *so* good."

"Let's get you back to your party then."

"Can't we have five minutes alone?"

"No. Not really. There is a party you are supposed to be at."

"I know, but…" I crawled to his lap hitting the release lever to move the seat back.

"Girl, what are you doing?"

"I'm giving you some leg room."

"But…" he resisted.

"I would rather be here with you all night, *alone.*"

"Even if I wouldn't let you do *this*?" He kissed me softly under my chin.

"Yes, even if you wouldn't let me do this." I breathed in his ear and kissed his ear lobe gently. He tried to push me off his lap back to my seat. I didn't want to let go, "What's wrong?"

He closed his eyes, "You just made me *so*…I need you to give me some cooling room."

I opened the car door and carefully climbed out and leaned against the car with my back to it, "I'm sorry."

He took a deep breath, sat there for a minute, and then got out. He stood in front of me and put one hand on each side of me resting them on the car, "You did nothing wrong."

"I caused you pain."

"It's not pain, just agony."

"I'll stick to lips, I promise."

"That makes me want to…here, now is not right. Sarah, if something happened between us right now, it would not be right and you would hate me. I have never cared enough for someone to wait." He closed his eyes shamefully.

"I could never hate you."

"Trust me, you would. Just try to stay away from the ears, please?"

"I am so sorry."

He put his arm around my waist and pulled my body to his. I could feel him. It took my breath away. I closed my eyes and let my heart race. The tingling started and I was enjoying this way too much. My breathing deepened, I bit my lip, and the wanting was overwhelming.

"This wasn't supposed to turn you on. It was supposed to scare you."

"It does scare me a little, but…I, um…" I couldn't finish my sentence the sensation was growing and so was my breath, "If this happens, it will happen right here, right now. I am really hot and I know your weakness."

He completely fell backwards, pulling me with him into the wet snow.

"What are you doing?!"

"A quick cooling off, that's what you need little girl!"

"*Shit!* I'm going to be soaked."

"Do you feel better?"

"No!" I stood up and tried to brush off as much of the wet snow as I could.

He laughed at me. "I mean *that* way."

"Well, yeah, but now I'm cold and wet. What is everyone going to think when we get back?"

"We'll get in a snow fight when we get back so it looks like it happened there."

"Is that what you feel when…?"

"We'll talk more about *that* later. You've got to get back to the party."

As soon as we got back to the party, I jumped out of the car and grabbed some snow. I ran around the car and threw it on him.

"All righty then!" He picked me up and put me over his shoulder and sat me right down in a snow bank.

"You are so mean. Can I kiss you?"

"No! And you are soaked."

"You are going to get it!" I chased him up the hill, "You are asking for it!"

"Bring it on! Any time!"

"I'll get you when you least expect it!"

"I'm scared of you little girl!"

I got up to the pole barn and a bunch of guys I didn't know were sitting at the fire. I walked past them to go in and dance. The girls were already dancing and I was thankful they let me join them. Brian came in shortly and started dancing my way.

"Are you Okay?"

"Just fine. Why?"

"You're all wet."

"James sat me in a snow bank."

"Do you want me to…?" Brian tried to make an angry face to impress me.

"No, I started it. So…it looks like Mykala seems really interested in you?"

"Really? She usually doesn't give me the time of day."

"Playing hard to get! Besides, she is so pretty, way prettier than me."

"Really?"

"I think so. You should go dance with her."

"It's your party."

"But I like to share."

He smiled, and then he moved over to dance with her. I now saw Sue, Pat's girlfriend. She was in here and Pat was outside. I wanted to know what was going on. I danced over to where she was sitting, "Do you want to dance?"

"Not much of a dancer."

"You're in here, and Pats outside. What's up?"

"He's been drinking."

"Good point, but if you were out there with him, he might not drink as much."

"You may be right."

"Go give it a try, especially if you don't want to dance."

She went out to the fire pit. I snuck over to the door and watched. James came up behind me, "What are you doing?"

"Playing matchmaker."

"Who?"

"Brian's on the dance floor with Mykala. I hope she likes him, because he thinks she does."

"You are evil."

"I'm good." I nodded toward Pat, "That's phone number guy over there and that's his girlfriend. But they're both really shy. Look! It's working. Now they're going for a walk."

"You are really good."

"I know."

"Do you see whose coming?" I didn't look because I already knew.

"Do they look happy or irritated?"

"A little of both."

A great song came on and he insisted, "First, you're dancing with me." He danced a little old fashion mixed with funky. He could move, but he twirled me and pulled me close and moved.

"This is one of my criteria for the perfect man."

"Dancing?"

"Yes, I want passion in my life. That comes with dancing."

"I'll give you passion."

"You already do."

Pretty soon all the girls were dancing with us too. He twirled me close again and sang with the song, "I know one thing is that I love you."

I looked at him kind of serious for a moment. He smiled and twirled me again. When the song was over he gave me a half hug, and kissed my forehead like an adoring father, "Thanks."

Then he walked away. I stayed and danced some more with the girls. Brian and Mykala were dancing off by themselves. I was happy this was working out so well. I still had to deal with Jason and Kylie, but how long would they stay anyway? The older crowd was showing up, so more people were drinking the keg. I continued to dance the night away.

A country song came on that I hadn't heard before. James butted in and twirled me away from the group, "This is my song for you."

"What is he saying?"

"You've got whatever it is."

"What?"

"Just listen to it someday when you can really hear it."

"Okay."

He moved so smoothly, turning me around and moving together. It was like we had been doing this for years, "Do you like a lot of different music?"

"Yes." The song was over and he took both my hands like a gentleman might do from the movies and said, "Thank you, now go have more fun."

I knew he was right, but I would have enjoyed it more if I could just be with him.

My dancing partners were dwindling. Brian came up to me, "Thank you."

"For what?"

"I don't think I would have been brave enough to dance with Mykala if you wouldn't have pointed out she was really interested in me."

"Friends?"

"Friends."

"I was planning on staying, but if I go now, I can ride with Mykala."

"Go for it. Take it slow." I gave him a wink.

Another song came on and there were still a few people left to dance with, so I moved over to them. As we danced to this I would occasionally look over at James and smile. I turned in his direction and danced, and then I would move back to the group and look at him. Every time I looked at him I would smile.

It was after 1 a.m. and most of the older group was out by the fire and keg. There was no one left in the pole barn, and I didn't really want to go outside yet. I began picking up some of the garbage lying around and danced as I picked stuff up.

"Uh, hum…"

I turned to see who was there. James was standing in the doorway watching me. He was leaning against the doorframe and his hand was resting on the doorknob. His body was so muscular. The look of him took my breath away. I smiled at him approvingly.

"What are you doing?" he asked

"Picking up a little."

He looked outside, then closed the door, and locked it. He walked slowly to me, and took everything out of my hands tossing them aside. He put one hand around my waist and the other took my hand and brought it to his chest with his, "One last dance." We danced slowly, but he still turned me in circles.

"What song is this?"

"It's one that fits my heart."

"I like this." I put my face to his shoulder and neck area and closed my eyes. I just enjoyed the movement. As the song came to an end, we hear somebody at the door.

James yelled, "Can you get it?"

The voice replied, "No."

"Just a second I'll get it."

I went back to picking things up. He played with the handle a little bit before unlocking it. I was laughing to myself.

"Sorry about that. It must have gotten stuck from the cold," as he pulled the door open. Jason was standing there.

"Yeah right. Just thought I would let you two know we're leaving and we're the last ones."

"Okay," I said without looking at him, "Thanks for coming."

Jason looked at James as he shrugged his shoulders, "Uh, do you think we can talk sometime this weekend?" he walked a little closer to me.

I turned and started walking toward him. James was still at the door holding it half open.

"Jason thank you for everything and you will always be special to me. You are with Kylie, and you need to give yourself to her completely or you will never be happy and neither will she. You can't keep me on the side *and* have a girlfriend until I grow up. That's just wrong. I am sorry I am so young, but you kind of made up your mind already. Now you have to stick to it."

Jason looked at me so sad, "I am so sorry."

I turned to walk away. As I got to the door, I was surprised to see Kylie was standing there. I realized she had been standing there and had heard everything. She looked at me with no reaction. James still tucked me behind him for protection.

I could see Jason was just as surprised to see her standing there as I was. Jason walked out grabbing Kylie's hand as they left.

15. Pleasure

James smiled at me.

"What?"

"That was *very* mature."

"He needed to hear it."

"Yes he did, and so did she."

I went back to picking up. He started helping me.

I had to ask, "What time is it?"

"It's 2:30 a.m."

"We should put the fire out."

"Your mom and dad crashed about midnight, so we might wake them if we go in."

"Yeah, so."

"I was thinking… we should grab a couple of sleeping bags and lie by the fire?"

My face lit up, "I would love that, but I have to warn you I am kind of a wimp."

"Good, I'll tell you about the feather."

"Okay."

"What did you do with the feather?"

"Do you really want to know?"

"Yes." He was on the other side of the pole barn now. I turned to him. He stopped and looked at me worried.

"I will show you if you stay where you are, but you can't move. Okay."

"Okay." He was looking at me puzzled.

"Promise?"

"I promise." He rolled his eyes.

"No funny business, mister."

"Will you tell me already?"

"No, but I will show you." I started lifting my sweater a little on the left, then on the right, and a little in the middle. I was walking very slowly toward him. I lifted a little more on the left, then on the right. I stopped and pulled up the middle again. I was getting closer to him. I started on the left again, then the right. I was almost to him, when I exposed the middle, to reveal the feather, the quill of the feather tucked in my pants. I stood there looking at him as seductively as I could.

He dropped to his knees, "You are going to drive me crazy!" He put his hands on my waist.

"*You're* the one that wanted to know where it was."

"You had it here all night?"

"I didn't know when you were going to tell me, so I wanted to be prepared."

He looked up at me, "May I?"

"Yes."

He traced his mouth up one side of the feather and down the other. Then he used his teeth to pull up on the feather until it came out. I had my eyes closed enjoying him touching me. I wrapped my hands in his hair. When he stopped I looked down at him. He moved up to kiss me so passionately. My breathing was so shallow and I could hardly take any air in.

He whispered to my lips, "Fire… lay down… feather…" I kissed his lips with mine. I didn't want to move. He stopped, grabbed my hand, and the sleeping bags, and pulled me to the fire. It was so cold I could hardly stand it. He folded one sleeping bag in half and laid it on the ground. It must have been 2 degrees; I was freezing. He took off his jacket, rolled it up and put it down, "Okay there you go."

I lay down with my head on his jacket, "Aren't you cold?"

"Yeah, but I won't be for long." He lay on his side facing me propping his head on his hand, but looking at me. He covered us with the other sleeping bag, "Is it too cold?"

"I'm okay for now."

He pulled the feather out, "Now I am going to tell you, but don't read into it. I only wanted to give you something of mine."

"I am happy about that."

He started tracing my face with the feather, I closed my eyes, "The feather is part of our wedding tradition. It is used to bless the new bride on her new walk in life as a woman. It's actually used on the wedding night. I gave this to you so you would have it the first time you... I am hoping to be part of it whenever it happens."

I put my hand on his to stop him from tracing my face with the feather. I opened my eyes to gaze at him, and he was scanning my face. I wrapped myself around him as much as I could. I placed my lips gently below his ear on his neck and whispered, "I would be honored to have you share that night with me." I was shivering more than ever. It wasn't only the cold. I was very nervous.

"You are trembling again. We need to get you inside."

"You get the fire. I'll take care of the sleeping bags."

"Ready, go!" He got up and helped me up and he put his jacket back on and started dumping snow on the fire. I grabbed the sleeping bags and put them back in the pole barn. I came out and he was just finishing putting the fire out. I ran and jumped on his back, "Oh, I see how it is."

"I'm tired," whining a little. I nuzzled my face by his cheek, neck, and ear. Then I couldn't help myself and I started to kiss him. He pulled me to the front of him. I didn't know how he did it. Now I was face to face with him.

"You're stepping on dangerous ground girl."

"How dangerous?"

"Very."

I kissed him so deeply; I couldn't get enough of him. I clung to him as tight as I could. His hands and arms were holding me, but I was distracting him from walking and he kind of tripped and we were close to the trailer, "You have to get down. We have to be really, really quiet."

Of course, the door squeaked. But we got inside and didn't hear any movement. He walked down the hallway. I stopped in the living room. I was asking for it. *Shit!* He waved me to the first room. I walked in and he swept me into his arms, kissing me passionately. When it slowed, I opened my eyes to look at him. I was so scared.

He must have seen it, "You need to sleep in here tonight."

"Why?" I protested.

"I can't stay with you tonight. I have to sleep on the couch."

"I don't understand."

"We have all the time in the world. Trust me on this one, please?" I crawled on the bed. It squeaked a little, and we heard dad move a bit. James looked at me in panic. He kissed me quickly, "I'll see you in the morning."

He disappeared. I listened, and heard dad sit up and then he got up and walked to the kitchen. It sounded like he got something to drink, then I heard him say something, "Hey! You may need a blanket, boy." And then I heard him walk back down the hall.

I was really sad, but if I was going to sleep in here by myself, I was going to be comfortable. I changed to shorts and a t-shirt. I sat back down on the bed, it squeaked. I stopped and listened. No movement. I lay down, and it squeaked again. I covered my face with my hands. I didn't have any covers on yet, and every time I moved the bed squeaked. I just sat there and thought of James' face today. I was trying to get to dream about him and I was getting frustrated. I wanted to feel good and fall asleep. I wanted to know if James was sleeping, but he needed distance, at least for tonight. More than anything I wanted to spend every second of everyday with him, especially since it was so long in between seeing him. What was I going to do now? I rolled to my side, and closed my eyes. I curled into a ball and hugged my pillow. Every movement made the bed squeak. *How was I ever going to sleep?*

"Can't fall asleep?" His whisper came over me, so quiet and precious. I smiled and slowly opened my eyes. He smiled back at me and put his finger to his lips, hushing me. I tried to sit up, but the bed squeaked. He smiled with a smirk on his face. He took his blanket and laid it on the floor. He held his hands out for me to take them. I put my feet on the floor, and put my hands in his. He pulled me off the bed, and it squeaked again. We both stopped and listened. No movement. We both started to laugh silently.

He took one of the blankets off the bed and laid it on top of the other one on the floor. He grabbed a couple of pillows and put them on the floor too. He pointed to the door. He pushed it shut without a sound. I sat down on the floor with my knees pulled to my chest. He came and lay beside me on his side. I was self conscious because I had shorts and a t-shirt on. I grabbed the other blanket and set it in front of me. I touched his cheek. We were both afraid to talk. I had an idea; I placed a pillow on the floor, so he could lie back, and pushed him down. I grabbed my feather off the bed. I realized he was still clothed. I pulled him up and put my hands under his shirt, asking him with my eyes if this would be okay. I pulled his shirt up and he helped me by taking it off. Oh my God! He was amazing! He was more muscular than what showed through his clothes. I gasped, but I covered my mouth. He sat back up looking at me. My eyes were wide open as I looked at him.

"What?"

"You're amazing."

He smiled, shook his head, then lay back down and put his hands behind his head and closed his eyes. He was so much bigger than I imagined. I wanted to feel his body next to mine, but not tonight. I took the feather and started tracing every muscle I could. His stomach had a line down the middle, and he had four lines across. I used the feather as I traced back and forward tracing each one, coming back to the middle tracing upward to his chest. He was cut. I went around each muscle, and moved to his side. He flinched and he moved his hand to stop that.

He put up one finger and moved it back and forth as to say no, but he kept his eyes closed. I smiled and giggled to myself. My legs were cramping a little so I scooted down and stretched them across him below his stomach. He placed his hand on my ankle. I continued to trace his collarbone and moved back down to retrace everything. He moved his other hand down and placed it on my back, under my shirt. I went over his abs again. I did this so slowly so I could watch his muscles flex, as I touched each one with the feather. I found this fascinating that each muscle reacted individually to the touch of the feather.

As I traced under the bottom muscle I felt him tense. His hand on my ankle gripped more tightly and his hand on my back now grabbed my waist. He was getting turned on and I didn't really want to do that, so I moved back to his chest. Each muscle moved individually, as I traced the feather over them. This was amazing that the body was reacting without any movement from him. I wanted to touch him, but I kept to the feather. I moved to the abs again. His hand on my back moved and he grabbed my wrist. I looked at him. He sat up and pulled me into him more. He kissed me softly, not luring at all, just a soft caring touch of his lips.

He smiled at me, "Your turn."

"I don't know if I can handle it."

"If I can handle it so can you."

I shook my head no. He looked at me with puppy dog eyes. I smiled, nervously. He traced my leg with his hand down to my knees. Then he lifted them off him and moved them, so I would turn to lay down straight. I kept my eyes on his. He didn't look away; if anything wasn't okay in my eyes he would stop. He moved very slowly putting both hands by my waist and he began lifting my shirt. I raised my arms, as he pulled the shirt over my head. We lost eye contact, but he did not touch me at all until our eyes were in contact again. Then his hand traced my back until he was scooting me down further so my head would be on the pillow. He placed his hand in the middle of my back to lower me to the pillow.

He moved to lie on his side resting his head on his hand, but closer to my face, so he could see my eyes. I just looked at him. I was so nervous. I was afraid of what I was going to feel. I couldn't even think of it, and I tried to get it out of my mind. I tried to think of school subjects, anything that would help me to get some control over what I was going to feel. He just lay there for a long time looking into my eyes. I didn't know what he was looking for, maybe for the fear to go out of my eyes. My heart was pounding so hard and I was just waiting. He put his head down next to me.

His lips were close to my ear, "I have a feeling if I start this something may happen." I closed my eyes, as he continued, "I want this to be the best night of your life, but I don't see it in your eyes."

I turned to look at him. My heart was pounding so hard I didn't know what to do. He placed his hand on my cheek and kissed my lips, *"I don't know if I can stop"*.

My chest was heaving. I closed my eyes. He took his hand slowly moving it down to my heaving chest, and rested it in the middle like he was feeling my breathing. I wanted him to taunt me, but I didn't want that either.

I knew if this went much further, I would beg him to be inside of me. *Was I ready for that, how would I know?* He now moved his hand to grip my waist and pulled me to my side to face him. He pulled my body to touch his. My breathing increased, but I stayed there very still, with our bare skin touching, and he just held me. He looked into my eyes. I didn't know what to do or say, so I continued to just look into his eyes.

He finally said something. "I need to go to the bathroom."

I giggled.

"I'll be right back." He got up and left the room. I rolled onto my stomach. I was so confused. If we did it then we wouldn't have to worry about it anymore. But would I hate him for it? I don't ever want to hate him.

I heard him walk back in. I laid there waiting for him. He crawled his way back up me, he kissed my back seductively. I rolled over to face him. He kissed my stomach moving upward, kissing between my breasts, my chest, my neck and then my lips. The whole time he was keeping his weight completely off of me. I placed my hands on his chest. I closed my eyes, "If I'm not ready, you said I would hate you."

"I did say that."

"But if I want you as bad as I do, am I ready?"

He was kissing me so passionately and I could hardly catch my breath. He slowly traced his hand down my neck, the middle of my chest down my stomach and over to my waist, "There is nothing more that I want than to give you every pleasure I can, but even if you are ready now, its 6 a.m., and I think your dad is going to want me to work in an hour."

I smiled at him, "You need sleep."

"I do, at least a little."

"I am so sorry."

"Don't be. What you gave me tonight was better."

"But we didn't do anything."

131

"Oh, but we did. I saw your soul."

"What?"

"Lift your arms please." He put my shirt back over my head and lowered it tracing his hands down my side as he did this. He grabbed his shirt and put it on. He got up, and pulled me up and wrapped the blanket around me. He grabbed the other blanket and two pillows, then took my hand and led me out of the room.

"But you need to sleep."

"If you think I'm letting you go now, you're a little crazy."

"Okay."

He put the pillows on one end of the couch, and he lay down. I stood in front of him and I opened the blanket.

"No, actually, keep it around you and come lay down with me."

I went to face him.

"No, your mom and dad will be suspicious."

He lay with his hands behind his head and I was curled up next to him.

But, he did kiss my head, "Good night."

"Until tomorrow, I will be dreaming of you."

16. Games

"So, what time were you guys up 'til?"

"I'm not really sure. We started to pick up a little before everyone was gone."

"Yeah, I saw that. Did she keep you up playing cards or something when you two came in?"

"No, but I did tell her about an old Indian tale."

"Oh, that's what I probably heard."

"That, or maybe the squeaky bed; its why she ended up out here. Every time she moved I could hear it out here."

"Yeah, they are kind of old."

"If you want to hold her so she doesn't fall off the couch, I can get up. I'll go finish cleaning."

"I think maybe we'll go in a little while. I'm not feeling the greatest. I think I'll go back to bed for awhile."

"Don't be afraid to wake me."

"I'll let Paula know about the squeaky bed, so she doesn't get the wrong idea. She's not feeling well, either."

"Let me know if I can get you guys something."

"Thanks. You look a little stuck." Dad walked back down the hall to the bedroom. It was quiet again. James took a deep breath.

"What time is it?" I quietly asked.

"It's a little after 7 a.m. Why are you awake?"

"I heard voices. Did you sleep at all?"

"A little."

"Are you comfortable?"

"Okay."

"Something is wrong, I can tell."

"A…little."

My heart sank. I closed my eyes and sat up. I turned to look at him. He was a mess. I went to touch his face.

"Um, you really need to not touch me right now."

"But…"

"It's really not a good idea."

I got up and moved away from him.

"I just really need a shower."

I looked at him quite puzzled.

"Don't get the wrong idea, but I need a shower right now and Karla's is the closest person with a shower. I promise nothing will happen except for a shower."

I looked at him desperately.

He warned, "That makes it worse. I'll be right back and then I can explain."

He was out the door. I sat at the kitchen table and looked out the window. I wondered how long it would take him to return.

It wasn't that long before he was back. He looked much more relaxed and in control, "Are your parents awake yet?"

I shook my head and replied, "No."

He had a look of concern and called down the hallway to their room, "Are you guys doing okay?"

My mom spoke up, "Well I'm doing better, but we should take Tucker to the hospital."

James was calm as he helped get my dad out to the car. He could tell I was confused as to what happened. He yelled to snap me out of it, "Sarah help!"

I immediately jumped up to help get my dad to the car. Mom came out. She had thrown on some clothes and didn't even bother to run a brush through her hair. She got into the car quickly and made sure dad was comfortable.

James was concerned, "Are you sure you don't want us to go with?"

"No, it will be fine," mom replied.

They drove off. I just stood there. He swept me into his arms and kissed me so softly. As he did that he said to my lips, "I told you I wouldn't be gone long." He picked me up by my thighs to his waist and walked in the trailer kissing me.

"So, you have all day and no work, what should we do?"

"Do you really want to go anywhere? We only have the four-wheeler. It might be too cold."

I grinned devilishly, "So you're stuck here with me, oh what ever should we do?"

"Not what you're thinking."

"What? No cards, board games, or movies?"

"You're a funny girl."

I wrinkled my nose at him, "Are you hungry?"

At that very moment his stomach growled. We both started to laugh. I grabbed both his hands, switching them around so they were behind me, and pulled him to the kitchen, "Let's see what we've got: milk, a carton of eggs, but only on egg, a couple slices of cheese, ketchup, mustard, relish, and pickles." I looked in the freezer where there was only a small bag of tatter tots and a bag of ice. I turned to the cupboards. There were only a couple of cans of peas, and a couple cans of corn, and a small variety of soups and a jar of peanut butter.

I looked at James, "Well, I think its peanut butter sandwiches and milk or the four-wheeler."

"I *am* hungry, but I don't think I can chew a four-wheeler."

"Okay its peanut butter sandwiches then."

James smiled at me and sat at the table. I tossed the bread on the table in front of him. I gave him two napkins, a knife, and the jar of peanut butter. I grabbed a couple glasses for milk and poured some for each of us as he put peanut butter on the bread.

"I only want a half please." I sat at the table across from James. James dug into his sandwich right away. He must have been *really* hungry. I smashed my sandwich flat, breaking off each piece.

"What are you doing?"

I swallowed, "Eating my sandwich." I took a sip of milk. I did it again with the next piece and took another sip of milk. He laughed at me.

"What?"

"You are just so…" He started chuckling and shaking his head.

"What?"

"I think if your mom and dad take too long were going to have to take the four-wheeler for more food."

"I think you're right." I finished my milk and closely observed him, to see his quirks.

He caught me, "What are you doing?"

"I'm looking for something funny that *you* do when you eat."

"So, how is it going?"

"Not very good. You're kind of perfect."

"Far from that."

"In my eyes you are."

"You only see me when I am with you."

"So you're not perfect when you're not around me?"

"Sometimes, but I'm working on it."

"Working on what?"

"You make me want to be better."

I got on my knees on the chair and leaned over the table. I kissed his lips, "You taste like peanut butter."

"So do you."

I got up and poured two glasses of water for us. We had to brush our teeth. I hated brushing my teeth in front of people, but it seemed like James always did this with me. He kissed me with his toothpaste mouth. I rubbed it off with my hand and smeared it on him.

He muffled to me, "You're going to get it!"

"Yeah, I bet."

"You think I'm kidding?"

I tried to egg him on, but he didn't take the challenge. "So what's next?" I asked and waited with excitement for his answer.

"I think we should go the whole day without touching."

I frowned at him, "Why?"

"I want to see if we can spend the whole day with each other with no intent at all."

I didn't say anything. I just got up to put stuff away. My mind was all over the place. We probably have as much time as we need and he wants to not touch. What was he up to? I walked around the table and he turned his chair so he was facing me. I stood there for a moment wondering how I was going to handle this.

"Sarah?"

"Yeah."

"What are you thinking?"

I sat on his lap facing him. I looked at his face, but didn't provoke him. I just sat there.

"Are you going to tell me what you are thinking?"

I just looked at him. I wanted to kiss him all day.

He closed his eyes and moved his hands behind his head, "Sarah, please let's not do this today, this morning was very hard for me."

"There is one more thing I need to know before I agree to this."

He kept his eyes closed and his hands off.

I leaned to him, not touching any more than I already was, but I whispered in his ear, "How will I know?"

He opened his eyes, "You'll just know, until then: cards, board games, and movies. We have lots of time." He stood up holding me and kissed me softly as he walked to the living room. He let go of me, so I would have to stand, "Movie and board game for now?"

"Fine," I said frustrated. I put in Terminator avoiding any girly mushy movies. He was laying a blanket on the floor. I looked at the board games, "We have Monopoly, Life, Sorry, and Pictionary."

"Whatever."

"Life?" I was being playful. I knew he wouldn't like that one.

"Okay, maybe not *that* one."

"Sorry?" I chuckled a little.

"It's a good place to start."

I pulled the game out and set it up. We sat across from each other not touching at all. Every time I got the card Sorry, I looked at him pleading, "Sorry," implying that I was so terrible to him.

Every time he would tell me, "No you're not," and lean over the game like he was going to kiss me, but he would stop and say, "Oh yeah, no touching," and he would pull away.

"You are just mean!"

He would laugh. The game didn't take that long. The movie was still going when we were done.

"Now what?" I looked at him.

"Cards, I have a better chance at winning that."

I got up and went to the kitchen to find two decks of cards, while James put the other game away. The movie had just ended while we were switching things around. I squatted in front of the TV, "We're dwindling away at the movie supply."

"What do we have left?"

"*Signs,*" as I looked at him.

"Very funny."

"The movie?"

"What else?"

"*What a Woman Wants?*"

"I don't think so."

"*Casanova?*"

"Definitely not."

"*You've Got Mail?*"

"Maybe later."

"*A knight's Tale?*"

"Is it safe?"

"I think so. Well, maybe a little much for you, but if you can't handle it, I'll turn it off."

"Stick with Signs. It's very safe."

"Fine." I put it in.

We played cards through the whole movie, but I wanted to know more about him, so I asked questions casually, "So, why don't you believe in your heritage?"

"It's like they are still living in the past, and I live for today."

"When you don't work for my dad, or entertain me, what do you do with your time?"

"Hunt, fish, hang out with *the bad crowd.*"

"Where do you live?"

"On the reservation."

"But where is that?"

He looked at me suspiciously and said, "You know the area that has totem poles on one side of a field and a tepee on the other?"

"Is that the one we pass on the way here, before we turn to the county road that leads to the lake?

"Yeah, that's the one. I live about two miles behind that."

"That's not that far from here."

"No, not really. It depends on if I have a car or not."

"I thought you had a car?"

"I do, but we share a lot, and sometimes other people have more important things to do than me."

"That makes sense. Do you have any brothers or sisters?"

He looked at me suspiciously, "Yeah, why?"

"Just wondering."

"I have two brothers, and one sister."

"How old are they?"

"Will is 17, Sam is 15, and Tamara is 10."

"There are a lot of years between you and your sister."

"Yeah, she has a different mom than us boys."

"Oh."

"By the way, you are not meeting them."

"Okay. Why?"

"My brothers...," he looked at me, "...they would be taken with you."

"So they wouldn't be able to keep *hands off?*", I smiled mischievously.

"You're not starting that again." He shuffled for the next hand.

I crawled toward him.

"Sarah. Stop it." He warned.

"But if I get this close..." I moved closer, my face less than two inches from his, "Are you sure no touching?"

"Yep, so behave, and sit down."

"Not even playful today?"

"I'll give you playful!"

I smiled looking at his lips ready for it.

"I said not now, please sit down."

"You are so strict."

"No, I'm just trying to stay in control, and like I said this morning was very hard for me."

"You were really fast about it. I was nervous about it."

"Why? I told you I would be right back."

"But..." I looked at him not wanting to tell him what I was thinking. "The state you were in and you have been with her before. I thought maybe you..."

"No, and how did you know that?"

"I heard you and Jason talking."

"If you thought that how come you let me kiss you when I got back?"

"Well three reasons really." I looked at him for reassurance that we could talk about this.

"Go ahead."

"Well, first of all; I was thinking it didn't happen, because we take forever and never get that far, and you weren't gone that long." I paused to see how it was going with him.

"That's a good assumption, but *'that'* actually doesn't take that long, especially when it's not meaningful."

I looked at him puzzled.

"Next..."

"Um-okay, if you *did* you were only doing it because you had to. Because I made you miserable and you had no choice."

He was frowning, "There is always a choice."

I looked at him suspiciously, "You were pretty miserable this morning."

"That's what the shower was for." He wasn't looking at me, but he was smiling a little, "And third?"

"If you did do it with her, you came back to be with me."

He had a great big smile now.

"Can I ask you a question?"

"Since you have been honest with me, ask away?"

"How *did* you get by with just a shower?"

"Karla wasn't there, but her new boyfriend was. We were friends before and he understood."

"I am so embarrassed. Someone knows I made you miserable."

He chuckled at me. He put the cards down and he was now crawling towards me.

"Remember, no touching." I teased him. He came closer and I leaned back to avoid his touch. "I am following the rules. What are *you* doing?"

He hovered over me looking deep into his eyes, "You thought I did it with someone else, you weren't mad, and you let me come back to you?"

"Yes."

"No touching rule is out the door." He laid his body softly to mine and put his hand to my face adoring it. He kissed me long and hard. Then his kisses came slowly, and were soft and gentle. I moved my hand to his back softly tracing it.

17. Emotional Roller Coaster

We both heard a car drive up. We stopped and James stood up and gave me his hands to help pull me up. I looked at the clock and it was already after 5 p.m. I walked to the door and James was putting on his jacket and boots.

I looked back at him, "What are you doing?"

"I'm going to help get your dad in the house."

"I don't think it's them."

I went out to hold the outside door and Brian came in. He looked a little worried until he saw James standing there, "Um, your dad…"

"What, what's going on?" I was worried.

"He might have food poisoning. They pumped his stomach and they're going to keep him over night. Your mom said she was going to stay with him."

"Okay. Wow."

"Did you eat the same thing?"

"No, remember it was my party and James took me out to distract me for the surprise."

"That's right, so you feel fine?"

"Yeah, I'm good."

He looked at James.

James took the clue from Brian, "It's going to be a long night and it's getting cold in here. I'll go get more firewood." He went out the door, but looked at me for approval.

"Thanks." I grabbed Brian's hand and made him sit down with me, "So, did my mom say anything else?"

"No, not really. He was doing a little better by the time she called, but she said you may need a few things and asked that we check on you."

"Well, actually, there isn't hardly any food here."

"I could go get some. Your mom said you might need something, and she would take care of the bill tomorrow."

"Cool." I grabbed a piece of paper. I wrote down: two cheeseburgers, two fries, bag of Doritos, and popcorn, and a 12 pack of Coke.

He looked at my list as I wrote it, "Either you're really hungry or you're getting enough for two."

"Well, yeah, he's been babysitting me all day."

Brian chuckled, "Danelle kind of filled me in."

I leaned into him just slightly, more like I was excited about something, "How did it go with Mykala?"

He smiled guiltily, "Really good."

"Did you kiss her good night?"

"I'm not telling you that!"

"Why not?"

"This friendship is going to be a little hard."

"You can do it, now did you kiss…?"

James walked in with wood. He tried to not look uncomfortable, but he did anyway. He moved to put the wood by the fireplace.

I looked back at Brian, "So, did you kiss her last night?" I was quieter. Brian was looking at James. "Just tell me, James doesn't know who I am talking about, right James?"

"What?"

"Nothing. I told you, now tell me."

"Yes."

"Was it short and sweet or…?" I smiled waiting for an answer.

"Maybe a little longer than short."

"Alright, that is so cool, but you have to make her feel special, you do know that, right?"

"Well, yeah."

"Don't be pushy."

"I'm not."

"*Really?*" I was giving him a disapproving look.

"Okay, I guess I can be a little pushy."

I looked at him, "Confident maybe, but just take it slow. You'll do great."

He smiled at me and stood up, "So, I guess I'll go get this stuff. Do you want to come with me?" He looked at James.

"Thanks, but I'm really not dressed to go anywhere, so if you don't mind I'll wait here."

"I'll be back in an hour or so with this order."

"Thanks again." I let him out the door.

When he pulled away, I watched to make sure he was gone. I turned back to James. He still had his coat and boots on, but was looking at me with a disapproving smile.

"So, what was that about?" He gave me a probing look.

I walked to him and pushed his jacket off, "He left with Mykala last night." I pushed him in the chair, "I asked him if he kissed her." I pulled his boots off, "He said he did and a little more than a peck on the lips. *Now,* can we get back to the touching thing, I miss this." I sat on his lap and traced my hands over his beautiful cut chest and moved in for the kiss.

James cupped my face with his hands and kissed me so passionately. I was hot instantly, I pushed to his lips harder. I loved to kiss him. He let go of my face and let his hand trace down in front of me until his hands were at my waist where he gripped and pulled me closer to him. I could feel him and I wanted this exciting feeling to keep going. I was finding it hard to breathe. He sat up more, so our bodies were almost touching.

He wrapped his arms around me so intensely. He was kissing my neck and traced under my chin. I wrapped my hands in his hair. I really wanted to keep this going. I liked how it made me feel.

He held me tighter to hold me still, "I have an idea."

"No, no stopping, please."

"Yes, stopping. I have to go."

"Where?"

"I have to go get something."

"What?"

"Trust me."

"How long?"

"As fast as I can."

"Karla's again?"

"Not this time."

"How?"

"Four-wheeler."

"It's cold."

"I'll be okay."

"I have food coming."

"Don't wait for me… I mean wait for me, but eat." He sat me on the couch, put on his jacket very quickly, and then his boots. He threw a couple small logs on the fire. He swept back to me and kissed me very passionately, "You are going to drive me insane." He looked at me before he was going to rush out the door, "You're a mess."

"Because of you."

"Well, get it together and fix your self up. I may need to bring you out into the public eye."

"What? We already have the whole trailer to ourselves. Why do we need to go anywhere?"

"Quit asking questions and just trust me." He walked briskly to me and pulled me up to him. He kissed my lips, as I stood completely frustrated. "Be a good girl, and go get cleaned up, please?"

"Okay."

And he was out the door and I heard the four-wheeler leave. I put on pots of water, so I could wash my hair. It was pretty bad, since I had been lying around all day. When the water became reasonably warm, I washed my hair. I wrapped my hair in a towel. I went to the back and threw on an old pair of jeans. They were a little looser, and they looked good. I put on a long sleeve t-shirt that had a short v-neck, and was long enough to come to my waist.

I heard a car. I let my hair down and toweled it a little, sprayed it with spritz a little and almost jogged to the living room. Brian was walking in with two bags of stuff. I ran up to help grab stuff and helped him put it on the table.

"Thank you so much!" I opened one of the burgers right away and took a huge bite.

Brian looked at me funny, "Hungry?"

"Starved. Sorry."

"That's okay." He put the coke in the fridge, the chips and popcorn on the counter. He put a gallon of milk in the fridge, and a couple of frozen dinners in the freezer. He got out the ketchup and handed it to me.

"Thanks."

I sat down and kept eating, "You don't have to do that."

"I know, but you're kind of busy."

"You brought more than what I asked for."

"Yeah, my mom insisted." I smiled at him, "So, what are you getting ready for?"

"I just needed to clean up."

"Where's James?"

"He had to go visit a 'friend' for a couple of hours. He said he would be back later."

"So, he went to see a girl?"

"I think so, its kinda boring to hang out with me, I think he does it to keep dad happy."

"I'm sure that's not the only reason."

I pushed him a little, "You're a funny guy."

I wanted to get off that subject so I asked, "What are *you* doing tonight?"

"I'm going roller skating with Mykala."

"That sounds like fun."

"We could skip that and come hang out with you."

"No thanks, you guys need private time."

"Yeah, I really like her."

"That's good."

"Do you want me to stay until James gets back?"

"No, I don't need a babysitter *all* the time."

He laughed at me, "Are you good now?"

"Yep. Thanks."

"See ya later; make sure you come down tomorrow, Danelle is bored."

"Tell her I promise."

"Bye."

I went back to blow-drying my hair. Wow, it looked really good. I wish I could do this all the time. I put some makeup on, just a little, because I didn't like a lot. I went back to the kitchen and finished my burger and fries. I looked out the kitchen window, paced to the TV then back to the window. Nothing, not a sound, and now it was so dark outside. I put in a movie and lay down on the couch placing my hair carefully over the pillows so it wouldn't get flattened. I closed my eyes. I just needed to relax. Time would go by a lot faster if I don't think about it.

I must have dosed off. My eyes were shut, and I stretched my arms over my head, I turned a little and opened my eyes to look at the TV. James was sitting on a chair from the kitchen, resting his elbows on his knees with his hands crossed in front of him. He was just sitting there looking at me.

"You're back?" I grinned at him.

He returned a sweet smile.

"When did you get back? And has anyone ever told you its kinda creepy to watch someone while there sleeping, especially when they don't know you're there?"

"You're so cute when you sleep and the noises you make when you're sleeping, sometimes I wonder what you are dreaming about."

"I mostly dream about you."

"Were you just now?"

"Yes, why?"

"What was it about?" I closed my eyes and smiled. He probed for an answer, "What! Tell me what it was about, please?"

Keeping my eyes shut, "We always go further in my dreams." I opened my eyes to evaluate how he was going to take that.

He put his head in his hands, "Does it ever hurt in your dreams?"

I sat up, and leaned forward. Facing forward next to him, "No, what do you mean?"

He turned his head to me, "That's why we have to be careful and not do that hastily. We have a lot of time to be together, but that can wait. Sometimes the first time hurts and I don't want it to be that way for you."

"Okay."

"You need to stop pushing me. I can only walk away so many times." He looked at me like he was warning me to be good. He took my hands in his, "Let's go."

"Your food?"

"I ate while you slept."

"Good."

"So, let's go."

"Where?"

"It's a surprise."

"On the four-wheeler?"

"Nope."

"You have your car?"

"No, but I borrowed a truck so I could bring the four-wheeler back."

"That's cool."

I got up and put my shoes on and my coat. He put the chair back in the kitchen. We walked outside with my hand in his. The truck was beautiful. It was a newer one, black, very sleek. It had a full size back seat, so when they worked in the fields they could get more full sized guys in it.

"Wow, they must trust you?"

"He owed me a huge favor."

We drove a long time, and I messed with the radio. James smiled at me the whole time like he had a secret. We pulled into a bar-night club. I felt bad, "I can't go in there."

"Why not?"

I looked at him disapproving and saddened that he didn't think about my age, "I'm not old enough."

"The owner knows me and I promised no drinking."

"Really?"

"Let's go."

We walked in, with him holding my hand. A lot of people greeted him and one guy even asked who the little lady was. James looked at me and said, "Ignore them, they're stupid."

He led me to the dance floor and twirled me around to start. We danced for a while. He was so good at dancing, and I didn't think I compared, but I really loved to dance with him.

A slow song came on and he pulled me close, "You want a soda?"

I nodded. He led me to the far end of the bar near the back. The bar tender walked over to us, "James."

"Hey Tony, this is Sarah."

"Hi Sarah."

"Hi," I shook his hand.

"Can we get something to drink?"

"James, I told you."

"Just a soda, nothing else."

He came back with two sodas. He stayed awhile to converse with James a little. Tony addressed me, "I heard you had a birthday. How was the party?"

"It was okay, but I don't like being the center of attention."

"Well you're kind of the center of attention here, too. Didn't you notice?"

"Nope." I looked at James.

"So you like to dance?" Tony asked.

"I *love* dancing."

"Well, have fun. No drinking."

"I'm good with that."

He went to serve someone else, and James grabbed my hand, "Ready?"

"Any time!"

We got up to move back to the dance floor.

Tony came back and grabbed James's arm, "I understand now."

James laughed as we moved to the dance floor. He twirled me onto the dance floor, and we moved together so smoothly. Every movement I could move with him was so natural. It had been a while before we went back to our sodas. They were a little watered down, but very refreshing. "We only have a little over an hour, shall we?"

"Love to."

Tony came down by us in a rush, "James! Door!"

We both looked, and saw that it was Jason and Kylie.

I looked at James, James looked at Tony, "Thanks Tony, we're out of here. I promised no trouble, back door?"

"Through there."

"Thanks."

"Nice to meet you, Tony!"

"Same here, now hurry."

James took my hand and led me out the back way. We were almost to the truck and we heard Jason, "James!"

He stopped, looked at me, then turned around tucking me behind him, still taking small steps to the truck, "What do you want, Jason?"

"I want to talk to her."

James looked at me, I shook my head no, "You know it's up to her and she already said no."

"James, you need to let me or I'll have to tell her."

"Jason, stop! I will talk to her; let me try."

I was shaking my head no when James turned to me, "I will not make you talk to him, but he's going to tell you something that will make you mad and maybe sad, but it's not going to happen. I will tell you the whole thing, just promise you will let me explain. Don't talk to him if you don't want to even if you're mad at me."

I nodded.

He turned to Jason, "Can't help you; she still says no."

"James, does she know about Katherine?"

James looked at me, I looked at him puzzled. We were by the truck, and he opened the door.

"Does she know you're getting married in the fall?"

I just looked at James. Tears began to drip down my face.

Jason called out again, "Sarah, did he tell you that?"

I got in the truck, and James closed the door behind me. I saw him walking toward Jason and they were arguing. I crawled into the back seat, and curled up with my knees to my chest and began to sob. I didn't want him to see my face when he came back. I wanted to die. I tried to contain my crying, and looked to see how much longer I had.

Kylie was out there now between them sticking up for James by the look of things. I put my head down resting it on my arms. I heard a tap on the window. I didn't want to look. It was persistent and tapped again. I lifted my head a little to see who it was. It was the bar tender, Tony. I rolled the window down an inch.

"Are you okay?"

I gave him a reassuring sad face and nodded.

Tony looked at me and said, "Let James explain." Then he winked. "This will be over in a couple of minutes." He lifted a bat and walked over to them. James turned to Tony, and I could see him say, "Thank you." Then he shook his hand and came running to the truck. He stopped, and took a deep breath before getting in.

He noticed I was not in the front seat, "Sarah?"

"Yeah."

"What are you doing?"

"I just need…" I couldn't hold it in. I was trying, but the tears wouldn't stop flowing. He sat on the seat with the door open facing outward.

"You said you would let me explain."

I couldn't say anything.

"I told you I don't believe in my heritage. I told you I was part of the outside world. Sarah?"

"I'm here."

"They are still picking our partners for us. It's how they believe. She doesn't want to be with me anymore than I want to be with her."

"What happens then?" I sniffled.

"Katherine spends a lot of time at our place, they try to force the relationship, but I am never there. My brother Will and she actually have fallen in love."

"So what happens then?"

"If I leave, she goes to the next one in the family."

"So, you have to leave?"

"Yes, but when I go I can't ever go back. I will not be part of the family anymore."

"That's why you haven't left yet?"

"Yes. I have a few things worked out, but I need to get everything finalized. Come up here, and I will explain everything to you. Please?"

I crawled to the front seat.

"Thanks for letting me explain."

"Why didn't you tell me? I would have understood."

"I was afraid you would push me away, like you did to Jason, and I can't…"

"Can't what?"

He turned his body to face me. He ran his fingers on my cheeks wiping the tears, "I can't live without you."

My tears started to fall again.

"I find everything about you amazing and I can't live without you." He scooted closer to me and pulled my face toward him. His lips were tracing mine. I started to kiss him back.

"Let's go."

"Okay. So, what do you have worked out so far?"

"I am going to go to firefighting school for six weeks in Colorado. I leave June 6th. After that, when I come back, Tony said I could stay with him. I guess I did pretty well on my entrance exam, and I will be going to school for forestry after that. I won't have to pay a cent. The Indian foundation is paying for half, and the other is a scholarship due to my test score. If everything goes well, I have a job lined up in Forest Lake. It pays really well, and if I want to be with you, I have to do better than this."

"So, time frame, how long are you talking?"

"About two years."

"How… when will I see you?"

"I will try to figure all that out, but as much time as I can."

I lay down on the seat and put my head in his lap. I closed my eyes letting the numbness overtake me. He traced my face as long as I could remember.

18. Losing You

I woke up in his arms as he was carrying me into the trailer. I wrapped my arms around his neck, "I could have walked."

"I know. I just like to have you close to me." He sat me in the chair, and pulled my boots off, "Jacket please."

I took it off and handed it to him. He put in a movie, grabbed a blanket and put out his hand for me to take. I gave him my hand and he pulled me up and moved to the couch pulling me with him. He lay down and directed me to lay with my back to him, but he scooted me down so my head was resting on his chest.

He lifted my shirt slightly and found what he was looking for, "My brother has already shared his with Katherine. She was the one who told me to share mine with you."

"You two have talked about me?"

"Yes, when she was trying to break it to me gently that she loves my brother. It works better for them if I leave."

"I understand."

He slowly unwrapped the feather, taking it very gently in his hand and placed it on my chest, letting it sit there as we watched my breathing move it. We laid there without saying anything. I had so many emotions;

I couldn't keep up with them all. My mind was racing, and I couldn't straighten anything out.

"Sarah?"

"Yeah."

"What are you thinking?"

"I don't know. It's all scrambled."

"Do you want to talk about it?"

"No, I really don't know where to start."

He reached for my hand and entangled my fingers with his, "Do you know how I feel about you?"

"Yeah, I think I do, except for normal insecurities on my part."

He cuddled in closer and wrapped his arms around me. He kissed my cheek, "I was really afraid I was going to lose you."

I nuzzled my face into his neck, "You almost did." I kissed his neck. We laid there in silence so long I was starting to get sleepy.

"Sarah?"

"Yes, James."

"I was checking to see if you were sleeping?"

"I am sleepy, but I can't really fall asleep. How about you?"

"I can't sleep either. I was wondering…"

I nuzzled into his neck some more and kissed him, "What are you wondering?"

"Is there anything I can say or do that will make up for today?"

I kissed his neck more luring, "I…" *kiss* "actually…" *kiss* "had…" *kiss* "the…" *kiss* "most…" *kiss* "wonderful…" *kiss* "day…" *kiss* "There was only one little part that I did not like."

"You know, that's the part I'm talking about."

"I know, it would have been nice to hear about it a different way."

"I am so sorry. What can I do to make it up to you, anything?"

"Anything?" I gave him and evil grin.

"Not *anything*."

"But you said…"

"Within reason."

I raised myself to look at him directly in the eyes, full of sadness, "Please," I closed my eyes, "don't hurt me again." I placed my lips on his.

"Are you going to torture me with this?"

"Nope."

"You didn't even yell at me."

"Why would I yell?"

"Normal girls do! Look at Kylie. She yells all the time at poor Jason. He can't even cross the street without getting yelled at."

I laid back down putting my face at his neck again. He could see I was feeling bad for Jason, "How come he keeps going back to her?"

"I'm really not sure, but he almost made it the last time. That's why he said he would wait for you. It was more like he was hoping that when you were a little older, you would be his escape."

"That's really sad. The only way he would leave her is if he had someone else to go to?"

James pulled my face up so I was looking at him. He looked as if he was really worried, "I wanted you to let Jason explain, so if you wanted to change your mind to be with him..." He was ashamed of what he was saying.

"I was already evaluating my pros and cons, and you won my heart before I even realized it."

"Really!"

"Remember the day on the snowmobile? I couldn't believe you felt the same way I did. I thought you would keep me at a distance because of my age, too."

"I couldn't stay away. I listened to Jason talk about every little part of you. I was fascinated before meeting you. I had to see for myself, because what he explained was so unbelievable. You were perfect before I met you."

"*Far* from that."

"No, really. You are not the normal crazy girl type. You're so much more mature than girls *twice* your age."

"Now, I know that's not true."

"You look at things different, and you evaluate everything before reacting."

"If you remember correctly, I tremble and cry a lot."

"Only when you get hit with some big situations."

"No, more like when I feel insecure."

"You're so strong."

"It only seems like that, because when I am with you I am brave."

"You're so adorable, I can't stand this anymore." He started kissing me so passionately I could hardly breathe. I traced my hands over his chest. We broke apart and I laid my head on his chest.

"You are still upset with me?"

I propped myself up on his chest resting my chin on my hands, looking at him, "I am not mad. I have no reason to be mad."

"But, you're not eager to tease or taunt me?"

"What I really need is for you to just hold me."

"I really almost lost you today, didn't I?"

"I was hurt. You nearly broke my heart. I just need you to hold me, so I can make sure this is real."

"If I hadn't figured things out, if I didn't have a plan, would I have lost you?"

"Maybe, I'm not sure, but we don't have to think about it, because you do have a plan, right?"

"The first part is definite."

"Well, then we don't have to worry about what might have happened."

"I have never seen you like this."

"Like what?"

"Mellow."

"Is that bad?"

"No, just different; harder to read."

"This is how I usually am when I am not with you. You bring me life, something I look forward to."

"I don't want you to leave tomorrow."

I looked at him, "You know, if dad is better, I'll have to. I still need to go to school."

"I am worried."

"About what?"

"If I let you go, you won't come back."

I was a little angry. I didn't want him to assume I wasn't coming back. He might go back to his old ways! "That's it!" I got up and took his hands to pull him up.

"What?"

"Come here right now."

I pulled him to the kitchen. Then I took a piece of paper from a notebook, and I wrote down my address and phone number, "Now, this is where I live and this is my phone number. If you have any doubts you know how to find me." I folded it up and was handing it to him.

He grabbed it from me, put it in his pocket, wrapped his arms around me, and twirled me around, "You just made me so happy." He cupped my face with his hands and kissed me softly, moving to trace my lips with his. He was taking my breath away. I wrapped my arms around his neck. *Oh how I loved to kiss him*! I could taste how sweet he was. My mouth was moving perfectly with his, and he picked me up and walked me to the couch. He laid me down without stopping the kissing as he knelt by me. He took my hand and turned it over to kiss it. Then he traced his lips up the inside of my forearm. He was being so gentle and adoring. I touched his face as he looked at me. His look completely melted me. His hand moved to my bare stomach as he glided his hand over it. I closed my eyes. His touch was so gentle and sweet. He leaned over me and kissed my neck moving up to my ear, "You are so…amazing."

I opened my eyes and wrapped my hand around his head, "What are you doing?"

"I want you to have a reason to come back to me."

"I already do because you have my heart."

He sat back on his feet still kneeling before me, looking at me with a questioning look on his face.

"What is it?" I reached to touch his face.

He took my hand and started to kiss it. His eyes closed in agony. He seemed to be torn with what he was thinking. I was getting a little nervous. He pulled me up, "Come here."

He pulled my waist so I was facing him. My legs were on each side of him, and my back was resting on the back of the couch.

"Don't, I just want you to hold me."

He scooted me down, so I was almost lying down. He unbuttoned my pants, and unzipped them, then traced his hands over my stomach.

"James, we can't."

"I won't, I promise." His face came to my stomach and traced his lips across it.

"You said you wouldn't be able to stop…"

"I will."

"But you'll be miserable?"

"I deserve it." He kissed my stomach.

"Really, you don't want…" I bit my bottom lip.

He laid his head on my stomach, "You're right. I can't do this."

I ran my hands through his hair. I tried to slide down, so I would be sitting closer to his face.

He lifted his face, "What are you doing?"

"I needed to kiss you… kind of hot right now." I put my arms around his neck and kissed him softly.

He stood up pulling me with him until we were both on our feet, "I need a shower…*badly.*"

"What?"

"I think my self control is getting worse."

"I'm sorry."

"You tried to warn me, but I will be right back."

I let go of him sadly, and then watched him put his boots on and jacket. He came back and kissed me on the forehead.

I didn't want to know but I asked, "Karla's?"

"It's closest, unless you want me to be longer?"

"No, not really, but it's weird."

He smiled at me, "Be right back." He was out the door.

I looked at the clock. It was 2:30 a.m. That's going to be a really bad thing. I took the feather and wrapped it back up, and put it in my bag. No more temptation for today. I curled up on the couch and hugged a pillow, as I watched the movie. I didn't like being here alone. I dozed a little and the movie ended. I threw in another one. I looked at the clock. It was 4:00 a.m., *it didn't take this long last time,* or maybe it did, but it didn't seem this long.

I walked to the kitchen window and looked out. I paced a little walking to the TV and then back to the window. I was getting impatient; 4:10 a.m.

"*Great.*"

I paced again, looking at the clock every time I passed it. Did it stop? Oops, no, there is moved; 4:15 a.m. *She trapped him!* Shit, he would have refused, right? *Of course he would have.* I looked out the window again. *Dam it!* I should have stopped him, completely refused. *Now look what I have done!* Now it was 4:25 a.m.

I felt the tears starting and I curled up on the couch again, hugging a pillow. *I didn't want him to be with her.* He was supposed to be mine now, that's what he was saying to me, right? I tried to convince myself that he only wanted to be with me. *He had been a player before, so could he give that all up for me?* He wasn't getting what he needed here. I closed my eyes.

"Sarah?"

"Yeah?"

"You've been crying."

"Self doubt…"

"I'm sorry it was so long."

"I drove myself crazy."

"When I went to Karla's…they were kind of busy, so I had to go all the way home."

I basically attacked him, throwing myself into his arms, kissing his whole face.

"You didn't think…?"

"I told you, I was driving myself crazy."

"I TOLD YOU, you have ruined it for me. No one is good enough anymore."

I kissed him all over his face until I reached his lips and the luring, hot, passionate kisses came through.

"Sarah."

"Yeah?"

"If you keep this up, I will need another shower."

"You're not leaving again, no matter what happens."

"You don't mean that." A guilty smile came over his face.

"I do, and if that happens again, we'll just have too…"

"Then we're back to *no more touching.*" He was smirking.

"Okay, okay." I let him go.

He sat down on the couch and had me sit in front of him again. His body was so relaxed. I wish I could do that. His muscles weren't flinching at all anymore. He was so strong and amazing to look at.

He pulled my shirt up a little, and traced my stomach with his hands softly, "Where's the feather?"

"I put it away, to get rid of *temptation*."

"Good idea." I relaxed into him and tilted my head to the side a little, as he kissed my shoulder and then my neck, "Sleep Sarah, I will be fine."

19. The Chief

"Sarah, your mom and dad are here."

I jumped up and looked at him in a panic. He got up and put his boots and jacket on really quickly, then stopped and looked at me.

"Sarah, pants."

I zipped and buttoned them. I looked around for any evidence, but there wasn't really any. I went to the door to hold it open and James was already helping him from the car.

"So you're ready for a beer, Tuck?"

"Yeah, almost."

James laughed. My mom and I didn't find the humor in it. He helped my dad through the door and sat him in the chair.

Mom went to the kitchen to make a list of food that dad might need over the next week or so, "James?"

"Yep?"

"Can you go shopping for Tucker?" As she handed $100 to him, James nodded, "Try to get some food you like too. You'll stay and take care of him, right?"

"Of course, until he kicks me out."

Dad started laughing, "Boy?"

"Yeah?"

"Did you take care of my little girl?"

"She's tough to handle, but she's still alive."

"What? You're the one that was tough to handle."

Dad started to laugh a little, "I can see nothing changed around here."

"Yeah, actually it has," James started to say. I gave him a nasty look. He had an evil grin, "You really don't have any food left."

"I knew that before we left."

"Okay, so I am off to get food. Can Sarah go...?"

"Of course, but before you two get going I want to give Sarah her phone."

"A *cell phone*? For *me*?"

"Yes, it's for you. After this weekend dad decided it was necessary for you to have one. Besides, you'll be driving soon and we'd feel safer if you could get a hold of us."

I kissed dad on the cheek, "Thanks dad! Glad to see you're better." I hugged mom too, "What time are we leaving?"

"Not too long after you get back."

I grabbed my new phone and put on my boots and jacket, "James we have to stop at Sherburn's. I need to tell Danelle I can't come hang out with her today."

"You're the boss."

"Thanks."

James was already out the door. I ran out the door after him and jumped on his back. He asked, "What do you think you're doing?"

"What I would normally do."

He smiled, "You're right." He started to spin me around. I had to hold on tighter. He dropped me at my side of the car.

"You're not going to open the door for me?"

"Don't push your luck."

I stuck my tongue out.

"Be careful that might end up somewhere." I got in and so did he. "Did you want to stop first or later on the way back?"

"First please!"

We pulled into Sherburn's, "Do you want me to come in or stay in the car?"

"I don't care. I will only be a minute."

"I'll wait here."

"You sure?"

"Yeah, I don't like watching you talk to Brian. I get jealous."

"I want to kiss you."

"Don't you dare!"

I laughed, opened the door and ran inside. Danelle was at the counter. Her eyes brightened, and I felt bad I was going to let her down. Brian came out, "How did it go last night?"

He looked at me, "So-so."

"Be patient, and dazzle her." He smiled at me a little and walked into the bar. I looked at Danelle, "He doesn't seem that happy about last night."

"He got to second base, but then talked about it, so she's not talking to him."

"Oh, stupid guy!" Then I told her, "I can't stay, I am on my way to get food for dad. We're going into town to get more supplies for him."

"*We're?*"

"Yeah, James is taking me."

"You are going to like him."

I rolled my eyes.

"I think you already do."

I smiled at her, "Well, if I'm a good girl, I get to go with grocery shopping."

She smiled at me.

"I will come spend a whole day the next time I come up, okay?"

"Sounds good, but no babysitter."

"Okay. Bye!"

"Bye!" she called back to me.

I walked out the door, but I heard it open behind me, "Hey, wait up!"

I turned to see it was Brian. I saw James roll down his window so he could listen.

"What's up?"

"It didn't go well." He looked down.

"If you do something with her, you definitely don't want to share that info." I tried not to scold him, but it was difficult not to.

He looked back at me with an embarrassing smile.

"Yes, I heard. Stop trying to impress your friends and just hang out with her. Don't push for anything, and if you do something keep your mouth shut."

He looked at James and then back at me, "Is that why you spend time with him?"

"Knock it off Brian. Sometimes you are a jerk."

"Sorry."

"That's okay. Ya know…if you would listen to me, you'd do better."

He reached for my left hand and leaned in to kiss my left cheek, and then he whispered to me, "That was to piss off the boyfriend."

I hit him as hard as I could with my right fist.

"Shit! That hurt!"

"Good!" I pulled my left hand from him.

James started laughing in the car as he yelled, *"Don't piss her off!"*

"Sorry, it was a test."

"Don't test me again."

"I wasn't testing *you*."

I glared at him, "Just try harder to be a gentleman."

"Friends?" as he smiled.

"Only if you behave?!"

"Okay, okay."

"Well, we gotta get going. See ya!"

I got in the car. James was laughing, "I told you."

"What?"

"They find you adorable." He started to drive.

"That's not what that was about."

"*Oh really?* What was that about then?"

"He knows. Shit! My hand is swelling."

"Let me see it." He looked at my hand, "It sure is. Did you break it?"

"I don't think so, but it hurts."

"We'll get some ice on it when we get there."

"To the store?"

"No, were going to the reservation. I can get twice the amount of food for the price."

"Oh, shit! This really hurts."

"What did you mean? *He knows.*"

"He was testing his theory by kissing my cheek. He was looking for a reaction from you. Shit! I think it's turning colors."

"Yeah, it is. So, he thinks we're together?"

"Yep, but that's why I hit him, because he was testing you."

"You defended me?"

"In a way. Shit! This really hurts!"

He put his hand out for me to hold. I took it with my good hand. He kissed it, "We're almost there."

We drove up to what looked like a very small cabin. He stopped and got out. He pulled me out of the car through his door. He took my hand and looked at me like he was going to kiss me, "Hope you're ready for this."

"I'm not, but I have no knuckles left."

"You shouldn't punch people." He gave me a disapproving grin. He walked through the door into the kitchen. It was very small. He grabbed a towel and went right to the freezer, and started putting ice in it.

A little girl came running into the kitchen, "James, you're here!"

He bent down and picked her up, "Tamara, this is Sarah. Sarah, this is Tamara."

She leaned into his ear to whisper something to him and started to giggle.

Out loud James replied to her, "Yes she is."

I gave him a questioning glance.

He smiled at me, "You're pretty."

He sat her back down and she ran into the other room, "She's here, she's here! Will, Sam, Katherine, she's here!"

"Well, here we go!" He grabbed the bag of ice and took my hand and tried to place it on it carefully.

"Ouch, sh…,sh."

"This is not a good way to make an impression."

"I know it. Just take it off."

"No! You may have broken it."

He held my hand and the ice on it. Will and Katherine walked in holding hands. She was stunning. She had a beautiful face, contoured with high cheekbones, deep brown eyes, and extra long eyelashes. She was breathtaking. I looked at James, like he was stupid or something. He shook his head at me.

Will walked up to me and put his arms around me, "Holy shit brother, she is gorgeous!" as he ran his hands down my back while holding me. Katherine hit him in the back of his head.

He turned to her, "Well she would have to be to take him away from you." Then he began to kiss her passionately in front of us.

James grunted with disgust, "Hey guys take it in the back. Tamara's here." They broke apart and left the room together laughing.

Sam came over to me and took my good hand in his, "James, I get this one, okay?"

James kicked him in the butt, "Out! Don't be stupid."

"But Katherine's a year older than Will. Sarah's only a year older than me. I get this one.

James stomped at him, "Out!" Sam ran out of the room. Tamara was standing there, staring at me. James noticed it too. He let go of my hand and squatted down so his face was even with hers.

"What's up little girl?"

She put her arms around his neck, "How long can you stay?"

"Not long. Why?"

"I love you, and they're not nice to me."

He looked at me, "Just one minute." I nodded. He walked out into the other room holding her, "Where's dad?"

"He's out back."

"What's he doing?"

"Praying you'll come to your senses."

"Hey, if you guys aren't nice to Tamara, I am going to beat the living shit out of you. Hey, I'm talking to you!"

"Yeah, sure."

"Whatever *the chosen one* says."

"Knock it off! And Katherine, you're older than both of them, could you quit with Will long enough to discipline them a little. Shit guys! Try at least."

"Okay."

"Yes sir!"

"The great Chief speaks."

"Not for long, and Will, it's your job now, so start acting like it."

He walked back in the kitchen and walked over to me and checked my hand. I really didn't feel anything. I just stared at him. *Did I really hear what I thought I heard?*

"How does it feel?"

"I don't know, numb. *Chief*?"

"No, not now, not ever, and don't think I will be if you push me away Sarah. I am still leaving, if I have you or not." He looked at me with anger in his eyes. I looked back at him puzzled. He leaned into me a little and whispered, "I don't believe in the same things they do. I'm different." I was speechless. "This is going to be hard and I don't know how he will react, …but do you want to meet the real Chief, my dad?"

"I'm scared."

"I was leaving before I met you. I was leaving when they decided my partner."

"She is beautiful!"

"I don't want this life."

"Okay, whatever you want. I would love to meet your dad."

"How's your hand?"

"I don't know. I don't really feel it anymore."

"Good."

He took my good hand and led me outside to a large shed. He opened the door and held it open above my head so I could walk in. I clung to him a little. James had me somewhat worried. I could see his father's legs sticking out from under a truck.

"Hey Chief."

"Are you here to help me?"

"Not really, Sarah's with me."

"Oh?" He pulled himself out from under the truck. He stood up and brushed himself off. Now I could see where James got his looks from. He was stunning, muscular everywhere, and a chiseled jaw line.

"Well, this is the little lady that has distracted him from us. I would shake your hand, but I'm a little dirty."

"That's okay," I held up my hand and gave him a wave.

"What did you do there?" his father looked at my swollen hand.

James stepped in and replied for me, "She slugged a guy that was getting fresh."

"Good for you!" He gave me an approving nod and smiled at me. "So, did my son fill you in on his duty to this family?"

"Dad, knock it off."

"If he did, I hope you help him get his head straight, like his mother did for me."

"Dad!"

"You are as beautiful as she is. I can see why, but sometimes we have to…"

James interrupted him, "Dad, that's enough! Will is the one now. Let it go."

"But, I don't think he will ever be ready. He's not like you."

"He will have to be. I just wanted you to meet her."

"Uh yes. Very pretty, but I have to get this done. Nice to meet you."

James pulled me out of the shed. He stopped and turned to me, "Please do not push me away. I cannot live without you." I just looked at him. "Please tell me you won't."

"I won't, but you need to explain this more."

"Later, we have to go get groceries for your dad."

He led me back to the car.

Tamara ran out of the house, "You can't leave, you just got here!"

"I have too sweetie," he kissed her forehead, "I love ya little one. See ya tomorrow. Okay?"

"Yep," she grabbed his face, "I love you chief!" He rolled his eyes.

We headed to the grocery store. It looked small, but it was very well stocked. James held my hand the whole time. My mind was still racing from everything that his family had said while I was there. We went up and down every isle grabbing everything on mom's list, and a little more.

"Are you sure you can stay and take care of my dad?"

"I'm there most of the time anyway."

"I was thinking we could stay another day, if you can't."

"If you stayed another day, I would be there anyway."

"Okay!"

"What are you thinking?"

"I don't want to leave yet."

He smiled and pulled me closer, "I think we need to be done."

He only spent $85 and he had 15 bags of groceries and 4 gallons of milk. We got in the car as James said, "I told you we could get a lot more for the money here."

"Yeah, I can't believe it."

"I forgot something at the house. We have to stop there, real quickly though."

As we pulled back up to his house, he looked at me, "You're coming with me." He pulled me out his side of the car. My right hand still really hurt. He grabbed a bag that was rolled up, and led me in holding my hand. Tamara came running. He pulled out a sucker and gave it to her. She took it and ran to the living room. We walked into the living room where Will and Katherine where cuddling on the couch, "Where's dad?"

"He went to get parts."

"Good." He pulled me down the short hallway.

"Dad's going to be pissed you brought her back here!"

"I don't care, Will!" He opened the door to a room. Sam was in there. James yelled at him, "Out!"

"But *you're* never here."

"I know it's yours for a couple days, but out for now."

"You're going to be in so much trouble."

"Out!" He closed the door behind Sam. He pulled me in front of him.

"Okay, close your eyes."

I did what I was told.

"Open your mouth."

"What?"

"Open your mouth, trust me.

I did it.

"Now put out your tongue."

So I stuck my tongue out. I put my good hand on my hip. He squirted cool whip on my tongue. I opened my eyes and tasted it, looking at him confused. He held it up to squirt it again. I opened my mouth sticking out my tongue. He squirted a little and started kissing me. I laughed a little.

"You didn't forget anything, did you?"

"Yes I did. If I am staying with your dad I need clothes." He threw some stuff in a bag. "Ready?"

"No."

"Why?" he asked and pulled me close.

"When I get back, I'll have to leave."

"Yeah, but we have groceries."

"I just don't want to leave." I grabbed his shirt in my fist, pulling him closer.

"I will give you 15 minutes, but that's it."

"Is this your room?" I looked around. I didn't have to move; I could reach every side of it if I stuck my arms out.

"Do you really want to waste 15 minutes looking around my room?" A grin came over his face as he lifted the can of cool whip.

"What are you thinking?"

"Lay down."

I obediently listened to him. He pulled my shirt up a little and squirted cool whip on my stomach. He began to trace letters in it. First an S then smeared it, A then smeared it, R then smeared it, A then smeared it, H. Then our eyes locked.

"Well, that was interesting."

He had a very mischievous look on his face. He scooted down, leaned over me and began licking it off of me.

"I thought we needed to be more careful than this?"

Then he was sucking it off and licking at the same time. I arched my back. It felt so amazing. I moaned a little, "This will get you in trouble."

"But I have a shower right across the hall. We have 15 minutes."

I looked at the clock, "Yeah but, we're down to 8 minutes."

He squirted a little more.

"We don't have time for this." I warned.

He spread it out with his finger and drew a heart in it. He looked at me and smiled, "Are you ready?"

"For what?"

He began licking and slowly sucking. I was breathing very heavy. I tried to scoot up to stop him, but it felt so good. He brought his face to mine and kissed me. I wanted to attack him! I looked at the clock; 2 minutes left, "You are mean."

"Why?"

All I could say was, "We have 2 minutes."

He laughed. He got up, grabbed my good hand, and pulled me up, "Let's go".

20. On the Phone

I started grabbing bags of groceries to carry into the trailer. I realized my hand was still hurting, so I looked at it. It was still pretty swollen. James grabbed two bags with each hand. We walked in and sat them on the table. Mom started putting stuff away. James and I headed out to get more bags.

As we got to the car, he hip checked me, and I almost fell over. He offered, "More whipped cream?"

"Yep!" I held my mouth open; he filled it. I tried to grab the can, but he wouldn't give it to me. I grabbed another bag of groceries and we headed back into the trailer.

We walked in laughing. Mom noticed I wasn't using my right hand at all, "What did you do?"

"She punched a guy for getting fresh."

"James, it wasn't like that!" I scowled at him.

"Okay, the guy kissed her cheek and she punched him." He looked at me with a sarcastically, "Is that better?"

"No."

Dad yelled from the living room, "That a girl, keep them away."

"Dad!"

James started laughing, "Yeah, now all I have to do is get another dumb boy to try and kiss her, so she'll hit him with the other hand. Then she will be totally defenseless."

"Down boy." Dad said from the other room.

We both started laughing. I grabbed the can of whipped cream and took a shot.

"What are you doing?" Mom watched me with a funny look.

"Eating whip cream." I held it up for James to take a shot. He opened his mouth. I gave him a shot. I shot a little on my finger and put it on his nose, then ran out to the car to get more groceries.

He looked at my mom and dad, "See what I had to put up with while you guys were gone?"

He followed out the door. I already had a bag, so I scooted by him. I sat it on the table and rushed back out. James had two in each hand again. All that was left was four gallons of milk. I waited for him to come back out. He looked at me, "What?"

"I just want to watch."

"Watch what?"

"You carry all four milks."

"What's the big deal?"

I walked pass him to go inside. As I passed him I whispered, "I just like to look."

"You are bad, a very bad girl."

"Sometimes."

Mom looked at James coming in with more stuff, "How did you get all this food? You didn't spend your own money, did you?"

"Nope, the Res."

Dad turned to look at him, "You're not supposed..."

James interrupted, "Well, I figured I am eating here all week, so it's okay."

"As long as you don't get in trouble."

"Me? Never."

I glared at him and I wasn't thinking when I blurted it out, "Is that what your brothers meant that your dad was going to be mad about?"

"I will be fine. Dad will have a whole week to cool off."

"That was very nice of you, James. Thanks again." My mom gave him a hug, "Now that everything is put away and it's getting later, I think it's time we get going."

"Okay," I went to the room to get my things. I took a deep breath. I did not want to go.

I heard his voice beside me, "1...2...3... breathe."

I smiled

"Here, I'll take your bag."

As I walked pass him I kissed his lips softly and quickly, "I will miss you."

He grabbed my arm and looked at me. He took my hand and kissed my palm. He nodded for me to go.

He put my bag in the trunk.

Mom asked, "Can you drive with your hand like that? I didn't get much sleep."

"Yep, no problem." I was glad to drive. It helped me to not cry. I felt like my world was ending.

Week One – Monday I had to get my hand looked at. It wasn't broken, just badly bruised. Swelling should get a little better within a few days. Pat called on Wednesday. That helped a little.

Pat asked, "What did you say to Sue?"

"Nothing really."

"Well, whatever it was, thank you."

"You're welcome. Now tell me why you're thanking me."

"She actually kissed me."

"Well, good."

"I wanted to spend more time with you at the party, but I think Brian was up to something."

"He was, but I diverted him with Mykala."

"I was wondering."

"Yep. Danelle gave me a heads up."

"I knew I liked her."

"Me too, but I have to go. I have lots of homework." I had to get started on homework, and with a bum hand it was going to take forever because it hurt to write.

Week Two – I was determined to work hard at school stuff, so I wouldn't think about *James*. I did fine during the day, but I found myself not getting much sleep. I would fall asleep and then the dreams would keep me up. I found a job answering phones at a car dealership in afternoons and early evenings. It was great. I was making pretty good money and not sulking about not going up north. I had no idea how long it would be, so I needed to stay busy.

Week Three – First week of work went well. I liked talking to different people and looking at the really nice cars. The best part is that if I worked there for three months I could get a car at twenty-five percent discount. I was having a really hard time not thinking about James, his muscles, his smile, and the kisses. All day on Tuesday and Wednesday I couldn't get my head clear. I was miserable. Pat called Thursday. He was going up north for a snowmobile run. My mom didn't want to make the trip because of the snow and ice that was predicted. So, we were staying home *another* weekend.

Three weeks! And now I will have to make it another week? I thought I was going to lose it and just confess that I needed to see James. I was going crazy wondering how much longer it would be until I could see him again. My mind was racing with all kinds of thoughts. Then my phone rang. I heard his voice, "Hey little girl."

"Where are you calling from?"

"I am calling from Tony's place. I needed to know if you were coming up here this weekend."

"Not this weekend. My mom doesn't want to chance the weather. I am miserable and missing you."

"That's why I called." My heart was jumping. *Was he coming to see me?* The guys want to take me skiing in Duluth, but if you were going to be here I would stay."

"I wish I was, but I'm not."

"I really don't want to go, but Will says I need to do something."

"You should if you are as miserable as I am." There was silence. "James?"

"Yeah?"

"I love you."

"Don't say that now. It hurts not being with you."

"Do me a favor?"

"What?"

"Close your eyes. Are they closed?"

"Yes."

"You're lying to me, close them please."

"How did you know that?"

"I can hear you. Are they closed?"

"Yes…," sounding like he was giving in.

"What do you see when you hear my voice?"

"It's not the same Sarah." He sounded so miserable, "I take three showers a day, because I think about you all the time."

"So you really need to get your mind off me, right?"

"I don't want to."

"I know, but you need too, are you and dad working?"

"No, not much."

"You need another job, something that will keep you busy."

"Tony said I could bartend at his place."

"Do it! That will help kill some time. Tell him tonight as soon as we hang up. I miss seeing you and hearing your voice. You can call me anytime you want. I don't care if it's 3 a.m., I will answer."

"I have to go. Tony is pushing me to hurry up."

"Hey, if you're bartending for him you could afford to call me more."

"Yeah, I guess."

"I'm glad you called. I really do love you."

"Sarah, please don't. I have to go."

"Bye."

Week Four – Every day after James called was torture. I tried to immerse myself in my schoolwork. I had a large packet of science, and there was always reading.

Pat called on Tuesday, "I wish you would have been there. All of us, the whole group rode from tavern to tavern. We all hung out."

"Did Mykala go with Brian?"

"She went, but she was with someone else."

"Dam it, I told him to take it slow."

"You wanted him with *Mykala*?"

"Yes."

"So, you don't *like* him?"

"Not that way."

"Good."

"Hey, that's not nice."

"He can be a jerk to girls."

'Yeah, I told him that."

"You did?"

I looked down at my hand, "He needed to hear it."

"You're so cool."

"Not really, but I better go, got lots of homework."

Matt from school called. He said he needed help with the math packet. I really didn't believe him since he was the smartest guy I knew and *he* usually had to help *me,* "Can you come over this weekend so we can work on it together?"

"I'm not sure. It depends on if I am going up north to see my dad. Can I let you know tomorrow?"

"Yeah sure, talk to you tomorrow."

"Bye."

Mom had plans this weekend, so no James. I made plans with Matt and we decided on 11 a.m. Saturday. I got home from school and I was pouting. I went to work and put on a fake smile. I would have to make it another week.

James called me at 4:30 p.m., "You're not coming are you?"

"Nope."

"Then I feel better, because I did what you told me. I'm bartending for Tony. I start in a half hour."

"That's so good."

"I can't talk, but...Sarah?"

"Yes, James?"

"Tell me I can do this."

"James, you can do anything."

"Sarah, my sweet Sarah."

"Yes, James."

"I love you... got to go, bye."

I didn't get a chance to say anything, and he was gone. I went to bed extremely sad. I woke to my phone ringing at 3 am, "Hello?"

"Sarah."

"James," I took a deep breath of relief, "What are you doing?"

"I had to call you. Tony said I could call you as much as I want to as long as I pay the phone bill."

"So, you're going to call more?"

"If that's okay?"

"Yes! It keeps me alive."

"I did really good; over $300 in one night."

"Oh my God, that's amazing."

"I should have done this a long time ago."

"I wish I could make that kind of money."

"Tony said it's usually not that good during the week, but the weekends seem to be this good. If you want to call me, call Tony's phone. I'm here all the time now."

"Have you seen my dad?"

"Yeah about that, this is a little rough on him, but I brought him a little more food."

"You're the best. How is it going with your dad?"

"Sarah."

"What? You really haven't explained anything, especially since you're supposed to be the chief."

"You caught that?"

"Yes, I think they were pretty clear on it."

"It's not going well at all, that's why I am here all the time now. You sound sleepy. I will call you tomorrow."

"Okay. I miss you."

"I will be dreaming of you."

I smiled, "Goodnight."

Weeks Five and Six – I continued to work as much time as they would give me at the dealership. It helped to keep my mind off of James, which was more difficult since he was calling a lot. He called almost every night. I would fall asleep and wake to his soft voice. I was able to sleep without feeling the pain in my chest from missing him. Still, I had no sign of when we were going up to see dad. *How did mom handle it?* I just don't understand.

Week Seven – On Wednesday I took James phone call. "Are you coming up to see your dad this weekend?"

"No, my mom's really busy again. She is working three jobs right now."

"Well, I was thinking…"

I started to smile. I could tell he was up to something, "What were you thinking?"

"Tony is going to 'The Cities' for supplies next Tuesday. He said we could stop by to pick up some things for your dad if your mom wanted that."

"You're coming here?!" I could hardly contain my excitement.

"If you…"

"Yes! Yes! I want you to come! I will get some things together for you to take back for him."

"Don't you want to check with your mom?"

"Nope. What time?"

"Sarah?"

"What?"

"It's not until next week."

"I know, but you're coming here!"

"Sarah?"

"Yeah?"

"You want me to come there?"

"Yes, yes, and please! When, what time?"

"I'm not sure."

"How long will we have?"

"Sarah!" He was firmer.

"What?"

"You need to settle down."

"I know, but I haven't seen you in so long. It's just I can't wait to touch your lips, your chest, your hands, everything. I just want to kiss you."

"Sarah, I can't wait to see you either."

"I'm not going to sleep for a week now."

"You still need to sleep."

"I will try, but I'm sure it will be filled with no-no's."

"Sarah, you drive me crazy. I'm working soon, so I will call you later."

"Okay."

I started plotting right away. I could have a box ready for dad. I would make Tony a steak dinner, and then I could steal some time with James, but only if they came before mom got here.

Week Eight – Monday I spent all of my time running to get stuff for dad and for making dinner for Tony. I got together a huge box of food and paper supplies. I also bought some steaks. I didn't know how much they would need to eat. I spoke to James and confirmed they would be here between 2-3 p.m.

I had gotten mom to write me out of school at 1 p.m. She totally understood that I wanted to spend time with James. He was like my best friend up north. He was my keeper there, so it would be okay. I was so ready to see him. I was pacing all night.

Mom asked, "Why are you so excited?"

"I just haven't hung out with him in so long. I miss him and all the fun we have arguing."

21. Cayuse

I went to school, and I was watching the clock ticking extra slow. I can't handle this. I wished I could skip, so I could go home and wait. I was so irritable and in math class Matt asked, "What are you so antsy for?"

"A friend from my cabin is coming for a visit today and I haven't seen him in two months."

"Him?"

"Uh, yeah."

"Boyfriend?"

"Kind of."

"Oh," he sounded a little disappointed, "That explains why."

"That explains what?"

"Why you're not responsive to me."

"*What*?"

"It's nothing."

"No really, Matt, I had no idea."

"I know. No interest on your part."

"That is so sweet, and if I didn't have him, you definitely would have my attention."

He smiled.

I left school at 1 p.m. and got home as fast as I could. I got the grill ready and put in the potatoes, since they take the longest to cook. Everything was going as planned. James called, "Hi, our plans are a little off."

"Please don't tell me you're not coming?"

"No, according to the directions I think we're here."

I looked out the window, there they were. I hung up the phone without saying a word and ran out to him. I jumped into his arms wrapping my legs around his waist and kissed him so hard.

I looked at Tony, "Thank you!" he smiled at me.

I could feel his face at my neck, "I smell food." He said.

"It was a bribe, so I could keep you longer."

He set me down and whispered, "Good idea." I took his hand as we walked to the back of the house. He pulled me back, "So, you cook?"

"Not really."

"So, what are you not cooking?"

"Steak, veggies, and potatoes."

"How long ago did you put the steaks on?"

"Right before you guys got here."

"That's good."

When we got to the back yard, James went to check the steaks, but never letting me go.

I turned to Tony, "I hope you're hungry?"

"I am starving. We haven't eaten yet."

"Good. Well come on in."

I held the door for Tony to walk in front of me. James was walking in behind me and I still had his hand in mine. He grabbed my stomach and pulled me back into him as we walked in. He kissed my neck and ear. I pulled his other arm around me as we tripped up the steps. I still had his hand in mine as I walked to the stove to check on the veggies. James leaned against the counter next to me, still holding my hand. I stirred the veggies and looked at Tony, who was now sitting at the table. James pulled me in front of him and kissed my neck.

"So, James' bartending for you, is that going good?"

"Yeah, it's going fine."

James put his hand around me to the front of my stomach holding me tighter still kissing my neck.

I scolded, "James stop it!"

Tony stood up, "Excuse us, James outside, the steaks need to be checked."

James held my hand to bring me with him.

"No, I want to talk to you alone, James." They went out in the back. I followed to the steps to listen in on their conversation.

"You are not going to be alone with her, you know that."

"I know, I thought I could, but she just…"

"Yeah, I would have reacted the same way."

"I swear she gets better every time I see her."

I smiled. My working out was paying off.

"She is, but I think our stay is going to be short. You made me promise to not let you do anything you would regret."

My heart was pounding. *They can't leave already. They just got here!* I need to kiss him, to hug him.

"I need more time, *please*?" James pleaded with Tony.

"Can you handle yourself?"

"I'm doing much better now."

"Yeah, but for how long?" Tony questioned.

"Until I look at her. *Shit!*"

"What do you want to do?"

"I didn't think it would be this hard."

My heart was ready to jump out of my chest. I didn't want him to leave, but I didn't want it to be impossible to be around me. I went to get the potatoes out and I put them in a bowl and set them on the table. I got the butter and sour cream and set them on the table. I got the veggies and two plates and put them on the table too. They walked in.

"Are they ready?" I asked.

"Yep." James brought the steaks in and set them on the counter.

I got the remote and handed it to Tony, "How long are you planning on staying?" I grabbed James hand, and looked at him, "He's mine now."

Tony looked at James, "I guess if you're too long I'll close my eyes, but your mom will be home by when?"

"5 or 6 o'clock."

"I wasn't planning on that long."

"Okay."

I led him to my room. I closed my door.

He looked leery, "Sarah, that's not a good idea."

I stood by my door looking at him, "I know, but I miss you so much."

He looked around, "Huge bed!"

"It was cheaper than the small one I wanted."

"It takes up your whole room."

"Pretty much."

We were both afraid to touch each other. We were afraid the desire would be too powerful.

"Sarah?"

I stood there looking at him. He walked over to me and put his hand on the door on each side of me. My breath was escalating and my heart was beating so hard.

"Sarah, do you have a shower?"

I smiled a little, "Yes."

"It's the only way." I nodded, took his hand and led him out of my room to the basement bathroom.

Tony asked as we passed him, "Where are you two off to?"

"I have to show him something. We'll be back."

We walked into the small bathroom. I grabbed two towels out of habit. I set them on the toilet. The shower was in the corner behind the door.

I turned to leave him and he grabbed my arm, "Please don't go." I stopped. He turned me around to face him, "Well, if I have to take a shower anyway…"

He took off his shirt. My heart was almost pounding out of my chest. He unbuttoned his pants. I kept looking at his eyes. *He was so beautiful!* He pushed his pants down over his hips so they fell to the ground, and stepped out of them. He moved closer to me. He wrapped his arms around my waist lifting me to him. I wrapped my legs around his waist, holding myself up. He kissed me so passionately that I could hardly breathe. I didn't realize I could be so torn how I felt. I want to feel his body against mine so bad, but if we did that, there would be no stopping what would come next.

He whispered to my lips, "Shower."

I was relieved. I didn't think I could turn him away.

He set me down softly and I turned to leave, but he stopped me, "I don't want to spend one minute without you. Please stay." He turned me to face the door, more for me than for him. He turned on the water and took my hand entangling our fingers, and then he was in the shower. I turned my body to face the outside wall of the shower and rested my forehead on it. What was I thinking? I was making him miserable. Why can't I just give myself to him? It would be so much easier. *I love him!* I didn't want to live without him, so why was I doing this to him?

His grip lessened, he was holding my hand still but it wasn't an intense grip, "Shit this is cold." The water shut off, "Towel please."

I let go of his hand and grabbed a towel. I unfolded it and held it up. I'm glad I did because he opened the curtain without covering himself at all. I turned my head as he walked into the towel, grabbing it and wrapping it around his waist.

He came very close to me, "If we are ever going to be together you will have to see me naked."

I didn't say a word. *What do you say to that?* I grabbed the other towel and dried him off.

He stared at me, "Okay, turn around and I'll get dressed." I turned away.

When he finished putting on his pants, his arms wrapped around my waist with his hand on my stomach, pulling me back into him. He kissed my neck and whispered softly, "Let's go back upstairs."

We started up the stairs and he grabbed the back of my pants and pulled me back.

I fell into him, "James!"

"Can't walk either?"

I started going up again and he bit my butt.

"James!" I turned around and sat down, "What are you doing?!

"I couldn't help myself."

"You can and will." I turned and ran up the stairs.

As we walked through the living room, Tony laughed, "I guess that's one way to handle it."

James laughed too, "It works."

"It's 3 o'clock guys."

We walked back into my room. He was still shirtless, and I stopped at the door to watch him roam around my room looking at everything. Not much walking room, but he managed.

"Are you going to spend our precious time looking at my room?"

He laughed and crawled on my bed, and then he laid down putting his hands behind his head, "This is cool. Are you going to stand there?"

"I can't believe you're here."

"Please come here."

I crawled slowly to him with my heart pounding out of my chest, "Are you better?"

"I am now."

I sat cross legged next to him tracing my hands over his chest and stomach, he closed his eyes, "Why the cold shower?"

He pushed himself up turning his body to face me. He unzipped my sweatshirt and pulled one sleeve off at a time. He started to explain, "When a guy is getting excited he can stay in control for a while." He reached for my waist and pulled my shirt over my head.

"James, you don't want to have to take another shower."

"I am really good now, it's okay."

"Are you sure?"

He explained further, "As the excitement increases to desire, he starts to lose control. Once he loses control, nothing else matters; not what the girl wants, not even what they want. The desire is so extreme that there is only one goal. That rush you felt before is the only way for a guy once he reaches that point. It's so much more than that, but it gets to the point of no stopping."

He took my hands in his and laid back pulling me to him, "He will say anything and do anything he can to get there, sometimes…"

He took a deep breath as I laid my body to his resting my chin on his chest to look at him. "Sometimes that's how it ends up hurting and the girl changes her mind and then it's too late." He closed his eyes and traced my back with his fingertips. "The cold shower stops it. It helps get rid of that desire, cools me off to think sensibly again."

"So, isn't *this* hard for you?"

"Not exactly; there's a difference."

"What do you mean?"

"I care about you. I don't want to ever lose control to that point with you."

"I have faith in you."

"I'm glad you do, but sometimes it's so hard. *You get to me.* And you look better and better every time I see you." He put his arms around me and rolled me over and started tracing my stomach with his fingers. He kissed me so softly and whispered, "You like horses?"

"Yes, I do."

"What is your favorite?"

"It's a tossup between the Black Arabian and a Mustang."

He chuckled a little. "Tell me why?"

"If you watch them they are cautious, but they lead. They are amazing. The muscles control their every movement. And they are free."

The grin on his face grew as I spoke. He came in for a deeper kiss. His hand was more aggressively touching me. It slowed again, "I have something I wanted to give you. It's really mine, but you may appreciate it more than I do." He looked over my head, "See, I was right. You take better care of my stuff than I do."

"What?"

He gestured to my headboard, "The feather."

I smiled at him. He was kissing me softly again as he reached into his pocket. It was something really small wrapped in a tissue. He unwrapped it and held it up. It was a two tone gold necklace, maybe from black hills gold. There was a word in the middle of it, 'Cayuse'. "This is my Indian name."

"How come you don't wear it?"

"It's the heritage that I am running away from, remember?" He stared putting it on me.

"Does it mean something?"

He was smiling, "Mustang."

"You're kidding, right?"

"No, I'm not."

"That's just weird."

"Or, is that a sign?"

I nuzzled into his shoulder and he put his hand on my face and traced it. He looked at the clock, and the disappointment in his face made me look too. It was already 4 p.m. He kissed me softly but passionately, and then he was scooting away from me.

"Not yet," I pleaded.

"No, not yet." He moved so he was over me but not touching. He leaned over and started kissing my neck. He scooted down more and was tracing my body with his breath, still without touching me. And then his mouth touched my stomach, very softly. He started to suck like there was whip cream, the taunting was overwhelming. I gripped the blankets at my sides to hold back the desire. He was more aggressive, making the desire in me grow even stronger. I couldn't stop feeling the wanting and the yearning, and the tingling was so intense. I was squirming beneath him, and I couldn't seem to stop. I was very excited, and wanted to feel the rush. My breathing was so intense I was moaning and my breathing was erratic. James came up to me swiftly laying his body to mine. I was still gripping the blankets, "Are you okay?"

"Um, yeah."

"Do you want me to do anymore?"

"No." He was kissing me so passionately.

I wanted so much more, but I stayed as still as I could because the trembling had started, "If I did, would you turn me down?"

"Probably."

"That would be hard for you?"

"Yes."

"I don't want to cause you agony."

He kissed me so softly and I wrapped my legs around his waist. I could feel him better this way. I didn't realize this was pushing his pants down a little.

He stopped and looked at me, "Sarah."

I pulled him closer, and the tingling even more.

"Sarah–we have to stop, right now." He pulled away from me.

"Just… a little… longer, I'm so…" I was losing control.

"I am sorry. I have to stop."

"I don't want you to."

"You do, you're just caught up in the moment."

"I want to feel the…"

"No more, I won't be able to…" He had moved and was sitting on the side of the bed.

I crawled over to him, "I'm sorry, I was feeling so good. I couldn't help myself."

"Sarah, it's too soon and if we keep this up it will happen soon."

"Okay, so hands off for a while?"

He turned and crawled at me so I was lying down again, "I don't just like you Sarah. You are so much more than that to me." He kissed me so softly. He slid my shirt back over my head, and kissed me when it was over my head. He hugged me so tight. He slid off the bed, and pulled on my hands to help me up. He hugged and kissed me again.

"You are so amazingly beautiful. But…"

"But what?" I sounded disappointed.

"But irresistible, and getting too hot to try and control myself around you."

"In a good way?"

"No, not good."

I kissed him on the cheek. He took my hand and led me out of the room. Tony was sleeping on the couch, quietly snoring. James sat down in a chair, and I sat at his feet. He picked on me, kissed my hands, and rubbed my back until mom walked in.

He tried to pull away and I grabbed his leg and held onto it so he couldn't move.

"What are you doing?" he whispered.

"She has seen me hang on you before, it's fine." I leaned my head on his leg.

Mom walked in, "So, you guys made it."

Tony woke up and looked at us sitting in the chair almost questioning us, but didn't say a word.

"Yeah, Tony here was taking a nap, but we were just going to wake him. It's getting late and we should get back."

"Oh, I see Sarah here fed you?"

"Yep."

"Did you get stuff ready for dad?"

"Yep, it's in the truck."

"Tony, all rested up now?"

"Yeah, I'm good. James did you nap?" Tony was grinning at James with an accusing smile.

"I closed my eyes a little, Tony."

Mom sat in the other chair, "Thanks, James and Tony. This was so nice of you two."

"Yeah, no problem, but we should get going."

As I realized the time, "Oh, shit I have to work at 5:30." I got up and ran to my room. I grabbed my purse, and my phone. I got back to the living room just as the guys were up and moving toward the door.

"I'll walk them out. Then I have to go to work. Love you mom!"

I jumped on James back once we were outside.

"Sarah."

"I do this all the time to you, so stop fussing unless you can't cuz you're weak."

"Very funny, you're so skinny I could pick you up with one arm."

"Yeah, whatever."

We got to the truck, and he set me down. I walked over to Tony and I hugged him and kissed his cheek, "Thank you," then I walked over to James. I wanted to hug him and kiss him, and I didn't want him to leave. He took my hand, "I think your mom is watching?"

"Yeah, probably." He took a pen and wrote a phone number on my hand, "I got a phone."

He put his arm around my neck like a big brother would and turned to the truck so he could get in, but he kissed my hand, "I love you so much; you have no idea." He got in the truck and looked at me.

The tears swelled in my eyes.

"Don't do that, or I won't be able to leave."

"I'll be okay. I have to go to work anyway. That will help."

"Bye."

Tony started to drive off. Suddenly I got a text, "1- 2- 3- breathe."

I looked up, laughed and waved.

22. The Protector

I was really confused on how to count down again. Was it a countdown until I went up north, or was it a countdown until I saw James again? If that was the case, I would have to start my countdown over again.

Week One – The phone calls were all the time now that James had a phone. I was even receiving texts all day long. It was great. It helped make it so I didn't miss him so much. The late night phone calls only happened on nights he worked. I was so much happier after seeing him. I was talking to a lot more people at school. I felt like I fit in better, and I wasn't being so judgmental of myself and how people saw me. Matt filled me in that people thought I was a snob, when actually I was so shy. I really didn't care what anybody thought. James was the only one that mattered. No cabin this weekend since dad just got supplies from James.

Week Two – I was really getting back into my schoolwork now. It was going well, and I was acing everything. I was working four days this week, and I planned to work both days this weekend. Mom was working too. Danelle had to be wondering what happened to me. Hopefully, Pat told her about mom working all the time. Mom promised we would go up soon. I was happy with that. I would have my new car, maybe we could drive it.

I really didn't know what I wanted yet. At work the salesman were having me try different cars. There was one used car that was two years old, that I was falling in love with. It was a Ford Mustang, gray metallic two-door. James would get a kick out of that.

Week Three – I wouldn't have the car until Friday after 4 p.m. I really wanted plans set up before I went up north, but James was working Friday night, and he said he would talk to Tony about Saturday. I was okay with that because I could spend time with Danelle. I was so happy to be leaving The Cities and go to my escape from reality. I was excited about all of it, getting my car, going up north, seeing Danelle, and my Cayuse (James).

The week went by really slow. I even wrote two essays for scholarships. I was trying to find a way to pay for college and be ready when it came. The time was just not going fast enough for me. Every day was a countdown, and the clock must have stopped at least 200 times this week.

On Friday I was bubbly and anxious, and I couldn't wait to get going. Mom and I went to get the car at 5 p.m. Mom was impressed. It was a used vehicle, but had low mileage. The best part was that it was a Mustang. We were headed on our way by 6 p.m., after dropping mom's car at the house. The only thing she didn't like was it sat too close to the ground.

We didn't go to the trailer. Instead we went right to Sherburn's. We found dad there, and he was looking really thin. Danelle was there too and she gave me a huge hug.

Laura grabbed my hands, "You are getting really skinny! You need to eat more."

Danelle was smiling at me, "You look good, ignore her."

"Do you want to see my new car?"

Danelle looked at her mom for approval. Her mom smiled and nodded, "Just a little ride."

We went for a small ride up by the trailer, around the circle and back to the resort. She was impressed. We went back in and played video games. They just got a new table game that we could both play at the same time. When we were bored, we went in the back to the living area.

Brian walked in with Pat, Zack, and Tommy, "Did you guys see the Mustang, and who was driving it?"

Danelle began telling him, "It's…"

I gave her a look like please don't tell him.

"You guys know. Whose is it?" Brian lay down between us and smiled looking back and forth between each of us.

Finally Danelle gave in and pointed at me.

"No way! You are taking me for a ride, right now. Can I drive?"

"NO, NO, and no. I am hanging with Danelle tonight."

Brian chided Danelle, "You know she's our age. She should be going to the party tonight with us."

Danelle looked at me, "If you want to go you can."

"Are you sure?"

"Yeah, Jess is supposed to be up soon and we can hang."

"We'll hang out more tomorrow?"

"I'll be here. I don't get to go anywhere."

I looked at Brian, "Okay, I guess I can take you to the party."

Brian was ecstatic, "Shotgun!" Pat looked disappointed.

We all got into my car and Brian directed me all the way to the party. I had to take orders from him until we came to a huge sand pit. There were about twenty cars in a circle around a fire and the keg. There were a lot more people than cars. Brian got out, and so did the other guys. I stayed in the car, "I'll be right out." I text James, *"I drove Brain and a couple of his friends to a party; I'm at the sand pit."*

As I got out, Brian brought me a beer. I leaned on the hood of my car. Some of the girls I had met at my birthday party came over and were talking to me. I felt a little better about being here. Mykala came over and was a little smug, "So…Brian's with *you* tonight?"

"Um-no. I just drove him here. Actually, I drove the four of them here together."

"So, you're *not* here with Brian?"

"Not together, together. Why?"

"Well, I think he's making it sound that way."

"Great." I wasn't too pleased with that, "I thought you two were still together?"

"No, he's kind of a jerk."

"I told him you might like him better if he wasn't such a jerk."

"You told him that?"

"Yes." I held my hand out to remember punching him.

"Thanks."

She leaned against my car next to me, "So, do you like anyone here?"

"No, I'm not really into this."

"Yeah, Brian told me you were into older guys."

"*What?*" I took a big gulp of my beer.

"Is it that one you danced with at your party?"

"Kind of, but it's not like that."

"He's hot; I'd be into him."

I took another big gulp of beer.

Pat came and leaned on the car close to where I was sitting. My phone buzzed.

I looked at it, and I knew who it was. >*"You're at a party?"*

I typed really quickly, *"Yep."*

Pat asked, "So, who was that?"

I smiled a little trying to make it look like a grimace, "My babysitter."

"It's the guy from your party?"

"Yeah."

"So, do you have to check in with him, or is he your boyfriend?"

"Dad asked him to watch over me, and he takes it seriously." I took another gulp of my beer. It was gone; I was done since I was driving. Brain walked over with another beer for me, "I can't. I'm driving."

"We'll stay longer. It's okay."

"You just want to drive my car. I won't give in. I just got it."

I took the beer, but had no intentions of drinking it.

My phone buzzed again. >*"Try not to have too much fun without me?"*

I text back, *"I feel stupid here, I really don't fit in, wish you were here."*

Brian was on one side of me talking to a bunch of people and Pat was on the other, sitting quietly.

"If you guys get too drunk, you're not riding in my car, I don't want anybody getting sick in it." I warned them.

Three more cars pulled in. They were all guys, and the girls at the party swarmed to them. I found this entertaining. Then a few of them noticed the car and walked our way, "Whose ride?"

Brian put his arm around my neck, "That would be hers."

The guys were saying things as they looked at it: "This is sweet.", "What year?", "How many miles?", "You have to let me drive it."

I was so wrapped up in them talking to me that I didn't notice right away that Kylie and Jason had shown up. When I did notice, Jason was leaning on his truck looking right at me; Kylie was over by a group of girls.

I pulled my phone out to text James, *"Jason and Kylie are here."* I tried to look like I didn't notice he was there. I avoided his stare, and I was really uncomfortable. I stood there for a while, and then Jason started walking towards me. I pulled my phone out to see if James had replied. Nothing yet. *Shit! James, where are you when I need you?*

Brian looked at me. He could tell I was nervous. He looked around, and saw Jason coming over. He turned to look at me. I was watching Kylie, who now saw that Jason was walking toward me.

Brian saw it too, "You're in deep shit, aren't you?"

"Maybe. Can we go?"

"Now?" Brian smiled at me, "I'll take care of it."

I looked at Pat, "We need to leave now."

Pat looked at Brian and then at me, "We'll take care of it."

Jason looked at the situation and addressed me, "So exchanging the older model to a new one?" I didn't say anything, "A Mustang, how ironic."

I mustered up enough guts to say something, "Jason, you need to go to Kylie; she's getting mad."

Brian and Pat were standing now. Jason eased up a little, "I just want to talk to you."

"And Kylie wants to kill me, I don't think so."

"Where's James?"

Brian looked at me, "I knew it."

"Shut up Brian, he's just trying to get to me."

Jason was probing more, "Where is your protector when you need him?"

A truck drove up and James got out of the passenger's side door. After he got out, the truck drove off. He slowly walked over as people said hi to him.

"Jason."

"James."

James looked at me, "Where is your car?"

I looked down at the car I was by.

"This is your new car, a Mustang? You are looking for attention."

Jason spoke up, "I just wanted to talk."

"I know, but Kylie's here. It's just wrong."

Jason turned to walk back to Kylie.

James called out, "Okay who are the guys that rode with Sarah?"

Pat, Zack, and Tommy spoke up. Brian looked at me, "I'll find my own ride home."

I felt really bad, "Are you sure?"

"Yep." Brian nodded.

"Sarah." I looked at James. He motioned, "Keys?" I tossed them to him. "Sorry guys, no more fun for Sarah. If you want a ride we're going now." The three guys piled in the back seat. I got in on the passenger side. James started in right away, "Damn it, Sarah, what were you thinking?"

"What?"

"A Mustang! Good way to draw attention to yourself."

"I wasn't trying too."

"And a party, what were you thinking?"

"Yeah, but I just drove." I looked back at the three guys, "Sorry guys."

"You should be sorry, Sarah. Drinking?"

"Yeah, a little."

"How am I going to explain this one?"

"You're not."

"Do you want to make a bet on it? You'll get grounded and you won't be able to go to parties."

We got to Sherburn's, and I got out to let the guys out. James said out loud to me so the other could hear, "If there is anybody you need to say good night to, do it fast."

I looked at him with a glare, as he cracked a smile. I closed the door half way, "Pat?" He turned to me. "Sorry I ruined your fun."

He walked back over and leaned on the car not looking at me and said really quietly, "You are crazy about him."

I was dumbfounded, and I didn't know what to say. *Why did he think that?* I looked at him puzzled.

Pat must have read my mind, "You let him drive your car, but you wouldn't let anyone else drive it."

"Yeah."

"He doesn't know?"

I shook my head no.

"You are headed for heart break."

I smiled at him.

"Night Sarah, good luck."

"I'm sorry, Pat."

23. Free Labor

"James, how mad are you at me?"

"I'm not mad at all."

"You seem mad."

"Well, I think there will be a few that will stay away now."

"Keep me untouchable," I smiled.

"Come here, please." He motioned for me to come closer.

I leaned to him, but tried not to distract him from driving.

"Okay, just kiss me, will ya?"

I wanted him to keep his eyes on the road, so I just kissed the side of his lips. He seemed pleased enough with that under the circumstances.

"So, why did you get a Mustang?"

"It seemed fitting. It makes me feel like I have you around me all the time." I wasn't sure where we were headed, "Where are we going?"

"I have to go back to work, so you'll have to hang at Tony's for awhile."

"Oh really?!" I was excited. I get to spend the whole time with him.

"I have to work."

"Oh yeah." The disappointment must have shown.

"Come on Sarah, what were you expecting? You knew I had to work."

"I know, I just… I want you to myself."

"This drives so nice."

"It's my Cayuse. Just like you!"

"Sarah, do you realize I leave in a little over a month?"

"No, I guess I didn't. Thanks, now I'm sad."

He took my hand, brought it to his lips and kissed it. "The only reason I'm telling you is I need for you to beg to be here every weekend. I need enough to get me through."

I leaned over the center console, "I will do my best."

We pulled into Tony's. James came around the car and took my hand. He led me through the kitchen, up the stairs and into his room where I sat down on the bed.

"You may get bored there's no TV."

"It's okay, I'll behave. Can I dig through you draws?" I smiled.

"You can do anything you want."

"Nothing to hide?"

"Nope, have fun with that." He gave me a quick kiss and ran down the stairs.

I looked through every draw and nothing. I really wasn't looking for anything, but it was something to do. Now I was bored. I wandered down the stairs and stood by the kitchen door, just listening to him work. Tony walked into the kitchen, "What are you doing?"

"Just listening."

"Sarah, you're as bad as him."

"Tony, can you give me something to do, please?"

"Like what?"

My heart raced, he was going to help me out, "Anything. Cooking, cleaning, or dishes? Please?"

He gave in, "I have an order to fill. Come here and I'll show you how to do it."

"Great!" I listened to everything he said. I watched carefully in case he let me do the next one.

All night Tony let me help make food orders. I also washed dishes and danced around the kitchen listening to the music. I caught James watching

me every once in a while. Tony had me bring out a tray of glasses. I walked
out and started putting them away.

James looked down at me, "What are you doing?"

"Free labor." I smiled.

"You don't have to do that."

"I know, but then I'm not bored."

He smiled and shook his head.

"Hey, that one down there looks like she has money, better tips."

"You are so bad little girl."

I stood up with the tray, "Cha-ching." I smiled and walked away.

It was only a few minutes later he came storming into the kitchen.
He grabbed my waist and pulled me into him, kissing my neck. I turned
and pushed him away, "Stop that! You're working. Go back out there." I
scolded him.

He groaned.

Tony laughed, "You're working. She's right."

James stormed back out. Tony was still laughing, "Thanks, that was
good. I told you; he's got it bad."

The music was playing, and I couldn't help but dance around the
kitchen. It was the end of the night, and the last tray was ready to go out.
I got to the door, and I heard him talking to two women, "It's bar close
ladies time to go."

"Why do you kick us out every day?"

"Because you *stay* until I have to kick you out."

"We're going to an after party, do you want to come?"

"Nope, I have to clean up here."

"Here, if you change your mind, we'll make it worth your while."
They placed something on the bar and turned and walked out.

"Goodnight ladies."

I could feel the jealousy, but he turned them down. They were both
really pretty. *Why would he choose me?* I wouldn't even blame him. I can't
think about it. I will get more upset. I walked out with the glasses and
started putting them away. I could feel the anger building, but I needed
to hold it in. I stood up with the tray, and he was behind me again. His
hand was on my stomach pulling me to him again, but instead of kissing
my neck he whispered, "You will dance with me."

He took my hand and led me to the dance floor, then hit a button on the music system and the music started. Nothing to fast but not really slow either, he moved with me and twirled me for three songs.

Tony was getting frustrated, "James! Clean up! Sarah you've earned it. Go ahead and dance all you want." I stayed on the dance floor. I was wrapped up in the music. I wasn't paying attention to the guys at all. I went to change the music and James was standing there watching me.

"What?"

"My sweet Sarah, it's time to go."

"Where?"

"I've got to get you home. Your mom and dad are going to be pissed." He took my hand while we walked to the car together, and he opened the passenger door for me.

"It's my car." I protested.

"Sarah, get in."

While we were driving James started with, "I have something for you."

"And what would that be?"

"Put your hand out." He put a $100 bill in my hand.

"I don't want your money."

"It was your idea."

"What do you mean?"

"That girl you said had money; you were right."

"But I can't take it. You earned it with all the flirting." I tried not to sound jealous.

"You're the one that told me to, and, well, it has her number on it. I don't want it, so it's yours."

"I still can't take your money."

"Put it away then and we'll have it for later."

"Fine, but I'm not spending it."

"Fine."

I was a lot quieter, "Does that happen often?"

"Sometimes, but I usually give those to Tony. You sound jealous?" He had a playful tone to his voice.

"No, not really, but the jealous kid in me kicked in when I heard it."

"You were listening?"

"Not on purpose."

"I told you before, you have ruined it for me. I only see one person I want to be with."

"Can we stop?"

"Why?"

"Because I haven't gotten to kiss you yet?"

"You are so late, we really shouldn't, and if we do you'll attack me."

"No, I won't. *Please?*"

"No begging, that's not fair."

I leaned over the center console and whispered in his ear, "*Pleeaasse?*"

"Definitely not."

I kissed and nudged his neck.

He pulled over, "Promise you'll behave."

"You are so angry; what's wrong?"

"I don't want you to do this just cuz you're worried what's out there."

"I just wanted to kiss you. I haven't really gotten to do that today, and I love to kiss you."

"So, it's not about those girls?"

"Nope."

He took my face in his hands, tracing my lips with his thumbs, and then the sweetest lips were kissing mine. This was the best kiss ever, making my breath completely gone. He was right, I did want to attack him, but I wanted to prove him wrong. I was determined to make this last as long as I could. His hands moved down as I entangled my fingers with his, and the kiss deepened. I could do this for hours. He pushed my hands back, and I wanted to let him advance. I hugged him and kissed him deeper. I couldn't breathe anymore. I broke the kiss, but I was so bummed. I wanted that to last all night. He started kissing me again. He wrapped his hands on my neck and tried to pull me closer. He broke away, "This car sucks."

I started to giggle, "It's perfect when you're trying to be good." I smiled at him and leaned over to kiss him softly.

"We have to go. We're going to have to make this good or I will never see you again. We're going to stick to the truth."

"What?"

"You were being naughty, and I stepped in to protect you."

"I wasn't being naughty."

"Let's see. Sixteen and a drinking party?"

"I really don't think they have a problem with the drinking."

"We'll see."

"What are you trying to do, get it so I can't leave the trailer at all? I won't get to see you either."

"Just trust me; I won't make it that bad."

"It wasn't that bad."

We walked in, and mom was in bed already while dad was sitting on the chair snoozing, "Sarah, where have you been?"

James stepped in, "Tucker she has been with me most of the night."

"I thought you were working?"

"I was, but I went to get Sarah at a party at 11 p.m."

"Why did you do that?" Dad seemed to be getting angrier as James explained.

"I heard she was drinking."

"How much were you drinking, Sarah?"

"I only had one. That isn't the real reason, I text him."

"Okay, now we're getting somewhere."

I smirked at James to say I told you so, "Kylie was there with Jason."

"Oh yeah, she doesn't like you much since you went on that date with Jason. It was probably a good idea to call for backup."

"I got nervous when I saw them. Brian and Pat didn't want to leave. They wanted to handle the situation, but I just wanted to leave."

"So, you're here and not hurt, everything went okay?"

"Yep, James showed up. The guys weren't too happy that we had to leave."

"I can imagine that. So how is it that it's so late?"

James took over, "Well that's my fault. I was at work when I left to get Sarah, so I had to go back to work. She helped Tony in the kitchen. I still had to cleanup, but we came here as soon as we were done."

"I loved helping Tony. I think I should help Tony all the time when I am up here."

"NO!" They both said at the same time. Dad looked at James, and James smiled back at him.

"Hey Tuck, can I crash on the couch? I don't have my car. We drove Sarah's here."

"Yeah, no problem. Sarah in the room."

"Dad, you know I hate that bed."

"But James needs to sleep."

I stormed off to the front bedroom. I didn't even change my clothes. I just crawled in bed and pulled a blanket over me. I knew this was safer, but it wasn't what I wanted. I tossed and turned, with every movement the bed squeaked.

I waited as long as I could stand it and went back to the living room. He was lying there with his eyes closed. I walked quietly up to the couch, and he put his hand out. I crawled into his arms. I nuzzled my face into his neck and closed my eyes.

He took my hand raised it to his lips and kissed it, "If you get in trouble; it's your own fault."

24. The Explanation

I woke up slightly, with my eyes still shut. I felt for James, but he wasn't' there. I opened my eyes a little and rolled over.

I heard my dad's voice, "Don't get up; you'll step on him."

I leaned over the edge of the couch. I put my hand on him and fell back to sleep.

When I finally really woke up he wasn't there, again. I sat up and looked around. Mom was in the kitchen, and it looked like she was cleaning up from breakfast, "Sorry we didn't wake you for breakfast, you were sleeping so peacefully."

I got up and stumbled to the kitchen. I grabbed a bowl and some cereal. I was sulking a little because I didn't know where James was. I sat down to eat my cereal and realized I didn't get the milk. I just sat there wondering if I could get up to get the milk.

Mom grabbed the milk for me and poured it, "So, you've gotten kind of attached to James?"

"Yep."

"How attached?"

"He's like a best friend, mom."

"That's all?"

"Yep."

She looked at me suspiciously. I love my mom. She has a free heart and is always happy. Compared to her I am very moody.

Dad and James walked in. I looked at him with my sleepy eyes and tried to have no expression. I didn't want to show my excitement, especially since mom was noticing, "So you got the good food?"

"Hey, I had to sleep on the floor."

Dad came in and grabbed another cup of coffee and offered one to James. James shook his head, "No, I'm good." He came to sit by me, "So how's the little partier?" He patted me on the head.

"I had one beer before you showed up. I was done anyway."

He bent forward to the table putting his elbows on his knees, his hands below the table, "Are you crabby today?" He reached under the table and traced his fingers on my thigh.

I stood up, put the bowl on the counter, and put him in a headlock, "If you keep picking on me, I'll have to take you down."

He stood up lifting me from the ground with the strength of his body. He looked at my mom and dad, "I think she's good now, and as for you little girl, you're not that strong."

I slid off his back, "You big bully." I wanted to hug him so much. I was in a bad mood, if only I could kiss him. Not a good time for that. I poured a glass of water to brush my teeth. He set a glass next to mine, so I poured him one too. I grabbed mine and started walking to the bathroom to brush my teeth. James followed right behind me.

Dad called out to James, "So, you're going to work with me for a couple of hours this morning?"

"Yep. No problem, teeth first?"

"Yeah, go ahead."

Mom had to give her input, "You two even have to brush your teeth together?"

We both laughed. He put toothpaste on his brush and offered to put some on my brush. I poured a little water over it and started brushing. I looked at him in the mirror. He turned towards me and brushed the hair from my face. I took a sip of water and spit and started brushing again. He turned to the sink and spit too and started brushing again. He peeked out the door and moved behind me, putting his hand on my stomach pulling me back to him. He closed his eyes and put his face to my hair, breathing in like he was taking in my scent. His grip was tighter. I couldn't brush any longer; I had to spit. I rinsed and smiled. He let go of me, rinsed his mouth and spit too. He grabbed a towel and dabbed my face with it. I took the towel and wiped my face. Then I moved to wipe his face, and he peeked out the door. I wiped his lips softly with a towel. He looked out the door again, and than he swept quickly to me, wrapping one hand around my waist to pull me closer, and the other finding my cheek. I was getting warmer by the second, and he kissed me. I wrapped my arms around his neck.

He whispered to my lips, "You're crabby?"

"I'm frustrated."

He smiled.

From the other room, "How long does it take to brush your teeth boy?"

"I'm coming!" Then he tauntingly bit my bottom lip, "Later."

I just nodded. I was so absorbed in hotness I couldn't answer. He was off. I shuttered to shake it off. I went to my room and got changed. I put on a clean pair of jeans, a t-shirt, and sweatshirt. I walked out and looked at mom, "So what's going on today?"

"We're meeting your dad and James at Sherburn's at noon. I thought we could leave a little early and have a visit with Laura and Danelle."

"So, I've got a couple of hours?"

"Yes, you do, why?"

"Homework."

I pulled out the homework. I tried to focus, but I found my mind wandering off thinking about James, his smile, his muscles, and his touch. I tried to make my brain stay focused, but my thoughts about James were driving me crazy. After about an hour of torturing myself, I decided to try and stay busy some other way.

"Hey mom, can I go riding for a little while around the circle?"

"Yes, I will be ready to go in about an hour and a half."

"Okay, I'll be back."

As I drove the trails, I had no desire to drive fast. I looked around the woods as I drove through them. I stopped, pulled out my phone and wondered. I really shouldn't bother him if he is working, but I couldn't help myself.

"What are you doing?"

I sat and waited for a couple of minutes and nothing. I knew that he probably didn't have time to talk to me if he was working. I put my phone back in my pocket and shifted the gears to go. A buzz came from my pocket. I stopped and shifted back out of gear.

>"I'm missing you."

My heart raced; that is what I needed to hear. I was torturing myself. *"I was thinking the same thing."*

>What are you doing?"

I smiled and text him back, *"Sitting in the woods on the four-wheeler thinking about you."*

>"My heart aches for you."

"I hate when I am up here and I can't be around you."

>"Have to go, your dad needs me."

"Wait, I just wanted...okay."

>"1- 2- 3- breathe."

That made me smile. He always knows how to make me feel better. I went back to the trailer, and mom was ready early. We went down to Sherburn's. Laura was more willing to sit at the bar with my mom. Danelle and I sat with them. This was getting to be a regular thing when we are up here. Danelle and I wandered off by ourselves.

"Did Brian get home safely last night?"

"Kind of, but it was late, and my mom and dad were pissed you left him there."

"It wasn't like that. He wanted to stay."

"How was the party?"

"I really didn't fit in."

"Pat told me James scolded you?"

"Only a little."

"You let him drive your car?"

"Yeah, that's how I got off so easy."

We walked down to the dock, she was telling me about all the people that come to stay at her place regularly.

-Jess, she was 13, but still liked to play with dolls.

-Tracy, she was 15, but not very cute, the boys didn't pay her any attention.

-Gabby, 14, whose name was fitting because she talked too much.

-Sherri, 16, not pretty at all.

-Tabatha, 17, so gorgeous she doesn't give the guys here any attention; she's too good for them.

After hearing about all these girls I had to ask, "Danelle, where do I fit in your list?"

"Honestly?"

"Yes, completely honest, I just need to know."

"Way better than average, but not stunning." She stopped and waited for me to say something.

"Is there more?"

"You definitely look older than you are, especially since you lost weight…"

"Okay, anymore?"

"You're nicer than your looks, so you are even better."

"Wow, are you done now?'

"Yeah, that's about it."

"You rated me way better than I thought. Are you sure you're not just being nice?"

"You said you wanted me to be honest."

"I know, but I really didn't think I was that great. Thank you."

"Are you thinking about James?"

"A little, but it was like nobody noticed me till dads workers were paying attention to me."

"Yeah, but your different."

"What do you mean different?"

"You're more outgoing than you were before. It's like a confidence thing."

"So, you're so pretty, do you like any of the guys up here?"

"I'm *not* pretty and they are all dumb."

"You *are* pretty and it's like that kindergarten thing when they pick on you cuz they like you."

"Don't be stupid. They're just immature jerks."

"That's one way to look at them."

Brian was walking down the dock with Tommy and Zack. They got to us and Brian looked at Danelle, "Can I talk to Sarah?"

"Nope, it's my turn."

Tommy picked Danelle up and put her over his shoulder and walked away with Zack. I knew it wasn't going to be long because they were only on the shore.

"So, I heard James yelled at you?"

"Yep."

"I heard he was going to tell on you?"

"Yep, he did, but he didn't get the reaction he wanted. I'm not grounded."

"So, are you going to tell me the story behind Jason?" I knew I would be safe talking about it if I could keep it simple. But I was trying to think the best way, with the least info.

"Come on, it got really bad last night after you left. Jason and Kylie were fighting so bad it took a lot of guys to stop her."

"Her?"

"Yeah, he just takes her shit."

"That is so wrong." I shook my head. I felt really bad. I felt guilty for liking James, but I wasn't going to change my mind.

"Well, are you going to tell me?"

"Okay, here it is. I went on a date with Jason. It was nothing. We just went fishing in the middle of the day." I was still doing okay. I wasn't getting any looks from Brian, so I continued, "I found out how old he was and he found out how old I was. After that he stopped coming around." I stopped to look at Brian, still no reaction, so I kept going, "I didn't know there was a Kylie at all, but that's probably when he went back to her. I found out about Kylie the night of my party."

"So, why does she hate you so bad?"

"From what James has told me, it took Jason a long time to go back to her after our little fishing trip, and then Jason told Kylie about me."

"So, how does James fit into this?"

"The night of my party, James was given the task of distracting me before the party. He took me to get something to eat when Jason and Kylie showed up and Jason introduced us."

"I bet that didn't go well."

"It didn't go well at all. In fact, it went extremely bad. She almost attacked me in the bar, but James stepped in and stopped anything from happening; hence the protector."

"That's what Jason was talking about?"

"Yeah, it's kind of annoying, but I also like it. I know you guys would have tried to protect me, but Jason keeps pushing to explain things to me. I really don't want to hear any of it, because it doesn't matter. He was too old for me anyway, and now Kylie wants to kill me."

"Wow, I guess you shouldn't go to parties."

"Probably not."

We sat together looking at the lake. It was so peaceful.

"So, how did James know to show up when he did?"

"That was my fault; I text James as soon as I saw them there."

"You guys talk on the phone?"

"Yeah, I get in trouble and he comes and bails me out. I guess I take advantage of it sometimes. I think he feels responsible for me, working for my dad and all." I looked at him to see how this was all going with him.

"You know he wouldn't do that if he didn't already like you?"

"What?"

"Stand up to protect you."

"What?"

He raised his eyebrow at me to suggest something.

"Oh, I didn't realize…" Realizing he was standing up for me last night to protect me because he really did like me. I scooted on the bench closer to him and nudged his shoulder with mine, as I looked back at the lake. He was hitting on me in a sweet way, "I really didn't think you felt this way."

"You do now, what do you think?"

"Brian, there are so many cute girls that are so hot for you, and I am just a silly little girl. Besides, you only are interested because you think it's a challenge. You can do so much better than me. I never had a chance with you and you know it."

"You're just into this knight and shining armor guy aren't you?"

I nudged him again, "No I'm not. You can do better than *me*."

He looked at me, "If you ever change your mind or need someone to talk to?"

"You will be the first to know."

217

"Okay, well thanks for telling me."

"Yeah, anytime you need to question me I am right here."

He got up and walked away. Tommy let go of Danelle.

I got a text: >"*What are you doing?*"

"*Sitting on the dock, are you here?*"

>"*Yeah.*"

"*I'll be right there.*"

>"*No, that's okay, who were you with?*"

"*Brian, he was asking about you and last night.*"

>"*What about it?*"

"*Can I explain later?*"

>"*Yeah.*"

"*Be right there.*"

>"*We're eating. Take your time.*"

Danelle sat down next to me, "What was that about?"

"I had to explain a few things and apologize to your brother about last night." I did feel bad.

"Oh, that's all?"

"Yep, sorry they were picking on you."

"That's okay. Who was text-ing you?"

"James. He was making sure I was okay."

"Why?"

"He saw me with your brother."

"Is he mad?"

"No, why?"

"No reason. I suppose you want to go up there?"

"Can we?"

"Yeah." She sounded a little disappointed, but we went anyway. We walked into the store area, and I didn't see dad or James sitting at the bar. We walked down and into the bar area, where they were sitting at a table. I went to the table and knelt on a chair across from James. I took one of his French fries. He scolded me, "Those aren't yours little girl."

I grinned at him, "I know."

"You don't want to do that again."

I grabbed another one, "You are such a bully."

I walked around the table and gave him a head lock. He pulled me forward to say something in my ear. I wasn't paying attention to anyone else. My world was focused on him.

"Behave little girl," and whispered, "People are watching."

Dad had to give his input, "You two sound like you're married."

"Thanks dad!"

James began to chuckle, as he went back to eating.

I backed off, took Danelle by the hand and dragged her to the back to watch Brian and his friend's play pool. We played music on the jukebox, and hung out with them. Brian was making little comments to me, quietly, when he was near, "It seems like more." He teased and gave me a serious look, "You're going to tell me more, later."

"So, where are all the groupies today?"

"I don't know."

"Maybe you should find one."

"Maybe I will." I was play fighting with Brian, but I was watching James every chance I got. He was watching me too. I don't think he minded Brian as much as I did. I didn't want to be back there; I only wanted to be with him. I think he knows that. Tommy was picking on Danelle too. He was seventeen and Danelle was only fifteen, but I think he has a crush on her. It was cute. Then I realized that is how James and I were at first.

"Hey Sarah," James called me over to him.

I got up and went to the table leaning on it, "What's up now?"

"Do you want to see if Danelle can go to the county fair? Your dad said you could take me."

"What?"

"It's your car, so *you* have to take *me*."

"Okay!" I ran back to Danelle, "Can you go to the county fair? James is going with so we'll have a protector?"

"Hey, we'll go too," Brian said from behind me.

I glared at him, "You're funny. I'm sure Danelle will give you a full report if you need one." I gave him a *yeah right* smile.

"I don't know if my mom will let me?"

"Please, go ask!"

We went to the bar to talk to Laura, she asked, "Until what time?"

I turned my stool to look at James for the answer. He replied, "Only 'til 5 or 6 o'clock because I have to work tonight."

I turned in my seat. I was heartbroken. The only time I would be with him was going to be supervised. *What was he up to?* I wanted to be with him alone. I wanted more kissing. Now Danelle will be with us the whole time.

25. The Chosen

We walked out to my car, and both James and I went to the driver's side, "Sarah, can I have the keys?"

"No, you said *I* was taking you."

"Sarah, give me the keys."

"No James, *I'm* driving."

"Sarah quit playing and give me the keys. Please?"

"Why do you always win?" I handed the keys over and went to get in the passenger side. Danelle was laughing at us.

We got to the fair and the three of us walked around, got some food, and went on a few rides. Every chance James got he would touch me; my arm, the small of my back, my fingertips, and my thigh. He was driving me crazy. I wanted to feel his kiss and his arms around me. I was so frustrated. I wanted to scream.

We ran into Will and Katherine. Will wrapped his arms around me seductively. I looked at James for help. Danelle's eyes brightened up in amazement that James didn't have a fit.

"Will, knock it off!" Katherine pulled him away from me.

I looked at her, "Thank you." Danelle was standing there taking this all in.

"James, you have to go see dad. Things are really bad since you've been staying with Tony. You might want to bring her with you." Will gestured toward me.

Danelle was very confused by this and looked at me, "James we're going to go get mini doughnuts, so you can deal with this. We'll be back."

James looked at me in desperation, but now was not the time to discuss anything.

Danelle waited until we got some distance from the others before asking, "What was all that about?"

"To be perfectly honest, I don't know." I hoped she believed me.

James didn't wait for us to return. He came and found us, "Ladies, I am sorry to say, but we need to go."

I looked at Danelle as if to say I was sorry, but she shrugged her shoulders and was fine with that, so we walked to my car. On the way James took my hand. *What was he thinking about that would allow him to not be careful about our affection for each other in front of all these people?* We got to the car and he opened the door, Danelle crawled in the back and I got in the front. He closed the door. When he got in to drive, he put his hand up waiting for mine. If he needed me I was there, so I put my hand in his. Once we hit the highway he was driving way too fast.

"James."

"What?!" he sounded almost angry, certainly annoyed.

"Um, you're going kinda fast and you're scaring us."

He looked in the rearview mirror to look at Danelle. You could tell he felt bad. He pulled over, "Sarah, you should drive. Danelle, I am so sorry."

We got out and switched spots. He didn't extend his hand to me this time. I didn't know how to take him this way. He just looked out the window.

We pulled into Sherburn's and I looked at Danelle and said, "If my mom and dad are in there, can you tell them I'm taking James to the reservation."

James blurted, "No! I need to go in and talk to your dad. He might be able to help me."

I was really confused by this, but we all got out and went inside. James said to me as we walked in, "I'll go talk to your dad, and you go with Danelle and play video games. I'll come get you when I'm ready to go."

Danelle looked at me as I shrugged my shoulders, "Okay."

My parents were sitting at the bar and James walked over to them. I went with Danelle to find Laura. She was in the kitchen cooking for a customer. She filled her mom in on everything we did, leaving out the part where James was holding my hand. I was thankful. Her mom was impressed that we were only gone for 3 hours. She suggested that James was responsible and she appreciated it. Danelle looked at me without saying why we had our outing shortened. We went back out to the video games. I could see James was sitting at a table with my dad. Dad didn't seem mad or anything. They were just talking. He wasn't telling him how he felt about me, that would end all our alone time. *What was he talking to him about?* I hated not knowing what was going on.

"Sarah!" It was dad calling me over to the table. I walked over to meet them. Dad put his arm around my waist, "Can you help James today? He needs to go to see his dad and then he will have to go to work."

"Yeah, anything he needs."

"Call me to give me updates please, so we know where you are and just in case you need more help." He looked at James.

James stood up. I moved to leave, he waited until I was in front of him before he followed me out of the bar. I stopped in front of the car because I didn't know what he was thinking, and I wasn't going to push any issues. He seemed to know what I was thinking, "You're driving." He insisted.

I got in and started the car, "Where to?"

"Your trailer."

I looked at him puzzled, and started to drive.

We pulled into the driveway at the trailer. We both sat there. I didn't know what to say or do. He got out so I did too. I was watching him to see what we were doing. He walked around the car and took me by the hand and led me into the trailer.

We didn't even make it in the door and he turned and started kissing me, "You have been driving me crazy all day."

I didn't say a word because he was taking my breath away. I didn't understand how he could be here with me when he needed to take care of something, and then I was lost. He was so aggressive that it made me really nervous. He was walking down the hall with me to the back room. He was almost carrying me with his kiss. *Has he lost control? What was he doing?* Oh, how the kissing was distracting me, and making me feel so good with his arms around me. He lifted one of my legs to his waist as we entered the bedroom. And he laid me down on the bed leaning over me. He pulled his shirt off, and started to kiss my neck. His hands traced down to my sides pulling my t-shirt and sweatshirt off at the same time. He was kissing my chest and my breathing was uncontrollable. He was pushing himself into me. I was getting hotter, and I could tell he wasn't thinking, "James?"

He didn't answer. He just kept touching me and kissing me.

"James!"

He kept kissing me to quiet me. He didn't want to hear it. I responded by kissing him back, but I said to into his lips, "You're scaring me."

He stopped and looked at me. The shame showed in his eyes, "I don't want to live without you."

"Good, I don't want to live without you either, but..."

He released me and sat on the edge of the bed. We were less than a foot apart, so he wasn't that far away from me. Our legs were still touching. I sat up, and grabbed my t-shirt out of my sweatshirt and put it on. I scooted forward to be as close to him as I could be, "What is this all about?"

"Will and Katherine are leaving."

"Okay, so what are you saying?"

"Will is not going to take over the family business." I just sat there. *What was he telling me?* I couldn't figure out what he was thinking, "I am still leaving."

I was cautious, watching him, trying to understand.

"I am not giving you up." I could see he was miserable.

"You really need to help me out here I don't understand."

"The good news for now, with Katherine leaving, no one will expect me to get married in the fall."

I laughed a little and he smiled at me.

"That's way better." I was relieved.

"What?"

"You were really scaring me."

He looked down disgusted with himself, "I'm so sorry, Sarah."

I stood a little and crawled to sit on his lap, my knees on the bed. I lifted his chin so he would look at me. I pulled my shirt off again and began kissing him. He pulled me closer to him by grabbing my waist. He moved to kiss my chest, his hands cupping my breast. He had never really done that before. I leaned my head back. He felt so amazing. He wrapped his arms around my body and pulled me so our bodies were touching.

He could have anything he wanted. I wanted to be with him more than ever. He moved back to my mouth, kissing me passionately. He hugged me closer, and whispered into my lips, "You're right, not today. Not this way." He grabbed my t-shirt and helped me put it back on. He kissed me again and lifted me up so I was standing. He grabbed my waist and kissed my stomach through my t-shirt. "Not today." He stood up, took my hand and led me back out.

We walked out to the car, and I looked at him to see who was driving. He assured me, "I'm okay now; I can drive."

I smiled and tossed him the keys. I got it the passenger side. We started to drive.

"James?"

"What, Sarah?"

"You could have had me."

"Now you tell me."

I smiled, "So, can you talk about what is going on or will you just get angry again?"

"Will has just screwed me over by leaving. Basically, I am back to being the chosen one until Sam grows up."

"But that's only two years. That really isn't that long to wait to be free."

"But I need to take care of things now, so when you are eighteen, I'm ready."

"Ready for what?"

He didn't say anything, but I could see he was off in his own world.

"So, what does that mean for now?"

"I am still leaving Sarah. I need to get this training done, but when I get back I will have to be chief for a while."

"So, your dad has to be released from his duty?"

"That's what I am going to talk to him about. I wasn't ready at eighteen, and I am still not ready, so I am hoping that he will continue for awhile."

"What if you leave and he doesn't hand it over to you, what happens?"

"Nothing, really, it's just the belief and heritage thing. It's all really stupid."

"No, it's not. You may not want it, but it's part of your life. You cannot turn your back on it."

"Please don't push me away, Sarah, because I don't want it."

"Why would I push you away? I am only sixteen. You have lots of time to deal with this before I grow up." I smiled at him to try and lighten the mood.

"My mom left so dad would take his heritage. She didn't give him a choice. Please, Sarah, don't do that to me. I don't want to live like him and I love you."

I leaned over, "You can still have me today."

"Don't do that to me. You'll drive me crazy."

When we got to the reservation it was quiet. He took me by the hand and led the way. We walked in and Tamara came running, "James! My favorite!"

He picked her up and gave her the biggest hug, "Sweetie, where's dad?"

"You're not going to fight with him too, are you?"

"Not if I can help it."

"He's outside in the shed. Will made him angry, so be nice."

He set her down and kissed her forehead, "Stay inside, okay sweetie?"

Will and Katherine were sitting on the couch and Will had his head in his hands. It was obvious that he was agonizing over the situation.

"James asked him, "So, where are you with this, and how is dad?"

I knew they needed to talk, so I thought I would distract Tamara. I took her hand. I pulled on James shirt and looked down at her, "Your room, do you have a head set?"

He looked at me relieved, "Yes, thank you."

We went into James room. I put some music on and put the head set on her. I wanted to listen to what went on with James.

"Will, what is going on? You both have a future here. You both could have anything you want. Why are you doing this?"

"It's just too much."

"Then do what I did, I asked dad for more time. And if I go out there, I will be doing the same thing, asking for more time."

"I just don't know if I want it. You have the talent James, not me, not at all. I can't lead without it."

"You can and you will."

"If you're not going to do it, it has to be Sam. He has more talent than you. Have you spent any time with him? He's amazing."

"But Sam is too young."

"So, they will have to wait for their great leader."

"Do you love Katherine?"

"Yes, of course I do."

"What about her talents? She was born to be with the leader. Katherine, you know you possess the same talents as me."

"But I don't want them. You and I are alike; we don't want this, and if I leave, my sister, Amelia, will be next. She's perfect for Sam."

"You two are so selfish."

"Like you can talk, you have Sarah. You're more like dad than all of us, falling for her. You know dad is miserable, and we never get to see her let alone talk to her. You should help direct Sam. You would benefit from it too."

"Sam?"

Sam hadn't said anything. I didn't realize he was there.

"James, Amelia is my chosen even if I don't lead."

"You two aren't together already?"

"Yes, we are."

"She's only thirteen!"

"Well, I'm just that good."

"That is sick."

"Some people have more talent than others, and James I can do a lot more than you ever have."

I heard James move, "Show me!" And I heard the door.

Tamara took off the earphones, "Sam is amazing; we should go and watch!"

"Did you hear what they were saying?"

"We're family. We hear everything."

I looked at her puzzled. She took my hand and led me to the kitchen. Everyone was outside. We looked out the window to see Sam was standing there, and a whole bunch of animals were coming to him, like they knew him and trusted him. He was holding a squirrel, and a bird landed on his shoulder.

I looked at Tamara, "They understand him and he helps them?"

I was really confused. They can communicate with animals, this is so weird.

James' dad, Carl, came out of the shed, "Showing off again?"

James walked up to his dad, "You didn't tell me. Sam is the one and you know it!"

Sam was very smug, "There's more, James, but it's not something I can show you. I feel things. I would be able to do great things for our people."

James looked at his dad, "Dad, why do you want me so bad when you know he is better?"

"James, you can do those things too, but you just ignore them."

"No, I put them out. I don't want them. Sam does, and look he's amazing. Dad, please give me more time. I need time to learn about protecting the land and conserving it. Tell them that's what I'm doing. When I am done Sam will be of age. Dad, please?"

"James, that's too much time. You are needed now."

"Dad, you loved mom, please don't make me live the way you do. I know how you feel. You never chose another bride. Please."

"Will you help if I need it?"

"Anything, I can't live without her, and I don't know how you ever did."

Carl hugged James, "I will talk to the elders, maybe show off your brother."

James kissed his father's cheek. Carl looked at James, "Is she here? She reminds me of your mother. May I see her?"

James smiled, "See, I knew you loved her."

"I will always love her."

I took Tamara's hand and led her to the living room where we sat on the couch. They all walked in. James' dad said, "Where is this Sarah?"

I stood up and he hugged me, "My boy really must have it bad for you."

I smiled.

"Oh, you do remind me of her."

I didn't know what to say because this was the most I have ever heard about James' mother. She must still be alive. *If she was where was she?* I wouldn't ask any questions; I'd wait for James to offer.

We sat and visited a while longer, but then James said he had to go to work. I was bummed. That meant my time with him was almost over.

26. A Touch Of The Dream

We got to Tony's about 6 p.m. We walked in to the bar and were greeted immediately by Tony, "Well, how did it go with your brother?"

James looked at him with surprise, "How did you know?"

"They came in here looking for you. Will looked messed up."

"Yeah, I was able to talk to my dad. He is going to talk to the elders to extend the time to try and work something else out."

"Well good, are you two hungry?"

I looked at James, "No, I'm good."

"Sarah, you need to eat."

"Why? I'm not hungry."

"You're getting too thin." He had a look of concern on his face.

"I ate all day. You saw me."

"Tony, get her a cheeseburger please."

"And you?"

"I'm good."

"Why do I have to eat and not you?" I protested.

"Because, I eat more than two bites of something."

"Funny guy. You'll share it with me."

"You're kidding."

"Nope! Watch, you will." I leaned forward to kiss him. He stood up into my kiss, put his arm around my waist, and pulled me to him. He was walking us to the dance floor, "Hey, Tony, one song, okay?"

"You're killing me. The music doesn't start until 8:30 p.m."

"One song," he said. He left me on the dance floor and went up to the stage fingering through the CD's. "Yep, here it is." He put in a romantic song, so we could slow dance. He looked at me and smiled as he spun me around and danced with me. As the song came to an end, Tony clapped, "A real Fred and Ginger you two."

"Who?" I didn't know what he was talking about.

"Forget it."

The cheeseburger was on the bar. I cut it in half and looked at James. I took only half out and broke off a bite size piece and put it in my mouth.

"Don't tell me you eat cheeseburgers the same way you eat peanut butter sandwiches?"

"No, I don't smash the burgers."

"Look," he picked up the other half, "Now watch me." He took a regular size bite.

I smiled, knowing I had won the argument.

James said, "Oh my goodness, Tony, I love your food. I am going to get fat living here."

I was almost done when he finished his half, "Are you happy I ate?"

"Are you happy you only had to eat half?"

"Actually, I think I won that one."

"Actually, you did, didn't you?"

I was beaming with satisfaction. "So, Tony, what am I doing tonight?" I insisted.

"What do you mean?" Tony looked puzzled.

"James is working, so please let me do something!"

"Well, I will even though there isn't much left to do. So, it's probably a good thing you don't have to start for a couple of hours."

"What, why?"

"James doesn't have to start tonight until 9 p.m."

I looked at James and got a big smile, as I entangled my fingers in his.

"What are we going to do with two hours together alone?"

"We're not alone, Tony's here."

"You have to get out of here. If the ladies knew, your tips would go down, so get out," Tony warned.

I pulled him towards the kitchen.

Tony scolded us, "Remember, none of that stuff under my roof."

James smiled at me, "Tony said no."

We walked into his room, and I turned to face him. After earlier today I wasn't going to push it anyway. I kept my fingers entangled with his, "So, if we're not going to get hot and bothered, what are we going to do?"

"I didn't say it wouldn't get hot. I'm that way whenever you're around."

I wrapped my arms around his neck and kissed him. *Oh, how I loved to hiss him!*

James tried to pull away, "Oh, this wouldn't be good."

"Oh, yes, it will!"

He held me at a distance, "No, it won't."

I eased up a little, "Fine. Do you want a back rub?"

"Really?"

"Yeah. Why not?" He lay down and complied with my wishes. "Shirt." So, he took off his shirt and lay down again. I crawled up and sat on his butt and started to massage his back. Every muscle was amazing. There were a few knots, so I worked on them first.

"Ouch!"

"Don't be a baby."

After rubbing the knots out, I went over his whole back. I don't know how long I was rubbing his back for, but he pushed up and sat on the edge of the bed.

"What's wrong?"

He put his head in his hands, "I'm going to fall asleep."

I scooted around him with my legs on each side of him. I wrapped my arms to hug him, "That's okay. I'll wake you up when you have to work." I kissed his back.

He rolled over to face me, pulling me to lay down with him. I propped myself up on my elbows looking at him. His eyes were closed. I traced my fingers over his chest. He was sleeping. I smiled. I hadn't really seen him sleep, at least not when I wasn't sleeping.

At about 8:30 p.m. I decided he should start waking up, so he would be awake for work. I whispered in his ear, "James?"

"Sarah," he moved closer to me.

"James you need to get up."

He nuzzled into my neck, "Will you be mine forever?"

"James, are you awake?"

He said nothing; was he dreaming or was he waiting for me to answer? "James?"

He started kissing my neck.

"James!"

"Huh."

"Are you waking up?"

"Yep."

"You only have a little bit to wake up."

"I'm awake."

His eyes still did not open, but his kiss was searching for my lips. I kissed him softly and said to his lips, "James, you need to get up. You need to work soon."

He opened his eyes and looked at me, "Why did you let me sleep?"

"You were tired."

"I needed to spend time with you."

"I was with you, and we were good. So, it's all good." He pulled my leg up to his waist rubbing my thigh. It was too close to work time to get hot, "James, work." I reminded him.

"I've got 15 minutes." He brought himself closer. He was taking my breath away. I was by his ear, and I couldn't help myself, so I started to kiss and nibble.

"You're on dangerous ground little girl."

I wrapped my legs tighter around him and kept nibbling. I could feel the heat and my breathing quickened.

He moved his body toward me. He took my hands and pinned me down leaning over me, "Damn it girl, 10 minutes before I have to be down stairs."

"It's safe."

"That's torture."

"I wanted too…" I just looked at him. I felt bad seeing the look of agony on his face. He kissed me so passionately that I could hardly breathe.

He got up and grabbed his shirt, "Gotta go!"

"I know. I'll be down in a minute."

"Hey, call your dad. He'll be mad if you don't."

I got my phone out to call dad. *How was I going to talk him into letting me stay?* "Hey dad, we just got back here, James is working."

"So how did it go with his dad?"

"I think really well. His dad, was going to try and bide more time with the elders, so James can go to school."

"That's good. So you're on your way?"

"Can't I stay and help Tony in the kitchen?"

"Sarah, you're sixteen and I don't like when you're out that late."

"Please, dad, I get to listen to the music, and dance all night and it's not like I'm at a party?"

"Sarah, you need to let James have grown up time."

"I know, but *please*?"

"This is not going to be a regular thing."

"I know. *Pleeaase*?"

"Okay, but get home right after you help clean up."

"Thanks, dad. I do have my phone, so you can call and check up on me."

"That's fine."

"Love ya, dad!"

"Bye, and behave."

"Oh, I will, Bye."

I hung up the phone and lay back on the bed and closed my eyes. When I opened them it was 12:30 a.m. *Shit I fell asleep!* I got up and stumbled down the stairs.

Tony looked at me, "I missed all your dancing. What happen to you?"

"I fell asleep. What do you want me to do?"

"You can wake up first."

I stretched and started to dance to the music. I made my way to the sink and started washing.

"You really don't have to do that."

"Thanks, Tony, but you fed me."

He smiled, "You need to be here when James works all the time. He's really working it today. Making lots of cash tonight."

I smiled, "That's good."

"Are you okay?"

"Yeah, still waking up."

Tony walked over to me and gave me half hug, "Wake up."

"I am slowly."

It was already closing time, and I took a tray of glasses out and stacked them away. James was wiping things down when he looked at me. "Sleepyhead, you're awake?"

"Yeah, no, not really."

"You could have slept longer."

"Nope, music."

He laughed.

I heard something from the other end of the bar, "So, she *is* here."

I turned to see who it was, and it was Jason. I was too tired to deal with this.

He was moving towards me, "Sarah, do you wonder what he does when he's done working? He has all these women hitting on him every night. Doesn't that make you wonder?"

I stopped just short of the kitchen. I thought about it and smiled, as I remembered the phone calls. I looked at James. He wasn't looking at me, but he was smiling.

Jason continued, "Sarah, don't be stupid."

James jumped over the bar and got in Jason's face, "Don't ever say she is stupid, and she does know exactly what I do every night after work."

"What, you call her?" I could see the surprised look on his face.

"It's none of your business."

I pleaded, "James, please don't, it really doesn't bother me, please lets…" I tried to pull him away from Jason. At this point I hadn't noticed Kylie was there until she began hitting Jason. This was getting out of control, "James, please stop her; that's just wrong."

Jason was letting her hit him and scream at him. James and Tony grabbed her and held her back. Jason took this opportunity pleading with me, "Sarah, I just wanted to be your first!"

"Jason, it's too late for that!"

"Are you telling me you already have? Please, don't tell me it was James?"

I could see Tony look at James. James shook his head no.

I reminded him, "Jason, none of that matters. You will not be my first or my anything, but thank you for bringing me James. If you stay with Kylie, she needs some help, it's wrong for her to hit you! And it's wrong for you to put up with it. Jason, I want you to be happy, but it will not be with me. You should try to give Kylie as much attention as you give me. She might not act this way if you did." I looked at Kylie, "I am so sorry. I didn't know about you at all. I would never have gotten between you two, but you need help. You can't beat him into loving you." I walked away and into the kitchen. The other room was really quiet. I went back to finishing the dishes.

I could hear Jason, "James, you shouldn't have, you know she's too young. That's the only reason I..."

Tony started in, "That's enough Jason. Have a good night. It's time for you to leave now."

I felt James behind me. He reached around me and turned off the water, "Why did you let Jason believe that we did it?"

"Because when it does happen, it will be you. Besides, if he thinks I did *it!* He might let me go."

He hugged me for a long time, "Are you okay?"

"I am doing fine, just still tired."

"You're really honest when you're tired."

"What?"

"You were brutally honest, and you were kinda...I can't find the word for it."

'Tired?"

"Do you want to go lay down? I can come get you when I'm done cleaning."

"No, I don't want to be away from you right now, okay?"

"Uh yeah, so what do you want to do?"

"I'll finish here, and James?"

"What?"

"I really am okay."

"I believe you are."

Tony walked over to us, "I still own the place and you're done. Get out of my kitchen; I made you some fries, go sit and eat."

"It's not good to eat this late."

"No complaining, go." Demanded Tony.

I went and sat at the bar with my fries. When Tony was done he came to sit by me. James kept looking at me and when James wasn't Tony was.

I was getting irritated, "You two are making me paranoid. Did I do something wrong?"

Tony looked at James, "May I?"

James nodded, but walked over to stand in front of me.

"It's like this; what you did was very mature. Not the reaction of a sixteen year old. You handled that better than people my age would. That makes you a little fascinating, and that's why I can't take my eyes off you. I am amazed."

"It's not that amazing because it was the truth."

"But people don't usually speak the truth; they hold back. They don't want to offend anyone. James tried to explain this characteristic you have, and I didn't understand it until I saw it. I'm sorry I made you uncomfortable." He smiled at me.

James pulled himself to lean over the bar and kissed me.

Tony got up and walked around the bar, "James, you take her home I got the rest."

"Are you sure?"

"Yes, go before I change my mind."

He didn't take time to walk around the bar, but he came over the top. He took me by the hand and brought me to the car. He opened the passenger side. I got in, but had no intention of staying there. When he got in I crawled to his lap, leaning as far as I could into him. I rested my head on his shoulder with my mouth to his neck and rested my hand on his chest. "Sarah, I don't think I can drive like this."

"Try."

He kissed my head and started to drive. I wanted kissing. I started with his collar bone and moved to his neck and under his chin. I felt the car stop. His hand came to my face to hold it while we kissed. Our mouths moved together, so soft, yet in perfect timing. He took my breath away. I was dreaming of an empty room, with lots of wood and he was holding me and kissing me. There was a fireplace with a beautiful fire.

I felt movement. I opened my eyes a little. He was driving. I nuzzled in, but wanted to feel his kiss again. I nudged his neck, kissing it, moving under his chin again, searching for his lips. I felt him stop the car, and I could feel his hand on my face kissing me. I nibbled on his bottom lip and the kiss became deeper. It was difficult to breathe and I was tired. The beautiful room had a table, a kitchen table, with candles lit, and the smell was like roses in spring. The floor had a rug of some sort, like fur. It was white and fluffy.

I opened my eyes. He was holding me in the car again, and I nuzzled closer. I smelled his neck, he smelled wonderful. I could hardly stand it. I wanted to attack him, but I was so tired. I kissed his neck, and then I moved to his ear. I felt him stop again. He put his hand to my face kissing me. He traced my lips with his. This was so dreamy. I was moving down a lane and it was a tunnel in the middle of the trees. The trees had lights everywhere. They were all white and lit up the lane. We were floating on air. He had his arm around me. I could feel the night air on my face, as I moaned with pleasure. This was so beautiful.

I woke again. We were in the car, and he was still holding me while he was driving. I didn't know where we were. I couldn't keep my eyes open long enough to tell. *What he's stopping again?* Nope, he was turning. I wanted more kissing. I moved to his chin which was the closest I could reach without him coming to me. The car stopped and his hand was on my face. He was more aggressive. I liked it. I moved more swiftly to his mouth. The tingling started. I wanted to feel his body, but I still couldn't move. I was absorbed in his kiss, and the movements were perfect. I reached to him more so the kiss could be deeper. He was moving in his seat and turned me more to him.

On the rug were two body pillows. I was lying on the floor. He was tracing his hands over my body. I was in pleasure, moaning a little with each breath. We were not wearing anything, but I really couldn't see anything. It was so perfect, I moaned again under my breath. He pulled me to him. I was sitting in his arms, and we fit perfectly together as one. I had to open my mouth to breathe. I took a deep breath and gasped when I released the air.

"Sarah?"

I moaned, "Yes?"

"Sarah, you have to wake up."

"Huh."

"Sarah, I think your dreaming, comeback to me here."

I opened my eyes. I was kissing him before he stopped the car. The dream was so good I wanted to feel the pleasure I had felt in my dream. He was slowing the car.

"Sarah, I am getting too…you're driving me crazy. You have to wake up and stop this."

I opened my eyes and I was looking right into his.

"I think you were dreaming, and you have to stay awake. You are making noises and breathing hard, and you're really turning me on. I want to tear your clothes off right now! Sarah, do you understand what you are doing? You have to stop, please."

I closed my eyes and put my head on his shoulder, "It was perfect."

I heard him, "Shit, I don't know if I can get you home."

I woke slightly as he was lifting me out of the car and was carrying me to the trailer. I heard dad at the door, "What's wrong with her?"

"Nothing, she's just sleeping."

He laid me on the couch. I reached for his hand, and he pulled it away from me, "Sarah, you're home, so you can sleep now."

He leaned over whispering, "No more dreaming, please."

I heard him talk to my dad, "I was thinking I could use Sarah's car to go home, is that okay?"

"Yeah, it's probably a good idea."

I reached for him because I didn't want him to go.

"Sarah, you're home. You need to stop and sleep because your dad's here with you."

He left and I rolled over and went to sleep.

I felt his mouth at my ear, "Hey?"

Was I dreaming again and if my dad was still in the room I didn't want to show him anything, "James?"

"Yes."

"Are you really here?"

"Yeah." He placed his hand on my stomach and pulled my body to his.

"After my dream, how do I know you're real?"

"I don't know."

"Where did you go?"

"Shower."

I laughed a sigh, "This is real; in my dream you didn't stop."

"I was afraid of that."

"Afraid of what? You were perfect. It felt amazing and we fit together."

"Well, it's not going to happen anytime soon. Your dad probably thinks we already did it, the way you were acting when I brought you home."

"Why, what did I do?"

"Let's put it this way; we won't be left alone for a long time, and you won't get to wait for me when I'm working."

"It was that obvious?"

"Sarah, I had to take a shower and I didn't even touch you."

I turned to him and wrapped my arms around him under his shirt, "I am so sorry."

"I'm glad you enjoyed it, but it's not going to happen for awhile."

"If they think that," I wrapped my leg around him, "We should jus…"

"No, we shouldn't. I want it to be special."

I moved my hands to unbutton his pants. He grabbed my hands and brought them to his mouth kissing them, "Not now, not today. Behave, or I will leave."

I curled into him and closed my eyes.

27. Supervised Time

I woke early about 7 a.m. James was still sleeping with me on the couch. I eased myself off the couch and got my homework and started to get some of it done. I decided to start with government. I really didn't enjoy the subject, but it was easy enough.

Dad came out at about 7:30 a.m., "Up already?"

I smiled, "I fell asleep after talking to you last night. I didn't even help Tony."

"See! You should have come home."

"No, cuz then I would have gone with the group of kids that hang with Brian. It would have been worse." I smiled

He shook his head with a disapproving look, "Getting your homework done?"

"Yep."

"That's smart."

"No, just have a lot to get done."

"What time did he get back?"

"I don't know, but I woke up when he got here and gave him the couch." I was done with government and pulled out some math.

"Do you want some French toast?"

"Yeah." I grabbed my book and moved to the table. I love math because it was so simple. We had another huge packet that we got on Thursday. I had gotten two pages done by the time dad had some French toast ready.

"Why are you making so much?"

"You should wake James."

"Really?"

"Yeah."

"How about mom?"

"Yeah, since I'm already cooking."

I went to the back first to wake mom. It was a little after 8 a.m. I came back out, and James was already sitting up. I walked by him and grabbed his hands, "Come on sleepyhead." I pulled him to the table. I went back to my corner where I was working on homework. I took one slice of toast, three pieces of bacon, and started working on homework. I cut the French toast in tiny pieces. James got himself and me a glass for milk and poured it. He sat down. I handed him a plate, the syrup, and butter without looking. After a little bit I saw him take another piece of French toast, and then I passed him the stuff again without looking. As we passed stuff between us mom and dad were laughing at us.

We both looked up, "What?"

"Do you two do that all the time?" mom asked.

I looked at James, "What are we doing?"

Dad replied, "You two act like you're already married, reading each other's minds or something. It's quite funny to watch."

I looked down at my math homework, "Well, since we already act married, when's the date, James?"

He looked down at his food, "Two years."

I added, "Now you two don't have to worry for two more years." I kept working on homework, and he kept eating. We didn't look up to see their expressions. I finished eating, folded up my math homework for today, picked up my plate, and put it in the sink. Then I poured boiling water in the sink. I reached over James's shoulder to grab his plate, "Hey!"

"Do you want more?"

"No."

I tapped him on the back of his head and held up his glass for him to finish. I washed the dishes, and James stood up and dried them. I grabbed two glasses and he poured water into them. We both grabbed our glasses and walked to the bathroom. Dad said in disgust, "Do you two do everything together?"

I stopped, then turned to look at James and then at dad, "No, not really."

We both started walking down the hall laughing. I grabbed the toothpaste, put some on mine and some on his. We began brushing our teeth looking at each other smiling. He quit brushing, put his hands at my waist, and peeked out the door.

He leaned into my ear, "You scared me with the marriage thing."

"Relax. I was trying to play along with them."

"You know this is probably our only time alone today."

I smiled and rolled my eyes. I turned and spit, then rinse, and started brushing again. He looked out the door, and turned me to face the mirror. He put his arm around me placing his hand on my stomach, and put his face near my ear.

Then we heard from the living room, "Brushing your teeth should not be a marathon!"

I smiled and leaned out the door looking down the hallway, "Dad, it's good not to get cavities!"

James was rinsing and spitting. He took a towel and wiped his mouth. I leaned over the sink. He traced his hand down my back. I spit and rinsed, and then I stood up. He was looking in the mirror at me.

He looked out the door, and turned me to face him, "I do want to marry you, but I will ask properly later."

I couldn't help myself. I threw my arms around his neck and started kissing him.

He took my hands and pulled them from around his neck and kind of pushed me away still kissing me, but saying to my lips, "Later, go, I'll be a minute."

I walked out and grabbed my book. I sat in the chair. Mom and dad must have felt better that I was in the living room again. Dad walked outside to do something, and mom followed. James came and sat on the floor in front of me, clicking through the channels. I picked on him until mom came back in. She grabbed her book and sat on the couch, supervising or observing us, I'm guessing.

James was getting antsy, "I'm board."

"Cards?"

"Yep."

"Kitchen or floor?"

"Floor."

I got up to get the cards, and he laid a blanket on the floor. Mom watched us, smiling.

"Kings or Rummy?"

"No thinking, Kings."

Mom got up and walked outside.

"Rummy might distract you."

"No. I don't want the distraction."

I smiled.

We played for awhile. At one point when mom was inside, I had my legs stretched out, and he laid his head on my leg, "Why do you always have to win?"

"I don't have too, I'm just that good."

"You are infuriating."

"I have to have one thing I am better than you at."

Mom really started to smile, I could see over her book. She set her book down. She was enjoying watching us spend time together, "I think we have to get going."

I looked at her, "Did you want me to take James to Tony's now then?"

James spoke up, "Or you can drop me at the reservation on your way out because my car is there."

I gave him a poutty look. No alone time was what I was thinking.

"That would be great; we'll do that." mom replied.

I got up and made my way to the room where my bags were. I was putting everything away.

James came in, "Can I get that for you?"

I whispered angrily, "That was our only chance. Why did you say that?"

He put his finger over my lips, "Gaining their thrust. Be good."

I looked at him pleading. He walked out with my bag and walked all the way outside and put it in the trunk.

We walked back in and mom said to us, "I didn't mean right now, I just meant soon."

James and I looked at each other. I turned and smiled at my mom, "How long do we have?"

"I don't know, a little bit."

I looked at James with energy and a great big grin came to my face.

"What are you thinking, Sarah?"

"Four-wheeler! Let's go for a ride on the trails." I looked at mom, "We'll stay on the trails out here on the point, please?"

"Go ask your father."

I took off running to the pole barn, and left James behind. He wasn't excited as I was. I wanted alone time and he was trying to show my mom and dad that we just hang out. Oh well, hopefully I will get my alone time.

"Dad, mom says we're leaving in a little while. Can I take the four-wheeler out?"

"You have a car now."

"I just want to ride the trails up here on the point."

"Is James going with you?"

"Yeah, I'm making him. He's not too excited about it, but I think he will."

"You should pack your stuff."

"It's all done and in the car."

"What did mom say?"

"To ask you."

"I suppose, for a little bit."

"Great!"

I jumped on the four-wheeler and drove down the hill to where my mom and James were.

Mom looked surprised, "He said yes?"

"Yep! James, are you coming?"

"Are you driving?"

"Yep."

"I don't know." He hesitated.

"Stop it, or I'll leave you behind. Come on!"

He got on and I drove away. When we got out of site, his hands were rubbing my thighs, his mouth was at my neck before I could get to the trail. Oh how I wanted to feel his touch all day, every day. We got to the trail, and I turned onto the path. I was going a lot slower now. His hand moved to my stomach, but under my shirt, so his hand was on my skin, pulling me back into his body. I could hardly keep my mind on the road. I wanted to close my eyes and enjoy his touch. I turned where it would take us farther from the trailer. I let off the gas and let it roll to a stop. His other arm wrapped around me, and his hand came to my face, so he could turn it enough to kiss me. My chest was heaving while I grabbed for him like a stretching cat. I wanted to enjoy the moment. He let his hand trace down my neck to my chest. He whispered, "Your heart is racing."

I breathed out, "It's all you."

"You know they are going to know we stopped."

"I don't care. I want to stay here with you."

"Sarah, we need to start moving. They're thinking of walking down the trails."

"I can't drive like this."

"Okay, switch."

He moved to the front. Than I laid my head on his back and rested my hands around his waist. We turned to get closer behind the trailer.

"This helped, they can hear us. They still think we're doing it."

"Can you just ignore what they're thinking or doing and come back to me."

"Sarah, I am sorry. You're right." He put one hand on my thigh and drove around. I squeezed him as tight as I could and kissed his back. We got to the furthest point again and he stopped, "Come up here."

I went to get in front, but he directed me to face him. He took my face in his hands and kissed me. It was soft and luring. We must have sat there for fifteen minutes kissing, and then he said with his mouth on mine, "We have to go back now. Your mom wants to go."

"How do you know that, or all the other stuff for that matter?"

"It's just a very strong feeling."

I grabbed at his shirt to pull him for more. He started kissing me again.

It was soft and tender, not eager, and he took my breath away, "Okay, let's go."

I turned around, but I was pouting. He drove with me sitting in front of him. We pulled in and he whispered, "They are so worried about you."

"Stop that, will you?"

"What?"

"Sometimes not knowing is easier."

"I agree with that although I didn't realize I did that as much as I do."

He pulled up to the pole barn and parked the four-wheeler. We got off and headed up to the trailer.

He encouraged, "Come on!"

I got on his back.

He walked into the trailer with me on his back, "Since I am lugging your kid around, is there anything I can take to the car for you?" He asked my mom.

She looked at us, "You two weren't gone for very long."

"I said a short ride, mom."

"I thought you'd be longer?"

"Nope, I got the riding out of my system."

"So, you're ready to go?"

"Not really, but if you are?"

"Okay then, everything is ready."

We walked out to the car. I gave James the keys to drive to the reservation and I would drive after that.

We pulled in and mom turned to James, "May I use your bathroom?"

"Yes, of course, let me make sure it's decent, with four men in the house." He ran in the house and came out holding Tamara. He sat her down, "Tamara, this is Paula; Paula, this is my little sister, Tamara. Sweetie will you show Paula where the bathroom is?"

Mom looked back at me, "Say your goodbyes. It will be a while before we come back. I'm working the next three weekends."

As my mom walked away with Tamara, I looked at James and tears welled up in my eyes.

"Don't do that, Sarah, you'll break my heart."

He wiped the tears from my cheeks, as they welled over. He kissed me softly, then brought my head to his chest and hugged me. We stayed that way until mom came out. He took my hand and led me to the driver's side. Mom was smiling as she got in.

He kissed my hand, and encouraged me to get in, "See you in a month."

As I drove off, I felt like my life was ending. I hated to be away from him, and he was leaving in a month. *Would I get to see him before he left?* My phone buzzed, >"1-, 2-, 3- breathe." I smiled, that helped.

My mind was still racing. Why did my mom allow me to have that last little moment with James if she thought we were doing it? I was so thankful I didn't want to bring up the subject. We drove for awhile, and then she started-asking questions.

"So, you like James more than a friend?"

"Yeah, he makes me laugh."

"Do we need to get you protection?"

"What?"

"Do you need birth control?" I knew my mom was very open-minded, but this was too much.

"No!"

"Are you sure? You two seem extremely close."

"Positive. It's not like that." *Yes*, is what I was thinking, but if I did have birth control it may happen sooner. When I am with him I want to be with him, but in the back of my mind I know I'm not ready for that. But I can't tell her that.

"Well, when you need it please tell me. You don't want to have an accident."

"Yeah, I will. But this is weird, mom."

"I see the way you look at him, and he looks at you that way too."

I didn't know what to say. I looked at him like I wanted to kiss him. I knew that. *But I loved to kiss him!*

Mom didn't wait for me to reply, "You know, it's supposed to be special with someone you love and want to spend the rest of your life with. I think you might not know that right now."

"Yeah, I know. Don't worry, that's not happening."

"Okay, just be careful."

Mom dropped the subject. I couldn't wait to talk to James about this conversation. I really want to tell him about the birth control, but probably not.

28. No More Hiding

*W*eek One – I pulled out the calendar to see how this would play out. June 6th was a Tuesday, so we would have the whole weekend together before he has to leave. I felt better, but still my heart ached. I found it hard to socialize because my thoughts were drifting to James. My heart hurt all the time. I hated the reality of my life here without him. My days were mundane. I went to school, did my homework, went to work, and waited to hear from my Cayuse.

Matt at school, noticed that I was off in another world, "Sarah, are you okay?"

"I'm fine."

"After school you are coming with me. I'm not taking no for an answer. We are going to DQ, so bring your math. If you don't show up I'm coming for you."

"Fine, I will be there."

I don't remember where the day went. I was so numb. After school I went to DQ to meet Matt. He bought me a hot fudge sundae. We talked about math, but he didn't push to find out why I was so gloomy. After we finished our math we went for a short walk. When we got back to the parking lot, I walked to my car.

"Holy shit, this is yours?"

I had forgotten about the car, my Cayuse. I suddenly felt better. I had my Cayuse with me all the time.

"Yeah, I just got it Friday."

"You are *so* taking me to the beach on Saturday!"

"What?"

"Yeah, you are."

"We'll see. I may have to work. I still have to pay for it."

We parted ways, and I felt better getting in my car. The rest of the week went better. I tried hard to be sociable and couldn't wait to get to my car each day. I worked all week, and I worked on Saturday, but only until 2 p.m. I told Matt I could take him to the beach after that.

James called me almost every day, and during Saturday morning's call I told him I was going to the beach.

"You're going with a guy?"

"Actually I am, but he's just a friend. He knows I have…," I didn't want to say it this way. "…a boyfriend."

"I think I'm more than that."

"Well, I can't tell him I found my life partner. A teenage boy wouldn't understand that."

"Life partner, so you really feel that way?"

"James, how can you ask that? I have been devastated this week without you."

"I'm sorry. I just hate being away from you."

"My heart hurts too."

"So, why is it that you mostly end up hanging with boys?"

"I guess I never really looked at it like that."

"No girlfriends?"

"No, they're mean. Guys are usually stupid, but they're not evil. I do have Danelle."

"You really don't have any girlfriends?"

"Not really."

"I'm sorry."

"For what?"

"You don't have anyone to talk to about us."

"Why do I need to?"

"Never mind, I love you."

He continued to talk to me until I fell asleep.

Saturday went just fine. Matt and I met up with a bunch of people and played volleyball in the sand. I got tired and decided to sit out for a bit. Matt came and sat by me.

"How are you doing?"

"Better, thanks."

"Well I was thinking..." he hesitated.

"Matt just spit it out."

He was a little reluctant, "Alissa is here and we've been kind of talking lately."

"Do you want to leave with her?"

"Not if you will be mad."

"Go, I'm fine. Don't be a jerk."

He ran off to her and took her hand. *Oh how I missed James.* I was feeling a little blue. I shouldn't have, but I pulled my phone out and text James.

"Thinking of you." I didn't wait long and there was a reply.

>"I thought you were at the beach?"

"I'm a good matchmaker."

>"What?"

"He's leaving with another girl."

>"That's weird."

"They were holding hands."

>"Did that bother you?"

"No, it just made me wish I could feel your hand in mine."

>"I miss you too."

"I love you."

>"Try to have fun, please."

"You know you're the best."

>"No, only when I'm with you. Call you later, try to have fun."

I knew the next few weeks were going to be a struggle, but I think I can make it until I have time with my Cayuse.

Week two – I just realized school was almost done, then wondered how I would preoccupy my time. I will have to worry about that later. My nights were still ending with James whenever he could. I got a letter for a scholarship I had won. It was only $500, but I got it for writing an essay. I need to do more of those. I worked every day this week at the dealership. I was hoping to pay off my car bill early. I didn't get a phone call, but I got a text.

>*"Lying here thinking of you."*

"Then call me."

>*"Can't."*

"Why not, can I call you?"

>*"Won't answer, I'm at dad's with Tamara. Elders in the kitchen."*

I took a picture of my lips and sent it. I waited a while there it was.

>*"What was that?"*

"A kiss."

>*"Cute, another?"*

I tried to take a picture of one eye. It was okay and I sent it.

>*"That's okay, more?"*

I took a picture of my fingertip.

>*"What was that?"*

"My fingertip."

>*"More?"*

"If you're looking for dirty pics I'm not doing it, too weird."

>*"LOL."*

I took a picture of my neck and sent it.

>*"I know that well."*

Next I took a picture of my stomach.

>*"Okay-I'm good unless you want me on your door step."*

I smiled, *"I do, more than you know."*

>*"Call U tomorrow."*

Thank goodness for cell phones. I felt closer to him when I could communicate with him.

Week Three – The pain of missing him was unbearable. I picked up two shifts at work to try and get my mind off of James. I have finals next week; I needed to study more. I met Matt a few times, and things were going well with him and Alissa. I was happy for him. It was nice to have someone to talk with.

He asked about James, "So, this guy you're seeing…"

"What?"

"Isn't it hard to have a relationship so far away?"

I held up my cell phone, "He calls a lot."

"What's his name?"

"His name is James. Matt, why all the questions?"

"You've been very moody, and if it's so hard, wouldn't it be better for you to have a boyfriend here?"

"No, he's more than just a boyfriend."

"How old is he?"

"It doesn't matter."

"He's a lot older, isn't he? Or you would tell me."

"No, he's just nineteen." *Shit! I just told him and I didn't want him to know that!*

"So, you guys make out?"

"Matt, I'm not answering you, and I'm leaving."

"Okay. But I'm having a pool party Friday after school. Please come, I promise no more questions."

"Maybe."

When James called I told him about the pool party, and he suggested I go. I made sure he was okay with it.

"I will be wearing a bathing suit. Are you sure you don't mind?"

"Sarah, I love and trust you, but do me a favor and hang with the girls."

"No problem."

Friday came and Matt couldn't wait for an answer. I let him know I could go to his party during the day, but I needed to be at work by 6 p.m. So, I could only go for a little while.

When I got there the girly girls were on one side of the pool sunning them selves. The sporty girls were in the pool with the jocks for water volleyball. The rest of the guys were on the other side of the pool checking out the girls sunning themselves. I really didn't want to be stared at, so I got in the pool right away. I was on the opposite team of Matt, so he came to the net to greet me.

"Thanks for coming." Matt was a gracious host.

I smiled, "Is Alissa here?"

"Why?"

"How's it going with you two, okay?"

"Good. You look hot."

"Matt!" I was stern in my disapproval, but secretly flattered.

After playing volleyball for a while, I got out and sat in a chair and toweled off a little. Matt came over, "Need anything?"

"Yeah, a bathroom."

He led me to the house, up two sets of stairs and into his bedroom. I stopped at the door.

"What?" Matt looked at me.

"*Your room?*" I questioned.

He smiled and pointed, "Right there."

There was a bathroom off of his room. I was relieved, but walked cautiously and locked the door behind me.

When I came out, he was leaning beside the door, "I have something to show you."

He held up a piece of paper with an 'A' on it, "All our studying paid off."

"That's great!"

He hugged me, almost lifting me off the floor, and set me down slowly as he whispered in my ear, "Do you miss him?"

I closed my eyes with my heart pounding. I could feel his mouth close to mine, "Do you miss his kiss?" *Oh how I miss his kiss, why am I still standing here?* He put his hand on my waist and moved closer, "Do you miss the feel of him next to you?" My heart was racing, and I wanted this to be James. *This feels so good, but so wrong.* He moved to my lips and said, "I can see that you do. I can help you with that."

Why am I still standing here? I opened my eyes, "Matt stop!" I tried to push him away. He held me tighter to him, "Sarah, I have never been with anyone, you could help me too."

"Matt, I'm still a virgin!" I shoved him and started to walk away. He grabbed my arm.

I turned to look at him, "No Matt, you were supposed to be my friend." I pulled away, got my things, and left.

I tried to hold myself together. I felt awful and so dirty. I took a shower and went to work. I faked a smile, and answered the phones politely.

I was done at 9 p.m. and went home. Mom was ready for bed. She was cheerful and asked, "How was the pool party?"

"It sucked, and Matt is a jerk!"

"Did something happen?"

"I don't want to think about *it* or *him*." I kissed mom on the cheek, "Goodnight mom. I love you."

"Sarah, it's Friday night, you should go out with your friends."

"I'm too tired, besides I have finals next week."

I lay down to go to sleep. I closed my eyes and put the phone to my lips. No matter how tired I was, I couldn't miss his phone call. I needed him so badly. I drifted off to sleep.

The phone rang, and I struggled to get it. "Hello?" I sniffled and my voice cracked; I had been crying in my dreams.

"My sweet Sarah."

"Hello James." I sniffled again.

"Sarah, are you okay?"

"I just miss...you!"

"You're crying?"

"My heart is aching..."

"I'm on my way."

"You can't James. Just help me get through this."

"How?"

"Talk to me, your voice helps."

"What do you want me to say?"

"Tell me a story."

"Like Goldilocks and the Three Bears type?"

"I don't care, anything."

"Did something happen?"

"James, please..." my sobs intensified.

"Okay, okay, on the spot...'There was once a young maiden that was so beautiful that everyone that laid eyes on her fell in love with her.'"

"James not that, please."

"Okay, remember the other day when we were text-ing, when I was with Tamara?"

"Yes."

"Dad was arguing my point; if I was schooled it would help everyone."

"Yeah."

"It was getting really irate and they were yelling. I didn't realize the pressure he has been under from them. He tried to explain; if they kept pushing there wouldn't be a chief at all because I would leave , Will would leave and Sam wasn't of age yet."

"Okay."

"Well, Tamara was getting upset. I tried to calm her, but she wasn't settling. She stood up and said to me, 'I can make them stop!' I didn't believe her, and I was trying to distract her. She got mad at me and told me to watch. She stood up and waved her hands in a circle and sat back down. I thought she had lost it, but everything in the kitchen went quiet. Then they were all agreeing with my dad; they told him he knew best and they all left."

I sniffled a little, "She has talents?"

"I guess so, but I think dad knew about them, because when he came and sat with us he told her she shouldn't have done that. It was really weird." He waited a little longer, "Sarah?"

"Yeah?"

"How are you doing?"

"Better."

"Can you tell me what has gotten you so upset?"

"I just miss you terribly."

"Is that all?"

"I can't talk about anything else, or I'll cry. Please, just talk to me, I feel better hearing your voice."

"One more week Sarah, that's all, one more week." He continued to talk to me. I don't remember anything after one more week. I fell asleep to his voice.

Week Four – Only five more days until I could touch him and kiss him. I was dreading math class. Matt usually sat in front of me, so I would have to look at him all during class. I tried to not think about it until I walked in the room. He wasn't there yet. Maybe he got sick for doing that to me.

That would serve him right. I got my book and packet out. There he was. I got off easy; he didn't turn and talk to me. Good! I didn't want to hear what he had to say anyway. A note dropped on my desk. I unfolded it, and the word was written huge. "SORRY."

I drew a circle around it and a line through it and tossed it over his shoulder. We made it through the lecture, but we had time to work on our study guides for the final. He turned sideways in his chair.

"Sarah?" He looked at me, "I am really sorry."

"Forgiven, but no friendship, I can't trust you anymore."

"How about not forgiving me, and keep the friendship?"

I squinted as I looked at him evilly, "You assumed and you took advantage."

"You can torture me all you want, I deserve it. At least think about it, please?"

"You'll have to keep your distance."

"DQ?"

"No!"

"Sarah, finals?"

"So, you're using me besides?"

"Yes, I guess."

"I'll meet you Wednesday, but only to review the packet, so have it done." I didn't want him to know I needed his help probably more than he needed mine.

"I'll take it."

Monday and Tuesday went by smoothly. On Wednesday, I met Matt at DQ, and we kept it professional. Matt didn't complain. I talked to James early Thursday morning. I should have been studying for finals, but he made my day bearable. I tried to get him to make plans, so I could see him, but he wouldn't. I think he was up to something.

"Do you realize I will see you in a little over a day?" *I couldn't wait to see him!*

Friday – I was impatient, we left at 3 p.m. and we were there by 5:30 p.m. We went straight to the trailer. I stayed in the car and text, "Where are you?" I was going to open my door, but he was already opening it for me.

My heart leaped, and I went straight to hugging him.

"I guess hiding isn't necessary anymore."

"I can't help myself."

He grabbed my stuff with one arm and held my hand with the other. We walked in, "Where would you like this?"

"Front bedroom, please."

He led me to the bedroom, and he set my stuff on the bed. He put his hands on my face and kissed me. It was soft and short.

Dad called from the living room, "It doesn't take that long!"

James smiled and took me by the hand. We walked out. I clung to his arm, and we were both grinning a mile wide. We sat down on the couch and looked at mom and dad. I think we were both waiting for a lecture.

Dad spoke up, "So, what are the plans for the evening?"

James answered, "We have none. We can hang with you two all night."

I was displeased, but I would take any time with him that I could. I just smiled.

"Okay, if you two are going to be..." he grimaced "...dating, there are rules!"

We both sat there listening.

"Number one! No hanging out in bedrooms."

"Dad, it's not..."

He interrupted me, "Yet, and number two! Alone time is limited, period!"

James spoke up, "That's fair."

Dad looked at James a little upset with him, "You're nineteen!"

"Yes."

"She is only sixteen!"

"I know that, but I can't stay away."

"There has to be respect and self-control."

"I got it handled."

"Do you really?"

"I think so."

"So, can you two can handle being good, if we allow you two to, *date?*"

"Anything you want, it's worth it." James eagerly responded.

"So, let me ask you again, what are your plans for tonight?"

"I would like to take her to dinner."

"Where?" dad said sternly.

"Timer Lodge."

"How long?"

"Maybe two hours."

Dad looked pleased, "Then what?"

"We'll meet you where ever you want us to."

"That's fine."

"Sarah, are you ready to go?" he asked so politely.

"Yes."

He stood up and pulled me up, "Let's go. Oh, where do you want us to meet you?"

"Meet us here, by 8 p.m."

"Okay."

We got in my car, but he was driving.

"That wasn't that bad." I said.

"Nope," he replied.

I was hopeful, "Can we stop, please, I need to feel your lips."

"Be patient, I have a surprise."

29. The Dinner Date

W e got to the restaurant and waited for them to seat us. Will and Katherine walked in, and he took my hand.

"Sarah, lets go, Will and Katherine are taking our place. They will never know because no one pays any attention."

He led me up the back stairs to a room and opened it. I was nervous but wanted to feel his touch. He held the door for me to walk in first. I turned to face him. He closed the door and came to me swiftly, kissing me intensely. He lifted me as I wrapped my legs around his waist. His hands were everywhere. He walked over to the bed, knelt on it, and laid me down. It was so crazy. I was really responsive, but this was so extreme. His pace slowed somewhat, and the kissing was intoxicating.

He pushed his body to mine, "James?"

He was kissing me harder, so I couldn't speak. He stopped and whispered to my lips, tracing them with his, "I hate being away from you. The desire is far more than I can handle."

"I'm glad you did this, but…"

"I'm scaring you?" He placed his hand softly on my face with admiration. Then suddenly, "Shower." He got up and went into the bathroom.

I edged myself to the end of the bed. I was the cause of his misery, and I hated doing that to him. Steam was coming from the bathroom. Steam? That means hot! What was he doing? The water shut off. I was nervous again. He came out with his jeans on but no shirt. He leaned on the doorframe looking at me, "This is breaking the rules."

"Yes, it is." I was scared now. What was he planning? Oh shit, I'm not ready. How can I want two things at the same time? He walked slowly to me and got on his knees in front of me, moving my legs so they were on each side of him. He put his head on my lap wrapping his arms around my waist.

"When you were upset the other day, what happened?"

I was tracing my fingers through his hair, "My heart hurt for you. I was missing you."

"That's all?"

I didn't have the heart to tell him what really happened. I didn't want to hurt him with my weakness. I didn't want him to worry. So I said, "Yes."

"You scared me."

"Of what?"

"I don't know, but I could feel your pain and it was more than just missing me."

He knew and he is testing me so I had to tell him.

"James, it was all about you."

"There's more?"

"Matt hit on me, but used you."

"What do you mean?"

"He asked me if I missed you, if I missed your kiss, your touch. I felt weak, but I walked away. I will not have guy friends anymore because they can't be trusted." The tears ran down my cheek, "James, I love *you, and only you.*"

He looked at me and wiped my tears. He pulled out a small box, "This is a promise that we will be committed forever. Will you please wear it?"

I kissed him without looking at it, "Yes," kiss, "Yes, my sweet Cayuse."

He took the box, "Scoot up."

I scooted to the pillows and lay down. He lay beside me leaning over me a little. He opened the box, and pulled out the ring. He took my hand entangling it with his, brought it to his mouth and kissed it. He slid the ring on my 'wedding' finger. It looked silver with a small diamond in the middle. Then he said, "The real one is much bigger."

I looked at it and it was very delicate, classy. I loved it. I looked at him a little puzzled.

He spoke without me asking the question in my head, "This is a promise ring. Your engagement ring is much larger."

"What?"

He looked surprised at my question, "The engagement ring, that one is bigger."

"You have one picked out?"

"Yeah, I have it almost paid for."

"What?"

"It's almost paid for, but I didn't think your mom and dad would appreciate their sixteen year old daughter getting an engagement ring."

"No, you're right. Are you *taking* me tonight?"

"No, I just over reacted. I am sorry about that. I can't control myself when I am not around you all the time. The intense feeling I have for you, after being apart, drives me crazy."

"I want to be yours forever. I want to be with you."

"You're not ready; I already saw that."

"We could try."

"Sarah, I can't. I tried to take care of it, but I don't think I could go there and not stop, even though I took care of it. My feelings are so intense right now, it wouldn't take much. Besides, this isn't the right place."

"What do you mean?"

"I have seen the place and this is not it."

"You have seen the place?"

"Yes I have. It's a room that is mostly made of wood like a cabin. There is a fireplace on one end of the living room, and no furniture."

I continued with his vision, "There are candles everywhere with a fluffy white rug in front of the fireplace, and there is a table off to the side." James looked at me confused, so I filled him in. "Remember the night in the car when I kept falling asleep? That is what I was dreaming of."

He traced my face with his hand, just looking at me.

I asked, "Would it be bad for you if we kissed?"

He leaned over me and traced his lips on mine and the kissing started. It was so soft and tender. I touched his chest, he flinched.

I whispered to his lips, "Too hard?"

He said softly to my lips, "No."

We kissed for so long, and I wanted him badly, "Can I…"

I pulled off my shirt, so I could feel his body next to mine. His hand went to my waist and he pulled me to him. I stopped kissing him just long enough to take a heavy breath. He traced my back with his fingertips. His kiss was deeper. I wrapped my arms around him. He pulled me so I was more on top of him. I kissed his chest, and he pulled my leg up to his waist and was squeezing it. He rolled over so he was on top again. His body hovered over mine, keeping his weight off of me. I tried to pull him closer. I could feel him.

I whispered, "Is this getting too hard yet?"

He nodded but didn't stop, neither did I. I was asking for it, but he knew this was not the place and so did I. He traced his lips down my neck to my chest. My heart was racing; I so wanted more. He kissed me there, and looked up at me for approval. I closed my eyes with pleasure. He cupped my breasts with his hands. I still had a bra on and he kissed over the top of it. My hand moved to the blanket, and I grabbed a fistful to endure my desire. He traced down my arm with his hand until he found mine. Our fingers entangled and he pushed one hand over my head, then the other. He leaned in to kiss me. It was deeper and much more intense.

I wanted him so bad, but this was not the place. He pushed into me, and I felt the tingling. Oh shit, I didn't want to stop anymore.

I want him it didn't matter where. He pushed into me again. I couldn't breathe. I wrapped my legs around him to pull him closer.

"Sarah, slow down."

I didn't care; I wanted to feel him so badly. He pushed to me again.

I was begging for it now, "Please?"

His kiss was not enough anymore, I had to have more. I pulled my hands free. I moved to unbutton his pants.

"Sarah, you can't do that."

Oh, my god, I wanted to feel him inside me now. I felt his pants move down with my legs. I tried to unbutton my pants.

"Sarah, not here, you know that."

I put my arms around him to pull him closer. He pushed to me again. "Sarah, I can't do this."

"*Please*. I am sure I want too. *Please?*"

His kiss was so deep and he lowered himself to me. My body was feeling his. I could hardly breathe, gasping for air. I went for the ears. I knew he couldn't refuse me anything if I did that.

He stopped completely, pulled away from me and went in the bathroom. I heard the water start. He left me there, and I was in total misery. I didn't want him to stop. I was still gasping for air. I walked to the bathroom and undressed. I opened the shower door and moved in behind him. I traced his back with my lips.

"Girl, you don't know when to stop."

I wrapped my arms around him with my body next to his, "I didn't want you to stop. Oh shit this is cold."

He turned around, so that every part of our bodies were touching, shielding me from the cold water. His arms were wrapped around me with his head next to mine, just holding me, "Now, you see why it works?"

I began to shiver. My wanting him had subsided. I no longer had the desire to feel him inside me anymore. I was too cold. Now, I realized I was naked next to him.

He looked at my face, "What were you thinking?"

"I wasn't, I just wanted to be with you."

"Your mom and dad were right to not want us alone together. It's just… we're getting too close, and you were not ready when I brought you up here. I knew that."

"But I *was* ready a few minutes ago."

"No, you were just caught up in the moment."

"I love you."

He grabbed a towel and wrapped it around me. He opened the shower door, and I stepped out. He grabbed a towel and wiped himself off. He put on his boxers then his jeans, "You are shivering so badly."

He walked me over to the bed and pulled back the covers, "I want you to lie down."

I crawled into the bed. He put the covers over me and sat down on the bed next to me, rubbing everywhere to get the circulation moving.

"How come you're not shivering? You never do."

"I'm getting used to it. Now it kind of feels good."

My eyes were tearing up, "I am so sorry."

"Sarah, it's not your fault." He leaned over and kissed my lips softly. "No more alone time, I can't control myself, especially after today."

We heard a knock, "James, it's been nearly two hours and we can't prolong the dinner anymore. We've even had dessert."

"Will, we'll be right down."

He looked at me, "Ready or not, you have to get dressed."

He went and got my clothes from the bathroom and set them on the bed. He turned away and grabbed his shirt and put it on.

I tried to get dressed fast, but I wasn't fast enough. He was watching.

"James, you're making me nervous."

"After what you did *this* is making you nervous? You always seem to amaze me." He came to me and took my hand, "Hope your hair dries fast."

"Shit, how bad is it?"

I went in the bathroom and fluffed it, "Shit they are going to know."

"You look fine; no one will notice." He took my hand and pulled me out the door and down the stairs. We walked over to the table and James put $100 on the table and asked Will, "Is that enough to cover it?"

"More than enough."

"Let's go."

We all walked out together, and as we got to my car, Will said, "Your hair looks really good like that."

I looked at James horrified, he assured me, "He's giving you shit. It looks fine."

We got back to the trailer with ten minutes to spare. He walked around the car and opened my door and took me by the hand, kissing it as we walked in the trailer. I was a little nervous, but James assured me, "This will be fine."

I smiled at him.

Mom and dad looked at us.

Dad was quite serious, "Back with time to spare."

James spoke up, "Yep, just following the rules. So, what are we doing tonight?" He had a big grin on his face. I nudged him.

Dad looked at us, "So, how was dinner?"

"It was the best I've had in a very long time," James said smiling. He was going to get us in trouble.

"So, what did you have?"

"Steak. We even had dessert." I began sinking in my seat. He was taking this too far.

"Oh really, what did you have for dessert?"

James smiled, "Cheesecake."

"Yeah, Sarah loves cheesecake."

"I found that out." He looked over and smiled at me.

How did he know that? He was full of surprises. *Oh shit the ring!* I didn't think how I was going to explain this. I tucked my hand under my leg. He looked at me and shook his head no. I looked back at him pleading.

"I hope you don't mind, but I got Sarah a little gift."

We were in deep shit now; what was he doing? I looked at him begging him to handle this with care.

Dad and mom looked at me, silently asking what he gave me.

James encouraged me, "Sarah, show them."

I pulled out my hand. Dad was instantly angry, and mom looked a little worried. Dad's voice was stern, "And what is that for?"

James looked at me, "We'll it's a promise: She promises to behave and stay innocent, and my promise is to protect that."

Dad took a deep breath, "Well that's a relief. You two are going to be the death of me."

I took a deep breath in relief myself. That was better than any way I could have explained it.

James was glad to get through that. He added, "So, where are we following you two? Since I have the night off, you're kinda stuck with me." I smiled. I didn't want him to leave. I really needed him to be around me, especially after earlier. I didn't want to let go of him ever.

"We were going down to Sherburn's."

"Did you want us to ride with you, or can we follow you in the car?"

"I guess you two can follow us, but no funny business."

"None."

While we waited for them to get going, we walked to the car and waited to leave. It gave me a chance to talk to him. "You scared the shit out of me in there. You were walking a very thin line."

"You think? I thought it was perfect."

"How did you know about the cheesecake?"

"I felt you telling me."

"I *did not*, how did you know?"

"You weren't telling me that?

"No!"

"I wonder who was." James looked confused.

"You're kidding, right?"

"No, I thought it was *you*."

"Mom!"

"You think?"

"It had to be. I wasn't thinking that. I was thinking you were going to get us in trouble."

He took my hand and kissed it, "I think your mom wants you to be happy, no matter what."

"Is that something you're feeling or something you just think?"

"Sometimes I can't tell the difference."

"Well, that's scary."

"Most of the time I'm right either way."

"That's even scarier." I loved that he was so amazing. I was still a little worried, "James, we have a problem."

"What?" He sounded a little panicked.

"I am starving."

He laughed, "Me too!"

"We'll have to wait for a late night snack."

"Yeah, it would look bad if we both ate right away."

He kissed my hand again as we pulled into the parking lot behind mom and dad.

30. Broken Heart

"Wait right there, don't you dare get out."

"What?"

"Just wait, please."

He got out and opened the door for me, taking me by the hand to help me out, "It's respectful, good for your dad to see. Can I hold your hand when we walk in?"

"I'm not letting go, are you?"

"No, just making sure."

As we walked by the bar I saw Laura and asked, "Where's Danelle?"

She looked down at me holding hands with James and gave me a disapproving look, "She'll be right out."

"Thanks." I looked at James, "That was unpleasant."

"Sarah, we're going to run into this all the time, what we're doing and the age difference is wrong to some people. I expected this. I don't like it either, but it's worth it." He kissed my hand and we walked to the backside of the game area behind the pool table, facing the rest of the bar. We were in plain sight of mom and dad.

I thought to myself, *did he do that on purpose?*

James turned to me and said, "Trust issue."

"That's fine." I was pleased he thought of these things.

Danelle came out bringing food to people. Her mom said something to her, and she came back to us leaning against the pool table, "So, you two decided to finally come out with it?"

I looked at James and back at her, "What do you mean?"

"You weren't spending any time here with me."

"I am so sorry."

She was looking at James suspiciously.

James tried to defend himself, "Danelle, I haven't done that crap in years."

"You know if you do and I find out, I am telling her."

"That's fair." James agreed; what else could he do?

She grabbed my hand, "Sarah, this is a promise ring!"

"Yes it is."

James was trying to explain it the same way he explained it to my mom and dad, but she wasn't buying it, "That's crap! You two are promising to be together."

"Someday," I said hopefully.

"This is too fast! How long have you two actually been together?"

"A little while."

"What do your mom and dad think?"

"Our time has to be supervised, no alone time."

"Well, yeah, I would put the same rules on you too.

"So, I was hoping you would chaperone us for outings."

"Like the fair?"

"Yes, and more."

She got really serious and looked directly at both of us, "There are going to be rules."

"We know," we said at the same time.

"No, these are my rules." We looked at each other and back at her.

"No mushy kissy crap; that makes me sick."

James spoke up right away, "Okay, that's a deal."

She looked at him to shut him up, "No excessive flirting with each other; that makes me gag."

James smiled, "Okay."

"And no stupid guy stuff, I get picked on enough."

"I promise. Cross my heart," James replied.

She pointed her finger at him, "And if you ever hurt her, I will get every guy I know to avenger her."

"Wow, okay!" He was taken aback by her threat, but he agreed.

"Then I will chaperone your outings as long as my mom will let me."

I smiled.

James leaned forward to Danelle, "How would you like to make $20?"

She looked at him cautiously, "Not that mushy stuff already?"

I knew what he was doing. I looked at him. Today already cost him way too much.

James continued, "No, I was suppose to take Sarah to dinner, but the mushy stuff got in the way and we forgot to eat. Sarah's mom and dad think we ate, but we're starving."

"You want me to bring you food?"

"Yes, please, but no one can see, so put it in the corner and we'll sneak it."

"Does the food price come out of this?" She was waving the $20 in her hand.

"Here's another $20, will that do?"

"Yep!" She left.

James set the pool table up, "I think this will work."

My stomach growled, "Hope so."

Danelle came out with two baskets of food and put them in the corner with a ketchup bottle. We played pool with her and snuck over to the corner between shots to take a bite. I didn't bother with food etiquette because I was too hungry.

He moved close to me, "She eats."

I gave him a nasty smile.

Danelle stepped in, "Too close for me."

James laughed, "She's strict."

Then we all laughed. We played pool all night until mom and dad were ready to leave. I hugged Danelle, "We'll find something to do that you have to chaperone tomorrow, okay?"

"I think I'm going to like this job."

We drove to the trailer and, he took my hand and walked me in. I was looking for cards while he put a blanket on the floor.

Dad interrupted us, "No."

We both stopped doing what we were doing and looked at him.

James spoke up, "Would you rather us play at the table?"

"No, James, you have to go home now."

James looked like he was hurt, "You're right, I forgot. No more all night games."

Dad could see the hurt in James, "Maybe next time, I'm too tired to stay up with you two tonight."

James lightened a little, there was hope. We walked to his car holding hands, and we stopped at his door. I wrapped my arms around his neck. He took both my hands and moved them in front of me and kissed them, and then one small kiss on the lips, and he got in and drove off. I was filled with joy; I felt like I could handle anything. Dad was standing in the door way as I walked up the stairs, holding the door open for me. I walked in, but I could tell he wanted to say something.

Then he spoke, "Do you need protection?"

I wasn't ready for that, "Dad, mom already asked me last time I was here, don't you two talk?" He stood there looking at me, questioning my sincerity.

"Dad it's not like that."

"Yet!" he blurted out.

"Dad…" I groaned.

"I see the way you two look at each other. Please, Sarah, try to wait longer."

"No problem."

"Are you sure?"

"Yep."

"Then I'm going to bed."

"Night dad."

I curled up on the couch. I really did hate the bed. I decided to dream of the house again, since it filled me with such happiness. Then my dream turned to something not right, something wrong, and something dark was in my dream. The pain was devastating, and James wouldn't respond to me. He was distant, far away. I sat up when I heard a screech into the yard. Dad came running out.

"Dad, there's something wrong. It's James and it's bad."

Dad looked at me, and went to the door, "James, I said not tonight."

James stopped on the steps and didn't say anything. Dad must have seen something in him, "What is it?"

As my dad opened the door to let him in, James was clearly panicked as he tried to explain, "My dad, at the reservation, ambulance…" and with a pleading look to my dad, "I can't go there, Tucker. Will and Katherine can't be there either. They are coming here, is that okay?"

"Yes. By all means, yes."

Mom came out from the bedroom.

James came and knelt by me, "Sarah, I need you to go to the Reservation."

He was helping me with my shoes, "James, I got it."

"I need to know what's going on."

I looked at dad, and he nodded, "Yes, go."

James was frantic, "Do you remember how to…"

"Yes James." I stood up not waiting for him to move. I took one look at him and ran to my car.

I drove as fast as I could to the Reservation while still trying to get there in one piece. As I pulled in, I could see the ambulance. I parked my car and ran to the stretcher now coming out of the house. The paramedics had Carl, and he was conscious.

I ran to him and grabbed his hand, "What is it?"

"My heart, it's been broken for too many years."

I kissed his hand.

"Call my Clarissa. I miss her so." He told me her phone number. I said it over and over in my head to try to remember it. They were putting him in the ambulance, so I had to let go of him.

I called back to him, "I promise."

I grabbed Tamara, and pulled on Sam. Sam didn't budge, but he looked at me, "I'm supposed to stay."

"Sam, snap out of it. Sam, now, your dad needs you there."

He wasn't responsive.

"Sam, get in my car now."

Finally, he pulled himself together and got in my car. We followed the ambulance.

I pulled my phone out to call James, "James it's his heart. We're heading to the hospital now. Tell my dad where I'm going, okay?"

"I'll be right there. I'm in my car now."

"James, don't hang up."

"Yeah?"

"He looks good, but he asked me to do him a favor."

"Never."

"James it's not what you're thinking. He wants me to call your mother."

The phone went silent.

"If I give you her number will you call her?"

He didn't say anything.

"Fine, I will call her myself. See you there."

"Sarah?"

"Yeah."

"What's the phone number?"

I gave him the number. "Promise me you'll call right now because he needs her. Everything else doesn't matter."

He was silent.

"James?!" I yelled at him.

"I haven't seen or heard from her in fifteen years."

"James, now, promise me."

"I promise." I could hear the pain in his voice.

"I'll meet you there. I have Tamara and Sam with me."

James:

I called my mother. It would be the first time I had talked to her since I was little. The phone was ringing. I didn't want to talk to her, but for Dad…"

She answered, "Hello."

I couldn't speak to her; how could she have left?

She answered again, "Hello?"

I took a deep breath, "Clarissa?"

"My sweet Carl, is everything okay?"

She took my breath away. I didn't know what to say. "This isn't Carl."

I heard her breathe with desperation, "James?"

For my dad, come on James. For dad, "Yes."

"What is it, has something happen?"

I couldn't let her into my life. She chose to not be part of it. "Dad's heart. We're on our way to the hospital."

I could hear the devastation in her voice, "He's not...?"

"No, but he asked for you."

All I could hear was a dial tone. She didn't say anything to me.

Sarah:

We walked into the emergency room waiting area. The ambulance went to a different door. I sat Tamara down by Sam, and I lifted his face, "Sam, you need to be here and be strong for her."

Tamara looked at me, "He will be fine."

I smiled at her. I was glad she knew that. I went to the desk, "I am here for Carl Swanson."

"Family only," the nurse insisted.

I'm sure I didn't look Native American. "I am. I'm the daughter in law." I held up my hand with the ring on it.

"Which one?"

"James."

"I don't believe you."

I yelled back to Sam, "Sam! James and I, are we married?"

"Yes."

"Fine." She hit the buzzer. I walked through the doors and she led me to Carl.

Carl looked at me as I went to him, "How did you...?"

I leaned to his cheek, "I told them I was married to James." I held up my hand for him to see. He took my hand and pulled it to his mouth and kissed it. I kissed his cheek.

"So what are they doing to help you?"

"Some tests, I might have a blockage."

"Why aren't they in here doing something for you? Are you in pain?"

"Did you call my Clarissa?"

"I asked James to."

"He won't, he was the one most hurt."

"He promised me."

"Maybe he will for you."

I kissed his cheek. "He promised me."

"Where are my boys? I want to tell them I am very proud of each one of them."

"Tell them later, you need to focus on being strong and getting through this."

He smiled at me, "I will be fine."

"That's what Tamara said."

"Well she knows things, so I guess I'll be okay then."

James came to his father on the other side of the bed taking his father's hand, "I am so sorry father."

"Boy, no need to be sorry."

"I couldn't come to the reservation when I heard."

"But you sent your wife." Carl reassured him. James lifted his head to look at his father. He smiled and kissed his father's hand. Carl continued, "Besides, Tamara said I was going to be okay."

James looked at me, I nodded.

"You stubborn old man, I told you to get that checked out."

I looked at James, "Where's Will?"

"In the waiting room, they will only let two in at a time. You were in here."

I leaned over Carl and kissed his cheek, "I'll be back, Will and Sam need to see you, okay?"

He nodded and gripped my hand tightly, "Don't break his heart."

I kissed his hand and took James by the hand and led him out of the room. As we walked to the waiting room, we stopped in the hallway.

"Did you call her?"

"Yes."

"What did she say?"

"She thought I was dad."

"Okay, did she say she was coming?"

"She said *my sweet Carl.*" Tears rolled down his cheeks. "I say that to you, I got it from her and didn't remember it."

"James." I touched his face to feel his pain, but this wasn't about him. This was what Carl wanted. "James, I am so sorry, is she coming?"

"She hung up without a word."

"James, you can feel this. Is she coming?"

He looked at me completely miserable.

"James, he's asking more and more. Think about it, hard, or whatever you do."

He didn't look at me, "She's on her way. Ouch!"

"What?"

He grabbed his chest. We both ran back to the room, "Dad! Dad!"

He opened his eyes.

Alarms were going off and a nurse came running in behind us. She yelled, "You two out, now!"

She pushed us out of the room. James stopped outside the door and leaned on the wall outside the room. His head was down. I didn't say a word as I stood beside him.

The nurse came out, "You two, back to the waiting room."

I took James' hand and led him down the hallway, "James, I don't mean to push, but you're the oldest. Sam's a mess and you need to be strong for them."

He pulled my hand to his mouth and kissed it.

We walked into the waiting room. Will and Sam looked at James. They asked, "How is he?"

"A little rough."

Tamara walked up to James and pulled on his arm, "He makes a lot of people run around crazy, but his heart will beat and he will be fine."

James chuckled a little with disbelief and relief.

We sat in the waiting room for what seemed a very long time, but it had only been a half hour.

31. A Destiny

The emergency doors opened. This elegant, beautiful woman walked through the doors escorted by two police officers. She was dressed in business clothes, a blouse, a suit skirt and jacket, high heels that I would fall off of if I even tried to walk in them. She had light brown hair that was long and wavy. Her skin was fair and very young looking. She couldn't be more than forty years old.

I found myself drawn to her. I got up and started walking towards her. James grabbed my hand to stop me.

I looked down at him, "James, it's okay."

She stopped and spoke to the officers then they left. She walked towards me. I spoke to her, "Clarissa?"

"Yes my dear. How is he?"

"They kicked us out; we don't know anything."

As I was telling her this, her eyes moved to the boys, looking at each one as tears streamed down her face, "It's been too long." She moved to them. First, she moved to Sam. She lifted his face. His eyes moved to me, and I nodded to him to allow her to look at him. Tears welled in his eyes, and he looked away. She allowed him to move away from her. Next, she moved to Will. James seemed to know what was coming. The look in his eyes told me he couldn't do this.

He said, "Excuse me." Then he walked out.

Her eyes followed him as he left. Her eyes fell on me, "I'm sorry."

I wanted to comfort her, but I didn't know what to say to her. All I know was that James needed me more right now. I followed James outside hoping to find him. He wasn't anywhere.

"James?" I said out loud.

"Sarah."

"Where are you?"

He stepped out of a shadow next to the building. I walked to him slowly. I put my arms around his chest to hug him. He turned me to the wall and started kissing me very hard.

"James?"

He was kissing me very deep.

"James, you're scaring me."

His kiss softened, but persisted.

"James, this isn't going to help."

He stopped and tried to turn away from me.

"James, I will do anything you want to, if that's what you need. But if you're doing this to get away from what's going on, if something happened you wouldn't forgive yourself." I turned him to me. I put my lips to his, "I love you."

He kissed me softly, and hugged me for a long time.

"James, we should go back inside. We need to find out what's going on."

He let go of me. I took his hand and I led him inside. We approached the others and I looked at Will, "Where is Clarissa?"

Will looked at me, "She's with dad."

James sat in the chair between Sam and Will, putting his head in his hands. I sat on the other side of Katherine. I hated being this far from James when he was hurting, but I was prepared to do whatever he needed.

Katherine turned to me, "That's their mother?"

I nodded.

"She's amazing! They weren't going to let her in, and then she called someone on her cell phone. Shortly afterward the phone rang at the desk, and they rushed to let her in."

Tamara stood up and walked over to me, "My mom thinks you're good for James."

I put my finger to my lips to hush her. Everyone looked at her, "What?"

"My mom likes you and thinks…" She walked to James and pulled him until he got up, and he moved him to sit by me, "…you're good for James." She pushed him to sit by me and took our hands and put them together.

James leaned forward to her, "You know her?"

"Yes, and she misses you the most; I thought you knew that." She shrugged her shoulders and sat between Will and Sam kicking her legs.

He looked at me with disbelief. I didn't know what to say, so I traced over his hand with mine.

The lady at the desk came over to us, "Carl will be going in for surgery soon. You all can go back and see him quickly."

She led us back to him.

I held James back as we got to the door, "They need a few more minutes."

We stayed in the hallway but could hear her, "Carl please give it to someone else. Even if it's not one of the boys, we have been apart too long. I love you and I want to grow old with you. Please come home with me. Please let me take care of you. I will walk away from everything if you say you will."

She leaned over to kiss his lips; she was sobbing. I pulled James in so he could see their love after all these years. James wrapped his arms around me as we walked to his dad. I took Carl's hand again.

He kissed it and looked at Clarissa, "Please don't let James live the way we do. Promise me you will help them, and I will give up all to be with you Clarissa."

She leaned over him and kissed his lips.

Will touched his dad's leg, "Be tough dad. I love you."

Sam didn't say anything, but he just touched his dad's arm.

The nurse walked in, "Okay, everybody out."

James and I were last except for Clarissa.

I stopped James and nodded for him to see how much his mother loved his father. We watched together as Clarissa said her goodbye, "I love you, please stay here with me. Our time has been short; I need more time with my sweet Carl."

I nudged James out the door, so they could have some alone time. He stopped me in the hallway before we got to the waiting room. He leaned on the wall holding my hands, "I can't live without you, like that. Please don't push me away."

I looked into his eyes, "I am not as strong as her, I can't and won't."

He pulled me close and kissed my forehead. I just held him there.

Clarissa walked out of the room and nearly fell to a bench in the hallway. I pushed James away and ran to her. I knelt down beside her, "Are you okay?"

"My heart has ached for many years."

As she touched my face and looked at James, "Do you love him?"

"Yes I do, with all my heart."

She cupped my face with her hands like James does and she kissed my cheek. James hurried to the other side and helped to lift her as we walked her to the waiting room. She sat between Sam and Will holding both their hands, but she looked at James a lot.

James and I were standing, and I turned to him, looking him in the eyes. I spoke softly, "I need to step outside. I need to call mom and dad."

"I will come with you."

"You should talk to her," I pleaded.

"Sarah, don't push."

He walked outside with me. I called and dad answered. "We're at the hospital dad."

"What's happening?"

"Carl is going in for surgery. If it's alright with you, I would like to stay for James?"

We were standing together. James face was next to mine, holding me from behind.

"I don't like you being away all night."

"Dad I know, but we're supervised."

"Can we bring anything, up?"

"No. Maybe in the morning, I will let you know."

"How is everyone?"

"It's a little rough."

"Are you two off by yourselves?"

"No, we're not alone."

"Sarah, it's the middle of the night. I don't really like this."

"I know, but dad please? I will call every hour. Just please, I need to be here for James."

"You'll call me every hour?"

"Yes."

"I am trusting you…"

"I know."

"Then okay, but I'm not happy."

"I will call you in an hour." I hung the phone up.

He turned me to him, "You were wonderful in there."

I looked into his eyes.

He traced his lips on mine, "I don't just love you. I am head over heels in love with you." He kissed me one long soft kiss almost resting his lips on mine.

"James," I broke our kiss, and looked.

Clarissa had come out to join us. He didn't look at her. He kept his eyes on me.

"James?" His mother spoke gently to him.

He looked at her and gripped me, "She stays."

"If she's a part of your life, then she stays."

He loosened his grip. We sat on the bench outside, and James kept me between them. He was holding my hand with our fingers entangled.

"You are angry with me?" She looked at him with concern.

His grip tightened on my hand. I traced my free fingers over his hand to remind him I was there for him. Any harder he would hurt me.

"You left me fifteen years ago, and nothing. I didn't even know if you were alive until this year."

"I am sorry about that, but it was for your father. I love you, but I loved him more than anything."

"How could you walk away?"

"I didn't, not completely. I see your father once a year. That's how Tamara came along."

"How come she knows you?"

"I get to see her when your dad comes to visit."

"How come we didn't get the same privilege?"

"Boys are different, you have a destiny."

"But I don't want it. He lived in misery for so many years."

"He had to. There was no other option; that's why there are three of you. One will take over. Then I can have him back. It was a huge price to pay, almost twenty years, but I will have him."

"Not me, I'm leaving."

"That is your choice. I will not deny you that. We made our choice, but it doesn't have to be yours."

"I thought we did something wrong?"

"Not you! You were my Cayuse my strong hearted."

They said nothing for a while, and she spoke again, "I heard you are going to go to school. If you need anything, I can help. Please, let me know, especially if you're not going to be part of that world. I have longed for time with my boys for many years. Just think about it, I am here now."

She stood up and kissed his head and walked back inside. I sat there. I didn't know how to help him. I traced my fingers over his hand again. We sat silently for more than an hour. I pulled out the phone. Dad answered again.

"We're still waiting."

"How long will you be there?"

"I'm not sure."

"Just keep us up to date on what's going on."

"Yep."

"James took good care of me when you and your mother couldn't come up here. I do care about him. Can I talk with James?"

I looked at James, "He wants to talk to you. Sorry."

James took the phone, "Tucker?"

I couldn't hear what my father was saying, just what James was saying.

"Yes."

He looked at me.

"Thank you." He stood up.

"Yep, one hour."

He pulled me closer to him.

"Okay."

He hung up the phone. He kissed me deeply like he was in pain. We broke the kiss and he rested his forehead on mine, "How can anyone feel so good and so bad in one day, I will be surprised if I survive."

I smiled, as we walked in, Will and Katherine got up to go outside.

Tamara spoke, "He's scaring them now."

We heard alarms going off and a bunch of people were running. We all held our breaths.

Tamara spoke again, "He's okay now."

James knelt on the floor with her. He lifted her face so she looked at him, "Tamara, is he alive?"

She tilted her head, "Yes."

He bent over her and kissed her head.

She stood up and took her little hands and placed them on his face. "Sam's the one."

We all looked at Sam. He had his eyes closed with his hands together just at the fingertips. He was moving his hands in a pulsing-like movement. He seemed to be concentrating very hard. James stood up, walked in front of Sam watching him.

Nobody said a word, but we are all staring at him. Sam opened his eyes and looked at James, "It's pumping on its own now."

He looked at the rest of us, "Why is everyone looking at me?"

We all sighed with relief, and James laughed a little. We waited a long time before the doctor finally walked out.

It was really early in the morning. Carl's doctor filled us in on his status, "Well, everything was a little iffy for awhile, but he is stabilized and holding his own. It will be a while before you can see him. You should all go home and get some sleep."

I called dad. He said everyone could come to the trailer. James pulled the keys to our hotel room out of his pocket and handed them to his mother. My heart sank; that was our place. He proceeded to say, "It's not great, but it's decent if you need to rest, and it's paid for through the weekend. Here are the directions and my phone number."

"I will stay with your father. We have been apart to long."

He wrapped her fingers around them, "Use it if you need to rest."

We got to the trailer and dad had food, coffee and sodas set out for everyone. He had made up the beds in the first bedroom. Sam went to lie down on the top bunk. James lay down on the couch with Tamara. Will and Katherine decided to take the bottom bunk.

I looked at the chair in the living room, "Is it okay?"

Dad looked at me, "Yes, that's okay." He smiled and looked at Tamara, "You have a chaperone."

I kissed him on the cheek, "Thank you." I curled up on the chair.

I woke about 8 a.m. It had only been two hours since I closed my eyes. James was putting Tamara on the couch, before he turned to look at me.

When he did he smiled a little, "I didn't know you were awake."

I smiled at him, "Did you sleep?"

"No, too much to think about."

"Like?"

"You know how I said I don't have all the plans worked out. I had an idea, but I need to talk to Clarissa."

"Yeah, but what do you need to work out?"

He pulled me to my feet and wrapped the blanket around me and led me outside. He sat down on the step. I sat down behind him.

I wrapped the blanket around him with my arms, "Do you want to share what you're thinking?"

"I was thinking, when I go to school, maybe I could save some money by living with her. But I want to talk to her to see if it is possible. The other thing is that I am supposed to leave Tuesday. I am still going, but I didn't quite know how I was going to get to the airport. She lives in the cities, so that might work out. Or maybe I will have to go home with you, and you can take me."

"Anything you want or need." I tilted his head back and kissed his forehead.

I just have to be brave enough to talk to her and ask."

"James, she loves you. Just ask."

He took a deep breath, "Here I go." He stood up and went to his car and drove off.

Dad came out the door, "That was good of you."

"He's confused; his mom showed up last night. He hasn't seen her in fifteen years. They didn't part because of a separation. She did it so James' dad could be chief."

"So…"

"Yes, she still loves his dad."

"Sarah?"

"Yeah."

"Isn't James supposed to be chief?"

"Yep."

"Then aren't you setting yourself up for heartache?"

"I'm not sure. Sam is the one that everyone thinks should be the one. So, I guess we'll have to wait and see."

"Do you really want to put yourself through that?"

"Dad, I don't know. I just can't live without him right now. He's my best friend, and we talk about everything."

"Even sex?"

"Dad! Yes, even that. He won't let anything like that happen, and I'm too young."

"Wow, I wasn't expecting that."

"He's really good at walking away."

"So, do you love him?"

"Yeah, I think I do."

"Do you want some breakfast?"

"Not yet, I think I need to sleep a little longer."

He held out his hand, I grabbed it and pulled myself up. We walked in. Dad started some coffee, and I curled up on the chair and closed my eyes.

32. Sam's The One

I woke to a lot of noise in the kitchen. Katherine and my mom were cooking although Katherine was doing most of it. Tamara was playing with my dad. She said he had sweet eyes. Then she worried us all. She stood up and said, "I can make you feel happy, do you want to see?"

"Sure." My dad chuckled a little.

"She waved her hands in a circle in the air. She stopped and looked at him and asked, "How do you feel?"

"I am even happier than I was. Thank you."

"See, I told you!"

None of us really knew if she did anything, but after she was done everyone seemed happier and went on with what they were doing.

I spoke up, "Did my dad tell you where James went?"

"Yeah, to check on dad."

I pulled my phone out and text him, "Where are you?"

My phone rang almost immediately. I walked outside as I answered, "So, how's it going?"

"Really good. She has room for all of us. She has been waiting for us. There is so much I need to talk to you about. We are going to have a great life together. I'm almost to the dirt road. I'll be right there."

I waited outside. When he pulled in I walked slowly to the car. He got out and hugged me. Dad came to the door.

"Hey, Tuck, can Sarah go for a ride?"

Will yelled out from behind the door, "James, how's dad?"

"Were suppose to be back by–*oh shit!* Tuck, never mind. Can she come with me to the hospital?"

I looked at dad in the doorway.

"Yes go," he replied.

James and I walked in behind my dad.

Dad looked over at mom, "Paula, do you need help?"

"Katherine's done most of it already. I will get the rest."

James interrupted, "Guys, I'm supposed to have you all back up there in forty-five minutes. We need to work out a plan of how we are going to take care of dad. Tamara and Sam you can ride with Will. Let's move guys."

He walked up to my dad, shook his hand and hugged him, "Thank you." Then he walked over to my mom, "Paula thank you." He kissed her on the cheek.

He picked me up and put me over his shoulder and walked out the trailer door. He slid me down in front of him almost tripping. He kissed me, while letting me down by the driver's side.

I looked at him funny.

He smiled, "Yes you're driving. Will! Hold up! Meet us at the house."

"But you said…"

"It's okay, meet me there."

James jumped into the car, "Let's go!"

"Okay, why am I driving? You always try to get my car keys."

"I want to get fresh with you," he leaned over and kissed my cheek then moved to my jaw line. I tried to turn to kiss him. "You need to keep your eyes on the road."

He took my right hand and kissed my palm moving slowly up my arm to my neck.

"Thing must have gone well?"

He just grinned.

We turned into the reservation, "Are you sure we should be here?"

He smiled, "Yes."

"James, I couldn't live like they did for so many years." I pulled up to the house and stopped.

He turned to me, "Stay here, and don't get out yet."

He got out and came around to open my door. He took my hand and helped me out of the car lifting me to the biggest hug. I wrapped my arms around his neck and hugged him as tight as I could. He moved so our faces were touching, resting our foreheads together, and he carried me in the house like that.

We moved down the hallway, and James yelled to the others, "You guys have fifteen minutes to freshen up!" He lifted me as we entered his room laying me on his bed. He lay down beside me never taking his face from mine.

We entangled our fingers, "James?"

He inhaled deeply, "Yes, my sweet Sarah."

"What are we doing?"

"I needed to look at you for fifteen minutes." He inhaled another deep breath close to my face, closing his eyes and shuttered. When he opened his eyes he looked deep into mine. His eyes were full of desire, but he kept our hands together, "You are intoxicating and I need a refill. I always do better when you're around me. Today has been so..."

I moved to kiss him, but he didn't seem to want the kiss. Instead, he studied my face like he couldn't get enough and traced it with his hand. I closed my eyes.

"Sarah?"

"Yes, James."

"Open your eyes."

He was making me dizzy, but I opened them and looked at him.

"I can't explain the feelings that are building in me for you. I think I am totally in love with you and then it grows even more."

I whispered to him, "You're my Cayuse."

Then, what I was waiting for, he moved to place his lips on mine. But this wasn't just a kiss. He rested his lips on mine like he was home.

"I suppose we should go."

"Yes," I said quietly.

"I'm not full yet, but I'm almost full." He kissed me softly as he lifted me to my feet.

"James?"

His eyes closed as if he enjoyed hearing me say his name, "Yes, my sweet Sarah?"

"When are you going to tell me what is going on in your head?"

He opened his eyes, they were saddened, "I'm sorry, I was so absorbed in taking you in, I forgot about everything else. We'll get to it, but we've gotta go now."

He took my hand and we walked out.

Sam got up and looked at us disgusted, "No heavy breathing!" Then he stormed out. James let go of me and ran after him. I went to the kitchen window to listen.

When James caught up to Sam he turned in anger on James, "Our father is in the hospital and you're so selfish! All you think about is her and being with her. You don't take care of things. I am better than you and I can do so much more than you. Why do you get to boss us? You're never here, and you're not chief yet!"

"Sam."

"What?"

"You're right, it's all yours, whenever you're ready."

"What, how?"

"I talked to the elders and they agreed that you would be the better choice."

"What are you saying?"

"Chief, that's why we can be here. They are ready whenever you want it. They will train you, today, tomorrow, in a week, a month, or a year from now. It's all up to you whenever you're ready."

"I am ready now."

"Can it wait until dad gets better? I think he would like to be part of it."

"Yes. Good idea."

James grabbed him around the neck and rubbed his fist on Sam's head, "I am still older than you and wiser, that's why I get to boss."

"Not for long!"

"Oh yeah? I'm still your older brother."

Sam grabbed James around the waist and lifted him, "I think I am stronger!"

James and Sam walked in. James was happy and it was so good to see him smile, "Is everyone ready?"

We left for the hospital and Sam rode with us. James put his hand up for me to place mine in his.

Sam laughed in the back seat, "I told you, all you think about is her and being with her."

James looked back at Sam, "You need to shut up."

"You guys don't do *it* for a long time."

"Sam!"

"Be patient brother; it does happen for you two, and it's really good."

I looked at him in the rearview mirror horrified by what he was saying. He already saw it happening, that's scary.

Sam looked in the mirror at me, "Yes, I've seen it and so have you."

I couldn't say anything.

James said quietly, "The dream?"

Sam looked at James, "So, brother, you've seen it too?"

"Sam, I think we've heard enough about our future! We'll leave it to chance."

"You don't have to James. Now that you have seen the dream, no other place will be right." He sat back and laughed.

We got to the hospital and Sam was still heckling us. James finally put a stop to it, "Sam, you're not riding with us anymore; you give off too much info."

"Come on, James, this is the most fun I've had in a long time."

"Let's go."

We walked in and met Will, Katherine, and Tamara at the door. The hospital was way busier during the day. We got on the elevator. When it stopped, we all filed out once the doors opened. Clarissa was sitting there in a chair talking on her phone. She smiled and waved us over to her. "Yes,

Wilson, yes please take care of it. I may be gone for a while. She hung up her phone and got to her feet first hugging Tamara.

"Hi, mom!"

Then to Sam, who was in a great mood, "Am I supposed to call you mom?"

"Mom, Clarissa, hey you. I don't care as long as I get to spend time with you."

She moved to Will and Katherine smiling at them, "My boys do have good taste." She placed her hand on Katherine's face, "You are so beautiful, and I understand you're already eighteen."

"Yes ma'am."

"Now, you have to call me mom."

"Yes ma'am...mom."

"What are your plans if you and Will are running off together?" Katherine shrugged her shoulders. "Oh honey, speak up. You have a lovely voice, and I bet you would be good at anything. Would you like to go to school?"

"Yes I would, but I don't know what I want to do."

"Well, I may have some friends that will help you figure that out."

She moved to Will, "Will, what are you going to do with yourself?"

"Well, I'm at a loss. I thought I was stuck here for so long that I really haven't thought about it yet."

James stood up, "Excuse me, but I would like to see dad, can we go back?"

"Yes, please do. Sorry if I distracted you."

He laughed a little, "Thanks."

What was he doing? I hope he didn't ask her to help him like this. He put out his hand for me to take. I moved to him as close as I could get. I looked at him with concern. He pulled me closer, putting his arm around me. He kissed my cheek, "Don't worry, everything is going to be fine."

We entered Carl's room. He was on a respirator, which was a big tube down his throat, multiple IV's in his arms and a whole bunch of other things he was plugged into. I don't think James was expecting this because he stopped as soon as he saw him. I pulled James arms around my waist and moved to Carl's bedside, holding James there with me.

James whispered, "I can't see him this way he's always been so strong."

"You have to do this."

I took Carl's hand in mine and traced my other over his forehead. I bent down to his ear and I kissed his cheek, "James is here." I felt Carl squeeze my hand. I pulled James hand to his dad's wrapping mine around theirs together. My hand didn't come close to covering half theirs. Their hands were large and strong, "Carl, you have James' hand; he is here with you."

His hand gripped again, he was trying to open his eyes.

"Carl it's okay. Rest your eyes, we're here."

I nodded to James to grab a chair. He pulled it as close to the bed as he could and sat down. I sat on his lap, talking to Carl explaining how Tamara was playing with my dad making him happy.

I leaned back to James, "You need to tell him not to worry, Sam's the one."

He looked at me scolding, "You listened at the window?"

"I have to, I don't get *feelings*."

He smiled at me. I kissed his cheek. James pushed me up so he could be close to Carl's ear, "Dad, you don't have to worry about anything. I talked to the elders; they agreed with everything I said. They will take Sam as chief. He can take it whenever he is ready. They will start to train him when you are well enough. Dad, I still have to leave, but you will be well taken care of. Mom is still here and dad, she is so beautiful, I wish you would have told me more."

I felt Carl's hand squeeze James hand. "I love you, too. But rest, all is taken care of."

Will and Katherine came to the door, "Dad, Will and Katherine are here. We'll be back later."

As we walked out he whispered to Will, "Try not to say too much Will, we don't want to upset him."

"I know!"

We were sitting in the waiting room. Clarissa was having a difficult time staying awake. James got up and went to her side, "I think we should take you to the hotel."

"No, I'm fine. I'm not leaving him."

"Let me put it this way. You can't take care of him if you get sick. We're taking you to the hotel. You can sleep for a few hours, and we'll bring you back."

She smiled, "Now that's your father talking."

James cracked a smile. He told Sam he was in charge and we would be back. We walked Clarissa out to my car.

"Um, why don't we take my car? There's a little more leg room." She smiled at me and began walking away from us, and we quickly followed her. She was parked in the Reserved for MD's. It was a beautiful silver gray Denali. I thought about it; we have the same taste.

She handed James the keys.

"I can't drive your car!"

"Yes you can, remember I'm tired."

I must have had a disgusted look on my face when she looked at me, "Honey, your car is perfect. I'm just too old to be in a sports car."

"Oh, I'm sorry. It's not that."

"What dear?"

I looked at the reserved sign.

She smiled, "Oh it's nice to have connections."

"I guess."

We got in and started on our way. I sat in the back, but in the middle because I wanted to hear as much as possible. Clarissa started as if she was on a mission. She pulled out a brown envelope, but it was larger than a letter size envelope. She sat it on her lap, "Now, have you talked to Sarah about riding with her to the cities tomorrow?"

"A little, but we haven't talked to her mom yet."

I interrupted, "I'll take care of that, begging if I need to."

"You are a sweet girl, are you going to be able to take him to my house?"

"Yes, I'll work it out with my parents. They won't have a choice."

"Good," she turned to James, "I like the way she works."

He smiled at me through the rearview mirror.

"Okay, I have the address to my home, and here are the keys. The basement is yours; I have changed it as you all have grown. It's like an apartment. You have your own living room and kitchen. There are two bedrooms. One is for Will and one for you. Yours is the farthest back; I think you will like it."

"Why have you done all this?"

"I have been waiting." She smiled. "Next, if Sarah can't drive you to the airport, there are four cars in the garage. There is one for each of you including Sam. You will know which one is yours."

"How will I know that?"

"You just will." She turned to me and winked; I didn't know what that was about. "If you need anything, my houseman comes in the morning between 9-10 a.m. and leaves about 2 p.m. He knows you are coming. If you have to park at the airport, use the extended monthly parking, and here is the rest of the info."

She held the envelope out to him. We pulled into Timber Lodge and parked. He opened the envelope and pulled out the packet of info, but it was mostly money.

"I can't take this! You have already done so much."

"Yes, you can."

"I have saved enough for this."

"If you don't need it, then tuck it away for emergencies." Then she turned to me and gave me an envelope; I was happy it was flat. I opened it and pulled out my cell phone bill. Across the front it said 'Paid in Full – One Year.' I looked at her quizzically as if to ask *why?*

She replied without me saying a word to her, "The hardest part is being apart. I hope this will help you keep in contact with James."

The tears welled up in my eyes. I leaned forward and gave her a huge hug. We got out and James grabbed her bags. We walked her up stairs and to the room. I had forgotten we had been in there yesterday. I was worried we had left a mess, and she would realize it. James opened the door and it looked untouched. He placed her bags on the dresser, and she took a seat at the table.

"James, why did you have this room?"

The guilt must have shown on our faces. We both looked at her and then she realized.

"Oh, I see. I shouldn't take your haven."

"No, it's yours." James hugged me, "We're waiting."

"Oh, I do remember the passion. James, I met your father when I was fifteen, and he waited three years for me to be ready. He said it had to do with being respectful. But there was passion every minute we could sneak off. I don't know how he ever managed." Her mind drifted off remembering.

James spoke up, "Well, try to sleep a little. We'll be right up the road. Call me when you're ready."

She looked at James with tears welled in her eyes, "Yes, I will. Thank you."

33. The Pain Of Desire

When we were walking out he stopped to give me a piggyback ride. I nibbled on his ear, "I bet *you* couldn't wait that long?"

He laughed, "Not if you keep doing that."

We got in the truck and started heading to the trailer. I called mom and dad to update them on what we were doing, "Dad, we just dropped off James' mom at Timber Lodge."

"Oh, that's why you were there."

"Yes, dad that is *why* we were there, you're sick sometimes. Anyway, we're heading to the trailer. James is going to crash for awhile."

"That means you will be alone?"

"Why, where are you guys?"

"Um, we're at one of the lodges down the road."

"Well, if you don't want us alone, you can come back or send someone to supervise."

"I just might do that."

"Well, okay, then."

"Bye."

"Bye!"

We pulled into the driveway. I started to get out but he grabbed my arm, "Wait." He got out and came and got my door for me.

"I really can't get used to that."

"Sarah, please just let me." He picked me up out of the truck in a front piggyback, *would that be a piggy front?* He struggled to carry me all the way in. It didn't help that our lips were locked. I didn't have much of this, this weekend. It's been to stressful.

"Either I gained weight or you're really tired."

"I don't think it's you."

He lay down on the couch, "Come be my pillow."

I turned the TV on and sat so he could put his head in my lap. He nuzzled in, and it tickled.

He scooted me down so his lips were resting on my stomach. I reminded him, "Don't do that if you need sleep."

He quit moving and dozed off. An hour went by and I was resting my eyes too. I heard a car pull in the driveway. I eased myself out from under James' head, propping a pillow under him.

I walked to the door, it was Brian, "I heard you need a chaperone?"

I put my finger to my lips to hush him. I opened the doors for him.

"I guess your mom and dad were wrong, no sex going on here."

"Nope."

Brian sat at the end of the table. I sat down on the side.

"So, do you two have sex, especially since you're not allowed to be alone?"

"Brian, that's none of your business."

"Are you just a tease then?"

"Shut up or you can leave."

"*We* would have done it already." Brian had a devilish look in his eyes.

I looked at James, and he didn't move, "You're a jerk."

"I mean you get hotter every time I see you. I wouldn't be able to keep my hands off." He moved a little closer.

I put my arm out, "That's the difference. He's a gentleman, and you're a dumb jerk. So, how is it going with Mykala?"

"She's finally talking to me."

"You would have gotten a lot further if you had kept your mouth shut, but the jerk had to come out."

"You're not nice to me."

"I'm sorry, but you hit on me and you know how I feel about him."

Brian grabbed my hand, "What is this?"

"It's a promise ring."

"He's trying to control you, do you know that?"

"What are you talking about?"

"He made you promise to be his. He will be your first. You still haven't done it; you're a virgin?"

"I told you, it's none of your business."

"He's nineteen!"

"I'm *only* sixteen!"

"A guy had needs."

"So do I."

"What are you waiting for? Don't tell me it's something like *you're not ready* crap?"

My voice was a little higher, "I said, we're not talking about this."

"Sarah, no one is ever ready. You should just do it. Then you'll know he's not right for you, and you can move on to me."

"Okay, I'm done with you, you're out!" I stood up.

Brain grabbed my arm, "I'm sorry. Sarah, I'm sorry, please sit down. I didn't mean to make you angry."

My head was swimming. I wasn't even paying attention to Brian anymore. All I could think was, *was he right? Am I torturing James for no reason?*

Brian must have realized he hit a nerve with me, "I'm sorry again, Sarah. I'll leave now." He walked out.

I went and sat on the floor with my knees at my chest, looking at my Cayuse. I had a feeling that James was awake for the whole conversation.

He turned his head to me, "You were amazing."

I didn't feel amazing; I feel really bad. I was hurting Brian and torturing James, "Is that true that nobody is ever ready?"

"Oh, Sarah." He moved off the couch wrapping his body around mine, "No, well kind of, but Sarah, I would rather have three seconds to kiss you

305

then do something with you before you're ready. To me it's like taking something that's not mine."

"But I am one hundred percent all yours, so you *should* have that."

"Someday, but there is more, that's just the whipped topping on the sundae. The sundae is really good without it, but pure delight with it. I don't need that to be happy with you. We will wait until you're ready.

"James, how will I know?"

"I'm not sure, but I'm sure you will let me know."

His phone rang and he answered it. He pulled me so I was wrapped around him with my head on his chest. He listened for a moment, "One hour. We'll be there." He hung the phone up, "We have one hour." He grabbed the blanket off the couch and laid it on the floor. He guided me to the floor and moved over the top of me.

"Why do you do this if it's torture for you?"

He smiled, "I want you to want me as bad as I want you." He leaned down to kiss me but didn't. Then he moved his mouth to my neck, then to my chest never touching me. My heart was racing. His hands caressed my stomach raising my shirt with his movement.

"James?"

He didn't reply. He moved so his mouth was tracing my stomach.

"James?"

"Um hum," he was more aggressive.

"James!"

He moved to look at my face, and I told him, "I want to be with you."

His kiss was deep. He rolled me on top of him. I moved to kiss his chest. He traced my back with his hands. He pulled me up to his face again, rolling on top of me. He was aggressive and the kiss was harder as his body moved to me. He traced his hand down and pulled my leg up around him squeezing my thigh. His hands moved everywhere. It was like he couldn't move fast enough. He stopped, "You can't tell me stuff like that."

"It's okay, James. I love you."

His kiss was deeper and I didn't want him to suffer. I was ready to give him what he needed. Nothing else mattered. He pushed away and rolled over.

I turned to him, "What's wrong?"

"I can't."

"Why not?"

"I love you. I'm out of control, and I would hurt you."

He stood up and put his hand out for me to take, pulling me to my feet. He led me out of the trailer and down a trail.

"James, where are we going?"

He stopped and put his arms around me pushing his body to mine until we were against a tree. He pushed me so hard I could feel the tree digging into my back. His kiss was so deep my head was spinning.

"It's okay I love you."

He grabbed my hand and started walking to the trailer. I kissed his hand. He turned to me again. He lifted me so I could wrap my legs around his waist. His intensity was exciting to me. His arms were so tight that it was hard to breathe. I was against a tree again, him pushing to me.

"Ouch!"

He stopped and looked into my eyes, seeing something there that made him sad. He walked away from me toward the lake. I didn't know what to do. He dove in. *Shit! What is he doing?* I ran as fast as I could to the dock. I looked and didn't see him. I jumped in and he was there.

"James, what are you doing?"

He came up with the most passionate kiss. I was so confused, what was he thinking? He stopped kissing me and rested his forehead to me. His hand held my face, "We have to stop this. No more temptation, I can't handle it anymore. I will hurt you."

"You didn't hurt me the tree did. I *want* to be with you."

"Sarah, it didn't matter. I wanted to hurt you."

"What do you mean, you *wanted* to hurt me."

He couldn't look at me, so he closed his eyes. "I wanted to make you scream my name, but it would have hurt, I didn't have any control. If we would have been any less dressed I would have pushed in until." Tears were coming to his eyes, "I would have hurt you."

"James, I don't want you to go through this anymore. I want to be with you."

"You're not ready."

"How do you know?"

"Because when I start to get out of control I see it in your eyes."

"What?" I was protesting.

"You look at me and I see wait, slow down, you're scared of me." He looked away and started moving to the shore.

"James, please. Don't walk away from me. That would hurt me more."

He went under water and came back up looking at me but keeping his distance. We stood there in silence. He could hardly look at me, "Sarah I have to go."

"Not without me. We're not done with this."

He turned away to start to move out of the water.

"James, please!"

"Come on then, my mom is waiting."

I moved quickly to his side. He took my hand and kissed it as we walked to the trailer, "I love you too much, Sarah."

I stopped him on the trail, "Don't ever push me away again. I can't handle that. I would rather *not* be ready to be with you and do it, then lose you."

"Don't say that, or even think that way, Sarah, because if you're not ready, I will lose you anyway."

"James, you said you love me?"

"Yes, of course I do."

"Do you remember, I told you not to hurt me again? This hurts James."

I started to walk away. He caught up to me and pulled me behind a tree facing him, "That's my problem. I will end up hurting you either way."

I touched his face with my hand, putting my lips softly to his and whispered, "I asked you to be with me. This was not your fault."

He turned me around and lifted my shirt.

"James, that doesn't matter. I wanted to feel you, and I was asking for it."

He sat down putting his head in his hands.

I knelt in front of him, "James, we just have to stay away from trees." I smiled.

He looked at me and grabbed my face, "I love you too much. The scratches are kind of bad."

"Is it bleeding through my shirt?"

308

"Yeah, kind of."

"Okay, if my parents ask I will tell them I scratched it on the dock. It will be okay, James. Please don't push me away." I got up and pulled him up, "Promise you will not push me away."

"It would be impossible to push you away."

"C'mon, we have to get your mom. This discussion is not done." I reminded him.

We walked up to the trailer holding hands. He was gentle. I could hardly feel his hand. Mom and dad were there when we got back up the trail, "Oh shit, good thing we didn't."

James kissed my forehead and grabbed a towel off the line and wrapped it around me. Get changed but wear a shirt under a t-shirt because it's sort of noticeable. Meet me in the bathroom. We need to get something on that."

Dad came rushing out, "Where have you two been?" He stopped when he saw we were drenched, "Swimming?"

"Yeah," I looked at dad.

"In your clothes?"

James smiled slightly, kind of fake, "I didn't have my suit and I didn't think it would be good if she wore one and I didn't wear…"

"Nope, clothes are good."

"That's what I thought too."

Dad smiled, "Why swimming?"

"It was in public and better than being here alone, right?"

He shook his head, "Do you have a change of clothes?"

"Nope, didn't plan on swimming. I have to bring Clarissa back to the hospital, so I'll stop at home."

I went in and changed my clothes, but James never came in. I went to the bathroom to look at my back. Shit! I could see why he was so upset. That's not good. I couldn't reach any of them, so I just pulled the shirt down to cover them. I grabbed some antibacterial ointment and walked out, "I'm ready."

"You're not going anywhere. You've had enough play time today."

"But dad it's the hospital and I called and told you where I was. Brian even came and checked on us. You can ask him."

"No! Enough. You need a break."

"We'll have a six week break in two days. Isn't that enough for you? Besides, my car is at the hospital, so I am going." I was going to stand my ground on this. *Didn't he realize how important this was to me? I am not a child anymore!*

"Sarah, stop it right now!" He turned to James pleading, "James, if you guys keep this up you know what will happen. I don't think I need to remind you that it would not be a good thing for you right now."

"Dad, stop with the sex talk! If you don't quit pushing I'll make it so he can't walk away!" I was so furious and my body was shaking.

"Sarah, stop it!" James gripped my hand gently. He turned me to him, "We'll go get your car and you can cool off. He's only trying to protect you." He looked at my mom and dad, "You're right. She will come straight back after getting her car. She needs to cool down anyway. I am sorry."

I didn't wait for him. I stormed to the truck and got in.

"Sarah, I know you're upset, but if you keep it up I will never get to see you. I'm not ready for that."

"I have an idea."

"What is that?"

"I could leave and stay with you."

"I'm leaving and you're taking me to the airport."

"I could get pregnant. They couldn't keep us apart then!"

"Sarah, that's not funny."

"I don't want to be away from you, and we still have some things that need addressing."

"Your dad is protecting you, so I don't do what I did today."

"Stop that right now, it wasn't your fault. If you want I will push you aggressively to a tree next time."

"Next time is a long way off."

"What?"

"Sarah, I told you, you're not ready. You're just upset. Let's just get through the next six weeks, and then we can discuss what we are going to do or not do."

I sat back and pouted.

"How is your back?"

"I didn't even remember it until you said something."

We pulled into Timber Lodge and his mom was sitting on a bench waiting for us. James got out and walked with her to the truck. I crawled in the back seat. She got in and looked at us. She could sense the tension between us. She asked, "The passion, right?"

I was embarrassed. All these emotions were getting to me. My parents pushing us apart, James was backing away, and I was so confused as to if I was ready or not. The anger in me was building. By the time we got to the hospital I was ready to scream. James wasn't helping. He was treating this too lightly. We got out and James told Clarissa he would be right up and that I had to go home.

She hugged me, "If you love him, you will have your whole life together."

I smiled, but she was telling me to wait. *Was everyone against me being with James?* I loved him. It was our decision, my decision.

James walked me to my car, "Sarah, when you bring me home we will have time to talk. Please be patient."

I put my arms around him and kissed him seductively. He responded aggressively and pushed to me.

I wanted him to know how sure I was that I wanted to be with him.

"Sarah, I can't do this. I am so sorry. I pushed it too far this time. You're just so intoxicating. Forgive me. You need to go home. I'll be over later."

He opened the car door and I got in, "Please go home."

34. Time Alone

I left him and I was not going back to the trailer. I needed some time to think. I drove by Sherburn's. I could stop, Brian wouldn't turn me away. I could get it over with so James and I could be together. Then he wouldn't have to worry about hurting me our first time together. *I might lose James that way, I couldn't do that.* I drove out to the main road. *What was I looking for?* Hey, there's Jason's truck, I could stop, but that isn't what I wanted either. I wanted James. *Tony's! That's where I'll go!* When I got there I drove around back. I came in through the back way and I walked into the kitchen.

Tony took one look and walked over to me, and I began to sob. He was worried, "James dad is...?"

"No, he's okay."

"Did something happen with you and James?"

I shrugged my shoulders, "I just need time to think."

"Do you want to use James' room?"

"Yes please."

He walked me upstairs and I sat on the bed.

"Are you okay?"

"Please, don't tell anyone I'm here, Tony."

"Not even…?"

"No, I need time alone."

"He wasn't disrespectful?"

I sobbed more.

"Oh, maybe not disrespectful enough."

I looked at him pleading, "I just need some time alone."

"Okay, kiddo, sorry."

He left me there. I dug through James clothes. I put on his t-shirt and pulled it over my nose, so I could smell him. I curled up and laid down. I laid there for what seemed like eternity. My phone rang. I didn't look at it. It continued to do this every five seconds. I wasn't ready to talk to anyone. I tucked it under the pillow keeping my hand on it. I was trying to understand my confusion. *Was I ready or not ready?* How was that up to anyone else? I was the only one that could decide that. How could mom and dad understand? I wanted to be with James for the rest of my life. I closed my eyes. I didn't know how long it had been, but my phone buzzed. I pulled it out to look. A text I might be able to handle.

>"Where are you?"

"I'm fine."

>"Where are you?"

"Needed time alone."

>"Sarah, where are you?"

"You'll make me go back, need more time."

>"Your dad came to the hospital."

"Stay there, I'm fine."

>"Too late."

"Just tell them I'm fine. I'll be back later. Needed time to think about things."

>"Please, don't push me away."

"I'm not the one pushing away. I just didn't want to go to the trailer feeling this way."

>"They aren't mad at you."

"So, I am. I need time to think, alone."

>"They love you."

"Yeah, well sometimes that hurts? Besides, it's not only them."

>"Sarah, where are you?"

I couldn't reply; the tears were overwhelming and I couldn't see the keys anymore. I didn't know why I was so confused. The phone buzzed again. >"Sarah..." I ignored it. The phone rang. I avoided it and put it back under the pillow.

Tony came to the door. I looked at him wiping my tears, "I'll only be a little longer, and then I will go." I sat up and pulled my knees to my chest.

"Are you okay?"

"Yeah, just confused."

"Sarah?"

"Yeah."

"He knows you're here. He wants to see you."

Tony walked away and James appeared from around the corner. He was so beautiful. I wanted to run to him and wrap my arms around him. He walked over to me, "What are you doing?" He put his hand down to trace my back. I tried not to flinch but the scratches still hurt. He grimaced.

"You should be with your dad. I got this handled."

"Um, Sarah, you don't look so hot. What are you doing here?"

"I just needed time to be alone."

"I got that. Why?"

"I felt like everyone was pushing us apart, including you." I started to sob again.

"Sarah, I don't want to live without you." He pulled me up, taking his shirt off of me, and then he held me and kissed me in the most amazing way. He crawled on the bed to rest his back on the wall and pulled me to him, just to hold me.

I cringed again.

"Let me see."

I pulled out ointment out of my pocket and handed it to him. I laid over his lap. He pulled up the back of my shirt, "Sarah, did you see how bad this was?"

"Yeah, that's why I grabbed the antibacterial ointment."

He began putting some on each cut. His touch made me relax, "How can you still want to be with me when I've done something so horrible."

315

"It didn't feel horrible when it happened. If I remember correctly, I wanted to feel you inside me and was excited."

He bent his knees so I was closer to him he kissed every one of the scratches then covered them with the ointment. When he was done he carefully put my shirt down over them. He traced my face with his fingers.

"You know, if you want to be respected as an adult by your parents, than this wasn't the best way to handle things. Running away is not the answer."

"I wasn't running away; I just needed time to sort it all out."

"What exactly are you sorting?"

"How I can want to be with you so bad and not be ready?"

"Your mind is playing tricks on you, and you're trembling."

"But if it feels anything like I imagine, I want to be with you."

"You really think you're ready?"

"Yes."

"Okay, I don't leave until Tuesday. So, Monday when you leave for school come spend the day with me. I will make it perfect. I will take as many showers as I need to, so I stay in control."

I turned my face to look at him. I had no expression on my face. This was part of the confusion. He just gave into my demand and me. *But is this what I really wanted?* I wasn't sure, but I did want more kissing and feeling his body next to mine. I closed my eyes thinking about it.

James pulled his phone out and called my dad, "Tucker, I found her." …"Yes she's okay." …"I will bring her home shortly." …"No, I promised her I wouldn't say, in case she needs some time alone again." …"You'll have to ask her." …"We'll be on our way soon." …"Okay, bye." He put his phone away.

"Do we have to go now?"

"Nope."

"You need to go be with your dad at the hospital."

"He's got his eyes open. The ventilator should come out late tonight or tomorrow morning."

I put my hand around the back of his neck and pulled myself to his chest, "James, you really should have let me deal with this one on my own. I was selfish and you needed to be *there*, not with me."

"Sarah, that's the part you're missing. You are my life and nothing else matters. The reason I am leaving is so I can be better for you."

He held up my hand with the ring on it, "This was not for you to promise me that you would give yourself to me. It was my promise to you that I only want to be with you, for the rest of my life."

"See, now I am confused again."

"Why?"

"I want to be with you right now, more than anything in the world. It's so much more than the desire. I want to give you as much pleasure as you give me."

"Don't you see Sarah, you already do." He lifted my chin and placed his lips on mine, "You chose me."

I kissed him deeply and very long. He wasn't rushing me at all. When the kiss broke I took a deep breath, "I think I'm ready to face the firing squad."

"They're not mad, just worried."

"Okay."

"1... 2... 3... breathe."

I took a huge breath and smiled.

He got up and pulled me up to him. He looked into my eyes, "You're not ready."

"What do you mean?"

"I felt the doubt."

"I'm not ready to face my mom and dad. Are you sure you're not feeling that?"

He took my hand and pulled me down the stairs, "Sarah, I know what I felt and you hesitated. You're not ready."

"James, I know how I feel better than you."

We walked in the kitchen, and Tony kept his face down avoiding my eyes.

I walked over to him, "Tony?"

He looked at me. I could tell he felt bad.

"Thank you." I kissed his cheek.

"Sarah anytime, but you don't have to be upset to stop by."

I hugged him, "I don't deserve all this."

"Yes, you do."

James shook Tony's hand, "I will see you tomorrow."

"Sounds good."

We walked outside, still arguing over who knew how I felt more. Secretly he was right. I walked toward my car and so did he. He opened the passenger side.

"We're riding together?"

"If I have your car, they really can't refuse to let me see you again today." I smiled.

He drove to the trailer, "Stay there." He got out and went to open my door, offering his hand to me. I stood up.

"Ready?"

I shook my head no.

"1... 2... 3... breathe." He moved like he was going to walk in with me.

I stopped him, "Nope, you're not the cause of this. It's my doing. I can handle this on my own. Go see your dad."

"Are you sure?"

"*You* tell me, *you're* the one that can feel things." I smiled.

"Okay. You'll do great." He hugged me so tight and kissed my forehead.

"You're not getting off that easy." I turned to kiss his lips; he was responsive and I moved deeper.

He mouthed, "Sarah, they're watching!"

"I know."

"You shouldn't torture them."

I slowed for one last long kiss and released him, "Thank you."

I turned to walk in. Dad held the door for me. James stayed long enough to watch me walk all the way in.

Mom and dad just hugged me. Mom did press a little, "Don't you ever do that to me again!"

"I'm sorry, I wasn't running away. I just needed to sort some things out."

"Are you good now?"

"Not really, it's James leaving, his dad in the hospital, wondering if he is going to have to be a chief, and then you guys restricting our time, when he's going to be gone for six weeks. My feelings are all in a bunch."

Mom hugged me, "If you need time or help talking through things I am here."

"I know, but you two don't always understand."

"We can try."

"James says you're just trying to prevent me from getting hurt, but sometimes that hurts too."

Dad spoke up, "Where did you go?"

"Tony's, it was safe."

"We drove by there."

"I parked in the back. I didn't think James would look there if my car wasn't there."

"You didn't want James to find you?"

"No! He would make me come back before I was ready. He doesn't want to do anything that would be against what you guys want for me. You can call Tony." I handed him my phone.

"Why Tony's?"

"He doesn't treat me like a child. He left me alone and didn't hound me with questions."

Dad smiled a little, "Okay, I get it."

They finally let me be. I was still exhausted and I needed to rest. I put a movie in and curled up on the couch. Dad covered me with a blanket.

Before I could even stop to think, I informed dad, "By the way, James is riding home with us. He's staying at his mom's. I will have to take him there *and* I am taking him to the airport on Tuesday! If it's all right with you?"

Dad was a little angry, but mom stepped in, "That's fine."

I leaned my head on the back of the couch, "One last thing, can I go to the hospital in the morning to say goodbye to Carl?"

Dad replied, "Yes, I suppose. When is James coming back with your car?"

"Not sure. He didn't say."

I guess my direct approach worked. I smiled to myself and fell asleep.

I woke to James curling up with me on the couch. His mouth was to my ear and his hand on my stomach, "Your skin is like silk, smooth and soft. I love to trace my mouth across it."

319

I moaned, "I love the delicate touch of your strong hands tracing my back."

He moved his face along my neck inhaling, "I like the way you smell sweet; it makes my mouth water."

"I love when you hover over me to kiss me but wait for the approval."

I love when you tangle your fingers in my hair like a kitten kneading with pleasure."

"I love every ripple of your chest when it touches my skin."

"I love your little moans when you are pleased."

"James!" He was kissing my ear nudging my neck with his nose. I went to turn to him.

"Um, no you don't. I am so turned on right now; you can't move an inch."

I wiggled my butt just a little.

"Sarah, please help me out here."

I took a deep breath and said, "Can I breathe?"

"Sarah, stop or I'll have to leave."

"I was just breathing."

"Have you noticed when you are excited your body trembles? You're doing it now."

"Okay, let's think of something else. How about a two-year-old with snot drooling down into his mouth." I tried to think of something to take our minds off of how hot we were for each other.

"Yeah that's gross. I know, how about a nasty dirty diaper, so bad you gag?"

"Um, how about a kid throwing up all over the floor? Projection style!"

"How about a kid putting peas up his nose."

"James, did *you* do that?"

He smiled, "To Will."

"You are so mean."

He was waiting for me to give another one, "Your turn."

I looked back at James, "My dad's right behind you." I gave him a funny grin and looked over his shoulder.

"Yep, that works best. He's really there?" he looked worried.

"Yep." I said. Both of us sat up.

"James, you're back?" my dad said.

"Yep," James responded.

Dad walked into the kitchen and got a large glass of water. He stood in the kitchen while he drank it.

"Dad?"

"Yeah?"

"I don't know what to say."

"Well, I guess I am impressed with how you dealt with that situation, and I have a little, remind you a little more trust in leaving you two alone. Have a good night."

He walked back into the bedroom and we both started to giggle. I turned to James, "Movie?"

"Distractions are good."

He lay back down facing me. I laid down facing him, but the only two things touching was where my head rested on his arm and our entangled fingers. I smiled at him.

He smiled back, "I love you Sarah." He whispered, "You're still not ready."

"You don't know that," I protested.

"Actually, the feelings are getting clearer."

"Well then, I guess you'll let me know."

"It's looking like twenty-five," he said teasingly.

"You're lying, that's nine years! I don't think I could make it even one year."

He lowered his eyes. *What is he thinking?*

"It's more than a year?" I was disappointed at this thought.

"How about we leave it to chance?"

"I don't want to even ask about two years."

"We should watch the movie," he said changing the subject.

"I am so bummed."

"Why?"

"Two years? I could go crazy in two years."

"*You?*"

"Oh my god, *you* will go crazy." The thought of this made me feel bad.

"Good thing I am getting to like cold showers." He reassured me.

"That's just wrong."

I nuzzled into his shoulder a little more and closed my eyes. I don't know if he fell asleep first or if I did. I was so comfortable in his arms, even if we were only holding hands.

35. Heritage

When I woke I didn't open my eyes. I could feel him next to me. My back was to him but his arms were wrapped around me, not tight but gentle like you would hold a baby. His head was resting on mine, so I could feel the muscles of his chest against my back.

He must have felt me stir, "You're awake?"

My heart raced, I didn't say anything I wanted to stay this was as long as I could. He moved his hand and placed it in the middle of my chest.

"Sarah?"

"Uh huh?"

"Why is your heart pounding so hard?"

"Because you're holding me, that's what you do to me all the time."

"But I'm not doing anything to you."

"You don't have to."

He held me tighter and kissed my face. I turned my face to him as far as I could. He traced it with his.

"I really do have your heart?" he said this so tenderly.

I admitted, "Uncontrollably."

We laid there holding each other. My heart was racing the whole time.

I could hear someone moving about, and then my dad walked into the living room. I opened my eyes.

He stopped and looked at us, "How long have you two been awake?"

James must have opened his eyes too. He replied, "For awhile now."

He shook his head and went to the kitchen to start coffee, "So what's the plan for today?"

James released me. I grabbed his arms and held him tight to stay, but he sat up to talk to my dad, "I would like to spend time with my dad today. I hate leaving him while he is still in the hospital."

"I can understand that. Your mom is here too, right?"

"Yes. She is going to stay here with him. My dad can't go anywhere for about a month or so."

"*Wow,* that long? Your mom can miss that much time from work?" my dad questioned.

"I guess so."

"When's your flight?"

"Tuesday 1:20 p.m."

"Six weeks?"

"More like six weeks and five days," James added.

I sat up and looked at him. *Shit! That's five more days than I was mentally prepared to handle.* The tears welled up in my eyes as I looked at him.

He sat up closer to me, "Sarah, it's not that much longer, please don't do that. You're really not going to notice the difference."

I got up and walked to the front bedroom and started digging in my bag. I didn't know what I was looking for I just needed time to adjust. I was prepared for six weeks. I tried to tell myself that five days was not that much more.

I heard from the living room, "May I?"

"I suppose."

I heard him enter the room, and I felt him behind me. I kept digging feverishly.

"What are you doing?"

"I'm looking for something."

"What are you looking for, maybe I can help?" He traced his hands down my arms.

The tears spilled over, "I don't know."

He wrapped his arms around me and whispered, "It's okay."

"I'm fine, really. You're right, it's not really going to make a difference."

He turned me to face him, holding my face in his hands, wiping the tears with his thumbs. He held up a finger and moved to the door looking both ways. He moved back to me with the deepest kiss I have ever felt. It was so intoxicating that I felt it down to my toes.

Dad's voice rang out, "Okay, that's long enough!"

The kiss broke and I smiled, "Tomorrow."

He hushed me. We walked out to the kitchen. I got the bowls out, and he poured us cereal. I got spoons, and he got the milk.

Dad observed us and laughed, "I just can't get use to that."

We both looked at each other. Dad shook his head.

When I was done eating I got up and poured water in a couple of pots to heat them up and two glasses of water for brushing our teeth. I handed one to James and started for the bathroom. James stood up to follow, but dad spoke up, "Boy! Sit down."

James sat back down. I turned on him and said, "Would it help if we brushed outside?"

"Nope, go away."

"Dad?"

"Go!"

This is what I expected on Friday not today. *Why was he doing this now?* I looked at James. His smile reassured me. I walked slowly to the bathroom wondering what he was up to.

I heard my dad say, "On the other hand let's step outside." They both walked outside.

Shit, I hope he's not chasing him away. He's already leaving. Why chase him away now? I don't like this.

I heard mom, "What's going on?"

"Dad's talking to James in private."

"About what?"

"I don't know, but he better be nice."

"Sarah, he is."

"I'm not sure about that."

"Really, he is."

"Why? What do you know?"

"Dad likes James. It's just hard to watch him with you. He is a lot older than you."

"Well, he's been through a lot of shit this weekend, and he really doesn't need more negative drama."

"Sarah!"

"He maybe all muscles, but he has a heart too."

"Sarah, it will be okay."

"It better be. I can't live without him."

"Sarah?"

I went to the bathroom and started brushing my teeth. Mom looked at me funny when she passed me in the bathroom, but kept walking to the kitchen. I was almost done when James came in. I looked at him questioning him without asking.

He smiled at me, "Later."

I put toothpaste on his brush and traced my hand down his chest.

He leaned into me, "What are you doing?"

"Trying to get you to tell me what it was about."

"Sarah! I said later."

He started to brush his teeth. I moved to be behind him. I was going to do what he does to me. I traced one hand in front of him resting on his stomach and pulled him into me, without much luck. He started laughing.

He turned around with a mouthful of foam, "I told you *later.*"

I smiled and traced my finger along his stomach under the edge of his pants.

He closed his eyes, "Please don't tease me like that. I told you I would tell you later." He turned away from me and spit. I kept pestering him. I traced my hands up his back and leaned into him kissing his back. "Shit, Sarah, quit playing."

He turned to me he was trying to look serious, but the smirk on his face gave him away that he liked this, "I said later."

I traced my hands down his chest to the top of his pants and pulled him closer. I nuzzled into his neck to kiss him. He took my hands and leaned into me with his eyes closed, "Sarah, please don't do that. I won't be able to handle it."

"You were just supposed to give in to me and tell me what he said to you. I wasn't trying to get you turned on."

He kissed me and his hands were aggressive and moved everywhere. *Shit, my mom and dad were in the other room!* I didn't realize I could get him turned on so easily.

I whispered to his lips, "I'm sorry."

His kiss softened, "Sarah, you can't tease me like that. I need a shower right now, and I still have to get past your parents. *Shit girl!*"

"I am so sorry, James, what do you want me to do?"

He pushed me away a little and stood there with his eyes closed. "What should I do…?" I felt guilty I had done it to him again.

He put his hand on my lips to quiet me, "Your voice makes it worse."

We stood there not touching and not saying a word.

Dad's voice rang out, "It's too quiet in there."

James pushed me out the door. I walked to the living room.

"James isn't done yet?" dad questioned, looking at me.

"Nope," I said, then changing the subject quickly, "So, are you two still okay with me going to see Carl?"

"Yeah."

"Mom, what time did you want to head back to the city?"

"Well, I wanted to talk to James about that. How much time does he need?"

"I think he will take as much time as he can get."

My mom offered, "How about 4 p.m. that way we should be home before 7 p.m. That should give you time to drive him to his mothers, and not be out too late."

"I'm sure that would be okay. James, are you almost done?" I called to James hoping he had composed himself.

"Yep!" He answered sounding muffled like he was still brushing his teeth. *How was I going to help him get out of here? What did I do? I am so in trouble. I hoped I didn't have to stall too long. I will never do that again, not unless I am sure we can be alone.* Finally, James was coming down the hall. I was so relieved.

He looked very composed and said cheerfully, "So, it's alright if Sarah goes with me?"

Dad looked at James and said, "Yeah, we already said she could go."

"You want us back by 4 p.m.?" James said looking at my mom.

"Yes. James, do you remember what we talked about?" questioned my dad.

"Of course." James started walking toward the door without taking my hand.

My dad could see the disappointment on my face, "Sarah?"

"Yeah, dad?"

"I trust you. You do know that right?"

I understood what my dad was getting at. I didn't want to think about that right now. I quickly said, "Oh, okay. I love you guys."

I followed James out of the trailer. He was already in the car. I got in the passenger seat. I didn't say a single word and I just sat there as we drove to his house.

We pulled into the driveway of his house. It looked like no one was there. He didn't look at me but said, "You should stay in the car."

I didn't move. He got out and went in the house. After he was in the house, I got out of the car and sat on the car's hood. It took a lot longer than I had expected. Maybe it was really bad. I put my head in my hands. He should be with his dad not here because I made him miserable. I can't do that again. I am so bad. I don't want to do this to him again.

The door to the house opened and he walked out slowly to me, "Oh Sarah, what you do to me."

I felt so horrible. I didn't know what to say. I looked at him. He stood in front of me without touching me at all, "We need to go."

I slid off the car avoiding touching him at all. He let me move without stopping me. We both got in the car. I just looked out the window. I put my hand in his. I don't know how I knew it was there for me. We drove in silence all the way to the hospital.

I went to get out of the car. He reminded me, "Stop, remember you need to let me get the door for you."

I waited for him to open my door. He gave me his hand to help me out of the car. I avoided touching him other than his hand. He closed the door and stopped me, "Are you afraid of me?"

"No, just ashamed of what I did," I said sadly.

"Don't be ashamed." He touched my face leaning to me without touching anything else, "I enjoyed it too much that's all. You caught me off guard. I will do better next time."

"Next time?"

"Yes, I want you to touch me like that. You've never come on to me like that before; I was so turned on." He smiled.

"But it made you so miserable afterward."

"I will do better next time."

I looked away. I didn't want to do that to him ever again. I could feel his pain and misery.

He took my face in his hands, "It won't always be this way." He smiled and kissed me softly, "Let's go face the firing squad." He smiled and put his arm around my waist to walk in.

When we walked in, everybody else was already there in the waiting room.

Tamara came running to me, "I missed you!"

I took her hand as she led me to a chair, "Why haven't you been here?" she asked.

James spoke for me, "She had stuff to do. Now stop asking questions little girl."

Clarissa got up and hugged me, "I am glad to see you again my dear." She looked at me deeply. I think she could tell things weren't as happy as they were before. "It gets easier. Be patient with him."

I smiled at her and she hugged me again and reassured me, "Love will get you through everything." I looked at her desperately. She reassured me again, "It will be okay."

James put out his hand for me to take. We walked down the hall together to go see his father. James whispered to me, "You are so irresistible."

"James, I'm feeling really bad. Can't you just let me feel bad?"

"Nope, I loved what you did, get over it." We walked in. Carl smiled at us, "You did what you promised. You brought my Clarissa home."

"Anything for you."

"You have brought joy to my life again. I will never be able to repay you, my darling girl."

"I brought you something." I pulled it out and held it up for Carl to see. It was a charm of a single feather. It represented the forever life, in this world and the world after. I had it on a chain, but it wasn't a very sturdy one." James looked at me suspiciously. I had forgotten to show him that I stopped and got this for his dad. I was just so upset yesterday and I needed time by myself.

I pinned it to the curtain behind his head, "There," I said, "If you will wear it we will have to get a better chain, but I thought while you are here we could hang it. I hope that's okay."

I looked at Carl and he had tears in his eyes, "How did you know?"

I smiled at him, "A little research that's all."

We sat with him for hours. The rest of the family came in and out, but we stayed with Carl the whole time we were there. I pulled a page from my pocket and read it to Carl. It was on the interpreting dreams and visions. Hence the feelings that the boys all had were deeper than what James knew about. James looked at me so confused. Carl smiled. He knew James did not understand this part of his life. He was hearing it for the first time from me. He never wanted to listen or understand what he felt and was capable of until he heard me read this paper.

Carl knew that this was the first time James had let anyone tell him about his heritage. "Now that James has his future figured out its good for him to understand why we are the way we are. James, this does not mean you have to believe or live this way, but maybe you could understand my way."

James spoke, "I accept that this is important to you. I will try to understand."

Carl looked at me and pulled me closer. I leaned over as far as I could. He said softly to me, "You are good for my James."

I looked at James, but replying to Carl, "Not always."

Carl laughed a little, "Child you shouldn't make me laugh."

I kissed his cheek, "Sorry."

It was getting late so we had to go. I enjoyed my time with Carl so much. I watched James hug everyone. He promised them he would try to call at least once a week. He put his arm around me as we walked out of the hospital.

36. Best Friends

The car ride was quiet. I didn't know what he was thinking. I wished he would talk to me. I hope he didn't feel like I was pushing him away. I didn't exist without him. He was going to be gone in two days. When we pulled into Tony's I got out of the car without thinking.

"Sarah!" James scolded. I hadn't let him open my door.

"Sorry, I forgot."

He took my hand as we walked in.

Tony smiled when he saw James, "I began to think you forgot about me."

"You know I wouldn't let that happen." James hugged him then he warned, "I'll be back in seven weeks, don't give my job away."

"It's reserved for you. Maybe Sarah can come to cook and clean with me once in a while." He gave me a wink and a smile.

"Really?" I was excited that he wanted me here, "Tony, I just might take you up on that!"

James frowned at me. He turned to Tony and asked, "Tony, can we have one last dance before we go?"

Tony smiled and went to the stage, "You got it Fred and Ginger."

I wasn't sure what that meant. I really need to look that one up someday.

James took my hand and led me to the dance floor. He called out to Tony, "Make it a slow one please."

Our legs were in between each others, so we could stand closer. He led me with one arm. I rested my hands on his chest. I didn't even hear the music; I just felt him. I turned my head to look at him. Our eyes were locked into a deep stare. My heart was racing and it felt like I could see his soul and he could see mine.

He smiled and said softly, "I am so in love with you."

The music stopped and eventually we stopped moving. We were startle by Tony shouting as he walked back to the bar. I heard him say, "Jason, I don't want any trouble."

James turned to look and Jason was standing there. "James, do you have a minute for an old friend?"

James looked at me, "Always." He kissed my forehead and walked to Jason, leaving me behind.

Jason nodded at me, "Sarah."

They walked out of the bar together. I stayed behind and sat at the bar with Tony as he wiped down counters. He looked up at me, "They used to be friend, you know."

I knew a little, "How good of friends and how long ago?"

Tony kept wiping counters and didn't say anything. He pretended not to hear me.

"Tony, please answer me."

He didn't even look at me. I insisted, "Tony, tell me it wasn't because of me. Please?"

"Sarah, I can't tell you that."

"How can he love me so much when his world is turned upside down with me in it?"

"It was Jason's own fault."

"What do you mean?"

"He is in love with you, too. Can't you see that?"

"I shouldn't have... Tony, I am not worth all of this! This shouldn't be happening. Friendship and family is way more important than a boyfriend or girlfriend."

"Jason spent hours talking about you and everything about you in great detail to James. Compared to Kylie, you were perfect in every way. This was one girl James did not know and would *never* get. Jason had you all to himself. I am sure he tried to keep you from James."

As I thought back I remembered Jason telling me over and over to stay away from James. Tony was right.

"Oh," I said sullenly.

Tony continued, "James always gets the girl and you were interested in Jason at first sight."

"Oh, Tony, I am so horrible!"

"Like I said, it wasn't what you did, it was all Jason. He talked about you 24/7. James couldn't help himself, and he had to see you. He had to see if you were as perfect as Jason made you out to be. He tried to keep himself away from you. He had girls left and right trying to keep his mind off of you. He didn't want to be in love with you because Jason was his best friend. Then when Jason quit coming around you and you were sad, it broke his heart. James quit seeing all girls and when you were here he became obsessed with only you, even if it could only be a friendship. I don't know what happened, but somehow you returned his affections. He spent many nights here in misery for what he was doing to Jason. James tried to talk to him and explain what happened. Jason still pushes the issue that if you were given a choice, side by side, you would pick him."

The tears were running down my face, "I need a moment." I got up and went to James' old room. I felt horrible. I was making two men miserable and I was not worth all this. I paced and tried to get in control of my feelings and what was going on in my head. Okay, first of all, I do love James. I want to be with James the rest of my life. So, I'm okay. But this was so unfair to them and their friendship.

"Sarah?"

I turned to James. He was so perfect standing in the doorway. I ran to him and started kissing him so deeply and mouthing, "I am so sorry, James." I kissed him more deeply. "I cause you so much pain…" I wrapped my arms around him, kissing him frantically. I wanted him to know I wanted him more than anything in the world.

"Sarah? What's…?" The kissing took over, and he gave in to me lifting me and moving to the bed. He laid me down hovering over me, but still kissing me, "Sarah?"

I kissed him even more deeply. I wanted him to take me right now. I wanted him to know his pain would be rewarded. I love him so much.

"Sarah, this will have to wait."

I kissed him more placing my hands under his shirt touching his chest.

He pulled away from me and sat up, "Sarah."

"James, I need to have you right now."

"No."

I moved to him and started kissing his chest.

"Sarah, if you love me this much you will wait. We have to go now."

I wrapped myself around him and kissed his shoulder, "James, don't you see. I don't want you to suffer anymore. I cause you so much pain, and now I want to give you pleasure."

"Sarah, this is not right. I want it to be amazing. This will have to wait." He looked at me and said, "If you're sure this is what you want we always have tomorrow." He kissed my forehead and took my hand to pull me from the room.

"No James, now. I need to make this right."

"Sarah, that won't make it right. It's everything you do that makes it right, even without that. Remember, that is only the whipped topping on a sundae."

He kissed me hard but not luring then reminded me, "We have to go. It's about the time your mom wants to leave." He wiped the tears from my face and kissed my forehead, "Great, I need another shower."

I looked at him in agony, he rolled his eyes, "I'll be fine; it wasn't as bad as before."

We headed down the stairs.

James hugged Tony and said, "You shouldn't have told her. Good thing I have some self control. She tried to attack me."

Tony looked down, "I'm sorry. She's so good at dragging things out of me."

"I didn't attack you, and Tony I didn't drag anything out of you," I protested.

They both laughed and looked at each other but Tony said to James, "Call me if you can."

James nodded to Tony as I kissed Tony's cheek and told him, "You will see me as soon as I can run away again."

"James warned me, "No running away, I'm not here to bring you back. You'll have to be careful, Sarah. I won't be here to protect you. There are many guys waiting for me to leave."

"I didn't want to hear or believe it. James was the only thing that mattered to me

We got back to the trailer. I could tell James was nervous when he went in before I got out of the car. We were a little late and I tried to keep up with him, but he was rushing. James quickly explained why we were late, "Paula, I am sorry. I went to say goodbye to Tony and Jason was there. I had to talk to him a little because it's been awhile. Can I bring stuff out to the car for you?"

Mom had everything ready to go on the table and the couch. I went to the bedroom to get my things together. He was so eager to go. *Why was he acting so nervous?* He came into the room and grabbed my bag from me and said, "Not in your life." He took my bag from me and my hand as we walked out.

Dad smiled, "That didn't take that long. I always knew you two were in there kissing before."

"Dad!"

"Okay, maybe not every time."

"No, usually arguing," I lied a little.

James got everything in the car. Then he came back in the trailer, "Ready?"

Mom smiled at him, "Okay, then we should go."

Mom hugged dad and so did I.

James walked over to him, shook his hand and then hugged him, "Thank you very much."

335

Our drive home was a little weird. I drove, my mom sat in the front passenger seat, and James slept in the back seat. I kept looking in the rearview mirror for movements from him. I knew he didn't sleep much this weekend. I did find it fascinating that he never moves a muscle. Mom seemed to laugh quietly to herself every time I looked.

"He's not going to disappear from the back seat, Sarah. Keep your eyes on the road."

I smiled at her.

"So what is the plan?" she asked.

"I thought we would go to our house first and look up the address on the computer. James has never been there before, so we really don't know how to get there."

"She lives in Minnetonka?" my mom asked.

"Yes."

"She has money?"

"She was a lawyer, and now she is a judge. From my understanding she has always had room for them to live there. At least that's what James told me."

"How is he taking it?"

"I don't think it matters to him that she has money. He wants to do it on his own."

"Good for him." She looked pleased at this, "Are you going to bring him right away?"

"Can't I keep him for a while? He's going to be gone more than six weeks."

"Yes, I'm here, so dad would be okay with it."

I smiled, that was easy. *I hope she's ready for the next request.* I waited a few moments, "Then whenever we go can I have a little while to check out the house? If she lives in Minnetonka, I bet it's really nice." I hoped she would say yes to this too.

Mom gave me a disapproving look.

"Don't you and dad talk at all?" I pushed.

"Why?"

"Because nothing will happen."

"You're sure?"

"Yes." I really wasn't sure. I wanted to make him happy no matter what the cost was. I wanted him to have a reason to come back to me.

Mom looked at James and back at me, "Sarah, he's more a man than a boy."

My mind wandered to touching his chest, yeah I would agree with that. I said, "What is your point?"

"He has needs that you may not be ready for."

"We both know that. But like I told dad, James is good at walking away from me."

"If things change, please Sarah, take care of it. You are too young for kids, you're still one yourself. I know James talks to you about being together forever, but things change darling."

I wanted to pout, *what did she mean things change? This will never change!* I hope he wasn't really awake and just pretending to sleep. This would be so humiliating.

We pulled into the driveway. I looked in the rearview mirror and I could see he was still sleeping. My mom and I grabbed our bags and went into the house. When I came back out to the car he had gotten out and was stretching. He offered to help, "What can I grab?"

Mom and I had already grabbed everything, "Nothing sleepyhead, your stuff is all we have left."

He touched my waist. I turned to look at him. He smiled and whispered, "I have man needs."

I wanted to die. He followed me into the house and turned to my mom, "Paula, I noticed the lawn needs mowing. I'll take care of that for you."

"You don't have to do that."

"You're helping me, so I can help you in return."

I led him outside to the garage and pulled out the lawn mower. I started it for him and smile. He realized, "You usually do all this?"

"Yep!" I turned and walked to the front steps to watch. He would look at me when he could. I just stared the whole time. When he was done with the front, he came and sat by me.

"Time for a break?" I asked.

"Not really, you're making me kind of hot sitting here."

"Stop that. What are you up to with this anyway?"

He stood up and pulled me to my feet, "If I'm sweaty I won't attack you, and I can take a cold shower."

"How's that going for you?"

"Not good, your yard is small."

"So the attack is still on?"

"No, but the shower is."

I smiled and walked him to the back yard.

"Great, this is even smaller," he said with disappointment.

"That's city life for you."

He was mowing the yard and sadness came over me. Only forty-three hours left, then seven weeks without him.

When he was done he came and sat by me, "You're sad?"

"Only forty-three more hours."

"Sarah, think of it like this." He got a great big smile then continued, "Tomorrow will be a whole day of just the two of us together."

The confusion was setting in. I wasn't sure about how things would go tomorrow.

"Sarah, you're not ready. We will not go there, but we can still spend the day together."

"How do you know that? I can't make up my mind what I want."

"It's the doubt that tells me."

"I do love you, James."

"I know."

"You feel that too?"

"More than you know."

We sat there not saying a word for awhile just looking at each other. He broke the silence, "I still need a shower."

I smiled, "Okay."

He went to the car and grabbed his bag. We walked in, "Hey mom, I'm taking James to the downstairs bathroom, so he can take a shower."

"Aren't you taking him to his mom's soon?"

"Yeah, but he mowed."

"Okay."

I walked him downstairs and grabbed two towels.

He asked, "Why do you do that?"

"Do what?"

"Grab two towels?"

"I usually use two. It's a habit. Sorry."

"Sarah?"

I looked at him.

"You're getting mellow again, are you okay?"

"Yep, almost back to my boring life without you."

"Don't do that; you'll make me sad."

"I'm sorry, I'll try harder."

He cupped my face and kissed me so softly, "Later."

I walk upstairs and went to the computer and looked up the address. It seemed easy enough to get too. I showed mom so she wouldn't think I was hiding anything.

"That's a good forty minutes drive to her house."

"Wow, that far?"

"Yeah, so Sarah," she hesitated. She could see my depression already setting in. She added, "Sarah, you have school tomorrow. I know it's the last day, but I would like you home at a decent time."

"Okay, what time?"

"By 10 p.m."

"How about I leave there at 10 p.m.?"

"I suppose, but…"

"I know, I know…don't do anything stupid."

"Yeah, he is coming back."

"I know. It's just…"

"You have gone this long without seeing him before."

"I'll be home shortly after 10 p.m. I promise."

"Thank you."

James came up and walked up behind me. I showed him the map.

"That seems easy enough," he said. "Are you ready then?"

I shrugged and said, "Okay, yeah."

We said goodbye to my mom. He grabbed his stuff and we walked to the car. He was putting his stuff in the trunk. I stood next to the car waiting. I didn't know if he wanted to drive or not.

He looked at me and said, "You're the one driving. I'm not used to city driving yet."

"Okay." I went to get in the car and he stopped me. He opened the door and smiled. I could hardly look at him. I felt like everything was going to end soon. I knew he was coming back, but my heart hurt. I took a deep breath as he got in the car. I was trying really hard to hold the tears in.

He put his hand up for me to hold. I didn't look at him but told him, "I kind of need my hand for driving down here." He took his hand away and turned in his seat to look at me.

37. All Wet

I drove for a while without talking, but eventually the silence got to him and the staring was getting to me.

"What?"

"I can't read you when you're like this."

"Like what?" I tried to sound better, but it wasn't working. *Oh, I can't talk about this I'm going to start crying.*

"Are you okay?"

Oops there they are. The tears started to run down my face.

"You're not okay, Sarah, pull over."

"I'll be fine. I just can't talk about it while I'm driving. I'll be okay, talk to me or something, anything. Tell me a story."

"Why do you put me on the spot like that?"

"What?"

"What is with the storytelling?"

"It's just a way to get my mind off everything that is running through it." I wiped my tears and took a deep breath.

He told me a story from when he was a child, I wasn't really listening. I was concentrating on not crying and just listened to his voice. It was working.

When his story ended, I handed him the map, "Find the next turn, please?"

We turned down a road that was very secluded and curvy. I went really slowly because it was dark and we had to read the numbers on the mailboxes. I could barely see, "It should be right here somewhere. Oh, there it is." I turned in. The driveway was long. I pulled up to the house.

"Sarah I think we have to go past the house. There is another driveway that looks like it goes behind the house. We could go down that one."

"Okay."

"Clarissa said the key she gave me was for the back door." I drove past the house to the other driveway. I followed it down and around the house to the front of the garage. *This driveway was as big as a parking lot.* I looked at him, "Holy shit!"

"I had no idea it was going to be this big." He spotted a gate off the driveway, "How about through there?"

I parked the car and got out. He started walking up to the gate.

"James, your stuff?"

"Later. Come here."

I walked over to him.

He cupped my face with his hands, "I don't know what's wrong, but I am glad you are here with me to share this." He was kissing me as he pushed the gate open and pulled me inside with him, "Are you ready?"

No, I wanted more kissing, nothing else mattered. I wanted as much time as I could get, "James, wait. Not yet."

I took out my phone and called home, "Mom, we just got here. We haven't checked it out yet. I just wanted to keep you posted."

"Sarah, thank you. Call me when you're on your way home."

"Okay, love ya." I hung up the phone, "I am ready, are you sure you're ready?"

"No."

"There is one thing I want you to remember, James."

"What?"

"No matter how great this is, you still need to leave and get this done, right?"

"Well yeah."

"James, it might be really tempting to stay here. Promise me you are going to go no matter what."

"What are you doing?"

"James, Please!"

"Yes, I'm going no matter what."

"I don't care how much I beg you to not leave, you are still going!"

"What?"

"James, no matter how much I beg you to stay, I want you to promise me you will not give in to me."

His kiss came deeper and so passionate his arms wrapped around me gently, so as not to touch the sores on my back. I grabbed his t-shirt and pulled him closer. It seemed like we stood there for an eternity. He finally slowed, "Sarah, we can leave and go back to your house. I can stay on the couch. I would rather be with you anyway."

"That's not my point James. I don't want to let you leave."

"Is that what this is all about?"

The tears ran down my cheeks again. I just nodded.

"Oh Sarah, my sweet Sarah. I have to go, so I can be better. I love you, but I am not leaving, I'm just..." He took a moment to think of the right words. "I'm just up north away from you. I will call you every chance I get."

He kissed my cheeks where the tears had run, "You taste salty."

I smiled

"Okay. So, if it's not the house, can we check it out now?"

I nodded.

"Ready?"

"Yep!"

He took my hand and we both turned at the same time. The backyard was amazing. There was a huge pool surrounded by a patio. There were lounge chairs and two tables with umbrellas spaced elegantly around the perimeter. There was a set of stairs that went up to a deck that looked over the pool. The deck was almost as long as the house, with a gazebo at one end. I had never been at a house like this before; it was so beautiful.

We were standing by what appeared to be a door to the garage, "Sarah, she said there is a car in here for me."

I waved for him to go in. He opened the door. There were four vehicles. One was a hummer. James walked by it and traced his hand over it, "This one is for dad." I followed him. He moved to the car behind it, it was a Lexus RX 250, "I am assuming this is Will's." He took my hand and led me past a car that was covered in a tarp, to an Avalanche truck, totally decked out.

He looked at me, and I shrugged my shoulders, "Is this one *mine?*"

"Well Tamara said you were her favorite, maybe you should look under the tarp."

He got out of the truck and walked to the tarp on the other side of the car. He looked at me and gestured for me to take the edge with him. I grabbed it and we both walked the tarp back. It was a Mustang GT500 convertible. He looked at me as a smile came over his face. He knew this one was for him.

I smiled at him. It was way better than what I had. He moved to the driver's side and the keys were in it. A note was attached. He read the note aloud, *"Yes, James this is yours. Look out the back door, that's yours too."* He looked up at me puzzled and walked to the back of the garage, "Come here!"

There was a motorcycle and it was beautiful. I couldn't believe my eyes, "Do you know how to drive one of these?"

"You're a funny girl."

"What? I have never seen you on one."

"Jason said you were a natural rider."

"What?"

"I have three at home, but nothing like this. Holy shit! Do you want to go for a ride?"

"No!"

"Are you scared?"

"Yes! And I don't want you on it either. Do you know who many people die on these things?"

"Sarah!"

"James, I don't want to lose you."

He picked me up and set me on it, "Are you sure you don't want a ride?"

I could feel the adrenaline pumping, "Okay, well maybe after you get used to it. This one here has the torque of 8000 rpm's and the power of 10000 rpm's and this can actually do 168 miles per hour. These are dangerous. I can't believe she would even get you one of these!"

He turned me to him and started kissing me so deeply and passionately. He pulled me off the motorcycle.

"James?"

"You know about bikes?" He kissed me more.

"No, I just have an appreciation. I keep my distance."

He kissed me more and I was getting so hot. His kiss was, *oh my God*. I was gone. I could feel it all the way to my stomach. The tingling started.

"James?"

"Yes, Sarah." As he was gasping and eagerly kissing me.

"We still haven't seen the rest of the house."

"I can't help myself. You just keep getting better and better."

The kissing persisted and we were both getting very turned on. If there was a place for us this might be it. I wrapped my legs around him. I kissed him so deeply. I was so hot for him right now. I pulled him tighter to me. I was kissing him more, as if I couldn't get enough. He pushed me against the wall of the garage as I gasped.

"Oh shit, the scratches." He stopped but I continued to nibble at his lips. He asked, "Sarah, are you okay?"

I tried to get him back to the kissing thing. My gasp wasn't from the scratches. I could feel him and I wanted him, right now. I assured him, "James, I'm good." I kissed him more. His caresses slowed, "James, please don't stop now."

"No, I need a shower right now."

"Then so do I."

He carried me to the house, and stopped at the door with the keys. I was not letting him go. He pinned me to the door trying to get the key into the lock. He pushed to me. My hands were everywhere. I couldn't get enough of him. He stopped and put his head on my chest. His hands were extended to the door holding him away from me.

I wrapped my hands in his hair kissing his head, "James?"

"Sarah, please stop. I can't even open the door?"

I chuckled a little.

"Sarah, I am going to rip your clothes off right now. Then how would you explain that one? Stop."

I put my hands on the door, "James, pool?"

"Are you sure?"

"I'm going to rip the clothes right off of you, I'm too..."

He took my hand. "Let's go!"

We ran to the pool and both jumped in. It wasn't very cold, but enough to stop the desire. I emerged slowly from the water. I still wanted him.

"We are in so much trouble Sarah. You are all wet."

I moved to the side of the pool, "I am sure this place has a dryer James."

"We're both soaked, and we can't bring all this water in with us, not in this house."

"Okay, you've got a point."

He pulled himself out of the pool in one motion. He gave me his hands to pull me out, "Now don't touch me anymore. That only helped a little."

I smiled.

He walked around the pool checking everywhere for towels or something so we could dry off. The night air was cooling me off even more. The trembling started. I couldn't tell if I was cold or if it was from the surge of adrenaline. I pulled off my tank top.

"Sarah!"

"I'm wringing it out, James."

"Oh." He pulled his shirt off and threw it to me, "Here is mine." I wrung it out too, while he was still looking for a towel.

I unzipped my pants. James stopped looking for a towel and looked away from me, "Sarah, you might not want to do that."

"James, think of it like a bathing suit."

"Sarah, it's not a good idea right now."

I dropped them and pulled them off. I dove back in the pool. The water was warmer than the night air. I swam underwater to the other side of the pool, slowly coming to the surface. I looked around; I didn't see James, "James?"

"Sarah what are you doing?"

"The water is warmer than the air. I was cold and shivering. James where are you?"

He was walking from the gate, with his bags in his hands, "I'm right here."

I turned to his voice, "What are you doing?"

"I went to get my clothes. I can't see you that way and not...*you know*."

"I didn't want you to stop; you know that, right?"

"That still doesn't mean you're ready. It was the heat of the moment and you're still telling me wait."

"Only because I'm scared. I've never done this before. You have to expect me to be a little scared, right?"

"I don't know."

"Haven't you been with anyone for their first time before?"

"Do we have to talk about this?"

"No, I guess it just came up."

"No, I haven't."

"What about your first time?"

"Sarah, I really don't want to discuss this."

"Okay."

"Look what I found!" He held up towels.

I dove back under and swam the width of the pool, coming to the surface by where he was standing.

"Are you part fish?"

"No, are you going to tell me about your first?"

"No, if you are trying to get me turned off, it's working."

"Aren't you cold?"

"No, this feels good. Um, you might want to use the stairs."

"Why?"

"Um, I still need a shower and if I see you that way, I don't know if I can control myself."

"Really?" I pulled myself up and sat on the edge of the pool. I reached back, "Towel please."

He handed me one and started digging through his bag.

"What are you looking for?"

"The biggest, ugliest pair of sweats I have."

"Why?"

"It's better than seeing the curves of your body." I stood up and wrapped the towel around me." I walked over to where he was looking through his bag.

"Any luck?"

He pulled out a pair of sweats and a sweatshirt. He looked at me and laid them on a lawn chair. I unhooked my bra and pulled it off under the towel.

"Sarah?"

I reached under the towel and pulled off my underpants.

"Um, Sarah, do you have to do that in front of me?"

"Think bathing suit James, bathing suit. That's all." I grabbed the sweats.

He sat down on a lawn chair and watched me. I put the sweats on under the towel. I was holding the top of the towel around me and I couldn't tie the drawstring.

"Do you think you could handle tying them for me?"

"No."

"James?"

"Nope, can't handle that right now."

"They might fall if you don't."

"No!"

"Help me put the sweatshirt on then." He stood up and helped put it over my head. I held the pants and the towel at the same time and put one-arm through at a time. I pulled the sweatshirt down enough to let go of the towel. It stayed up, so I pulled it with one hand letting it drop. Then I was able to tie the pants, "There, are you okay?"

"Do you do that often?"

"Only when I'm swimming."

"So, you dress and undress in front of people with only a towel on?"

"Not all the time, only if I have to. Are you going to get those wet things off?"

"They're kind of keeping me cooled off."

"James, let's check out the house. I have to leave soon and I need to get my clothes dried and I would love to see the rest of the house."

He looked at me suspiciously.

"James, I am fully clothed and I won't attack you. I'm okay now."

"But I'm not."

"Give me the keys. I'll try to find the right key and you get something else on."

He smiled, "I think the keys are still in the door."

"Oh."

I smiled and went to the door, "James, put some dry clothes on and you will be fine."

I went to the door and it was already open.

"James?" I didn't turn around. I thought to myself, he knew the door was open. We would have done it. I must not be ready. He was protecting me and my virtue. I smiled to myself, *he really did love me.* I didn't turn around, "Are you ready?"

"Uh, yeah."

I walked back over and picked up my pants and wrung them out. I picked up my bra and underpants. He was wringing his stuff out too.

"Let's get these in the dryer first. Then we will check out the house."

"Yep." He grabbed his bags and we walked into the house. The kitchen was the first room we walked into. It was huge! Every appliance was stainless steel and there was a huge center island.

"We've only got about forty-five minutes." We walked in and put the wet stuff in the dryer. He took me by the hand and led me to the room adjacent to the kitchen. It was like a living room. There were two couches that faced a fireplace in the middle of the wall. The windows on each side of the fireplace were huge and looked out over the lake. It was a beautiful view. We could see there were two boats on the shore. James pulled me to a door that was situated straight across the room.

This definitely was Sam's room. It had a flat panel TV with game systems and DVD player. There was a desk with a computer sitting waiting for someone to use it. The window had a built-in bench to sit and look at the lake. We moved to the next room. It was a very large bathroom with doors leading to each bed room. There was a large tub and a separate shower with a long his and hers vanity. The toilet even had a separate door. I ran my hand over the marble countertops, "This is nice!"

The Next room was made up for a girl. It had a beautiful canopy bed with netting surrounding it. She would be like a princess here. James closed the door, "Tamara's room I'm sure. Clarissa said Will and I have rooms downstairs."

"Do you see stairs?"

We looked all over trying to find a door leading to the downstairs. There was another room off of this living area that was separated by French doors. There were stairs but they went up. Every room we saw was perfect and breathtaking. We found a door back by the laundry area. We thought this may lead to the downstairs, but it was a very large bathroom. It looked like it was for guests using the pool area.

"Should we go upstairs, or look for more stairs going down?" He asked.

"Definitely up. I can't wait to see this!"

At the top of the stairs there was another set of French doors, but curtains kept us from seeing in. As James opened the doors, my breath was taken away by a beautiful, spacious room. The bed must have been custom made because it seemed larger than anything I had ever seen. James could have laid on it in any direction and his feet would not have hung off. This bed had a beautiful frame around the top of it with curtains hanging around the whole thing. If Carl came here to see Clarissa this would be magical for them to get lost in each other. James hand tightened on mine, and I looked in his eyes.

He smiled at me, "They must still have passion."

We walked in farther into a large bathroom. There was one shower you could walk straight in without stepping into it. There were jets on every side of this shower and it even had benches to sit on. I moved to the other shower which was much smaller. All of Clarissa supplies were in this one. I felt bad when I saw this because I realized how lonely this must be for her. Her whole life was based on a couple of weekends a year when she could be with Carl.

James was still looking at the shower with the jest in it, "Can you imagine being in there together?"

I pulled him next to me, "We can't use it! She probably only uses it once in a great while and probably with your dad."

"Sarah, I don't want to think about that."

There was another room toward the back of the house. This also had French doors covered by curtains for privacy. He opened the doors and we walked in. There was a huge chaise lounge for two overlooking the lake through one window. There was a fireplace the same place as the first floor and a desk in front of the other window where she must have liked to do her work.

James turned to me, "I am mad at dad for not letting us know her. I have missed out on all this."

"James, they didn't have a choice."

He looked at me almost scolding, "You always have a choice."

I moved to him and whispered to his ear, "They didn't feel like they had one."

He looked down at me, "You are so cute in my sweats."

I reached up and kissed him softly.

"Now let's find the basement," I insisted. I walked out pulling him, "Are you going to be afraid if you are here all alone?"

"Why would I be? How about you?"

"Yes, actually," I admitted I was intimidated by all this.

"You don't want something this big?" he seemed surprised.

"No, but maybe the bathrooms, the master bedroom, and definitely the pool. I really don't need or want anything more."

"No kitchen?"

"Well, I guess we could find something to do in there."

"Oh, you are a bad girl."

I turned around to look at him as I walked backwards.

"Sarah, don't be playful. Not now."

I turned back around, "Okay." I walked down the stairs.

38. Vulnerable

I stopped by the laundry room to check on the clothes. They were still soaked. I walked around and around looking for stairs going down. I looked at James, "It looks like there should be a downstairs."

James shook his head, "She told me there was a basement apartment."

"You probably have to go outside to get to it." We headed out the back door. I went to the left, but there wasn't much there.

James went to the right, "Sarah, I found it!"

I ran over to where he was. There was another patio farther down from the stairs, almost hidden. There was a hot tub, currently covered. We found the door, and he held up the keys, "Which one would you guess?"

I shrugged my shoulders, "You may have better luck with this lock, since you're not busy thinking about something else." I smiled.

"Sarah?"

"Yeah?" I gave him a look of apprehension.

"The door was unlocked when I stopped."

"I know."

"You're not mad?"

"James, you were protecting me. Why would I be mad at you? It wouldn't have been perfect."

"I wanted you so bad," he admitted.

"James, I did too."

"You're okay with waiting?"

"Until tomorrow…"

"You shouldn't say things like that," he warned.

"You said, Monday if I come here."

"Sarah, if it's not right, it still won't happen."

"James, if it is, we'll leave it to chance, right?"

"Sarah, please no teasing. Behave when we go in."

"Okay, I will wait until tomorrow."

James found the key and opened the door. As we walked in James was overwhelmed. The room was very spacious; it was as big as the floor above it. There was a large living room set that looked like you could get lost on. On the one end of the room was the kitchen area. It wasn't a real kitchen, but it had cupboards, sinks, a fridge, dishwasher, and an oven. It looked like there was a pantry next to the kitchen, but when we opened the doors we were surprised to find laundry machines. In front of the living room set there was a large flat panel TV with built in surround sound. There was another room off to the left of the door that had a pool table, darts, and a small bar at the end.

To the right there were three doors. He opened the first door as he looked at me, "This one is Will's. Remember, she said my room was in the back."

The room was great! It had his and hers dressers, and a smaller flat panel TV on the wall. We walked into their bathroom. There was a shower and a toilet with separate door and his and hers vanities. No tub, but who takes baths anyway.

We moved to the next door. This was a large walk-in closet they could use for storage.

We moved to James' room. He turned to me, "Can you behave?"

"James, you're the one that gets overheated."

He opened the door. This was very different. It had an addition to it that gave him even more room. We walked in the rest of the way.

He looked at me, "We need to find the bathroom in case this gets hot."

"James, think of a snotty nosed kid dripping in his mouth."

"Sarah, I don't think that's going to work."

"Stop it, James. Just check this out." The bed was in a pit and there were three steps down to it on all sides. There was maybe a foot of flat surface around the whole bed. It also had a metal frame above it with see through drapes flowing to the ground. I avoided this area completely. To the left was a sitting area with a fireplace of its own. There was another chaise lounge for two for sitting at the fire.

There was a door to the left and I opened it. "I think I found the bathroom." It was enormous; the tub here was the same as the one in Clarissa's bathroom. In the corner there was a very large shower, not quite as big as the one in Clarissa's room. It had jet streams on all sides of it but only one bench in it. The toilet had its own door and the vanity was a single but it had two sinks in it. I looked at James, "Why would she have all this done? She didn't even know if you would ever come to live with her."

"I don't know, but I think I like this. I think I could stay here while I go to school. It might be a little tough, but I would suffer through it."

"James, I'm going to go check on our clothes, if they're not done do you want me to lock the upstairs and bring your stuff down?"

"I'll come with you; I forgot about my stuff."

He took my hand as we walked out of the huge apartment living area. We walked in upstairs and I checked the clothes. They were way more than damp. I grabbed them out. It was 9:50 p.m. and I told mom I would be home a little after 10 p.m., shit, the clothes were too wet to put back on.

I pulled out my phone.

James asked, "What are you doing?"

"I'm calling my mom."

"Why?"

"Because I am supposed to be home soon and I don't want her to worry." I dialed, "Hey mom.'

"So how is it going?"

"Good and bad. We got here and there weren't any outside lights on and I tripped and fell into the pool, so my clothes are in the dryer as we speak. I just checked them and they are still pretty wet. So I am going to be a little longer than I thought.

James yelled out, "Hello, Paula."

"I'm not happy about this." I could hear her concern.

"I know, but nothing is going to happen. This house is so amazing; I knew it would be. She has a room for each of them. I really wish you could be here. You would love this. The laundry room is on the first floor and she has three boats and five vehicles. I can't believe this place."

"Sarah, I'm still not happy about this."

"Mom, it's only going to be a little longer."

"So, you're just sitting around in a towel?"

"No, I am wearing James' sweats."

"Can't you wear his clothes home?"

"Mom, I won't see him until Tuesday and he's leaving then. I can't keep his clothes because he may need them."

"Sarah, your dad would be so mad."

"Mom, if we were doing anything would I call you?"

"No, you're right. Please call me when you're on your way home."

"You got it."

I hung up.

"You were amazing! Does lying come naturally or do you have to work at it?"

"I actually don't know where it came from."

"You are a very bad girl."

"We still need to get the clothes back in the dryer or I won't be seeing you to the airport."

He grabbed his bags, and I grabbed the wet clothes. I followed him out the door and he turned to lock it. We went down the stairs to the apartment. We walked in and I went straight to the dryer and put the clothes in.

He turned on the TV. It echoed from every inch of the room. "Wow, you can turn that down. I can't even hear myself think."

He fell onto the couch, "Oh my god, Sarah, you have to try this."

I walked over to the couch a foot away from him and fell onto it. "Oh, you are so right. This is amazing!" I traced my hands over the couch.

"So, how long do you think we have?"

"James, you said tomorrow."

"No, I'm saying not for two more years, but sometimes I can't hold you off."

"What. *Me?*"

He rolled over to me hovering, "Sarah, it's still not the right place, no matter how great this place is."

"James, remember you said we would leave it to chance."

He lay his head in my lap, "Sarah, I don't want it to just happen. I want to plan it out to try and make it perfect."

"James, nothing is perfect, and you said that you had planned this out."

"Sarah, are you trying to convince me or yourself?"

"Probably me."

"See, you're not ready."

"James, all I know is that I love you, and I want to be with you. I am scared, but I don't think that means I am not ready. I think it's because I have never done it before, and you have scared the shit out of me with all this talk about how it may hurt, and that I may end up hating you. Those are the only two things that are holding me back. The hating you part I don't believe. The hurting…does it get better?"

"Sarah, it's just I feel you telling me to wait, stop, and the big one is NO."

"I'm not saying those things."

"But you do feel them, and I can feel you. There is one other reason for you also."

"What's that?"

"You're afraid you won't be good enough."

"Oh."

"Sarah, that's the part you don't understand. You have my heart and anything we do together starting with kissing is better than anything I have ever felt in my life."

"So, you are set on not being together tomorrow?"

"I want to be with you more than you know, but no, we will not."

"So, you're not going to be disappointed if it doesn't happen?"

"Nope, anything you want."

"There is one other thing that is bothering me. You said you have never been with anyone for their first?"

"That's right."

"Why won't you tell me about *your* first?"

"I just don't want to talk about it; it's weird."

"Did you end up hating her?"

He closed his eyes.

"James, you *did* hate her. I am so sorry."

"It's not completely the same thing, Sarah."

"James, its okay we don't have to talk about it. I just wanted to understand." I scooted away from him, "I need to check laundry."

He reached out to hold my hand that was still laying there on the couch.

"It's okay, I'll be right back."

I checked the clothes and the jeans were getting drier, but pretty wet still at the seams. I pulled the rest out.

I grabbed my phone and called my mom again, "Hey mom."

"Are you leaving?"

"Almost."

"The jeans are finally getting less than drenched. I just wanted to give you an update, so you didn't worry."

"Sarah, it's already 10:20 p.m."

"I know, that's why I'm calling you. It should only be fifteen to twenty minutes longer. I will call when I'm on my way."

"Sarah, we trust you."

"Mom, I know you trust me, otherwise I wouldn't be here at all. And yes, I know you're worried about the sex thing, but James is a gentleman even more than guys my age. I don't know if that helps, but I just wanted you to know."

"Sarah, we do worry, but it's more about you getting hurt."

"I know. I love you too. Mom, I will call you when I'm on my way home."

I hung up the phone. I looked out at James, "Hey James?"

"Yeah?"

"The jeans are still wet, but I'm going to put the rest of my clothes on. I'll be right out." I went in his room and closed the door. I took off his sweats and put my underwear on.

He came into the room, "What did you say? Oh! Sarah, I'm sorry." But he just stood there. I didn't move.

His sweatshirt was hanging far enough down over me, but he wasn't moving, "Sarah?"

"What?"

He stood there and closed his eyes, "We are going to have to be very careful tomorrow."

"Okay."

He walked out of the room. I put the sweats back on. My heart was racing. I sat down on the steps to the bed. I was trying to get my heart to settle down. I was taking deep breaths. *What the hell am I doing?* James already said we weren't going to do this, so why did I want him to come in here right now, especially since I really had to go soon.

"Sarah?"

Does he feel what I am thinking all the time?

"Yes." He said out loud. He sat next to me, running his fingers through the hair that was hanging in my face.

"So, you can feel everything I am thinking?"

"Most of the time I can. Except when I get too…well you know. It goes a little fuzzy."

"So, earlier when you stopped, you didn't stop because you felt me say no or anything."

"That's why I am afraid of hurting you. If we get too far and you got scared or you want to stop, unless you say it out loud I can't feel you."

He was kissing my ear lobe, my neck, then down my arm to my hand. He turned my hand over and kissed my palm. I wanted to kiss him so bad, but if I did I knew I wouldn't leave.

"James, I have to go."

"But Sarah, you wanted me to come to you. To seduce you, I felt it."

"I do want you too, so badly James, but if I don't go home now, it will happen. You said that it wasn't going to happen, that it's not the right place, and I need to get my head clear before tomorrow."

"Okay, wait here just one minute please."

He jumped up and went to the dryer. He came back with my Jeans. "They are done."

He grabbed my bra and shirt off the dresser and came back to me. He sat on the step with one leg behind me and the other on the step, then turned me so I was facing him. He pulled his sweatshirt off of me. He moved closer to me. He put one arm through my strap and then the other one and started to push the bra up my arms putting it back on me. He leaned forward and kissed my neck. I tilted my head back a little. He moved even closer. His kissing moved down to my chest where my heart was pounding. I leaned back into his leg, which was supporting my weight. He continued to push the bra up further until it was very close to being on.

He looked at me for approval. I had nothing. His hands traced my breasts as he cupped them with the bra, kissing them over the top of my bra. He moved his hands, so he was clasping the bra. He took his attention off of me long enough to find my shirt. He put it over my head, but as he slid it down he was kissing everywhere that it was being pulled. I was absolutely speechless. He put his arms around me gently, and he stood up pulling me with him.

He untied the sweats letting them fall. He knelt down and helped me step out of them. He grabbed the jeans and gathered one leg and lifted my calf to help me put one leg in them. He gathered the other side and touched my calf to help me put the other leg in. He traced his face up my legs as he pulled the pants up. He pulled them over my butt. He was on his knees looking up at me so adoringly. I ran my fingers through his hair. He kissed me lower than he had ever done before as he zipped them up. His mouth moved to the top of my underwear as he pulled up to button my pants. He slowly arrived back to my face.

He parted my lips with his, and I responded. I was completely and utterly ready for him, but this was really weird; he was putting my clothes *back on*, whereas most guys try to get them off. At least that's what I thought. His arm was completely supporting my weight while the other was cradling my face. The kiss was so deep. He could have had anything he wanted right now and I was ready.

"Sarah?"

I tried to open my eyes, but I was completely melted.

"Sarah?"

"Yeah?"

"You have to go right now, it's been twenty minutes."

"I am so ready for you right now."

"I know, but not today."

I started to kiss him so deeply.

He broke the kiss. "Sarah, you will come back tomorrow, right?"

I was so lost in him that I didn't care if I went home or not.

"Sarah, you have to go home now. I love you, but you have to go."

He kissed me and took me by the hand and led me out the door and to my car. I sat in the driver's seat and took a deep breath.

"Are you okay to drive?"

"I guess I have to be." I looked at him.

"Oh, Sarah." He looked at me for a long moment. "You need to call your mom and then call me so I can talk you home. Okay?"

"Yeah, great. I have to go home."

"Sarah, give me your phone." I handed him my phone and he dialed my home phone. He handed it back to me.

"Your mom, tell her you are getting on the freeway now."

"Yep, mom."

"Are you on your way home?"

"Yep, just getting on the freeway. I'll be there shortly."

"That's good."

"I forgot the directions at Clarissa's house, so I have to call James to make sure I am not going the wrong way, but I'm on my way."

"Be careful, please."

"I will."

"Bye."

"Bye."

I looked at James and he put his hand out. I handed him my phone. He dialed his phone. It rang and he pulled his out and opened it. He handed mine back to me, "Put your phone on speaker." He handed me the keys to his door and said, "Let yourself in, in the morning." He kissed me softly and closed my door. I turned my phone to speaker.

"Can you hear me?"

"Yes."

"Good. I can hear you. I will be waiting for you in the morning."

I smiled as I drove away.

"Sarah?"

"Yep."

"Take a left out of the driveway."

"Okay, I'm on the road now."

"When you get to the lights take a right."

"Okay, just a second." I paused, "I see the light. It's Heron Street."

"Yep, take a right."

"Okay, now I'm on Heron."

"You're going to take a right onto 494."

"Yep, I see it." I paused again, "Okay, I'm on the freeway. James, you need to talk to me."

"Okay, on the spot again. Anything you want to hear?"

"I just need to hear your voice."

"I love you, Sarah."

"Tell me what happen with your first?"

"Sarah, I can't."

"James, do you have something else?"

"Not really, but I just can't."

"I feel so vulnerable right now James, and I need to feel like everything is going to be okay."

"Sarah, it will."

"Why didn't it work out with your first?"

"It's not that I don't want to tell you; I am just afraid to."

"Was it that bad?"

"Yes, and you know the person, and you may never look at that person the same way. It wouldn't be good."

"Was it Kylie?"

"No! Don't even think that way."

"James, Jason wanted me to stay away from you because you always get the girl; that's the only reason I thought maybe it was her."

"It's not, but it is worse than that."

"James, I don't know many girls, especially ones who are already active sexually."

"Sarah, do we really have to discuss this now?"

"No, but I need you to be as vulnerable as me."

"You really need to know this?"

"No," I said with reluctance.

"Where are you?" he asked.

"Highway seven."

"Okay, you're half way there."

"James."

"Okay, Sarah, I will tell you. I thought it was the first time for both of us. Katherine and I were supposed to be together, and I thought if we were together *that way* it would help me love her."

"James."

"It was supposed to be special, right?"

I didn't know what to say. "James, I love you."

"Sarah, it was awful. She did things I wasn't ready for and then told me she had been with Will many times already, and she couldn't love me like she did him. That's when I decided I couldn't live in that world anymore. I needed out."

"James, I am so glad you told me."

"Sarah, my dad doesn't know this, and neither does my brother, Sam. Please don't say anything."

"Does Will know?"

"I don't think so. I left that up to her to tell him because I couldn't."

"James...There is more, isn't there?"

"Just that, well, that's how I ended up with so many different girls. After that I was searching for something, but I didn't know what, until I found you. You give me so much more, without that."

"James, I don't know what to say."

"Say you will be here tomorrow."

"Without a question."

"What do you mean?"

"James, you shouldn't wonder if I will be there. I can't stay away from you. I wish I were older. We could go away together. I don't want to live my life without you, ever. You are my Cayuse."

"Sarah, I have done so many bad things in my life, how can you even want to be with me?"

"Because everything you do for me is good. You make me so happy on so many levels."

"Sarah, what time will you be here?"

"School starts at 7:45 a.m. I usually leave about 7:20 a.m. I could be there by 8 a.m. I just got off the freeway. I am less than five minutes from home. Do you want me to drive around a little longer, so we can talk?"

"No, I will close my eyes. Sarah, I am miserable without you."

"James, remember I made you promise to go no matter how much I begged you to stay?"

"Yeah."

"I won't live without you."

I pulled into my driveway, "James, I'm home. I love you."

"I know. It's time we say goodnight."

"Yes, goodnight."

"Sarah, you are my world now. I love you more than you know."

39. Valleyfair

M om was waiting for me when I walked in. I collapsed on the
chair, "What a long day. Sorry I kept you waiting."

"Sarah, I am very upset with you."

"Why?"

"It is 11 p.m., we talked about 10 p.m."

"I know, but I called and I kept you informed. I wasn't hiding anything
from you." I stood up and walked over to her, "Feel my jeans, they're still
damp at the seams."

"Sarah, we don't give you many rules, so we do expect you to follow
the few we do set. James is a lot older than you and even if he wasn't, if
you two are dating, we have to have an understanding what is acceptable
and what is not."

"I know, but I thought I was doing good by calling you."

"That was good, but you guys really shouldn't be alone. Sarah, you
may get in over your head, more than what you are ready for."

"Mom, I don't know how to explain this, but that is not important to
him. He just wants to spend time with me, and mom, I do love him."

"That's why you need to have rules, Sarah."

"I know I am too young to have these feelings, but I do and we will have to deal with them, because I am not giving him up. Remember the pool party with Matt? He made more of a pass at me than James ever has. His age is actually a benefit. He *wants* me to wait. Guys my age don't."

"Well, then. I guess we will try to deal with this. But Sarah, you really need to follow rules, and so does he."

"I will try harder. I have Valleyfair tomorrow with school, so I need to go to bed."

"What time were you going to be home again?"

"I'll go get the sheet." I got up and went to my room to get the sheet. It read, *leave Valleyfair 7 p.m., be back to school around 7:45 p.m.* My heart leapt. I had until 7 p.m. to be with James. I had forgotten that this went so late. This was going to be perfect! That's like four more hours. *Shit, a lot can happen in four hours.* I'm really not ready, I think. I want to be with him, but I'm only sixteen.

I walked back out with the sheet and handed it to her, "I guess not until late. I still want to see James tomorrow."

"I thought you weren't going to see him and that's why you couldn't wear his clothes home."

"It's definitely not in the plans, but I said I would like to. I wouldn't be home until 8 p.m. So, what would you be okay with so I can see him?"

"Sarah!"

"I will take *anything* mom. He's leaving for seven weeks, *please.*" I thought this would be more convincing, because if I was really going to Valleyfair with my class I would beg to see him afterward.

She thought about it, "Okay, but you will have to hang out here."

"Unless you want to go check out this house with me."

"No, Sarah!"

"Okay, here. That's it?"

"Sarah. We'll see."

"I will take it. Goodnight mom. I do love you."

"Yeah, Goodnight."

I crawled in bed. How was I going to handle tomorrow? I kept going over stuff in my head until it was so foggy. I think I was making it worse. He said if I wanted to, he would. But he said it wouldn't happen. But then he came to me when I wanted him too. He is worse than me! This was so confusing.

I closed my eyes again. I was dreaming of us playing a board game and laughing. I dreamt of us dancing, smiling and laughing together. I dreamt of him at the fair, the slight touches from him were so exciting for me. I dreamt of the arguments over stupid stuff, which infuriated me before we knew. I dreamt of the words, *Sarah he's suppose to get married in the fall.* The overwhelming fear of being hurt was filling me up. His first was with her, and it was bad. He had pain too. I couldn't handle not loving him and neither could he. What if it was too early for me and I would hate him.

I woke up to my phone, "James?"

The phone was silent so I tried again, "Hello?" It was still silent.

I hung up and checked who was calling. It was James. I called him back. He picked up but didn't say anything.

"James, you called me? What is it?"

"Sarah." His voice was so sad.

"James, what is it?"

"Sarah, are you still coming in the morning?"

"Yes, of course I am. Why?"

"You were dreaming."

"Oh, I'm sorry."

"I love you, and we have our whole lives to be together. I promise I will behave tomorrow."

"James, it's not..." I didn't know what to say. He had felt my thoughts. I didn't even remember all of them, but he was feeling the same way I was. "James, can you block the feelings? You said they were getting stronger. Can you make them go away?"

"Why?"

"Because, sometimes people may need their privacy. And James?"

"I'm here."

"It's just... I am hurting you with my insecurities."

"They are only clear with you, so I block everything else out. I will try, but I like knowing how you feel. If I didn't, we would have already done it."

"Oh, normal guy stuff."

"I will try to block them, but if you're not ready I can try and control myself better."

"Well, that is helpful, but if I am hurting you I don't like it."

"You weren't intentionally hurting me, and you weren't ending it, so I just wanted to make sure you are okay. My sadness doesn't matter."

"Oh, but James it *does* matter. You have been miserable since you met me."

"That's not true."

"James, you know you have."

"But I wasn't really happy before you either."

"I am totally in love with you, and do you want the good news?"

"What's that?"

"I am supposed to be at Valleyfair until 7 p.m., but mom will let me see you around 8 p.m., but here of course."

"Oh, really?"

"Yep. So figure out something for after I get back. Something we can do with my mom maybe."

"Oh, okay, but Sarah? That's a lot of time together. I will have to take a lot of showers."

"That's the price for seeing me. Are you okay with it?"

"Yes, I don't care if it's a hundred showers, as long as I am with you."

"I'm glad you feel that way. So, I will see you around 8:00."

"Sarah?"

"Yes, my sweet Cayuse."

"Try not to dream."

"Maybe only good ones."

"No, those are harder to get through."

I laughed. "Goodnight, James."

"Goodnight, my sweet Sarah."

I hung up the phone and closed my eyes. I was dreaming of the house. The *mystical* house. The house where we did not know of yet. I walked into the room and the candles were all lit. The fog was seeping in and you could see the light flicker off the fog showing its layers. I traced my fingers through it and it swirled around them. It was beautiful. I was wearing very little, just a silk nightgown. James was behind me, in silk boxers. He slid his hands down my arms. It was perfect; we were together as one. It was amazing.

I was floating down a lane with trees lit with white Christmas lights. James put his arms around me. He was kissing my neck holding me close. He was making me feel so good. I was with him again. I was with him floating on the clouds, nothing could be better. I tried to not think about it and I tried to make it go away and it wouldn't.

And then something that seemed bad... James was holding my stomach kissing it, not seductively, just adoringly. He rested his face on it as if he was listening to me. I was smiling at him and running my fingers through his hair. *Why did this feel wrong?* He was adoring me. That should feel amazing.

I woke to my alarm at 6:15 a.m. I woke up feeling so good, but a little confused. I went down and took a shower. I made sure to shave my legs. After all, I was going to the water park and wearing shorts all day. When I was almost done I turned the hot water off all the way. The cold water penetrated my body. *Shit! How could he do this all the time?* I shut it off. I went up to get dressed. I set out all six bathing suits and looked at them. I couldn't figure out which one would be best for a water park, but still make me look amazing, "Mom?"

"What Sarah?"

"I want to wear a really cute suit to the water park, but I will be going down waterslides and floating around on tubes. Which one do you think?"

"A one piece."

"Mom, I'm not swimming in the Olympics, please?"

"I would stay away from anything that has ties."

"Mom, they all tie. You just put a knot in it before the bow. That way when the guys grab the straps they don't get anywhere. I'm not stupid. Mom, just which one do you think looks best on me?"

She picked out the worst one.

"Okay, Mom, too conservative."

I grabbed one that would make me look tanner than pale white. Well, maybe not next to James. I got dressed and put my stuff in a beach bag. I grabbed the feather and tucked it into the bottom of my bag. I took off all my jewelry, except the ring James gave me. I couldn't part with it. I finished getting ready and doing my hair and makeup.

Mom walked in, "Why are you getting so dolled up if you're going to the water park?"

"Mom, we still have the time at school before we leave, and the bus ride there, right?"

"Is Matt going?"

"Mom, everyone is going. But Matt is on friendship probation."

"He did make a pass at you?"

"Well, just put it this way. I will not be attending any pool parties at his house, and were not hanging out anymore."

"That's too bad because I liked him."

"Mom, you liked *him* and he did what you and dad *wanted* me to stay away from. That's warped."

"Maybe it's the age thing."

"It has to be, because James would never have done what Matt did."

"What did he do?"

"Mom, I don't want to talk about Matt anymore. If you want to talk to me about men in my life, it's only James."

"Don't you like Brian, just a little?"

"Mom, no, he's another jerk, but I have told him that. I actually help him with his girlfriends, trying to help him not be a jerk. But like I said mom, if you want to talk about men in my life, it's only James."

"Sarah, you have your whole life, please don't settle for someone now. Take your time.

"Mom, I love you, but I gotta go."

It was about 7:25 a.m. If I were going to school I would be freaking out. I grabbed my bag and started to run out of the house.

"Sarah?"

"What? I have to go."

"Do you have money for food?"

"Yep, I have plenty. Bye mom."

"Bye."

I was on my way to my Cayuse. With all my thoughts this morning

I couldn't believe I remembered the feather. *Oops, no thoughts. James I'm on my way.*

My phone rang, "Hello?"

"Okay."

"Okay, what?"

"You're on your way."

"James, you need to block me some of the time."

"Yeah."

"You sound tired."

"Someone was dreaming most of the night."

"That's what you get for snooping."

"Two times Sarah? And now I have to be good around you all day."

"Yes. Now get some sleep. I'll wake you when I get there."

"Okay."

We hung up without saying anything more.

40. Floating Dock

I pulled up into the driveway and parked my car. I walked through the gate, and I scanned the back yard. It was even better than the night before. I looked around slowly as I walked to the basement apartment. I let myself in. It was still overwhelming. I looked around and it was so amazing. *How was she doing all this on her own?* This is just too much. I hoped it wouldn't go to James' head. I would be so tempted to stay here myself and forget about anything else.

I walked into James' room, and he was still sleeping. I smiled looking at him. *Why did he want to be with me?* He was so amazing and perfect. My heart raced. I set my bag on the dresser. There was a good size box on top with a note on it. *Sarah, yes this is for you. Only put it on if you are ready.*

Shit what did he do? I opened the box and unfolded the tissue paper. It was a white satin lingerie thing. It was very pretty, but I wouldn't put it on, not yet. I dug around in my bag to find the feather. I put the feather in with it and closed it back up. I looked at James lying there with the curtains draped around his bed. He was only partially covered.

I went to the steps, walked down two and sat down. *I wanted to kiss him awake, but would I be asking for it?* I didn't want to turn him on and then turn him down. I loved to kiss him. I sat there looking at him. I wanted to touch him. *Did he flinch? Am I going insane?* I had to test this. I thought about tracing my hands down his chest to his abs.

"Sarah not again." He rolled over. *Shit, did he live my thoughts?* Oh my god, I am sorry James. His muscles relaxed. James, I love you. He hugged his pillow a little more.

I moved to the bed crawling very carefully not to wake him and sat down. He was facing away from me. My heart was beating fast. I reached out to touch his back. The muscle tightened.

"James?" He didn't move.

I thought about lying down next to him wrapping my arms around him. He turned to me and opened his eyes. He looked at me and closed his eyes again rolling to his back putting his arm up to shield his eyes.

"How much do you know?"

I moved closer to him not touching his body with mine, but I did trace my fingers over his chest, "Enough to know I tortured you last night." I could see the smile under his arm. "James, can't you block it at all?"

He rolled to face me and moved closer, "Nope, I tried."

"James, you have to try harder; this could be torture for you."

"It's never been this strong before, besides, it was all so amazing." He smiled.

I closed my eyes and imagined what I had dreamt the night before. "Oh James, you must hate me."

He pulled the sheet up over him more and moved closer to me, leaning over me. He kissed me so passionately pulling me closer. I wanted him right now. He pushed to me. I wrapped my leg around him. I could hardly stand it. I traced my hands down his back, and the kissing was so good. *Yes, yes, I wanted to be with him right now.*

He moved down to kiss my chest that was heaving. I could hardly breathe. His hands came to my waist touching my skin pulling me to him. Then he stopped and smiled, "Shower."

"James, please, you don't have to. I want to."

"No, you don't; you didn't put it on. I'll be right back."

I held him tighter and started kissing him, begging him to stay. I moved my hands down his waist to pull him to me. *Oh shit! He didn't have any clothes on.* I stopped.

"See, you're not ready." He pulled the blanket around him and went to the bathroom.

What the hell am I doing?

I heard James yell from the bathroom, "Sarah, it's okay. You're allowed to change your mind."

I rolled over and hugged a pillow. Damn it, why does he do that?

"Sarah, I don't actually know *what* you are thinking, but I can feel your confusion. I can feel your feelings. You still have to talk to me, tell me what you're thinking."

I hate this, the confusion. I wish someone would tell me what to do. I am so use to people saying what I can or can't do, what I should or shouldn't do, what I should or shouldn't think. *Why can't this be that simple?* The house was in my mind. The *mystical* house. I was tracing my hand in the fog and watching it swirl, life was so simple here. I continued to swirl the fog. James was there, and he started to swirl the fog with me. I felt so amazing and comfortable.

I woke to him tracing my face with his fingers, "That was nice."

I moved to rest my head on his chest putting my arm over him. He kissed my head. I fell asleep again, dreamlessly.

I had so much passion for him that I started kissing his chest even before I opened my eyes. I moved on him. I wanted him so bad, to feel him. I was in such a great mood. I moved up to kissing his lips. The kisses were deeper and better. His hands traced my body. He rolled me over, touching my face. He was playfully kissing me.

He nibbled on my lips, "Sarah, are you sure?"

I looked at him a little scared. His kiss came deeper and very intense. I don't know what he saw or what he was feeling, but I knew I was asking him to take me. My heart was racing. That is what today was for. So we could be together. I wanted to hurry up and not be afraid to be with him. He was very aggressive, he pushed to me, and he was *more* than ready.

He kissed under my chin, his hands moved so quickly to help me take off my shirt, his kisses came to my chest as he cupped my small breast. He came back to my face he looked into my eyes, his kiss got harder. He moved his hand to my butt and pulled me harder to him. I opened my mouth to breath. I couldn't kiss him anymore. I couldn't breathe, and I closed my eyes to wait for him to take me. He pulled away from me. He turned and sat on the edge of the bed.

"James?"

"Sarah, don't tell me you want to if you're not ready."

He got up and went to the bathroom. I felt horrible. I was *scared* but didn't really want him to stop. I don't remember saying that or even thinking that. *What did I do wrong?* I needed to leave right now. I got out of the bed and grabbed my shirt. Actually I grabbed the sweats from the day before. I put on the pants and sweatshirt. I stopped at the door looking at the bathroom. I walked out and curled up on the couch putting my head on the arm. *What did I do?* I didn't have anywhere to run to. I didn't want him to see me. The tears were starting to well up in my eyes. I turned to face the back of the couch. I pulled the hood over my head. When I was hurt I only knew how to walk away, avoid it. If you ignore it, it will go away. I didn't want to lose him, but I didn't want to be here either. *I shouldn't have come.* He would have been better off with just a couple hours tonight not a whole day of torture, I am so bad.

I felt him kneel by the couch, "Sarah, please don't leave."

"I have nowhere to go."

"Sarah?" He touched my back, "Please, Sarah, look at me."

I couldn't. The tears were running down my face.

"I'm sorry I couldn't do that to you. You mean more to me than that and you weren't ready. Sarah, please I love you."

"James, I need some time to think this trough. I am so confused again and I am a mess right now."

He moved to sit on the couch next to me, trying to lean over me to see me. I cowered from him. I didn't want him to see my misery. He pulled me to his lap. He put his arms around me and began kissing my face under the hood. He traced his lips over my face, "Sarah, are you crying?"

"No, my eyes spilled."

He pulled my hood back, "Oh, my sweet, Sarah. Don't feel this way please. I love you and I can't live without you. Please don't push me away, I need you so badly. All of this, it's not important. Someday you will be ready and I will still be here, if you will let me."

"But…" I looked down, I felt horrible, and "…I make you miserable."

"Sarah you also give me so much joy. Let's just have a great day and this is *not* going to happen, so quit trying to make it happen. Okay?"

I nodded. His kiss was so sweet and soft. He made all the hurt slip away from me. I could stay this way all day. He kissed my cheeks, my nose, my forehead, my chin, and back to my lips. The tingling started. He was so intoxicating.

His kiss was deep and both his hands came to my face, "Nope, we need food." He stood up holding me until my feet hit the ground. He took my hand and led me to the fridge leaning into me, "You are so cute in my clothes." He smiled... I leaned into his shoulder.

He was looking in the fridge, "What are we going to do today?"

"James, I am supposed to be at the water park all day so something in the sun."

"The pool it is." He peeked at me from behind the fridge door. "It's not going to be easy if you're in a bathing suit." I smiled. He pulled out a huge tray of fruit, "Compliments of Clarissa."

There was a small envelope on the top with my name on it. He handed it to me.

My Dearest Sarah,

It's okay to wait. If my James loves you like I think he does, he will wait for you. Just like my true love, Carl. They are very good men.

Love,
Clarissa

The tears welled in my eyes again. I looked at James.
"What Sarah?"

I handed it to him and left for the bathroom. *Why was I crying again? Shit, stop this!* It wasn't bad.

He came in, "Did that make you mad?"

I turned to look at him, "James, why me if it's so hard on you?"

"You really need to listen this time. Are you ready?"

I nodded.

He took off the sweatshirt slowly, "Doing it, having sex, is only one small part." He untied the sweats and let them fall very slow. "It's only the whipped topping on the best sundae you've ever had." He pulled my shirt off, "It's the frosting on a cake that is so moist it melts in your mouth." He unbuttoned my shorts and let them fall to the floor. "You are everything I want. You give me so much pleasure without that." He kneeled down to help me step out of them. "Sometimes it's very hard not to have a taste or little nibble if it." He kissed my stomach, "But not necessary to have. I enjoy all of this without doing it." He stood up and kissed my lips seductively, "Sarah?"

I was a little stunned, "Yes, James."

"Will you please get the tray of fruit and meet me by the pool. I need to stay her a minute."

"Shower?"

He didn't say anything, but nodded.

"That's what I'm talking about."

"Sarah, it was a nibble, I deserve this. Go please."

I went out and grabbed a towel from my bag. I wrapped it around my waist. Grabbing the tray of fruit, I walked to the pool area. The tray must have weighed over ten pounds. It was very heavy. I sat it on a small table between two chairs. I walked over to the pool and dipped my foot in it. The water felt wonderful.

It was a while, but James walked out; I met him at the lawn chairs.

"Well that's better."

"Shower helped?"

"Yeah, so does your towel."

I smiled.

"Nope, maybe it's even a little sexier."

"James, don't do that to yourself!"

I sat down in a lawn chair and scooted to the back of it. He sat on the same chair facing me. He picked up a piece of pineapple and fed it to me. I took a bite. It was so juicy he came to my mouth to eat the other half kissing me.

"So, even this is going to get hot?"

Someone was walking through the gate. He looked at us, "I see company made it. Hello James, Sarah, I see you two found some food."

James got up and moved to shake his hand, "Hello, Wilson."

"Oh, she said you were polite." He leaned forward and shook James's hand. Wilson was a little bit older than Clarissa, you could tell by the gray hair.

He looked at me and back at James, "Is everything to your liking?"

"It's amazing, better than I could have imagined. Do you do the work yourself?"

He smiled. "Yes, it's a full time job. Clarissa has taken care of me and my family quite well."

"It looks like you take very good care of her too."

He smiled again, "Were you going to use the pool today?"

"Yes, if that's alright?"

He looked a little uncomfortable that James was asking, "Anything you want, but I usually do the pool cleaning in the morning hours. If I pull out the floating dock, would you mind being on the lake until I'm done?"

"Whatever works for you."

"I will get it ready." and he moved out the gate.

James looked at me, "A floating dock?"

I shrugged my shoulders, I had never heard of a floating dock.

"Eat up! I don't think we can bring this with us."

I started eating the fruit, it was so good.

"This keeps getting better and better."

Wilson returned to us, "It's all ready for you. Would you like me to take you down?"

We both jumped up. James started putting the tray back together.

"You don't have to do that. I will take care of that for you. Follow me."

We walked down to the lake. It looked like a huge solid inner tube.

"The cooler in the center has more fruit, a salad, and water if you're thirsty."

I looked at James, "I don't know if I can swim that far."

Wilson directed James to a garage for boats, "You may want to take that." It was a wave runner.

"Good idea."

"There is a latch to hook it to where the ladder is. I will let you know when the pool is ready."

"Thank you so much." James shook his hand again.

"Do you need instructions on the operation of the wave runner?"

"Nope! I got that one handled."

"Life vests are in the garage. You two have a good time."

James took my hand and we found vests in the boathouse exactly where Wilson said.

James guided me back to the wave runner, "Are you ready?"

"For *what*?" I was trying to be playful.

"The ride of your life little girl!" He had a mischievous grin on his face. I could tell this was going to be a wild ride.

He was having the time of his life. I knew he wasn't going to go straight to the floating dock. He twisted it, turned it and jumped over waves. I was holding on for dear life!

Finally, we ended up at the floating dock. He hooked it to the ladder like Wilson had instructed, then took off his life vest. I took mine off. James held the wave runner in place, so I could get to the ladder.

He was coming up right behind me, "This could turn me on."

I turned around sitting on the edge, "What are you doing?"

He was crawling over me, "Having your butt in my face was kind of hot."

"James, that's gross!"

"Actually, your curves are very…" He closed his eyes and kissed me; it was hot. We sat together on the floating dock looking around the lake, "Wow! People actually live this way?"

"James, *you* will be living this way. When you come back and go to school, right?" I crawled up to the center looking in the cooler.

"Are you still hungry?"

"Yes."

"The girl eats!"

"James, I told you I do eat. This stuff is all good for me. I can eat as much as I want." He pushed himself closer to me and laid there basking in the sun. It was still kind of early. I pulled out the salad, but it wasn't a lettuce salad. It looked like a crab salad. There were forks tucked in on the side of the cooler. I grabbed a fork and opened up the salad. I took one forkful. "Mmmm…"

James looked at me, "*That* good?"

I took another forkful, "Oh my god. This *can't* be good for me."

He propped himself up on his elbows, "That must be really good." I took another forkful and fed it to him, "Oh my god, this is better than…" He stopped and looked at me. We both started laughing.

I grabbed water, opened it and took a drink. I lay down by him close to his face, so I could feed him. I fed him another bite then I took a bite and continued to feed him two bites to my one until it was gone. "Was that really good or were we just that hungry?"

"Maybe both, but if I had any more I wouldn't need to think about your half naked body to get excited."

I offered him water. As he was lying down he opened his mouth. I gave him a little and poured a little down his front.

"That felt good."

I grabbed a piece of ice and traced it over his stomach with my fingertips.

"Sarah, that feels so…I love it when you touch me, but…" He sat up leaned forward and let himself fall into the lake.

"James, I think you like me to torture you sometimes!"

"A little." I heard his voice from underneath me.

"What are you doing?"

"From under here I can see every curve." He traced his hand down my front.

"James!" I could feel him tracing my curves. "James, stop that!" I lowered my voice, "If you want to touch me, come back up here."

"Sarah, people could see us. Come down here with me."

I stood up and dove in. The water was quite cold out here. I dove under the tube. He was waiting. He was holding the straps underneath to hold himself up. He took one of my hands and lifted it to hold on and did the same with my other hand. Then he traced his hands down my arms slowly. His kiss was soft and adoring. His hands moved down gradually tracing my body, and then his hands reached my waist and squeezed.

The kisses moved under my chin and to my neck. He pulled my legs around him, rubbing them and tracing them as his kisses grew more passionate. He brought his hands up to touch my breasts, his mouth coming back to kissing my lips. His kiss lowered more to my chest, which was now pumping so hard it felt like my heart was going to jump out of my chest. I let go of a strap with one hand and wrapped my fingers in his hair. This could be it. I wanted to feel all of him. He tried to untie the top in the back. It wasn't budging.

He smiled, "Booby trap?"

I giggled, "If you are with a bunch of teenage guys you do it as a precautionary measure. You don't lose your top then."

He kissed me, "You're cold."

"No, I'm not; I'm quite warm."

"You're teeth are chattering."

"Really I'm fine…I just need more of this." I moved to keep kissing him.

"I think we need to get back in the sun!"

He let go and dove under the tube. I followed moving to the ladder. I started up and crawled to the middle of the floating dock and lay down on my stomach. He came over, laid on his side next to me propping himself up on his elbow. He traced his fingers across my back, "You are my every dream." He kissed my shoulder. I smiled, I was warming again.

We heard a boat coming toward us. Wilson was coming with the pontoon. He pulled up, "The pool is done. Do you want to head up now?"

"Sounds good," James said as he got up and took my hand.

We both got up and got ready to get on the wave runner. James encouraged me to drive this time and try some tricks on our way back. He kept one arm around me. The other was tracing my thigh. I slowed and turned to shore.

"What are you doing?" James asked.

"Heading in."

He nibbled my ear and whispered, "Drive longer."

As I drove, his hands traced my inner thighs, and I closed my eyes.

"You have to keep your eyes open to drive." He tilted my head and was kissing my neck, "How are you doing?"

"I'm getting a little warm." As we drove around he continued to massage and caress my body. My temperature was rising, my heart was racing, and my breathing was almost moaning with pleasure. It was obvious that I was getting overheated, so he said, "We can head in now."

We moved onto the shore. Wilson called to us, "If you like I could put the wave runner and vests away for you." We looked at each other and started to walk toward the house. James waved back to him and yelled, "Thanks." James took my hand and pulled me closer. I looked into his eyes smiling at him. James could tell what I was thinking, he looked past me toward Wilson and scolded me, "Now, Sarah, why do you have to pick the worst time?"

"Because it's safe." I closed my eyes and put my arms around his waist as we walked back to the house. We walked through the gate. Now there were two floating lounge chairs in the pool. Another spread of food at the table outside the main part of the house and a large pitcher of iced tea. I let go of James and walked up the stairs, looking back at him again, "James, oh my God! More food!"

"You're hungry again?"

I blushed, "Yeah, kind of. I must burn a lot of calories when I'm with you and besides, it's all healthy."

I grabbed one of the sandwich rolls and took a bite. It was amazing too. "James, come here and try this."

"I can't handle anything that good again."

"Just come here." I fed him a bite.

"Oh my God!" He fell into one of the chairs by the table.

"I wonder who is making all this great food."

Wilson walked in, "I hope you didn't mind. I put some more food together for you." He looked at us already eating it, "So, what do you think of my food?"

I looked at him, "*You* make all this yourself?"

"Why of course. Clarissa has helped me publish two cookbooks, but she advised me to tuck all that away for retirement. I don't even know how much I have made so far. But she said she has people that are taking care of it in a trust and by the time I retire I will be very comfortable." He smiled and looked so proud.

"I don't like much food, but Wilson this is amazing."

He turned a few shades of red, "Clarissa also said you may need some alone time. So, unless you want me to make dinner before I go, I am to keep it to a minimum today."

"She gave you the day off?"

"Not really, I do whatever she wants, and she thought you may need alone time with James leaving for a while."

"Thank you." James stood up walking closer to Wilson, "You have already been so kind to us, thank you." James held out his hand to Wilson.

Wilson reached out and shook his hand turning even redder than before, "Well, I'll be on my way then." He turned to walk out the gate.

I started wrapping up the food. I had my fill; James didn't eat much. He mostly sat there watching me, "Should I put this in your fridge downstairs or the one upstairs?"

"Downstairs, we may need a quick snack later if you keep burning calories?" he chuckled.

"Are you picking on me, James?"

"I have never seen you eat like this?"

"I told you I eat. I am just careful about what I eat. You wouldn't want me to lose my girlish figure would you?"

He stood up and put his arms around me, "You are so thin; I was beginning to worry."

"James! Let's get this food in the fridge first."

He smiled and grabbed two huge plates of food, I and grabbed the other.

I opened the fridge and there was already so much food in there. James was only going to be here for a day and a half. *Why so much?*

He smiled, "I know, I think this would be enough at my house for at least a week for the whole family." He moved things around to make some room. He put the trays in and stepped away watching me. I put the tray in and turned around.

He was right there with his face next to mine, "Pool?"

"Please! I have to be in the sun, or mom is never going to believe that I went to the water park all day."

We still had seven hours. I was so happy; I didn't want this day to end. Everything was perfect.

41. Almost

I walked straight to the pool and dove in. I swam to the floating chair and turned to look at James standing there watching me.

I called to him, "How am I supposed to get in it?"

"I think from the side of the pool."

I tipped the chair toward me and put my foot on the edge to ease myself up. After one good push, I fell off backwards into the water. He stood there laughing at me.

"Fine, you're right."

I swam to the steps and walked out right into James arms. He wrapped his arms around my waist, "You are so cute."

He went to kiss me, but I pulled away, "Remember sun, James."

He smiled wrapping his arms around me trying to pull me closer.

"James, sun first…, play later."

I was trying to walk away toward the lawn chairs in the water. He was walking with me trying to hold my stomach, pulling me back kissing my shoulder.

"James! Stop it! Or else you'll have to go inside."

He turned me around, wrapping his arms around my back kissing me.

In the midst of this kiss I mouthed, "Alone."

He pulled me closer tracing his hand down my leg pulling it up to his waist, "I already need a shower, just a little more, please?"

I put my arms around his neck to get lost in his kiss. I wrapped both my legs around him as he walked back to the steps and sat down. His hands came to my face. He seemed content on the deep kissing. His hands traced my back moving slowly over the cuts, trying to remember what happened when losing control. His hands moved to my hips. He pushed a little and then pulled me harder to him.

As he breathed he moaned a little, "Sarah..."

"James?"

"I need a shower. Now!"

I moved away from him. I was getting the gist that he was close to losing control. I wanted to be with him, but when he loses control, it kind of scares me.

"*Shit!*" He got up and left for the bathroom.

This made me feel horrible, like it was dirty or shameful. My heart sank. I was in misery. It was time to take care of this and he either needed it from me or someone else. I knew he hadn't been with anyone for over six months. That had to be difficult. I loved him, so I should be able to do this. What was I so scared of? Oh yeah. *It may hurt and I will hate him.* How can that even be possible? I don't think I could ever hate him. I sat in the lawn chair with my eyes closed wondering how this was going to work out. I knew I would get hurt somehow. He couldn't keep doing this without hating me a little every time we got carried away.

I was glad James was leaving soon, but not quite as sad as the overwhelming depression setting in that he was leaving me for so long. *What am I going to do while he is gone?* This is too much to handle. *How can he know he wants to be with me the rest of my life?* That just doesn't seem possible. I know I want to be with him; the whole marriage thing scares me, but it also filled me with complete joy. I know I would be doing the right thing if we were together. I felt tears escaping under my eyelids. *Great! Overly emotional again. What the hell am I doing?*

"Sarah?" There he was in front of me in the pool leaning on the edge of the lawn chair. I looked at him. He knew what I was feeling, "I think your thinking too much about this. Can't we just enjoy where we are in the relationship?"

I nodded, but still felt horrible. He laid his head on the lawn chair between my legs not saying a word. He would splash a little water over my legs when they got dry. I ran my fingers through his hair. We stayed that way for a long time. He didn't look at my face. He could feel my depression, or maybe he felt the same way. I dozed a little in the chair. It felt so good with the warmth of the sun and the coolness of the water.

"I'm bored." He said as he finally looked at me.

"Okay, we can be done with the sun. I think I've gotten a little color."

He smiled, "You're pink everywhere, any more and you might get well done."

I pushed his head down to dunk him.

"You want to play like that?"

"No! You'd win!"

"I would let you win."

I was standing in front of him in the pool and the feelings started to rush again. *I want to be with him so bad.* I mean I wanted his arms around me all the time. I liked it when he touched me just slightly when we were in public to show his affection toward me. I liked it when he touched my face and looked me in the eye to see how I was feeling.

"I like *those* feelings better." He could sense my joy.

"James, can't you turn it off? It has to be annoying for you."

"It's not like that. I can feel what you are feeling most of the time when I am thinking about you or you are thinking about me. When we're apart it weakens a little, but if I need to know how you are doing or need to feel you all I need to do is concentrate on you."

"So, you can tune it out?"

"Somewhat, but when you are really emotional and need me, or if you are thinking about me really hard, I can't stop it. You have to take the good and the bad."

"So, James, you have to block me as much as possible when you're gone. You have to concentrate on what you are doing there."

"I will, Sarah. I am doing this so I have a future. That future will be with you."

I looked down. I was going to miss this. We have had so much time together for the last four days. I didn't want it to end.

"Can we get back to the kissing? I like the kissing!" We still had five hours and we could do a lot in five hours!

"Are you hungry yet?" He asked.

"No, are you?"

"No, do you want to go for a boat ride?"

"Not really."

"Do you want to play cards? I could go look for some."

"No, James, no cards."

"What do you want to do?"

I took his hands and started walking backwards to the steps.

"I know! We could um, take my new car for a drive?"

"Later, James." I backed up the steps and was moving toward his place, his *new* home with his hands in mine. I pulled him to the door.

"Sarah, we can cuddle and watch a movie."

"No, James." I opened the door and entangled my fingers in his pulling him past the couch.

"Sarah, look, the couch. It's so comfortable we could make out with lots and lots of kissing."

"James, there will be kissing."

I tried to smile, but my nerves were kicking in and I felt like my face twitched a little. *Look seductive, no smiling.* I know what I was asking him to do. I was scared and my heart was pounding so hard I felt like it was going to explode in my chest, but if it was going to happen we needed a lot of time. I led him to the room stopping in front of the dresser. I let go of his hands.

"Sarah, you don't know what you are doing."

I opened the box he gave me. First, I unwrapped the feather and I traced it down the front of him. He closed his eyes.

"You are going to have to excuse me, I need..." I kissed him softly tracing my lips on his.

"Look at me James. I don't want to be scared." I took the lingerie out of the box. It wasn't the one from my dream, but it was close. I slipped it over my head. James was still looking at my face.

"You want to take a nap?"

"If that's what you want to call it?" I untied the top straps of the bikini top and loosened it.

He smiled, "It's that easy?" He shook his head in disbelief, like he couldn't believe it was that easy. I let it fall to the ground. I reached underneath and pulled my bottoms down far enough for them to drop too.

"Um, Sarah shower..."

"Not this time, James." I took his hands and led him to the steps at the side of the bed. He slowly followed me. His body was very close to mine. I turned him to face away from me. I reached my hands around his waist and I traced my fingers along the front of his shorts. I was looking for the tie on the swimming trunks.

"Oh, Sarah..."

I untied his swim trunks and helped them slip to the floor.

"Sarah, shower right now."

"No, James, it will be okay."

I moved to the bed pulling him down to it. He willingly followed. I traced my hands over his back to his shoulders and down his front. I kissed his neck and pulled him back to lie down as I moved backward.

"Sarah. *Oh shit!* Sarah. Shower then board game?"

I leaned over his face and kissed his lips, "No, James, shhhh."

His hands came up to my face. I took his hands in mine and pushed them back to the bed.

"James, slow down, stay in control for me. Please?"

I kissed his chin and then I leaned more and kissed his chest, tracing my face across it. The muscles were getting very taught. His grip got tighter against me.

"James...slower."

He moaned quietly, I pulled him up more on the bed and kissed his abs while moving to the side of him.

"Sarah... shower!" He desperately pleaded.

"James, no, it will be okay." I kissed his lips more. I moved over top of him. I lowered myself to rub against him just slightly then moving away again.

He moaned, "Sarah!" as he pulled the gown up to my waist.

"Shhh, slower." I did it again. He moaned again very slightly.

I whispered to him, "Feels good?"

He pulled the gown up over my head, "Oh, Sarah…"

I lowered to him, but the desire was coming over me. I wanted him to be inside me. I knew he wasn't, but I was rubbing against him. It felt so good and I was so ready for him. I started to feel the tingling. He pulled his hands away putting them on my hips to help me with the movement, slowing it. His breathing was almost a moan, and then he was pulling and pushing me harder.

"Oh… Sarah… Oh… Shit!" He pulled me hard to him, "I can't…"

I felt the warmth of him spreading over my stomach. His movement stopped and he just pushed a little more. I still felt the tingles coming, and I wanted to feel the rush with him. I was so close.

"James, don't stop, help me." I was trembling, "Can you be in me, now?" He rolled me over and helped me with the desire. His movement changed. It felt even better, more enjoyable for me and the rush came. I wrapped my arms around his chest pulling him to me. I wanted more. His hand came to my face to adore me, reading my face. His kiss was tender as he traced my face with his, like he was trying to calm me. I couldn't stop the trembling; it was uncontrollable.

"James, I am so ready for you. Can you *try?*"

"I already came. You could get pregnant that way."

"So, we still haven't?" I was a little bummed.

"It depends on who you talk to. I'm sure according to your mom and dad this is definitely doing it." He was tracing my face with his fingers.

"How long can we stay like this?"

"As long as you like or until I get turned on again from feeling you…"

I started to move around, "We can do that again?"

He smiled at me and began to kiss me passionately. This went on for hours. I don't know exactly how many times. It just all felt so good. I really wanted to know if it was that much better inside. I knew I would have to wait, but I wasn't totally afraid anymore.

He rolled over to his back, "What time is it?"

"It's 5 o'clock, we still have two hours." I curled up to him.

"Sarah, don't even think about it, I have nothing left."

I smiled and put my lips on his shoulder, "I feel a mess, and I need a shower."

"That I can do." He smiled as he rolled out of the bed and reached for my hand pulling me off the bed. He grabbed the sheet and wrapped it around me walking to the bathroom. He turned on the water, and when the water was hot he let the sheet go and led me into the shower. He was so tender and adoring. He helped me wash up, but the entire time kissing my hands, my neck, my shoulders, and my cheeks. I felt so amazingly good everywhere, even my heart. This wasn't shameful at all. He was so beautiful, and we now shared something that was just ours. It wasn't what I had planned, but he made me feel wonderful by being so gentle and loving.

We got out of the shower and he helped me dry off. Everything he did made me feel like he loved me even more. He led me to the dresser where I had left my bathing suit. He helped me slip it back on. He pulled out boxers for himself and slipped them on. He held up one finger and ran to the bed pulling the comforter off the bed and came back to me leading me to the couch. He held up one finger again and ran to the kitchen setting the timer for one hour.

That would give us thirty minutes to get out the door. He came back to me and turned me to face away from him and sat down on the couch pulling me inward to him. I curled up in his arms. He kissed my forehead, my check, my hand. He traced his hands over my waist. He was very attentive. We didn't even turn on the TV.

"I don't want any distractions." Everything was perfect. I smiled at him and nuzzled in closer. I wanted this moment to last forever. I couldn't get enough of this. He made me feel so special and completely loved. I closed my eyes as he kissed my fingers individually.

He paused, "Do you want your ring before I go?"

"No, James! You have to come back to me first."

"Do you think I'm not coming back?"

"If I really think about it? No, but it hurts like you won't."

"You're not getting rid of me that easy."

He tilted my head up, so he could kiss my lips. I was lost. I loved kissing him. I moved so I could sit facing him more and wrapped my arms around him. We sat kissing the whole time, it was so intense.

Then we heard the alarm go off in the kitchen.

I smiled at him, "You have made this day so exactly what I wanted from you."

"Sarah, I am completely head over heels in love with you." He kissed me one last time. It was so passionate and the kiss was deeper, and much more intense than before. I wanted him right now again. I was advancing on him more aggressively.

"Sarah, we have to go."

42. Special Dinner

I was on my way home and I was feeling very sad. He was going to be gone in eighteen hours. *Eighteen hours! Then I would be alone.* I hated being away from him; my life is so empty without him. The tears started to fill my eyes. James would know I was sad. I didn't want to make him feel bad about leaving. I put the picture in my head of the mystical house and the fog seeping in through the window. I imagined his arms around me, swirling together in the fog by candlelight. My thoughts stayed there the rest of the way home. I pulled in and walked inside. Mom was sitting in her chair reading.

"How was your day?"

I smiled, "The best day ever."

"Good, it's okay to have fun outside of James."

"Mom! He's on his way here, please be nice. I've waited all day to see him."

"Okay, okay, but you need to get back to your old self while he's gone."

"I'll try, but it's not going to be easy."

He pulled up in the Avalanche.

"So, is that the car his mom got him?"

"No, that's not his."

I took off out the door so fast and jumped into his arms. I didn't kiss him. I just wrapped myself around him.

"What are you doing?"

"This is what I would do if I didn't' get to see you all day."

He set me down and wrapped his arm around my waist. As we passed part of the house where mom couldn't see, he kissed me urgently on my lips, neck and shoulder.

"Wait, I forgot something." He ran back to the truck and pulled out a grocery bag.

"What are you doing?"

"Making dinner."

"What?"

"Trust me."

He took my hand. As we walked in he whispered into my ear, "I am so in love with you little girl."

He always knows how to make me feel better. My heart almost jumped out of my skin. He pulled everything out of the bag. He peeked through the door at my mom, "Paula, did you eat?"

"What? Why?"

"If you're hungry, I'm going to make dinner."

She got up and moved to the kitchen, "What are you doing?"

"I figured since Sarah was gone all day she hadn't eaten real food. Are you hungry?"

"I could go for a little food. Do you want some help?"

"Nope. You go sit down. Sarah can help me."

She looked at me, shrugged her shoulders and walked back to the living room. He moved closer to me, but not touching and he inhaled. The grin on his face was sinful. I moved to wrap my arms around his neck. He stopped my hands and moved them back to my side.

"Not yet." He reminded me. Then turned to pull everything out of the bag, "Knives?"

I pointed at them.

"Cutting board?"

I grabbed one. He leaned over and quickly kissed my lips.

"Two fry pans?"

I pulled them out.

"You're going to help." He pulled the peppers out, and cut out the tops. He turned me to face the cutting board in front of him, his arms around me, "Cut it like this, small strips."

I started cutting. I felt him move closer, his face tracing my neck inhaling. It was difficult for me to concentrate, "This is going to be…"

He whispered in my ear, "Keep cutting."

I tried to cut, but he was breathing and nibbling on my ear. I said very quietly, "If you keep doing that I can't do this."

"Okay, okay." He moved back to the meat and other items. He bought stuff that was precut. He opened the two packs, "I wanted to get her really full and really tired." He put both of them in the pan. He pulled out spices and seasoned the meat, "Ooh, it's a little hot." He smiled, and looked at me, "You need to work a little faster."

He picked up a pepper and fed it to me, coming in for the other half, but it turned into a deep kiss, "This is going to be harder than I thought," said James.

"James, you're kind of…hyper?"

He wrapped his arms around me pulling my head to rest on his chest, "Do you feel that? That's my heart. It's been like that since you left."

Mom walked in, "I thought you two were cooking."

James turned with me, my head on his chest, "She's a little sad, sorry."

Mom smiled, "What about you?"

James went back to stirring the meat, "Nervous, happy, sad, excited, and maybe a little scared."

I stopped and looked at him, but he ignored me.

Mom put her hand on his shoulder, "You'll do great I'm sure. Now what are you making?"

"Fajitas!"

"It already smells good."

"Do you like it spicy?"

"A little."

"Okay, medium." He put the cover on one spice and threw it back in the bag.

"You sure you don't want help?" My mom asked again.

"Nope, I used to cook at home all the time."

"Well, okay, then…I'll go back to my book. Sarah, no more sadness because this is a good thing for James." She left the room.

"You get out of trouble so easily."

He smiled, "Okay, you are going too slowly. My turn." He moved in to cut the peppers faster. I traced my hands down his back and wrapped them around his waist.

I pressed my forehead on his back, "James, you're scared?"

"A little. I'll be a long way from home and from what I know."

"But you're so strong."

"Change is hard Sarah. Do you ever think about what you want to do after high school?"

"Yes, well sometimes. Too many options to put my finger on one thing."

"How do you do on your grades?"

"Okay, I guess."

"Let me see a report card."

"No, you're making me feel like a child, James!"

"Please. I have a theory I will share with you if you let me see it."

I relented. I kissed his back and walked out of the kitchen toward my room. As I walked by mom she looked at me funny.

"He wants to see a report card."

She laughed a little, "I knew I liked this boy."

"Mom!"

I retrieved the report card and brought it to him, "This really makes me feel like a child."

He pulled me close, "Planning a future is not childish." He kissed my forehead.

"It might not be what you're expecting, James."

"Okay. Hold on." He started the other burner and threw the veggies he had cut up in the pan and seasoned them. The he stirred the meat one more time. He picked out a piece, "Here, try this."

I tasted it. It was good, "It's *okay*."

"You're teasing me *right*?"

I smiled, and leaned to him, "The *best* I have ever tasted."

"Now you're playing." He glared at me as he opened the report card, "This is not the last one from this year?"

"Nope, don't get it for four weeks."

"I want to see that one too."

"James, what are you looking for?"

"Your grades can't drop because of me. If they do, I'll..." he leaned into me, "...cut you off."

"You won't see me?"

"No, I'll see you, but no kissing or touching, or *anything* else. We'll just have to see."

"I don't think I'll have to worry."

He looked at it, "Well, it's a little better than I thought."

"Did you think I was stupid?"

"No, I knew better than that but...a 4.0 with honors, shit are you a genius?"

"No. School is just stupid. They test you on things that they find in books. There is so much they don't even know about."

"Who doesn't know?"

"The teachers, they tend to get mad at me when I correct them."

"You actually correct them?"

"Only when they're wrong."

He looked at me.

I looked away in embarrassment, "James, you know I love you."

He turned to me and wiped the hair from my face, "And I you, my sweet Sarah."

I smiled at him.

"So, what do you like? I mean what do you want to do?"

"I don't know; if I could do ten things I would, but it's all jumbled in my head and I can't sort it out."

He turned me to look at him, "You can sort it out. List them out with the pros and cons of each. Then put it away and ..." he smiled, "...1... 2... 3... breathe."

He leaned into the living room, "Paula, food's ready!"

He pulled out the sour cream, guacamole, lettuce, and a special cheese. He took a flour tortilla, sprinkled the cheese on it, and layered the meat and then the veggies. He put it on a plate and placed it on the table for my mom. He made another one for me. We all sat at the table. James was waiting for us to try it first.

Mom looked at him, "Aren't you eating?"

"Not really hungry, nerves I think."

She smiled at him and took a bite, "James, this is so good!"

He smiled. I was still cutting a small piece.

James looked at me waiting, "Are you back to that?"

I made a funny face at him. My mom and James exchanged looks. He returned the look, "She eats like a bird." He looked back at me, "Did you eat at all today? I suppose only junk food there, huh?"

"Actually, I did eat today!" I glared at him. *He knew what I ate today. What was he doing?*

He shook his head, "I need to show you how to eat one of these." He got up and made another one for himself, topping it with lettuce, guacamole, and sour cream on the inside. He returned to the table with his plate, picked it up and took a regular sized bite.

Mom started laughing, "She works out too much also, James. She needs to eat more calories if she burns it all off."

"You two can quit talking about my eating and working out habits. I am healthy and slim." I took a big forkful of food.

My mom had finished hers. James offered, "Paula, another?"

"Yes, please." He smiled at me as he got up to put another one together for her.

When we were finished eating, James and I cleaned up the kitchen, and mom moved to her chair again to read. When we were finished, he looked at the clock noticing it was 10 p.m.

I looked at him, "Not yet, *please*?"

He smiled, "No, not yet, movie?"

I nodded. We went to the living room. My mom was sleeping.

"Mom? Mom? You should go to bed."

"No, I'm alright."

"We're going to throw in a movie." He sat on the floor looking at me as I held up movies. I really didn't care about the movie, so my attention was *not* on the TV. He finally nodded his head yes, I looked at it. *The Notebook*. I looked at him funny.

He answered, "You always end up with your true love."

398

I smiled. Mom was snoring a little. "Mom?" I touched her arm, "Mom, you should go to bed."

"I suppose so. I can't keep my eyes open anyway." She got up looking at James, "You know Tucker and I like you James, right?"

He smiled at her, "Yes?"

Where was she going with this? Please don't embarrass me, "James, please, be good and go home at a decent time."

He smiled, "Yes, ma'am."

"Mom!"

"Sarah, you don't listen to me, so maybe he will."

"Goodnight mom."

"Goodnight, be good." She warned before going to bed.

"Yes, mom."

I curled up next to James. We started the movie. After a little while he started to kiss my neck, "Is this good?"

I smiled and whispered, "Yes."

He lifted my hand to his face. He kissed my palm and then each of my fingers sucking on them, "How about this, is this good?"

I closed my eyes, "Yes."

"Sarah, what do you want to do?"

I smiled at him, "You *know* what I want to do."

"No. Not that. Even though I would love to do that, I am talking about life."

"I really don't know."

"Come on, Sarah, everybody has an idea of what they would like to do."

"Realistically? Or anything?"

"Anything."

"A dancer, model, singer, actress…"

"Really?"

"James, I think all little girls want those things at one time or another."

"Okay, realistically."

"I think maybe a doctor, lawyer, financial planner, or architect."

"No wonder you're confused."

"See, it all gets jumbled in my head and sometimes I need time to try and organize it, so I understand what is important to me and what's not."

"Most smart people are weird."

I looked at him feeling sad.

"What is it?"

"James, I *am* the weird one at school, or at least I was until I met you and Jason. My world has kind of changed."

"Jason?" he rolled his eyes.

I don't think he wanted to hear about Jason. I assured him, "James, he brought me you."

His hand came to my face and he tilted me a little to the side, so he could kiss me better, "You are so cute and irresistible and it's a little hard to believe."

I looked away from him, "I have been working on being better, and you have noticed."

"But, Sarah, you had me *way* before the changes. Some of the changes make me worry. You get more attention than you realize."

"I am getting more attention, but it's from my change in attitude. I feel better about myself. I have never, ever been hit on before Jason. Let alone had someone do to me what you have done."

"I am so bad, Sarah, I am so sorry." He looked away. I could tell he felt like he was corrupting me.

I lifted his chin, "Now people actually notice me as a person, James. People, kids at school, actually talk to me. I felt empty before you. I was numb to the world. I merely existed. I wasn't living."

He looked at me.

"James, do we have to talk about this anymore?"

"No, does it upset you?"

"My life is nothing when I don't have you in it."

"Sarah, I could scold you for feeling that way, but I feel the same way."

I wanted kissing, and kissing is what I got.

I went to the bathroom, just quickly. *I didn't want to miss out on the kissing.* When I came out I heard, "Sarah!" He was calling from my room. I smiled and walked into my room. He was sitting on the edge of the bed. I closed the door.

"Sarah, you don't want to do that."

"Why?"

"I won't be able to leave."

"*Okay.*"

"No, Sarah, *not* okay. I just wanted to tell you it's time. I need to go."

I walked over to him, and put my arms around his neck while his head rested on my stomach.

"Do you really have to go?"

"Yes, but we will have a little more time tomorrow before I leave."

He stood up and hugged me. We walked to the living room. Mom was sitting there, "Glad to see you have self control, the both of you."

I smiled.

"By the way, *no more bedrooms*." Her voice was stern.

"Mom, it's not like that."

"I know, but you're sixteen Sarah."

"Yes, mom." I went to walk James out.

My mom called out, "James, thanks for dinner!"

He smiled and yelled back, "You're welcome!"

I walked him to the truck. He got in and rolled down the window and said, "Come as soon as you can."

I kissed him through the window. He drove off. Shortly afterward I got a text, >"1- 2- 3- Breathe."

I took a deep breath to walk back in. Mom looked at me, "At least he has the common sense to know when to leave."

"Mom, I told you, he's really good at walking away."

"I told you before he is more a man than a boy."

"Mom, I need to go to bed."

Mom followed me into my room and sat on the edge of my bed. "Sarah, when you go to pick him up, please, don't do anything stupid."

"Like what?"

"Don't trap him."

"What are you talking about?"

"Some girls would do things, just to keep a guy."

"Mom, I wouldn't do that!"

"I didn't think so, but you are more attached to him than you let on. Let him go and he will come back. Have a little faith."

"I will try. But I need to sleep mom, please."

"What time does he have to go?"

"If he has to be there two hours before the flight, we will have to leave his mom's by 10:15 a.m."

"Okay, I'll see you in the morning."

"Good night."

"Love you, Sarah."

"Love you too, mom."

Mom walked out, and I heard her door close. I got up and closed my door too. I crawled in bed hugging my pillow and started to cry. All I could think about was, *I'm so sorry James, I can't help it*. I could hardly sleep. I was turning at least once an hour, worrying if I was going to be able to wake up in time to go get him. I finally gave in and got up at 6 a.m. I took a shower and fluffed my hair. I didn't' want to wake mom so she would worry more. I curled up in the chair and waited.

Mom got up at 7 a.m. She walked into my room then came storming out to find me in the chair, "Sarah!"

"I couldn't sleep. I gave up and came out here to wait."

"What are you waiting for?"

"Until I can go get him."

"But you're waiting, that's good Sarah."

"I would go now, but I'm too depressed and I don't want to make him feel bad. His leaving is good, right?"

"Yes, it's good for him, it's a future."

"Then why does it feel so bad?"

She sat on the arm of the chair, "Growing up sucks, doesn't it?"

I wiped my tears and hugged her.

"You know you are going to have to put on a happy face for him. He needs to feel good about this."

"I know. I'll try."

"Would it help if I said you could go now if you swear that you won't do anything stupid?"

"*Really?*"

"Yes, really."

"Yes, that would help!" I jumped up and kissed her, "You are really saying I can go?"

"Yes, it will be two hours together. Can you behave?"

"Yes, yes! *Oh mom, yes!*" I grabbed my purse and car keys, then ran out the door.

43. Forever Yours

I was so happy. I could hardly wait to get there. *I didn't have a key now, so how was I going to get in?* He must have thought about that. I pulled into the driveway. I got out as fast as I could. I quietly opened the gate, and gently shut it behind me. I turned to walk in and there he was. He startled me a little and I backed up into the gate, "James, you scared me!"

He leaned into me, but not touching, "You have been so sad since I left."

"I'm sorry, James. It's just so hard to let you go."

"I will stay if you ask me to."

"No, James, I'm not going to. You told me change is hard. We both have to be strong for each other."

"Ask me Sarah! Just say it and I will."

"No, I can't."

He wrapped his arms around my waist and picked me up. He was kissing me and walking to the basement apartment.

"Sarah?" he mouthed with the kisses.

"Yes?" I didn't want to talk. I wanted more of this. Time was not on our side anymore. When we got inside, he let me down so that my feet

405

were touching the ground, but never breaking the kiss. His hands moved to my face.

"Sarah, ask me please?"

His kiss was intense, and I was getting lost, "James…" Oh this kiss was too much, "Did you sleep?"

We were moving to his room. He pulled off my shirt only breaking the kiss long enough to pull it over my head, "No, just ask me."

The kiss resumed. We passed the kitchen. I reminded him, "James… set…the…timer."

He stopped walking me to his room. His hands traced my back so tender, "We don't have to." His kiss was so deep I could hardly breathe, "If you ask me to stay." His kiss moved to my neck and I closed my eyes as he moved under my chin.

I didn't want to be, but I was firm, "Timer James. Two hours."

He pulled me with him. He reached for the timer and pushed the buttons. I looked to make sure he set it right. His face came back to me to distract me, "Sarah, do you want me to stay?" His hands traced down my arms, kissing my lips, nibbling, luring me, "Ask me?"

I wrapped my arms around his neck and moved into his kiss more, tracing my hands through his hair. I mouthed, "No."

His hands moved around my waist lifting me to my toes and started moving to his room. As we moved through the door, "You know the answer, just ask."

The tears were starting to fill my eyes. I didn't want him to leave, all I had to do was ask him and he would stay, but I can't ask him that, "You promised me!"

He traced his hands down my side to my leg to pull it up to his waist. I put my other leg around him too. He was walking to the bed. He knelt on the bed to lay me down moving his hands to my face, wiping the tears that had fallen. His body was hovering over me as his lips found their way back to mine, "It's okay, Sarah, I'm asking you to ask me."

Why was he doing this? His touch felt so amazing, his kiss, but yet my heart was being torn into pieces by him. His kiss was passionate again. I was pulling his shirt up and over his head. He moved swiftly back to my lips, to keep me in his trance. The emotions were so confusing, but he was intoxicating at the same time. All he wants me to do is ask him to stay. That would change his future and I can't be responsible for that.

"James, you're making my heart hurt. I can't ask you that."

His face traced down to my chest, cupping my breasts. He kissed between them, and then moved down to kiss all the way to my stomach. I gripped the blankets at my sides.

He insisted, *"Please, Sarah."*

I shook my head no. *That would change his plans, and that would change our future.* I didn't want to mess up the plan, "No, James!"

He unbuttoned my pants moving away from me. He grabbed them by the cuffs and pulled them off. I sat up as he did this. I kissed his stomach unbuttoning his pants. His hands were running through my hair. I slid his pants down. He helped to get them off. He moved over me and I pushed his boxers down as he moved up to me still hovering. I used my feet to push them off the rest of the way.

"Sarah, ask me!" He lowered his face to kiss me.

I wrapped my arms around him to pull him to me, "James, I can't do this if you keep pushing, my heart is breaking!"

He lowered himself to let me feel he was ready for me. I closed my eyes.

"Sarah?" He lowered again.

"Just try, it's okay I want you to."

The tears fell from my eyes. This was too emotional. I needed him to stop; he was confusing me. I couldn't take it any more and I turned away. He lay down beside me. He wrapped his body around me and pulled the covers over us. His hand traced over my stomach tenderly, he kissed my shoulder and the back of my neck pulling me as close to him that is humanly possible.

"Sarah, you have to tell me what you want, or I have to go take a shower."

I couldn't talk. I would be sobbing if I said a word. I turned to look at him. He was hurting my heart.

"Okay." He got up to go to the bathroom.

I grabbed his arm, "Today was not supposed to be like this, so much hurting, and you're making it worse."

He kissed my hand and walked away. I rolled back over. Oh my god, he was breaking my heart! I closed my eyes as the tears were streaming down my face. He wasn't coming back. I couldn't do this. I had to leave. I'm not going to be the reason for him to give up something we were working toward. I crawled off the bed quickly to find my jeans and slipped them on.

I crossed the room toward the door to the living room, "Sarah, don't even think about leaving. Remember, I can feel you."

I grabbed my shirt and put it on. I was on my way out the door.

"Sarah, please!"

I didn't' want to leave. I just needed time to sort things out in my brain. Our time was so limited, but if he didn't come back, there would be nothing to sort out except my devastation. He deserved better, and I had to go. I ran out the door and out the gate. I got to my car and I couldn't get in. I sat on the ground. *Why can't I leave?* Get over it, move on. Go home and cry for a month or two and get back to my emptiness. I couldn't pick myself up. I heard him coming through the gate. I knew he was relieved that I was still here. He bent over to lift me.

I put out my hand to stop him, "No, James!"

He didn't listen to me. He picked me up anyway, "You're not getting away from me that easy."

He kissed me deeply. I turned into his shoulder. I can't go through this emotional roller coaster anymore. I can't get lost in his kiss. This was tearing me apart. He walked me into the apartment and set me down on the couch and turned to lock the door.

"James, don't." I could hardly breathe. I felt like I was going to hyperventilate. *Oh shit, I'm going to be sick.* I didn't even see what he was doing and I ran to the bathroom and locked the door.

I started throwing up. I heard knocking on the door, "Sarah, are you okay?"

"No, I'm not. Can I use your toothbrush?"

"Yeah. Sarah, what's wrong?"

"I'll be fine. Give me a few minutes."

"Sarah, open the door."

My head was spinning, and I felt really queasy. Too many emotions I wasn't ready to feel. I put toothpaste on his brush, rinsed it with cold water, and started to brush. I even did my tongue. I hated getting sick. *Thanks a lot James, this is just gross.* I finished, but I didn't' feel much better. I washed my face with cold water. I sat down on the toilet. I couldn't stop my head from being fuzzy. Shit. I went back to the sink and took more cold water and put it over my face, then in my hair. I needed to cool off.

"Sarah, what are you doing?"

"James, I need a minute please!" I took the towel and fluffed out my hair. Okay, I think I'm okay. I opened the door. He was standing in the doorway, looking down. Tears were coming from his eyes.

"James, what are you doing to me? You're confusing me."

"Sarah, are you okay?" He didn't look at me.

"Yeah, I think so. There are just too many emotions at once."

"You said you wouldn't push me away."

"I wasn't pushing, more like running." I smiled a little.

He looked up and smiled. He led me to the chaise lounge and sat me down. This helped. My head was still spinning a little.

He got down on his knees, "Sarah, I am so sorry. I don't want to leave. I want to be with you all the time. I wanted you to ask me to stay so I wouldn't have to make that decision on my own. I am sorry I was laying that on you.

He put his head in my lap. I ran my fingers through his hair, "James, I love you and I don't want you to go either, but these are your plans. You have to do this, for us, right? It's your future, and if we want to be together, you have to have a future, a plan, right?"

"Why do you love me still after what I did?"

"Remember, James, I don't exist without you."

"How are you feeling?"

I shook my head a little. The fuzziness was getting better. "A little better, I think."

"I have to ask you something. You don't have to answer it, just let me finish."

I nodded.

"You know I want to be with you the rest of my life. You are my *everything*, and I can't live without you. Do you know that, Sarah?"

"Yes."

He took my hands in his one hand and he kissed them one long kiss. He pulled out the little white box.

"James, no, not yet, you have to come back to me first. I love you and I will wait forever to be with you, but not yet. I need to know you are coming back because you want to not because you owe me anything."

He put his finger to my lips, "Shhh, I love you. You don't have to answer me yet, but please let me do this Sarah." Tears started running down his face, "Will you marry me?"

I wrapped my arms around his neck and kissed him so hard it hurt. I wanted him to be mine forever, and this was a promise that he would be mine. I couldn't say no, "Yes! Of course, James, yes!"

He took the ring out of the box and took my hand. I was trembling; my hands were shaking so bad he had to steady my finger to put it on me, "James, this is too much. It's too big!"

"It doesn't even measure how much you're worth to me."

Now the tears were streaming down from the happiness, "Why are you doing this now?"

"Your feelings were so mixed up. I was messing with your mind and you really thought I wasn't coming back. I am going and I don't want to be away from you, but I am going. I want you to know I will come back, and I will come back to you if you will still have me."

I kissed him deeply, "James will you make love to me?"

He eyes moved away from me, "You're not ready, Sarah, and I am not teasing. It's not the right time yet."

"James, please. I need to get my fill before you go. I need to feel like we are one."

"Sarah, I feel everything you feel. We are one."

"But I don't feel you the same way and my mind gets crazy sometimes."

"Oh, I have something else for you."

"No, James, it's already too much."

He pulled out another box and opened it. He pulled out a really long chain and put it over my head. "I know you really can't wear the ring yet, but this is so you can wear it and nobody will know."

It hung down so far that it came down below my breasts. He smiled at me. I laid my head on the side of the chaise.

"Do you feel okay?" he asked.

"I feel wonderful, James, why?"

"You got sick, and something just doesn't seem right. I've got this knot in my stomach that I can't put my finger on it."

"You just asked me to marry you. Are you sure it's not nerves?"

"With you? No. It's coming from you."

"Maybe I'm nervous, because of what I want from you. I want us to be together before you go."

He smiled, "Not today, Sarah. We have our whole life for that."

"No, James. I want you now!"

I slid myself onto his lap. I began kissing his ear, breathing deeply into it. He lifted me and walked back to the bed standing me beside the bed. He helped me get undressed, "Are you sure Sarah? I will be back and we will have plenty of time for this."

I traced my fingers inside his pants and unbuttoned them. He helped me undress him. We moved to the bed. Everything was beautiful. We tried, but it was harder than I thought it would be. We settled for what we had done the day before. We were too rushed and it would have hurt and James didn't want to leave if that happened. Our special moment would have to wait. We lay in each other's arms kissing and touching. It felt like we had all the time in the world.

The alarm went off. I looked at him desperate.

"It's okay, Sarah. 1… 2… 3… breathe."

I took a deep breath. He got up and pulled me out of the bed, "Sarah, quick shower."

After we showered, we moved quickly to grab everything. He got his bags and put his arm around me, "You ready?"

"No."

"Okay, let's go anyway."

We stopped at the door so he could lock it, and then we went to the car. I drove kind of fast. With us taking a shower, we were running a little over on time. I had planned an hour in the car to the airport and we actually only needed about forty-five minutes to get there. We were going to be okay.

I held his hand even though I liked to have both hands on the wheel for driving in the city. We got there and parked. I was going to stay with him as long as they would let me. We walked in and I stood in line with him to get him checked in. He spent his time holding me and kissing my hand, with my new huge rock on it.

"James, you sure you don't want to hang onto this until you get back?"

"Nope, you said yes." He cupped my face with his hands. I walked him to the gate. I sat and waited with him before he had to board.

"I'm glad you are here with me; I might chicken out if you weren't here to push me away."

"James don't start. I'm not pushing you away. I'm going to wait patiently."

They started boarding before the flight was to take off. I walked him to the gate. He kissed me passionately until the attendant interrupted us, "Sir, you have to board now if you are going to be on this flight."

We both smiled. He walked down the gate backwards to look at me as long as he could. I walked to find a seat by a window to watch his plane depart.

The attendant walked up to me, "He forgot to give you this."

It was a note, but I couldn't read it then. I didn't want to walk out of the airport crying. The plane pulled away from the terminal and out of my sight.

My phone buzzed, >"1- 2- 3- Breathe." It buzzed again. >"*I love you, more than you know.*"

I text him back, "*I'm forever yours.*"

Characters

Sarah Sullivan

Paula Sullivan   Mom

Tucker Sullivan   Dad

James Swanson   Tucker's Employee

Carl Swanson   James Dad

Clarissa Swanson   James Mom

Will Swanson   James Brother 2nd oldest

Sam Swanson   James Brother 3rd

Tamara   James Sister youngest

Katherine   James Betrothed/Will's girlfriend

Amelia   Sam's Betrothed

Danelle Turner   Sarah's Best Friend

Laura Turner   Danelle's Mom/Sherburn's Resort Owner

Paul Turner   Danelle's Dad/Sherburn's Resort Owner

Brian Turner   Danelle's Older Brother

Jason Gasser   Tucker's 2nd Employee

Kylie   Jason's Girlfriend

Karla   James's so called Girlfriend

Wilson Phallen   Clarissa's Houseman

Tony   Tavern Owner/James Employee

Mykala   Brian's Girlfriend

Pat Hanson   Friend of Brian's

Matt Erickson   Friend of Sarah's

Upcoming Sequel- Wasting Away

1. The Other One

I walked slowly back to my car. I needed to make a plan how to get through this time alone. I knew James had his phone, but I would wait till he contacted me, or I would just let him feel me. Now that I know he could block me a little when we're apart, if he didn't reply he was busy. I still didn't understand it all. I wish I could feel him, or maybe not. I didn't know what he was going to be going through.

Shit, I feel sick again. I found a bathroom and threw up again. I hope this isn't the flu, and James would get it. That would be really bad.

I walked out of the stall and someone form the airport staff was in there. She asked me if I was okay. I assured her I was fine now, but I washed my face with cold water and rinsed my mouth. I started for the car. I wasn't thinking about James anymore. I just wanted to get home and go to bed. Maybe all this stress was too much and I needed sleep. I got to my car and I was feeling a little better. I opened James's note:

Sarah,

There is an envelope on the side of your mattress where I was sitting last night. It has instructions inside. I love you more than you will ever know, and Sarah: 1- 2- 3- Breath.

With all my love,
James

This is amazing. I have made it this long with no tears, and I wasn't going to have a nervous breakdown. I drove home thinking about the envelope. What was he up to? By the time I got home I wasn't feeling great again. I was nervous about what he left me. I am glad that the anticipation of him leaving was over. I was driving myself crazy over it. I think that is why I am not feeling well. I got home and the queasiness was back. I drank a large glass of water. Mom wasn't going to be home for awhile, so I was going to go to bed. I lay down and reached for the envelope, shit! It was the one his mom gave him.

I opened it. Yep, the money was all there. I pulled the note out and tucked the money back under the mattress.

My sweet Sarah,

This is for our future and I didn't need any of it. Deposit $300 a week in a bank account until it's all in there. It may look suspicious so smile and say 'waitress'. They won't think anything of it that way. As for you, my little girl, I hope you will wear the ring even if it's only around your neck. I am so in love with you. There is another envelope, go ahead and open it. Each letter is marked with a date on it. Don't open each one till the day it says. Please follow the instructions and remember, Sarah, 1-, 2-, 3- Breathe.

Don't forget to put the ring on the necklace. You wouldn't want to explain this one to your mom and dad.

With all my love,

James

I gazed at the ring. It was too big on the top of my finger. I could hurt someone with it. I pulled it off. My heart was pounding like I was losing him when I did this. I took the necklace off and put the ring on it, tucking it in my shirt. The hole filled a little. I rolled over and hugged my pillow and put the paper to my face with hopes of smelling him. No luck, but I had to sleep now. I set my alarm for 5 p.m. I was working tonight.

I woke in a rush. What was I forgetting? Oh yeah, work. I didn't have time to think of how I was feeling but I didn't have to run to the bathroom. Good, I must have been tired. I went to work and managed to not think about James other than enough to make me smile, touching my chest where the ring laid. I got home at 10 p.m.

Mom was there in her chair, "Did you get James to the airport okay?"

"Yep."

"Are you okay?"

"Surprisingly, I'm doing okay. I was a little sick this morning at his moms place, but I think it was nerves."

"You got *sick*?"

"Yeah, it came on suddenly, but I didn't sleep much and I was a little torn over him leaving. I feel better now."

"You actually were throwing up?"

"Yeah, a few times today, but I took a nap and I feel better."

She looked at me funny, but didn't say anything.

"Well good night."

"You're going to bed already?"

"Yeah, I think I got sick from being so tired. I have to work all day tomorrow and I don't want that to happen again. I really hate throwing up."

"Okay, but let me know how you are feeling in the morning."

"Yep, I feel better already."

I slept almost dreamless. The dream was back, but James just held me. I think I was feeling very happy knowing we were going to be together forever, so I was content on letting it stay there.

Day 1 envelope:

My love is not found, until I lost
You may look, but never see
The love around you
Saying it was meant to be me.
With all my love,

417

James

Day 2 envelope:

Is it possible, or should I wonder
The thought of you
To forget, not possible
I will not try.
With all my love,

James

Day 3 envelope: I smiled as I opened this one.

You may hold my hand for a while
You may hold my eyes to linger
You may hold my body for a smile
But my heart
Is yours forever.
With all my love,

James

These three days went without feeling an ounce of being sick. Mom kept asking, but I was feeling fine. We were going up north to see dad. What was I going to do without James there? I would hang out with Danelle; she would be happy about this. She was feeling neglected. I remembered to grab days four and five. I hadn't heard from him at all, but I wasn't desperate in my thoughts, and he was busy.

We got up north about 8 p.m. We went to Sherburn's. I found Danelle and we went down to the dock. She wanted to ask me questions, but I think she was afraid I would be sad. I asked her about Tommy.

"So, does he come up here often?"

"Yeah, every weekend; why are you asking me about Tommy?"

"It's nothing."

"What?"

"Danelle, that's how James and I started, completely arguing and disagreeing about everything."

"Really?"

"Yeah, do you like him?"

She giggled, "No, he's like a big brother."

I smiled at her and raised my eyebrows. In a way, that's what I told her about James when she asked.

"No, no way, I don't like boys like that. Sarah?"

I was smiling at her, not believing her.

Danelle was trying to change the subject, "So, James left?"

"Yep."

"And you're okay?"

"Yep, so far."

"You really like him?"

"Yeah, I do." I couldn't say that without smiling.

"Did you have *sex*?"

I couldn't believe she was asking me this. "Yes and no."

"What do you mean?"

"Danelle, I really don't want to talk about it."

"Because it's too juicy or because it will make you sad?"

I tried to grin, but the tears started to well up in my eyes. Shit, I was doing so well.

She let me off the hook, "Let's go play pool, and be around people."

I was relieved, "Sounds good to me."

We headed back to the house part of the resort. She put her arm around my shoulders as best she could, "I kind of do like Tommy. Promise not to rat me out."

I smiled still holding back the tears. "Try to take it really slow, or you will be a puddle like me."

She laughed as we walked in. Brian and Pat were there. They both treated me like I was going to break. I sat down by Pat, "Haven't heard from you in a while, how's it going?"

"Good I guess, I didn't think it was okay to call you anymore."

"Pat, I can still have friends, right Brian?"

As I turned to him I noticed he was staring at me. I tried again, "Brian, I can still have friends, right?"

He smiled and avoided my gaze. "Yep, the best of friends."

I didn't know what his problem was, but I pulled Danelle toward the back to go play pool.

Brian followed us till we were in the kitchen. "The other one is here."

Danelle stopped and pulled me to stop walking. I had no idea he was talking to me, but I turned around to see why Danelle stopped me.

She said, "I don't think we should play pool."

This confused me, but I was up for anything, "What do you want to do then?"

Brian repeated himself, "The other one is here." Then he pulled me in front of him to look at me in the eyes.

"What do you mean the other one?"

He didn't take his eyes off of me as he spoke to Danelle, "Danelle, can I talk to Sarah for a minute?"

"No!"

She turned to me, "Let's go back down by the beach and hang out. Or we could, um. Brian we could play a game of basketball."

He smiled, "Danelle, that's a good idea."

They were acting really weird, "What is going on with you two?"

Danelle was disgusted, "Fine, but don't be a jerk. If you make her cry, I'll tell mom."

He finally moved his attention to her, "I won't, go get Pat and the ball. We'll be right out."

I crossed my arms and waited impatiently. He walked closer to me but leaned on the stove. "Did something happen with you and Jason again?"

"No!"

"Sarah, are you sure?"

"Positive. Why?" I was a little short because I didn't like what he was implying.

"He is here, sitting with your mom and dad."

"Oh, basketball sounds great."

I took him by the arm and led him outside. Danelle smiled. We played two on two. Danelle and Brian, against Pat and me. I sucked, so I felt bad for Pat. Brian stopped for a minute and I followed his eyes to the road. Jason was leaning against his truck watching. I hip checked Brian and took a shot. It knocked him back into play. That was the first basket I made. I got a high five from Pat. Jason wasn't budging.

I was guarding Brian and he was dribbling, "Do you want me to say anything?"

"Nope, play."

He took a shot and I stopped it. Pat ran over to give me a high five again, but Danelle grabbed the ball and Brian lifted her to get the shot.

Pat was embarrassed, "Sorry about that."

I laughed, but I glanced over to Jason. He smiled and walked back in.

Brian walked over to us, "What was that about?"

My mind was going wild thinking of all the reasons he would show up without Kylie. I smiled at both of them, "I have no idea."

I grabbed the ball and started playing again. We played until it was completely dark. I sat down on a cooler outside. Jason's truck was still there.

Pat walked over, "We could play pool?"

I didn't want this to be about me so I was going to leave it up to Danelle, "It's your day, what do you want to do?"

"Pool sounds good."

We started walking in and Brian pulled my arm. Pat saw this and stopped too. "Sarah, he's still in there."

I evaluated Pat and Brian and realized something. "Kylie is not here to kill me, and he is still friends with James, so I don't think he will push any issues. It will be fine." I put my arms around both their necks, "What are you guys afraid of? You're both bigger than him anyway, and if that fails dad's not going to let anything happen, right?"

I started walking in and Danelle was laughing. We filed out to the game room and played pool till it was time to go. I had a lot of fun, no flirting, but pure innocent fun. I did notice he was watching me all night long.

Mom and Dad asked if I was ready. I was more than ready to go, especially with Jason watching over me all night, "Yep."

Danelle walked with me to my car. Of course, mom was going to ride with dad. Jason was waiting by his truck. I didn't want to know for what, but Brain and Pat were right behind Danelle and me. I turned around, "Pat, did you need a ride?"

"No, I'm staying here tonight."

Danelle got a great big smile on her face. "Sarah, you could stay too."

I could see Jason from behind them. He stood up shook his head no.

"That sounds like fun." I would have liked to stay, but I saw Jason as he held up the ring finger. Was he here to make sure I was being good? "But, I am really *tired* and I would fall asleep anyway. Maybe I will tomorrow."

I got in my car and they were walking away. I was desperate to keep them there with me, "Hey guys talk to me until mom and dad are ready to go. I don't want to leave till I know they will get there the same time as me."

Brian smiled. Pat came back with him.

Danelle inquired, "What do you think he's going to do?"

I smiled at Danelle, "Nothing, I'm being paranoid, night then."

I closed the door and pulled away. Jason didn't get in his truck that I could see. I was relieved. I hate that James was not here to hide behind. This was going to be hard.

I pulled in and went in the trailer. *Okay, where are mom and dad? Why were they taking so long?* I turned on the TV and threw a movie in. I changed to lounge shorts and a t-shirt. I grabbed a really light blanket and curled up on the chair. I heard the truck pull in. *Good, mom and dad are here.* I took a deep breath and closed my eyes. They walked in and Jason followed. Great!

Dad smiled at me, "So, James got to the airport okay?"

"Yep."

"How are you doing?"

"I'm okay dad. I think I'll go to bed now."

"Wait. Tell me about his mother's house."

I was happy he was interested and couldn't wait to tell him how great it was. "It was really great. It had a big pool. She had rooms for each of them. There were three boats and a floating dock. Have you ever seen a floating dock? And it was beautiful all of it.

"I talked to Clarissa."

Oh, this isn't going to be good. "Really?" *Where was he going with this?*

Jason sat on the couch and watched my face as I answered dad's questions.

"So, James has his own apartment in the basement?"

"It's not just for James; it is also Will's apartment." Oh shit, I walked into that one; I was going to try and recover, "From my understanding."

Did I tell mom this? How much did I say and how much did Clarissa say? Shit. Jason, wipe the grin off your face was all I could think. *James, help me, I need you right now, so bad. Please, James, please hear me.* I pulled my phone out to see if he replied, but there was nothing.

Dad continued to ask me questions, "So, was it nice?"

"Yeah the whole house was nice. Clarissa's bathroom was bigger than this trailer."

"You checked out the whole house?" He was being careful how he was talking to me. I was getting irritated by it.

"Yeah, it's in Minnetonka; I couldn't help myself."

He laughed a little, "I heard you had a pool accident?"

I knew that one came from mom and he was getting down to the real questions, "Yeah, a little clumsy of me, but no lights were on and I didn't know there was one there."

Jason was laughing. I was more irritated that he was in on this whole conversation.

I knew dad wasn't pleased, so I tried to comfort him, "I *did* call mom multiple times to keep her updated."

"Yeah, she did say that."

I got up and headed for the door, I wasn't feeling very well. I really think it is the stress. Yep, I am going to be sick.

Dad asked, "Where are you going?"

I could barley answer, "Bathroom."

I ran out the door. I wasn't going to make it to the outhouse. I went to the side of it and threw up. *Great!* At least it was cooler out here than in the trailer. I leaned against the outhouse to gain my composure.

"Are you okay?" It was Jason's voice I was hearing. I really didn't want him here.

"Yeah, I think I might have a touch of the flu or something."

I walked past him to go back to the trailer.

"Sarah?"

I kept walking. I really didn't want him here.

He sped up to catch up with me. "You're not pregnant are you?"

"No."

"Are you sure?"

"Positive."

"How can you be positive?"

He was trying to be nice but it was making my stomach turn.

"Jason, I'm not feeling…" I ran back to the side of the outhouse and got sick again.

He came to stand by me holding my hair back, but not touching me anywhere. I didn't want him here; I wanted James.

I leaned up against the outhouse again. "Thanks, but I'm okay now."

He put his hand on my forehead, "You're kind of warm."

I didn't say anything and walked away from him towards the trailer. I needed to lie down. I went in and curled up in the chair.

Dad was eyeing me, "So, did you see the apartment?"

"Dad, I'm really not feeling good. You can ask me all the questions you want in the morning." I closed my eyes.

"Here you go." I opened my eyes. Jason was holding out a glass of water for me.

"Thanks." I took a drink and put it on the floor next to me and closed my eyes. I was thinking how bad I would feel if James were sick too. I hope I didn't give him whatever I had because this really sucked. *James I need you. Please let me hear your voice.* I covered with the blanket and held the ring in my hand under my shirt and concentrated on him as hard as I could. It didn't take long to drift off.

Forever Yours   Book 1 ☺

Wasting Away   Book 2

Growing Tears   Book 3

A New Beginning   Book 4

Manufactured By: RR Donnelley
Momence, IL USA
January, 2011